JANETTE TURNER HOSPITAL

BORDERLINE

WITH A NEW INTRODUCTION BY
HELEN DANIEL

Published by VIRAGO PRESS Limited 1990
20–23 Mandela Street, Camden Town, London NW1 0HQ

First published in Great Britain by Hodder and Stoughton 1985
Copyright © Janette Turner Hospital 1985
Introduction Copyright © Helen Daniel 1990

A CIP catalogue record for this book is available from the British Library

Printed in Finland by Werner Söderström Oy

We have been unable to trace the copyright holder for the painting "Self
Portrait" by Maruja Mallo reproduced on the cover, and would be
grateful for any information.

For
Blanche Gregory
and for
Jack McClelland
with gratitude and affection

INTRODUCTION

In *Borderline,* in a Dantesque scene, Felicity enters the subway miasma, "An underground world of equals, every face pale and phantasmal as the nimbus of a wandering soul. Felicity felt at home in such places." Throughout Janette Turner Hospital's work, there is a sense of being at home with the ambience of change and dislocation. Other places and times chafe at the edges of the present, the past colonising it, setting up sly outposts of another time inside its territories. Within a hall of mirrors, she explores rites of passage, transgressing the boundaries of time, space, character, place, country, art, figures.

Configurations shift from moment to moment, revealing gaps, crevices, filament fractures, stress lines running beneath the surface of an image, lucent spirals and silences. Language, she records, has "harmonics and half-notes, the music of the cracks between the keys"—and hers is a fiction of such harmonics and cracks between time and place. Expatriates, she writes, carry reverberations:

> They have echo chambers inside their heads and words rattle around in there, casting shadows. There is always static: Brisbane humming below Boston, descant pips from Canada and India, Australia in the 1940s seeping up through Australia in the 1980s.

A wheel spins and, just beneath the surface of the present, the shadows of other landscapes stir. With a constant awareness of the provenance of the present, Janette Turner Hospital's work is located in dislocation.

At the age of seven, moving with her family from Melbourne, where she was born in 1942, to Brisbane where she grew up and attended the University of Queensland, she discovered that "words do not have immutable meanings . . . Like wine, words do not travel well. They mutate as they cross borders, they curve through time, they generate astonishing proprietary passions." This sense of curvature and mutation across borders informs all her fiction. Her own life has crossed many borders and place has generated many proprietary passions. In 1965, after teaching in Queensland, she moved to the United States. Since then she has lived in Boston and Los Angeles, in South India, London, and in Kingston, Ontario, where she now lives with her Australian husband, a professor of religious studies at Queen's University, and their two children, "fellow dislocatees", to whom she dedicated her collection of short stories, *Dislocations*.

After postgraduate work in medieval literature, Turner Hospital began writing short stories in 1975. Her first novel, *The Ivory Swing* (1982), won Canada's Seal Award and was followed by *The Tiger in the Tiger Pit* (1984). In 1986, she was named as one of Canada's Best Ten Younger Writers and, a year later, *Dislocations* won the Fellowship of Australian Writers' ANA award. Both *Borderline* (1985) and the more recent *Charades* (1988) were shortlisted for major Australian literary awards. In 1989, Turner Hospital was writer-in-residence at MIT in Boston and—change of hemisphere—in Australian universities in Sydney and Melbourne.

The Australian novelist, Christopher Koch, once wrote of the strain of the "lost hemisphere" in Australian writing, the consciousness of "a ghostly negative image of another landscape": the lost landscape of European ancestral memories. In Turner Hospital's work, this lost hemisphere becomes Australia, its landscape underlying the icy surface of Canada; memories of Queensland emerge in multiple exposure in Toronto or Montreal.

In *The Ivory Swing,* she writes of "the hazardous, balancing act of someone born on the cusp between eras". Themes and shapes of Janette Turner Hospital's later work are anticipated there, as she explores the image of the swing, forever in motion between two poles. Living in a South Indian village with her husband, David, Juliet is besieged by memories of Winston, Ontario, and memories of her lover which clamour beneath the heat and the proprieties of the East. Already, borderlines are blurred "in the precarious terrain of slithering reality".

Through a sustained musical metaphor, *The Tiger in the Tiger Pit* presents themes of familial damage which also emerge in *Borderline* and in the later *Charades*; damage working in arcane ways, perhaps without balm. In the interweaving voices of a family, memories and images of the past uncoil within the framework of the present. These dissonant voices finally converge to produce a symphony composed by Elizabeth who, though wife and mother of three, lives incognito, her imaginative life tucked away inside a charged stillness. For tormented Victoria (foreshadowing Verity in *Charades*), she conjures a dark adagio; for Jason, haunted in the eaves of his dreams (anticipating Nicholas of *Charades*), an allegro, full of syncopation and discord; for Emily, concert violinist, a luminous and nomadic figure, scherzo, a keyboard hide-and-seek; and the taming of the furies is for Edward, her husband, raging against his Iago-body and the indignities of old age, a frantic dreamer of "alternative autobiography" who yearns for "a last Faustian toss with the Devil". With the grandchild Adam, the redemptive figure, the novel becomes a family composition of celebration and hope.

Characteristics of Emily and Elizabeth foreshadow Felicity of *Borderline*. Some notions of time and coevality, developed in *Borderline* and *Charades,* are also anticipated in that earlier novel, as Adam realises that time somersaults, "time and history rolling over and over on themselves, an acrobatic display". In *Charades,* time is a necklace. In *Borderline,* Jean-Marc, the narrator, records that "the past, as Felicity knows and I know, is a capricious and discontinuous narrative, and the present an infinite number of fictions." This baroque novel braids the boundaries and conjunctions of time, dream, memory, art and reality.

Borderline is a Borgesian work across frames of paintings and frames of lives, as dreamers transgress boundaries and enter one another's dreams. It is also a tense and intense mystery/thriller, with contestant versions of events double-dealing and forming new shapes at every shift of the plot. As rival worlds jostle and crowd, clandestine agencies move amid a Dantesque vision of the urban landscape.

From its beginning at the Canada–US border, when a refrigerated truck carrying illegal immigrants is seized, the perversities of chance weave through the lives of Felicity and Gus. Impulsive accomplices, Gus, the insurance salesman, and Felicity, art historian and curator of a private gallery, are caught up in the consequences of smuggling one woman across the border—Dolores Marquez, La Magdalena. Also known as La Salvadora and as La Desconocida, the unknown or unknowable one, her image is "like an icon, pale and luminous". This image hovers over the novel, with shifting patterns of meaning clinging to it. For Felicity, it is like Perugino's painting, "Magdalena", incarnating itself. Mysteries intensify and entangle both Gus and Felicity, as if they are marked, luring sinister figures across the edges of their lives.

In the nightmarish quest for the secret El Salvadoran network, Felicity feels she is playing "deduction roulette". Felicity's fascination with the absurd is her "immunization program", but the sudden link between her collection of bizarre news-clippings and her own experiences has shocking synchronicity, as if the newsprint has broken into the text of her life. Dogged by his own guilt, Gus is haunted by the image of La Magdalena, which summons him back to L'Ascension. As if overtaken by the political realities of Latin America, Felicity, Gus and La Magdalena become "los desaparecidos", the disappeared ones. The novel becomes an extraordinary blend of the political and the postmodern in a manner that suggests modes of Latin American fiction—the novels of Mario Vargas Llosa, or Isabel Allende's *Eva Luna*, or the passion and whirl of Luisa Valenzuela's *The Lizard's Tail*.

A year after their disappearance, Jean-Marc, piano tuner, "a priest of austere and inviolable computations" reconstructs the past. While the narrative moves forward with tightening intrigue, he is "tempering the data" with the dynamics and harmonics of events, among competing notions of art, truth, borderline chimera. Felicity herself seems:

not anchored to everyday, she floats away. Her days are baroque, they curl into each other like acanthus leaves, she lives somewhere between now and then. She moves in and out of her life.

To Jean-Marc, her disappearance seems insubstantial, momentary, because of her "quality of absence", her *otherness*. So he inhabits Felicity's memories, which "writhe and change and regroup in the way true memories do . . . a deluge of the ever-present past". The narrative moves in and out of Felicity's past in India as a child, in Brisbane with her grandparents, and later in Boston with her aunts. Images of her father in India, of her childhood in Queensland, crowd impatiently around the present, importunate.

Jean-Marc records, too, the guises of Gus's guilt, old masks Gus sloughs off, to uncover another self sustained by the image of La Magdalena. Yet the figure Gus glimpses in the orchard is also a glimpse of Felicity's mother and Jean-Marc's own dream of Felicity herself. Here dreams intersect, melting boundaries as if the characters have stumbled into one another's dreams and become locked in the frames of one another's worlds. Jean-Marc's quest for Felicity blurs with Gus's for La Magdalena. Felicity's love for the painter, Seymour, Jean-Marc's father, mirrors other family links. Kathleen's search for her father, Gus, echoes Felicity's yearning for *her* father and counterpoints, too, Jean-Marc's estrangement from his. Reflections shimmer at each other, as if putative selves in contest.

Jean-Marc is aware that "We impose our own lives on the world: the self as template." This is, he says, "the gospel according to Jean-Marc"; his version of truth, where "I temper, I stretch, I embroider." But he also knows the lure of centre stage, of crossing the borderline between character and narrator, dreaming Felicity's dreams and remembering her memories. While Jean-Marc insists all this conjuring is both true and not true, within the novel's multiple layers, intriguing possibilities are held in front of us: perhaps *Borderline* is a diaphanous narrative which clings to Felicity's memory of the Perugino painting; or else her nightmarish image of being entrapped within the frames of Seymour's paintings; or perhaps a Borgesian dreamer is being dreamed through those paintings, which themselves are figures in Jean-Marc's dream.

The tangled mysteries of origin in *Charades*—origins of the universe and of Charade herself—suggest Borgesian dreams. Through Charade's tales to her lover, the Boston physicist, Koenig, Turner Hospital draws on the age-old tradition of Scheherazade and the Thousand and One Nights. Koenig speculates that "he is being slept, or dreamed, and that she invented him. There is a certain elegance to this theory." The novel traffics in the indeterminacies of quantum physics, guises of guilt and damage in a meditation on time and reprieve, holographic memory, and the notion of matter as one of our most persistent illusions.

In *Charades,* there is a doubling of characters, Koenig and Nicholas, Kay and Charade. The doubling also runs into the frame of *Borderline*, the father quest here shadowed by Charade's quest for her father; Seymour and Felicity shadowed by Koenig and Charade; shadowed like Turner Hospital by memories of that landscape perpetually humming beneath the surface of the present, the Tamborine Rainforest of Queensland.

There is sheen and elegance in all of Janette Turner Hospital's work—in the fiery, dynamic prose, in the sensuous rendering of place and time, in the passage of dream and self across caesurae. In the chameleon world of her reality, with masks and spinning versions held in counterpoint, Janette Turner Hospital glides gracefully through paradoxes and circles of meaning, poised between contradictory notions and contestant worlds. With a passion for chimerical borderlines, hers is a baroque consciousness, her vision polyphasic, containing rivalries and revenants, each of which might break away and incarnate in a different context. Her characters inhabit other possible selves, shadow-selves waiting in the wings for an opportunity to dart onto the stage. With a prodigal richness, her work is charged with energy, whirling across absences and presences, constructing elegant whorls of contradiction.

Helen Daniel, Victoria, Australia, 1989

All one's inventions are true, you can
be sure of that. Poetry is as exact a
science as geometry.

Flaubert

Once Chuang Chou dreamed he was a butterfly,
a butterfly flitting and fluttering around.
He didn't know he was Chuang Chou.
Suddenly he woke up and there he was,
solid and unmistakable, Chuang Chou.
But he didn't know if he was Chuang Chou
who had dreamed he was a butterfly
or a butterfly dreaming he was Chuang Chou.

From *The Book of Chuang Tzu*★
4th century BC

Chuang Tzu: Basic Writings, trans.
Burton Watson (NY: Columbia Univ. Press, 1964)

1

At borders, as at death and in dreams, no amount of prior planning will necessarily avail. The law of boundaries applies. In the nature of things, control is not in the hands of the traveller.

Felicity had crossed more borders on more continents than anyone would want to keep a file on. She had the right documents, the right kind of charming smile, a knack for the smooth and non-detaining rite of passage. She was a veteran.

Nevertheless, in retrospect, she was not surprised by what happened. She had a veteran's knowledge and scars.

In the ordinary course of events, she would never have met La Magdalena—which was just one of the names of the woman so many people were looking for. Some said her real name was Dolores Marquez; others called her La Salvadora, perhaps because of where she was from; still others referred to her as La Desconocida, the unknown or unknowable one.

Nor would Felicity have met the man Augustine, whose life was to suffer dislocation. In the ordinary course of events she would never have put herself on the wrong side of the law, nor been obliged to hide from knives and shadows.

But at borders there is never an ordinary course of events.

2

I call them the Holy Innocents, *los desaparecidos*, the disappeared ones. Felicity, Dolores, and Augustine. They had a certain quality that made one think of them as soft-shell people. In a way, their disappearance (if they have really disappeared) was inevitable.

These are violent times, as Seymour says.

And yet, though a year has gone by, I am constantly expecting to hear from one or another of them. Kathleen also expects to hear. She visits frequently, she practically lives here now, she says I remind her of her father. (I am not entirely flattered by this, though she thinks of her father as a saint.) When I go on my rounds, she comes along. Mr. Piano Tuner, she teases. She sits quietly in a corner while I work with tuning fork and lever, and afterwards we tell each other stories. I tell stories about Felicity, she tells them about her father. Neither of us ever met Dolores.

We wait for letters. We wait for a telephone call.

They are the kind of people who lose track, Felicity and Augustine. Who trail off in the middle of a sentence. So I do not necessarily believe they have disappeared permanently. I resist believing it. I begin to ask myself if I dreamed the entire course of events. Every time the telephone rings I expect it to be Felicity. She will be calling from New York or Rome or Mexico City or wherever. (She travels a lot. It has always made her nervous to stay in one place for too long; she is only at ease in transit.)

I can hear the operator's voice: Long distance for Jean-Marc Seymour.

"Felicity!" I'll say. "About time! I had the most extraordinary dream about you. In the end you vanished without a trace."

"Oh dreams!" she'll laugh. Because no one has dreams like Felicity's. Her dreams are as beautiful and mysterious as a hand-painted tarot pack—the Visconti set in the Pierpont Morgan Library, for example. Lavish. Arcane. Felicity's dreams are as clear as runes. You could write a gloss on them.

"Seriously," I'll say. "An incredibly complicated dream. The exegesis would take a whole book."

"So," she'll say. "Write it down quickly, Jean-Marc, before it goes. I'll interpret it for you."

This is a joke. At the girls' school Felicity's aunts sent her to, an extremely proper New England one ("She was so *uncivilized* when she first came to us," the aunts said), there was a very Freudian counsellor, an Interpreter of Dreams (upper-case) who was also the headmistress's lover. Or so the girls claimed. He spoke of the "repercussions" of Felicity's "vagabond life" and made her hand in a daily dream on quarto with one and one-half-inch margins and all official Style Sheet niceties observed. "Before breakfast," he used to insist. "While it's fresh in your mind. Write it down quickly before it goes."

What a twit, I said.

A dream-sniffer, she shrugged. They're a prurient bunch.

To make things interesting for him, she invented a dream in which she slept with a young nobleman in a Rembrandt painting. The headmistress's lover told Felicity that though her feelings for him were understandable, she had a slight problem with reality. Her view of life was out of focus, he said.

He spoke to the headmistress.

The headmistress had a talk with Felicity in the chapel. She prescribed corrective measures and assigned an essay on St. Agatha, who had her breasts shorn off with pruning shears rather than lose her virginity. The topic gave Felicity an abiding interest in the iconography of medieval painting, and perhaps it was this very penance that led to her distinguished career as an art historian and curator of a private gallery. Which in turn led, in a way, to her disappearance.

13

The moral of this, Felicity would say, is that even the dreams you dream up are dangerous and should never be written down without due regard for the consequences.

Nevertheless, I *am* going to write it all down before it goes. For Felicity's delectation when she reappears.

And partly, of course, for Kathleen, who needs to invent her missing father.

But mostly, I confess it, for myself. To try to make sense of what happened. Not that this is going to be easy, since I have so little to go on: a few encounters, a handful of phone calls, a jumble of out-of-sequence information, and of course my lifetime knowledge of Felicity.

Felicity used to say . . .

Correction.

Felicity says: There are only three possible defenses: the first is not caring, and the others are irony and art.

Naturally, given the facts of my own life, I distrust art for reasons that must be obvious. What else would you expect of the Old Volcano's son? And yet I am, you will point out, an attendant lord. True. There are, in my opinion, far too many composers and performers, too few piano tuners. Too many prima donnas, not enough people to hold the props, clean the paintbrushes, build the perfect harpsichord. But I digress.

Felicity, I fear, relied excessively on art, altogether too much on not caring, and not nearly enough on irony. Though when explicators of Seymour's painting occasionally managed to track her down and asked about her early life, she would shrug and say: It didn't happen here. It's too foreign to be of interest to you.

Do you miss those places you came from? I sometimes asked.

Constantly, she said.

And yet, though you travel just about everywhere else, you never go back to those particular—

I can't afford to, she said. I keep a perfect image intact. I'm not going to tamper with it.

She felt at ease in airports and in the hearts of great cities. Because, she said, they are full of other people who don't belong—my closest relations.

14

Of course it is difficult, even for me who knew her so well—*knows* her so well—to separate Felicity from the welter of visual interpretations, footnotes, capsules of biographical speculation. Too many galleries and too many wealthy private citizens own an early work by Seymour (the Old Volcano himself). Far too many people have stared at *Blue Woman* or *Reclining Nude* or *Eve Fragmented* and read their catalogues and thought they knew something about Felicity: the childhood in India, the Australian grandparents, the Boston aunts, the famous affair much photographed in *Vogue* and *Life: "Artist leaves wife of many years for missionary waif."* (Journalistic nonsense, it goes without saying. God only knows how many women came in between my mother and Felicity.)

For the curious, there is a surprising number of these missionary waifs around. Grown up now, of course; relics of imperialist piety. Doctors, lawyers, artists, professors, secular missionaries all. They were born in China or India or obscurer parts of Asia, tossed about through childhood by itinerant preaching and violent uprisings and the whims of various missionary societies and emergent nationalisms. I know. I tune their pianos. I cannot tell you how many living rooms hold their coded mementos: the sandalwood carvings of Krishna, the jade statues, the African masks, the Indonesian shadow puppets. Oh, the owner will shrug with slight embarrassment, I grew up there. Haven't been back since I left at the age of fourteen.

Felicity left earlier than that. Her mother died of heat and childbirth. Her father "went native," a not uncommon indiscretion of that era. "Lost his sense of the uniqueness of the Gospel," as the missionary society put it. He died of further rashness. Australian grandparents (her mother's side of the family) rescued her and then rather carelessly, within a few years, succumbed to terminal old age. Enter, from Boston, her father's sisters, hitherto unaware of Felicity's existence. They restored her, as they put it, to the *respectable* part of the world.

"Don't ask about the years in the wilderness," she says tartly when asked. "It's too foreign. It wasn't in the Promised Land."

15

"Artist's model," gushes some asinine reporter, "hails this country as promised land."

"Honestly!" she says to me, and we laugh.

But the wilderness years are part of her, they seep up. It's like being a live transparency, she says, from a camera that was jammed. A multiple-exposure life.

It shows in some peculiar though secret ways.

For example, that file she keeps (privately she calls it her "wilderness file"): clippings of dark and bizarre events, world news, the familiar international insanities.

"Don't you think that's excessively morbid?" I've asked.

She shrugs. "It's a kind of proof that I didn't invent my own childhood. There are things I saw, things I think I remember . . . and such things still happen. Even stranger things, worse things, though they have no reality here. It's in bad taste to talk about them here."

It *is* in bad taste, in my opinion, but I don't argue with Felicity.

I am often tempted to argue with the twits who mention Felicity in art reviews and catalogues. The rubbish they write. But if I were to be cynical about my reaction—and what, after all, can one afford not to be cynical about?—I quite simply resent anyone else writing about her at all. No one else (besides myself) is *qualified*. I especially resent the presumption of those who think they have her located in the Old Volcano's acrylics. A painting? It's static, which Felicity never is. You speak of his "kinetic" brilliance? The whirlwind of tropical colors around her unmistakable lop-sided eyes?

I can assure you: This is not Felicity.

3

Felicity often overheard herself described as a painter's dream. For years the remark bothered her because it took on a life of its own. In a catalogue, below one of Seymour's portraits, she read: The woman is not real. She is an idealization, an embodiment of the painter's fantasies.

"Why do you tell people that?" she asked, hundreds of gallery openings and cocktail parties later. "What exactly did you mean by it?"

"Mean by it?" Seymour puckered his brows. By then he was in his sixties and weary with fame. Long ago he had moved on to other women, other canvases, other themes. "I don't suppose I meant anything much. I don't remember. I borrowed your eyes quite often." He reached over and touched each eyelid with the pad of his right thumb. "And once, after you'd gone, you appeared as a swan. Did you recognize yourself? Then for a long time you kept showing up as a shadow. But that's far behind us, isn't it? They all seem so pale now, those old canvases."

Now his colors came thick and violent. These are violent times, he was quoted as saying in a prominent art critic's column.

"But what exactly did you see as ideal about me back then?"

"I've never understood why you left," he said. "It was a savage act."

"Or were you claiming to have invented me? Implying that outside of your paintings I was . . . insubstantial?"

"You still creep into my blues," he said sadly. "My blues have always gone closest to the truth. But I don't

17

remember saying it. I don't know what I meant. It's irrelevant. A marginal comment."

"I wish they wouldn't keep quoting it," she said.

She laughed when she told me about it, a sheepish laugh, embarrassed. "I shouldn't let it rattle me, Jean-Marc," she said. "But still . . . when I'm right there, in flesh and blood, in front of his paintings . . . I get this queasy feeling that it's vulgar of me to insist on being literal."

"Oh well," I shrugged (casually, my blithe and bitter self), "my father can make anyone feel like a cipher. He has a knack."

Still, I have to admit, there has always been a quality of absence about her; which is why her disappearance itself seems insubstantial, merely a figure of speech, or a trick of the light, a momentary thing.

If I shut my eyes, I can see her waking in the apartment in Boston on the day that it all began. . .

4

Felicity woke beside her lover in an apartment in Boston. No one lived in the apartment, though they both shared the lease; it was purely for assignations. There were plants and rugs and Marimekko cushions and a waterbed, all the usual pretenses of permanence.

Felicity woke sweating because of the dream.

She was trapped in a painting again. She fitted snugly inside her black outline but there were 144 square inches missing from the middle of her torso. Between her breasts and her pubic hair, the viewer could see straight through to the tropics: mango trees, coconut palms, white sand. A conch shell where her navel might have been. White wave crests frothing like crabs up the sand, a little breeze off the reef stirring her pubic hair. There was a hibiscus behind her ear. Jasmine in fluted letters across her thighs announced: This is not a real woman.

Felicity slipped out of her painting and moved discreetly among the navel-gazers, staring through the tropical hole in her guts along with them, listening to the comments. What does it mean? she heard on all sides. According to the guidebook, someone said, the view could be South India or the Queensland coast of Australia. Felicity considered sticking small flags into the canvas to mark the sites of her hometowns. If you scratch the crotch and sniff, someone said, you can smell papaya.

No touching, please! called a guard.

There was a stain on the floor below the painting.

Felicity mingled with the crowd as it flowed toward the exit turnstiles. Escape was at the forefront of her mind. Passports, passports, the border guard said, and people held their documents ready for showing. Scrutiny, rubber stamp, pass on, that was the routine. But there was something wrong with Felicity's passport; a visa lacking, or a hole in the middle of her photograph. Step aside, she was told. Wait here.

Once the inspector arrived, it was all over. You again, he said, back you go. The man with the brush was waiting as usual and they pasted her back on the canvas, flattening the curves, elongating here, twisting there, making free with the placing of her eyes. She had not even settled herself properly around the empty space—through which the surf hissed and writhed—when the frame was clanged shut around her. Locked. All borders in place. The man with the keys shook the bunch in front of her face.

Felicity woke in a sweat.

Her lover had turned in his sleep and flung an arm across her breasts. She was pinned beneath him. Through the grid of her lashes and across the curved foreground of her cheeks, she could see the delicate hairs, luminous from the street lamp, crosshatching his arm muscle. A novel perspective—though perhaps it had been done in one of da Vinci's anatomical sketchbooks.

Her lover's body pleased her. She could sing it entirely from memory, curve by curve. She loved the taste of its hollows. For years now they had met here and slept here, a comfortable noncommitment. As she eased herself out, she kissed the flesh of his inner forearm—it was vulnerable and sweet—and the small tattoo that had been done in Korea and that tasted of knapsack musk and the 1950s and the Marines. Smooth as a salamander, she slipped past the tips of his fingers. No! he moaned in his sleep, groping at the air, but she tiptoed barefoot to the chair by the window and put on her clothes. The street lamp threw wings of white light on her shoulders, her dress fluttered and sighed. Nothing was left out of place: his shoes black as glass and his woollen socks under the chair, the pinstripe suit, charcoal gray, neatly folded, the silk tie quiet as a furled snake. Everything spoke of regret. In stockinged feet she slithered down to the street.

A deserted city at this hour, all her own. She loved it this way. On the bridge over the Charles River a man wrapped in newspapers whispered fond words to a bottle of Five Star whiskey. The concrete railings listened. Felicity thought of temple steps and beggars, another life. An emaciated hand with a begging bowl reached out through the windy space at her navel. She drove on through the dimly lit streets to her own apartment.

The phone was ringing when she entered.

"Felicity," her lover said. His name was Aaron. "I can't stand this anymore. I'm leaving my wife."

"I was afraid you were going to say that. I had a premonition."

"I'm coming over," he said.

"No! No, please don't do that."

She knew he was bitterly hurt. "If you knew the cost of this decision," he reproached. "The children. The chaos."

"I know." She was speaking gently, she felt relieved. "We cannot have that on our conscience. I won't let you do it."

"But we can't go on like this. We can't."

"No. We'll have to end it."

They did this once or twice a year, for greater or lesser periods of time. Rehearsals for termination. Eventually, no doubt, one of their abeyances would ripen into a permanent rift.

Nevertheless she would leave town for a few days in case he did anything rash. There was always a certain amount of grief to contend with, the knack of solitude to be reacquired. She roamed barefoot around her apartment, her own territory, free. She touched her arrangement of arcana: the Queensland conch shell; the sandalwood figure that smelled of monsoons; the lovers drifting in an ivory embrace; the photograph of her father—he was on a beach mending nets; and the one of the mother she had never known—a woman in white, walking away from the camera. (They were married under a frangipani tree, Felicity's parents. But there is no photograph of the wedding. No one in Trivandrum had a camera at the time.) And there is Seymour's portrait of her: the two eyes floating out of a sea of blues, one eye higher than the other. Below the eyes there is a suggestion of a woman's body, more an echo of one really, a sort of lapis lazuli shape swimming up through aquamarine—as though Seymour had layered his way into abstraction. The painting is called *The Ghost of Happiness.*

She turned to look at her reflection in the mirror. Her eyes, the right one slightly higher than the left, stared back. I am often distressed, she confessed to them, by the gulf between experience and the possibility of representing it in any medium other than memory.

Felicity, Seymour still says to anyone who asks (and of course they often do), is the sanest, the most real, the most ideal of all the women I have known.

Look at her, he says, when she's talking. The way she cannot refrain from touching: her listener, her own hair, the coat sleeve of the gentleman beside her. She lives at the tips of her senses.

And a cunt made for fucking, he sighs fondly (his hand on his interviewer's knee), a purely sensual being.

He slides his hand up to the interviewer's thigh.

Of course, he murmurs, muffled, into the valley between his interviewer's breasts, I rarely see her anymore, but still . . .

It is a matter of personal honor with him that an interviewer leave dishevelled. He is particular about interviews, rarely granting them. Wrong place, wrong time, wrong sex, he once snapped at Mr. K., the well-known art critic.

As the latest interviewer, flushed, her pupils dilated, is collecting her notes and clothing, Seymour lights a cigarette and sighs: Felicity ruined me for other women.

Felicity contemplated her lopsided eyes in the mirror.

Once upon a time, she remembered, Seymour had said: "I prefer the irregular."

"Well, I'm certainly that," she had laughed. She was just a green girl and blushing. "My entire history. Nobody even believes it's real."

"Anything's real once I've painted it," he said.

But it was his afterthought, so casually added, that

22

seduced her: "I knew your father. Before he went chasing God."

Felicity turned from the mirror of her past and opened her bedroom window. She watched the dawn leak between the buildings and into the streets and the sky, a capillary action of amber. Sadness oppressed her, and she felt an urgent need to flee it. She needed to be on the road, on the move, defying another border. I will spend the weekend at the cottage outside Montreal, she decided. She felt better immediately.

She showered and did her exercises.

She stepped into a pale blue sundress and a pair of sandals and went out to buy fresh rolls for breakfast. The phone was ringing as she left. Oh Aaron, she sighed, pausing, the key in her hand. But she decided not to answer it.

5

"Jean-Marc," Felicity used to say to me, "you are the world's most patient person."

Perhap it's true. One note at a time, that is my credo.

There are days, however, when I feel like Hercules emptying the ocean with a shell. Today, for example: two pianos, both recalcitrant. The first was a Boston Chickering about fifty years old, a fine old instrument, though much abused. God knows how it ended up in the home of a Montreal building contractor, but he is *nouveau riche* and believes a grand piano gives class. He lets his children bang the hell out of it. I had considerable difficulty repairing the action in the middle range, not that a soul in that house would know the difference.

Still, I have infinite patience. When I left, the jangled air was noticeably unsnarled. Tonight tranquillity will take the building contractor by surprise; it will seep into his thoughts like a perfume remembered. Such is harmony, the science of proper alignments. There is no problem too great for mathematics and the tuning fork.

Kathleen sat in a corner and watched while I worked. She dreams and smiles; when she thinks of her father she grows pensive until I say something paternal, and at such times I could live off the look in her eyes. I have discovered that admiration sustains—and also, I suppose, corrupts. When she goes off to college . . . well, I have begun to think of September as eclipse, which is foolishness, since she will be here at McGill and I will certainly offer my services as mentor and tutor. I ply her with books. The temptation to mold her is immense, though misunderstood by her mother and the formidable Aunt Marthe. I imagine a visit from the latter, her eyebrows

24

knitting together like offended caterpillars: What are your intentions? she will demand.

It's a question I ask myself.

In his studio the Old Volcano smirks. He laughs up his sleeve. He guffaws.

I have explained the craft of "tempering" to Kathleen because it applies to this attempt to set things down.

Piano tuning, I've told her, is both a science and an art (though not an art in the flamboyant and egotistical sense. Not the Old Volcano's style at all).

It is a science in that it follows exact mathematical laws: 440 cycles per second for the note of A. I strike the tuning fork, I strike the note, I show her how I bring the vibrations into agreement. When the two sets of sound waves are in flawless alignment (like two bodies locked in sublimely mutual climax), the A is tuned to perfect concert pitch. Then I turn to the fifths and the thirds, making precise mathematical emendations. I tap, I listen, I adjust the pins, I am priest of austere and inviolable computations.

But here is the crux.

When the octave is complete, each note mathematically infallible, the scale a paradigm of accuracy in beats per second, the total effect may nevertheless not sound "right" to the genuinely musical ear. To the sophisticated ear. The ear of the initiate.

This is where tempering comes in.

This is where art and intuition and musicality apply.

This is what distinguishes the master piano tuner from the mere technician.

An octave may need to be "stretched" to the minutest degree, a fifth augmented, a third softened. There are no guidelines now. Tuning forks and mathematics are useless. The tastes of a concert pianist must be taken into account, the pulse of a hall or a room taken, a quantum leap made into the souls of the composer and the performer and the tuner, into their dark corners and most secret desires. The absolutely accurate is too narrow; it is false and imperfect. I am after something more organic:

25

the truth. Which, as Oscar Wilde said, is never pure and rarely simple. I am after the whole of it, the messy unpresentable fantasies, I am going for the well-tempered heart of the matter.

This afternoon: an ancient and magnificent Steinway in one of the Westmount mansions. I wanted to be alone with it (they are so highly strung) and was very annoyed that a maid kept coming into the room to dust, to arrange the flowers, to bring me tea on a silver tray. Exasperating.

Though I confess my state of mind was not the best from the start. During lunch there was a *contretemps* with Aunt Marthe on the telephone. Kathleen thought it wiser to go home. Aunt Marthe does not approve of me. He may have a French name, she sniffs (so Kathleen tells me), but his heart is *anglais*. Perhaps this was why I had such trouble with the Steinway, why there was so much interference. But eventually I pulled concord from the old strings and pins, my gift to the mansion's chatelaine who was a frail sparrow of a woman in her eighties. When I left she took my hand in both of hers; they were trembling; thank you, she said, and then went on saying it. Thank you, thank you, thank you. A fitting sense of priorities, I thought. It is not after all a small thing. Only consider: the entire cacophonous universe could be tuned. This is a mathematical possibility and a great comfort, requiring only infinite patience.

I proceed note by note.

Kathleen and I have pooled our knowledge.

This is what I have done: the phone calls, such dates as we can vouch for, the occurrences real or believed to be real, have all been committed to file cards, a box full of three-by-five-inch information. The cards have been shuffled into chronological sequence. It was satisfying, this ordering and shaping of memory. Three lives on tap. The bald facts.

But the bald facts do not make sense, of themselves.

Now is the time to breathe life into them, to examine

the dynamics and harmonics, to look for patterns, resonances, meaning. Time for tempering the data. Time to begin at the beginning of the events that led up to the disappearances—well before I met Kathleen or her father. Before I was aware of their existence.

6

For Gus (christened Augustine, which he detested, by a pious mother) the border was a source of trepidation (what wasn't?) but also something of a reprieve, a compulsory delay while he took stock of the weather of his emotions. Forecast: instability. A clouded future. He was groping through anxieties: overdrafts, mortgage renewal, the stink of adultery on his underclothes, the dread of Therese's sharp nose, a rainbow of guilts—and all in pitched battle with a valiant little guerrilla flank of self-confidence, a novelty this, his fix from the sales conference. Success, success: it could be pulled from the air like dandelion puffs. So the speakers had promised.

At the checkpoint he was handed his duty-free liquor, a fifth of Scotch. As soon as he was through with formalities he would pull over to the shoulder of the road and imbibe comfort, just a little, to calm his nerves. A few more minutes and he would be through—although the crack in his windshield (courtesy of a stone on the turnpike) seemed to leer and promise delays. Border nervousness, habitual, drizzled into his thoughts. Not that he should expect trouble. After all, he was crossing north, he was coming back *in*. He expected any Canadian immigration officer to share his relief: home is the sailor, and the sheep to the fold, and the fellow citizen to safe haven; unscathed, unmugged, unseduced by kinder taxes south of the border.

On the other hand, difficulties would not surprise Gus unduly. Sooner or later he would be caught and punished for something, his dreams were full of disaster. He knew what caused this. His pathology had been defined in amazing detail only yesterday, in the conference room of the Grand Hyatt in New York: negative thinking. The source, said the speaker, of all evil. Gus knew he was

28

addicted. This came from being Catholic and Canadian; no one could say it didn't make a difference.

Ahead of him, like the monitoring eyes of electronic confessionals, the control-point lights blinked a summons. Only two of the six lanes were open, and as the blonde woman in the sporty Datsun ahead of him veered right into the neighboring line, he slowed to a halt behind a refrigeration van with "Beckett's for Meat" emblazoned across its rear doors.

Weird blue, he thought of the Datsun, eyeing its driver. Custom color, custom female, classy, both out of his bracket. The woman must have been wearing a strapless sundress, or else one of those things with shoulder-straps thin as spun sugar. From Gus's angle of vision she appeared naked, her tanned arms amber and tempting as duty-free whiskey. The blue of her car sang an exotic jazz note, disturbing. He thought of cornflowers.

(Not blue, Felicity would tell him in a near future as yet inconceivable. Lapis lazuli.)

Ahead of the woman with cornsilk hair and her excessively blue Datsun, a Winnebago with Ontario plates sprouted weekend fishermen. They were perhaps inebriated, not given to meekness, and they appeared to be having minor troubles. As did the Beckett's Meat man. Ah well, Gus sighed, dreaming of his Scotch, what else could one expect of those poor buggers in Customs and Immigration, obliged as they were to sit in a sort of upright coffin and wear ties in this summer's heat? Soon he would be through. He readied his driver's license.

Business or pleasure? the man would ask.

Pleasure, that scalding word. Probably the man had X-ray eyes, probably he could smell philanderers from three cars away. Gus fidgeted with his ID; its corners were curled and dog-eaten. *But did you take pleasure, my son, in your impure thoughts?*

Gus would lodge a not guilty plea: Business, sir.

But suppose the man persisted? Suppose he smirked: And what exactly was the nature of your business?

If that happened, it was entirely possible that Gus would answer like an obedient Christian Brothers schoolboy:

29

I cheated on my wife (though it was nothing, it meant nothing, an open and shut case of sexual starvation, what legs she had!). I am guilty. *I took pleasure.* Forgive me, Father.

He raked his fingers through his thinning hair, gave his head a shake, flinging off irritations. He concentrated on the carnations he would give to his wife. Thinking positively. Also there were the gifts for his four children. He cradled the fifth of Scotch and its duty-free pink slip on his knees. He held his driver's license between his teeth. He was ready.

At about that moment, the strangeness began.

The driver of the Beckett's Meat van got down from his cabin. He pushed back his Boston Red Sox baseball cap, gesticulating, asking the August sky to bear witness to bureaucratic insanity. Untouched, buttressed by uniform and badge, the officer indicated that an opening of the rear doors was necessary. Demurral. Argument. A crossfire of anger. For God's sake, man, Gus thought irritably, just *do* it and let's all get moving again. But the Beckett's man leaned his back against his doors, a martyr for Small Business, the Massachusetts plate glaring from between his straddled legs. He gazed heavenward, a real ham. Mouthed at Gus through the cracked windshield: *Jesus!* and spread his hands in an elaborate gesture of despair. The gesture said: This is the way they get their kicks, poor bastards.

It was, finally, the officer himself who pulled on the large chrome lever and pitched them all into shock.

Exposed: a roiling curtain of carcasses. Steers. Gutted, obscenely lanced on thick hooks, the lapels of their slit underbellies flapping and gaping like eyelids around empty sockets, they swayed in the sun. There was a metal screech as the officer shunted the hooks across a track, then silence, then something amazing: a group of people, perhaps ten of them, men and women, huddling together from cold. They gazed out like exhumed relics of another world. Like animal things still warm and faintly bleating in the midst of an abattoir's carnage.

Gus blinked and glanced at the whiskey bottle (no, he

had not yet broken its seal), then back at the freakish group portrait in its frame of dead cattle. He looked away, half afraid for himself. Hallucination? He gripped the steering wheel: solid. He cast about for other moorings—and in the eyes of the Datsun driver saw something he recognized. It's not just me then, he thought.

The look they exchanged was the look of strangers made suddenly intimate.

Felicity had certainly seen more distressing sights. Or almost certainly. It was so difficult to be sure on a continent where no one believed in the unpleasant.

At the time of her birth, in another country, people were killing one another over issues of land and language. You were riot-induced, her father said. Your mother was not prepared. Of course Felicity remembered none of this. Perhaps her father had invented details. What proof did she have?

Still, by the age of five, she herself had seen children die in the streets. Before her eyes, sores had flowered and unfolded like peonies on the skin of beggars. She had watched as a girl of her own age tore apart a dead rat and ate it raw. Years later, of course, the aunts in Boston said she must have imagined such things. Felicity, they told their friends, is *so* theatrical. Such a taste for the macabre. She will become an artist or a writer.

But this was happening in front of her Datsun, within the chrome frame of her windshield. Otherwise, perhaps, she would have the usual trouble knowing whether to believe. And even so the composition invited doubt: the blankets and shawls warding off refrigeration, the glitter of frost on raven hair. She thought of cave dwellers. Of refugees from another time and place—the Ice Age, say, or the age of myth.

The truck-travelling cave dwellers did not stir. They sat there blinking through their ice-crusted lashes like owls transfixed by dawn. The Beckett's driver and the immigration officer seemed frozen too. Motionless.

Felicity did not breathe.

Without knowing it, Gus rubbed the St. Christopher

31

medal that dangled from his dashboard and reverted to
Latin: *Mater misericordiae, ora pro nobis.* Now and at the
hour of our death, amen.

Silence, the weight of it, bruised.

Then pandemonium.

As though a starting gun had been fired, the Beckett's
man suddenly lunged away from the officer and began
sprinting back across no-man's-land. A whistle. Somewhere
a siren. Guns, warning shots, armed men. Herding: of the
cave dwellers, and of the drunken Winnebago crowd, who
waved fishing gear and outrage like flags. The official
building swallowed everyone whole.

Then a settling, and the kind of quietness that drops
milkily from the sky after thunder.

Gus stared at the abandoned control booths, at the driver-
less trucks, at the pallid blood-streaked rinds of cattle still
rocking gently on their hooks. He looked across at the
impossibly blue Datsun in which the fair-haired woman
was resting her head on her steering wheel. Stunned,
apparently. He looked behind him: there were no other
cars waiting. It was the tag end of a summer's afternoon,
and sensible travellers were sipping drinks in air-conditioned
road stops, postponing border irritations till evening. Gus
stared down Route 87, curling emptily back into New
York State and innocence. He wished he had stopped at
the last motel.

He turned his windshield wipers on and then off. He
was not sure why. To see if logic applied, perhaps. He
opened his door and staggered from his car as from a
fallout shelter. Avoiding looking at the carcasses, but feeling a puff of the dwindling refrigerated air, he walked
behind the open van and leaned on the front of his own
Chevy, facing the Datsun. The duty-free Scotch was still
in his hand and he broke its seal and put the bottle to his
lips. Sweet comfort. All this time he was watching the
woman slumped over her wheel and now he grunted in
her direction, dribbling whiskey, as though suspecting it
might only be possible to communicate at primal levels.

She stirred like a waking sleeper and turned to look at

him. He held out the bottle and she opened her door and swung her legs out onto the pavement, bare legs, smooth and tanned under her pale blue sundress. (He could see the spaghetti straps now.) Nice, he thought. And had a sudden urge to splash her with whiskey and lick it off. Dazed, she reached to accept the bottle and he watched as she swallowed a greedy mouthful, saw the muscles flinch and the eyes focus.

"Thank you," she said. Like a concussed patient reviving.

"Well . . ." Taking back his bottle, his voice shaky.

"Yes. A bit . . . bizarre, wasn't it? Illegal immigrants, I suppose."

"Oh," he said. "Yeah. Guess so." And then: "Weird blue."

"Pardon?"

"Your car."

"Oh. Yes. I had it done. Not blue, in the usual sense. Lapis lazuli, actually. Eccentric of me."

He took another mouthful of whiskey and began to find the situation extremely funny. "Wish I'd stocked up on duty-free. Not a soul left. Could have got a whole case through."

Laughter—it was as though he had been injected with it or had breathed it in, in some gaseous form—began to inhabit him. Any breathalyzer test would have verified: *hysteria cachinnata*, a helpless and immoderate mirth. They both gave in to it, leaning against their cars, holding their aching sides, gasping, rubbing their wet and salty cheeks with the backs of their hands. They were almost in pain.

Gus knew he was laughing partly from relief. What could Therese possibly smell from the far side of fresh-slaughtered beef? Red herrings, as it were. "F—f—fi . . ." fishy cows he tried to say, in a paroxysm of glee.

Felicity's laughter was that of someone waking in the night, not certain if the sound of revelry came from a dimly heard party or was part of a dream; not certain if the dream was good or bad.

"Those fishermen," she gasped, fixing firmly on the

33

particular. "They were so incensed. Did you see the big one . . . ?"

"Waving his fish! The way he . . . the way he . . ."

"As proof of his . . ."

"I'm not a . . . not a . . ." Gus mimicked.

They were holding on to each other now, weak with strained hilarity and dissipating anxiety.

"And then," Gus spluttered, "the way he slapped . . . kind of *slapped* that dead cow with his fish . . ."

But this washed them abruptly against the somber offside of their laughter. As suddenly as it had visited them, the demoniac merriment departed. They stared into the meat van around which a nimbus of flies now quivered, a pungent cave guarded by hook-hung carcasses as by a row of rotting pillars. Other carcasses (perhaps removed from their hooks by the stowaways) were stacked along the sides and back of the van, slit underbellies facing the walls, so that the remaining space resembled the interior of a sandbagged fort.

"Well," Gus said soberly. "Do we wait here all day? Or do we just drive through? Or what?"

"Under the circumstances . . . I'd rather not look as though I were trying to get away with something. Suddenly I feel . . . I don't feel so well." Sinking back on to her driver's seat but leaving her door open. "My legs feel like . . ." All this, she was thinking, because Aaron had threatened to upset the status quo again.

"Have another drink," Gus offered.

She grimaced. "Don't like Scotch, actually. Still . . ." Unsteadily she walked towards him again. "Perhaps I will. Thanks."

"Gus," he said.

"Excuse me? Oh. Mine's Felicity."

He did not even raise an eyebrow. It seemed to go with the lappy's leisurely or whatever the hell it was.

"Someone coming," he said. "Oh shit. We'll be nailed for opening the booze." Jerkily he screwed the cap back on, his eyes flitting about and fastening on the large garbage can beside the control booth. He was calculating his chances of disposing of evidence, but the man was upon them and absorbed in other matters. He stopped at the cabin of the Beckett's van, paused in mild surprise, noticing them, and said: "Someone will be out. All hell's broken loose in there. Got to impound the van."

He revved the engine. Gus and Felicity stared vacantly into the gaping hold where the carcasses began to jostle one another in agitation. Those that were stacked horizontally, like so many folded table napkins, began to slide and thump across the floor. There was a lurch, a screaming of metal hooks. The unfastened doors flapped to and fro, the hanging carcasses swooped up and out like playground swings. When the van gunned suddenly forward there was a horrible crowding of the floor-stacked meat at the doors, as of bodies panicking to escape from a burning building. A stampede of dead cattle: thump after thump, the grotesque smack of butchered flesh on pavement. And the hook-hung siblings careened violently away toward the immigration building, gymnastic on their tracks, keening a wild metal note of sympathy.

Gus reeled from the impact of three hundred pounds of bullock. Felicity covered her face with her hands. There was something quite appalling about this indignity to the great slaughtered torsos, something that affronted deeply and powerfully, like the desecration of a grave.

And then La Magdalena appeared, illogically, as in a vision.

I *must* be dreaming, Felicity decided. Or perhaps a disorderly fantasm was slopping out beyond the borders of sleep. It was, she told me later, so typical of her night-time collages, a multiple exposure, a Perugino superimposed on a Bosch or a Munch. Or one of Seymour's latest.

Gus blamed his duty-free Scotch.

They stared at the carcass nearest them. Its unzipped front, wilting in the hot air, curled inwards—a cesarean wound around a fetus. Something, someone, was *in* there. A woman. Across her forehead hung a tendril of intestine, ghoulish curl. Her knees were hunched up and her arms were crossed over her breasts like a careful arrangement in a coffin. There was no way of knowing if the eyes registered the two figures bending over them. Though they blinked every few seconds—the only sign of life—they were blank and unreflecting. Felicity was shaken by the face. She knew it from a painting. It was the kind of face that, seen fleetingly in a crowd, is not easily forgotten.

"Perugino," she said. "The *Magdalena*."

"What?" Gus crossed himself.

Afterwards, neither of them could recall any sense of making a decision, or even of being particularly conscious of what they were doing. Felicity dropped to her knees and took hold of the frigid hands. It was despair that she touched, an absence of all trust in warmth, as though the body, in abandoning hope, were backing quietly into a state of nonbeing. There was no movement, and no flicker of response from the eyes.

"We'll have to lift her," Gus said. "You take her arms. The trunk, I suppose? There's only one suitcase in mine."

"Don't be crazy. They always look in the trunk."

"Oh shit." He rapped his knuckles against his forehead. "But how the hell *will* we . . . ?"

They paused. It was not a simple matter.

Felicity said: "Back seat. On the floor. I'll cover her with a sleeping bag."

"My car, then. It'll have to be." His voice skittered momentarily, like a boy's voice breaking. He cleared his throat, recovered. "Yours is too small."

"What's your citizenship?" she asked urgently, as though the question were germane to the size of their cars.

"What?"

"Citizenship. What's your citizenship?"

"Canadian. Why?"

"Born there?"

"Yes. Why?"

"They always ask." She was rubbing the woman's hands, brushing wet strands of hair from her face. "Poor thing. Thank God she's lucked onto one person with no complications."

Gus had no idea what she was talking about, but who thought logic would apply? It came to him that he still had the whiskey bottle rammed into his coat pocket, and he put it to the woman's lips. Amber rivulets coursed from the sides of her mouth and down her neck, but some of the fire must have found its mark. There was a shudder, a swallow, a momentary focusing of the eyes.

"Hang in there, baby," he whispered. "Drink up."

Felicity looked at him, analytical, assessing risks at lightning speed. There was the larger space in his car, his uncomplicated passport, his ordinariness. Surely any border guard or policeman would classify instantly: Salt of the earth. An innocent.

On the other hand, there was his nervousness. And a powerful sense, somehow, of a child with one eye perpetually open for the big stick. A lousy liar if complications should occur. (And when, if not now?) Clearly someone who would blunder into unstoppable truth-telling.

"My car," she said decisively. "Pull this damned ribcage open, quick!"

He obeyed instinctively. There was a cracking sound, and Gus was six years old again, smelling the sawdust and guts of a butcher's shop: cleaver descending, bones snapping to attention on the block, the butcher—bloody to the elbow—reaching in to grasp handfuls of soft insides too awful for a boy to tear his eyes from. Gus extracted the soft bundle and cradled it against his chest as though it were his first-born, the one he had never held.

"Through here," Felicity said urgently, pulling the driver's seat forward.

He had always hated two-door cars. He had known, somehow, that he would never get Therese to the hospital in time, her hastily packed overnight bag jammed half in, half out, of the back, so that the passenger seat could not be pushed properly upright and Therese had to pleat herself forward over her own contractions. (A judgment, her sister Marthe always said, for not waiting until they were married. It must have been true. There had been no more sons.) He heaved and shoved, sobbing.

"Take it easy," Felicity murmured. "I've got my eye on the building. No one coming."

The body in Gus's arms settled like a rag doll around the hump in the floor. Felicity covered everything with a sleeping bag over which she scattered some books, a bag

37

of apples, a crumbling packet of cookies. Artless disorder. Traveller's junk.

"Right." She straightened up, brisk, rubbing her hands. "I'm not going to wait here sweating."

Gus watched her stride across the pavement, positive thinking personified. He wished he could get the knack of it, but his limbs and guts seemed to be liquefying. He managed to get back into his own car, but it was inconceivable that he would be able to move it forward, stop it, answer questions, and drive on again. He sat behind the wheel and waited passively for doom, though the St. Christopher medal found its way into his palm, a small comfort.

Movement and confusion. The fishermen returning like a swarm of bees from unsatisfactory flowers. A buzzing haze of resentment, he registered that. Also Felicity walking back with an immigration officer, her head tilted to one side: a deferential listener, the kind who encourages self-esteem and expansiveness in the speaker. From this distance the two had the appearance of strangers beginning a flirtation.

". . . told to watch out for a van, you see," the man was saying. "But we didn't know what kind, so we had to be very thorough with all of them. Got a tip-off from Boston." Gus missed the next bit, and then he heard: "served deportation papers last week. Trying to jump the gun."

Felicity's voice, on a falling inflection: "It doesn't seem possible, so far from the Mexican border."

"Nothing stops them," the officer said. "They'll cross twenty states, God knows how, bribe their way out of anything. You wouldn't believe. Fear of death, they try to tell you, but it's green stuff they want." He rubbed his fingers together. "Not enough to go round down there, so they come to nibble at our pie. Tens of thousands in Boston and New York, and now it's spreading to us. All this economy needs."

"And so you . . .?"

"Yeah. Round them up and send them home. When we can catch them."

38

"Poor things," Felicity sighed. "Rather sad work for you, isn't it?" She was giving him the full benefit of mournful but understanding eyes.

He appeared to be mesmerized. Coughed a little. "Well now," he said. "You get a bit cynical in this line of work." She lowered, for a moment, her sad eyes, and he added hastily, "Not pleasant, of course, though someone has to. . . . And we do get to be grateful for a bit of excitement." He seemed embarrassed by the admission and became brisk.

"Well now, young lady. Where are you headed? And for how long?"

"My cottage near Montreal. For the weekend." With a rueful laugh. "This was supposed to be a quiet interlude."

He clicked his tongue in sympathy. "And you've come from?"

"Boston." She realized instantly: mistake! Damn.

Almost imperceptibly the man stiffened. "Boston?" A pause. She could hear the click-click of association, hear his ponderous thought. "You've been following the meat van for quite a way then?"

She puckered her brows in concentration. Gus thought suddenly: What do I know of her? And sensed the liquefaction of his bowels reaching some critical stage. It would all be over in seconds. Scandal, complicity, trying to prove he'd never laid eyes on her before, trying to explain why he'd . . . (my God! what *had* he done?), criminal charges, God knew what.

"I do recall that the van tried to pass me about ten miles back," Felicity was saying thoughtfully, with the air of one summoning up intense powers of concentration. "I remember because I get these silly competitive urges, you know? We stayed level for a mile or so, before I realized what I was doing and let it get ahead. But before that"—she closed her eyes tightly—"no, I'm afraid I can't recall being aware of it at all."

"What's your citizenship?" the man asked.

She raised her eyebrows in surprise. "American." As though he had asked: What sex are you?

"Born there?"

39

Felicity sighed. "As it happened," she said apologetically, "no. I was born in India."

"India!" He looked at her sharply. She might have told him she was smuggling heroin. She was tempted to say: I know; very poor taste on my part. But border guards rarely had a sense of humor. She knew the rules.

(Border Catechism No. 1. Question: What shall constitute a legitimate and acceptable human being?

Answer: A person, preferably of Anglo-Saxon stock, with the decency to have been born in a country familiar to the presiding official, and respectable in his eyes. Such person shall be deemed to be largely above suspicion, provided he/she does not exhibit vagabond and philandering territorial habits. Past association with only one other country, two at the most, shall be deemed appropriate.)

It was the way the officer looked at her that goaded Felicity. She could not resist. "It was negligent of me, I know. But my father was preoccupied with medical matters, you see. A local epidemic. And then I arrived in the middle of a riot, which finished my mother."

"Finished her?" The immigration officer was bemused.

"She died. Terrible timing."

The officer was not certain whether she considered the riots or her own advent or her mother's death inopportune. He was not certain whether she was serious or joking. He observed her warily. Felicity, vulnerable, smiled into his eyes with lambent trust.

"Well," he said. He cleared his throat. "Still. Could I see your driver's license, please?"

"Of course."

He retired into the booth and typed something into a terminal. "Routine check," he said apologetically. "I need to look inside your trunk."

Gus held his breath, his guts seeping slowly from him, his head light. The officer's face was floating now, swaying away from its shoulders, performing arabesques. Were the movements benign? Gus watched Felicity drift to where her car lay at anchor. Everything fluid, the edges of objects undulating like sea anemones, Felicity's car shimmering and swimming to the oceanic Other Side of the border, lappy's something-or-other into wild blue yonder.

Now judgment.

Was the officer speaking to him? To Augustine Kelly, who had *taken pleasure* and was guilty of mortal sin? He could hear nothing. I can't hear you, Father, he whispered. And the priest, not unkindly, urged: Speak up. A strange vibration, a voice perhaps, but not one he knew, issued from somewhere inside his chest. "Too much for me," it said. "All this. Don't feel safe till I'm back on Canadian soil."

Did the priest smile? His face was flowing in the swaying air and difficult to read. Absolution was perhaps being granted, God's mercy being infinite. It seemed that the Chevy's engine was readying itself, a Gregorian chant throbbing from beneath his feet: Amen, Amen. His car was swallowing highway. He thought he saw a road sign in French.

Miraculously, he was through.

7

Across the border, some of the changes are immediate and obvious. Interstate 87 from New York City (catchment Thruway for the Massachusetts Turnpike from Boston and for I-81 from Philadelphia and Washington) becomes L'Autoroute Quinze to Montreal. The speed limit, to visiting Americans, seems to catapult into the stratosphere because it is in kilometers. Instead of Schuyler Falls and Plattsburgh and Coopersville, the little towns have names like Ste. Clothilde, L'Ascension, St. Jérôme du Bois.

But other changes are intangible.

Felicity's Datsun, like a spooked horse that knows the way home by instinct, left Autoroute 15 a scant ten miles north of the border and turned sharply east, lured by the scent of river pine. Felicity drove by some sixth sense.

Conifers crowded her. Maples, oaks, a commotion of sumac, even the occasional elm that had survived the plague, all jostled for roadside space. It was a country road she followed, narrow and rutted, winding at whim to mark the boundary of some old *habitant* farm or the bank of a creek—though Felicity saw none of it, having crossed another border.

Her life was much like one of those small lizards that Australian children chop into sections with penknives. The children do not believe they are being cruel because each scaly severed section wriggles away and becomes a whole lizard again; at least, so the children believe. So they used to tell Felicity when she went to school with them in Brisbane. She thinks she must have picked up the habit from the lizards; she is prone to incarnation into one of her segments.

In the country she has returned to, there are flame trees flamboyant as whores. Red petals are falling on her

42

shoulders, and a brick-colored dust rises from her sandals in soft plumes. She is alone. Her father, as usual, is off in some village with stethoscope and comfort. Felicity is watching two black crows and two Untouchables fighting over a not-quite-dead cow. The crows are going for the eyes: slash, slash, the beaks brutal. The men are beating at the crows with *lathis*, but they are afraid of them too; they flail out with their sticks and then dart back. Of course they are not permitted to touch the cow until it is dead. A caw of triumph: one crow swoops off on arrogant wings with its prize like an amber ping-pong ball in its beak.

Felicity screams and covers her own eyes with her hands and runs, slipping and stumbling, all the way back to their house where her *ayah*, her Didiji, is waiting. But the road is fiendishly rutted from monsoon runoff. The Datsun loses its footing, spins, lists dangerously, pitches into the dust and grass of the shoulder. Felicity brakes, trembling, and throws herself into the comforting arms of Didiji.

"Listen," Didiji croons, "you do not know the whole story. Listen, Felissiji. For many months the crow-demon has been tormenting our village. He has taken a thousand forms. Don't we know it? Haven't we snapped at all thousand of them with wet clothing when they swooped at us on the roof and in the courtyard? He has eaten the ears of new rice, that wicked crow-demon, and savaged the plantains and jackfruit before picking time. But listen, Felissiji: the goddess, who devotes herself to the prosperity of those who offer her *puja*, has taken the form of a cow to tempt the crow-demon to his own destruction.

"Listen, little peacock feather. If you had only stayed to watch, you would have seen that the crow-demon has choked on the eye of the cow and fallen to earth like a stone!"

In Didiji's stories, the demons always lost; the Untouchables, whose *dharma* it was to eat carrion, were fed as they should be; and the will of the gods triumphed. "As it always does, Felissiji. It cannot *not*." Didiji never knew any English; and Felicity, today, can remember only a dozen or so words of Malayalam, yet the story (in which language?) survives entire in her memory.

43

"But what about the cow, Didiji?" she cries into the past. "It was still alive. It was writhing in pain."

The monsoon is at her car window, an importunate battering. She winds it down and says vehemently: "It won't serve, Didiji. It won't serve."

"Are you *crazy*, or what?" Gus reached in and took hold of her by the shoulders and shook her. He seemed to be in a rage. As in: disgusted married man brings hysterical young mistress to her senses. "You're not even hurt!" he shouted. The final outrage, an affront to panicked concern.

Felicity is still arguing with the past: It's not just the question of suffering, Didiji. It's the problem of the proper response.

"That's the question, isn't it?" she said to Gus. "Just how accountable *are* we? You and me."

"Jesus," Gus said.

"Why us? Why me?" Felicity asked dully. "Why me? I mean, did I inherit this, or what?"

"Oh Jesus," Gus said. "Oh shit. Do I know how to pick 'em!"

He clambered out of the ditch and walked back to his car for the whiskey, twisting handfuls of his hair into peaks as he went. How he yearned for the known sins and miseries: the simple, guilt-fraught act of adultery; the tight lips (both sets) of his wife. How he wished he were sidling into Therese's kitchen, sheepish, flowers in hand, facing nothing more than a cold shoulder and a cold bed.

He shambled back, wiping his mouth with his sleeve.

"I've just realized what we've done," Felicity said. "I mean *really* realized. Do you?"

He was beginning to, whiskey and all. An alcoholic trance along the artery, illuminations of the lymph, visions of courtrooms and headlines like sugarplums in his head.

"It hasn't got through to you," Felicity sighed. "You've had too much booze to be upset."

"I'm upset, dammit!" He was shouting again, red in the face. "Crazy bitch, what got into you? We should have left her there. It was none of our business."

Her eyes widened, unjustly accused. "*You're* the one

44

who was frantic, *you're* the one said the trunk, and how will we smuggle—"

"What! I never suggested a thing. I just . . . You mean you wouldn't have if I didn't . . . ?"

She sighed heavily. "Yes, I probably would've. That's the trouble with me. I probably would've anyway." She said it as though acknowledging something shameful but hereditary. Epilepsy, say. Or congenital soft-heartedness. "Look. This is a mess." She began to pace the creased crotch of the ditch. "I attract messes, they gravitate to me, just your rotten luck to be in the vicinity. I mean, you wouldn't believe my life. Guinness Book of Records, a natural aptitude for foul-ups." Pace, pace. "But for the same reason I'm a veteran at handling them, a professional. So why don't you leave this to me? I mean, clear out, forget it happened. Go back to your normal life. I'll never breathe a word, I've forgotten already what you look like. I've never laid eyes on you. Scram!"

"Jesus!" he said, as though hit by the fast ball of truth. "What's the *matter* with us?"

"I told you. It's me. Clear out before—"

"She's *in* there. She might have suffocated, she might be dead."

"Oh God, yes, the woman!" Unzip, zip, a waving of wands: changes of costume came to Felicity in the twinkling of an eye as occasion demanded. There was a flurry of efficiency and concern, cookie crumbs and sleeping bag flying. Is she conscious? Alive? Can't very well get her out, can we? In case someone comes. Though couldn't we sit her up, prop her up? Who spoke what, neither knew. A humming party line. And both again incautious, forgetting consequences and implications, in the face of such abject need.

Afterwards, endlessly afterwards, they would replay this day and think: there, at that moment, or at this one, or at least by such and such a time, was the point where we should have, well, stood back at least. Ah, hindsight. In the now there is so little leeway for thought.

"Her hands are warmer," Felicity said. "So stuffy down there, but a good thing, maybe."

"Get her onto the seat."

"I'm trying, I can't. She's a dead weight. Here, you—"

And he managed it somehow, hefting her up into his arms. "She's still unconscious," he said. "The whiskey, quick."

Even white and blank, the face took his breath away. He brushed the matted black hair from her cheeks, her head in the crook of his left elbow, and endeavored to part and hold open her lips. Delicately, like a nervous father during a first bottle feeding, he let the whiskey trickle over her tongue. But the apparatus for swallowing does not necessarily respond well to unauthorized invasion. First, there was simply a welling back from the corners of the lips, a certain amount of messiness. Then violence: spluttering, coughing, a risk of choking. For heaven's sake, for heaven's sake, Felicity was expostulating. What are you trying to do? And Gus snapping: Get out, give us air! And thumping the invalid's back, holding her head against his shoulder, rocking back and forth with her.

When the storm quieted, the woman went suddenly rigid, aware for the first time of the man's hold on her. Catlike, she flared away from him and hunched up into the back corner of the car, knees hugged to herself, arms tightly around her legs, her limbs an instinctive system of fortification. Her gaze flickered from Gus to Felicity, back and forth, back and forth, intense, unwilling to let a microsecond's worth of information pass unmonitored.

In such moments spells are cast, the eyes as assiduous and seemingly neutral as cameras, the mind recording details that will float up into dreams, that the memory will rerun in close-up time after time, new elements announcing themselves as on a screen, sharp-edged and super-real.

Felicity had a fantastic sense of everything being outlined in light, or in some antique emulsion of gold leaf and egg white. It was happening again: a painting incarnating itself, Perugino's *Magdalena*, which was hanging at this moment in Florence. It was because she was negotiating for it, interfering with history; because she wanted it on loan in her gallery.

It's suspect, Seymour would say, this retreat to the

luminist past. They were all escapists, those fifteenth-century painters. Inappropriate for today. These are violent times, my dear.

And indeed, the woman was all blacks and bruised purples, an impasto of savage techniques. Pure Seymour, the latest phase.

But look, Felicity argued, the attention to minutiae. That isn't modern at all. Look: the small mole, a fleck of dark velvet, high on the right cheek near the outer edge of the eye. The high cheekbones. The eyes (brown-almost-black) that skitter in demented flight patterns. The black cotton dress that is badly torn at the bodice.

(Seymour might introduce—in brilliant verdigris, say—the hand that had defiled her, the hand that had ripped at the cloth.)

But look at the skirt, Felicity argued. Yes, yes, it is torn, it's done in your style. But it's also voluminous, archaic, outlandish, surely not of our time or place. There is something otherworldly about it: tented down over the jackknifed knees to the ankles, almost covering those broken shoes that make one think of moldering objects dropped from museum attics.

Felicity, hypnotized by eyes that seemed to be casting about for which language to say nothing in, thought dizzily: She is not a Perugino or a Seymour. She is a memory of myself.

She was the moment when Felicity knew she would never see her father or Didiji again, when she had said over and over—but apparently in Malayalam—to her distressed grandparents: I don't believe you, it isn't the whole story, Didiji will tell me the truth. He is only out in a fishing boat, he will be back when the tide turns.

(When Seymour heard this story he shut himself in the studio for three days, but if he had done a painting, she had not seen it.)

Gus reached out tentatively and touched the woman's cheek with his fingers, the merest feather-brush of an offering of concern. The woman recoiled, her mouth formed the shape of a scream though no sound came out, her muscles tensed so violently that the ears of her rescuers braced themselves for the splintering of bones.

47

And then slackness . . .

Unconsciousness.

"Jesus," Gus whispered.

"It was when you touched her," Felicity said sadly. "I think perhaps she's been raped."

"Oh Jesus," Gus said again, and crossed himself.

Nothing, Felicity thought, is so clumsy as the well-meaning gestures that pass haplessly from the safe to the totally unsafe.

8

What is one to do?

When recording fantastic events in which others have
believed, where does the reporter's responsibility lie? Let
me illustrate: In a bar once in New York I met a woman
who was convinced the CIA had implanted radio trans-
mitters behind her kneecaps. They monitor everything,
she told me in a fearful whisper. They chart my bio-
rhythms. I can't even use hiccups as a code. If you speak to
me they will hear every word, you are right to be nervous.

It was true that she made me nervous, but not, of
course, for the reason she supposed. This is an extreme
example, not at all a borderline case, and one for which a
flippant reportorial voice would be cruel as well as unnecessary. Every few seconds the woman felt her knees
compulsively, tapping out a morse code on the patella,
gently probing the crease behind her leg. I *receive* things
too, she confided; I pick up weather reports, I know when
people don't like me.

Such encounters, which are altogether too frequent in
the seedier sections of great cities, either sadden or irritate
depending on the speed and ease with which one can
disengage. But no one can deny that the woman's bizarre
behavior was logical once one accepted her premise; and
her biographer would want to know, indeed would have
an obligation to understand, how it felt to the woman
herself when electronic impulses buzzed in and out along
her calves.

This is my problem, compounded by the fact that the
protagonists are dear to me, and apparently of sound
mind.

Something happened at the border—and also at a
roadside ditch a few miles in on the Canadian side—the

49

details of which must remain unclear at least until the reappearance of the only witnesses, and perhaps beyond that. Whatever happened changed their lives, but I have little to go on. There were Felicity's overwrought and elliptical remarks; there were the drunken recollections of Gus some time after the disturbance; and there was (in both the *Montreal Gazette* and the *New York Times*) a small filler item which I do not suppose I would even have noticed if Felicity had not alerted me to improbable happenings:

(Associated Press)
Canadian–U.S. border: A group of illegal aliens was apprehended at the border today following an attempt to smuggle themselves into Canada in a refrigerated meat van. Two of the aliens subsequently died of hypothermia. The remainder, officials say, will be extradited back to the United States, where they had already been served deportation papers, following all necessary medical treatment.

All the aliens are from El Salvador, a spokesman said. Charged on two counts of smuggling and extortion was William Minton, aged 47, van driver.

Do you see what I mean? With what voice can such a news item be appropriately interpreted? I do not know, anymore, how a newspaper should be read. In the entrails of old pianos I can far more easily decipher signs and portents. Take these high-school uprights in a music room littered with gum wrappers. Here are the bass strings of a tired Baldwin, copper wound, slack with the day's depredations.

Today a senior (math major, but with wider aspirations) was assigned to a wrestling bout with Chopin, but slipped into hard rock. Thunder was what he gave voice to—it can be told in the dislocation between the metal core and the metal wrapping of the strings, a guttural warble of agony. His classmates predict a brilliant future: strobe lights, groupies, sold-out concerts, a fortune. Tonight he is shooting heroin into his veins in the washroom of a dive

50

on Dorchester Street. (I read it in the configuration of strings, and also in the flotsam of staff-room conversations.) That is the way of the untuned world.

It is wise not to care too much.

I do all that is humanly possible, note by note. Beyond that, there is nothing one can afford to take seriously. Sheer folly. One has merely to consider the vagaries and fashions of history, to peel back two centuries and look in on the court of Weimar. The A on Bach's clavier is vibrating at only 435 beats per second. So scholars have deduced. Today 440 beats per second is standard. Fashions change without rhyme or reason, history adjusts, old revolutions take on the glow of sanctity, new ones are blasphemous.

If I am tuning for an Early Music Consort or a Bach purist, I have to adjust the pitch downwards. Back to the "authentic" A. The "real" A. The A, some would say, as Bach and God intended it to sound. But such purists must play for a small audience of like-minded aficionados, for their music sounds slightly flat to the ear of the modern concertgoer. It offends. Some people may even walk out of the auditorium because the performance grates on them unendurably and they feel impelled to take compensatory action —in the same way that few can refrain from straightening a picture hanging crookedly on a wall.

Modes change.

Renoir did not like the work of the young Matisse; Matisse did not understand Jackson Pollock. Nonconformist troublemakers in England became the Pilgrim Fathers of hallowed memory. Today's illegal alien is tomorrow's Resistance hero. This fashion or that fashion, what difference does it make?

There are other pianists and conductors who lean away from the 440 norm, but in the opposite direction. Their quest is for a "brighter" intonation: the A at 442 beats per second. And some, defying convention, outraging the conservative ear, reaching for the most brilliant colors of sound, crave an A that is febrile with speed, 445 beats per second, a dizzy note, on tiptoe.

Do not dismiss these micro-changes as anything less

than cataclysmic. Nor as having any more meaning than the length of this season's skirts.

When I was five, my father was already famous and my mother was mostly distraught. Later she escaped. She made a quantum leap into banality, which is the true secret of happiness—a second marriage, a very ordinary life, other children. Naturally she does not care to see me, a revenant from that earlier bad time, and I do not blame her at all. I understand.

She taught me two things of importance: that the lime-light is a very bad place to be; and that, in dealings with luminaries, it is preferable to be in a position where you can tell them to go to hell.

But when I was five my mother had not quite learned these lessons herself. We were visiting the home of a concert pianist, a friend of my father's. The two men had a way of discussing things, as friends, that sounded like violent battle to the rest of us. The rest of us were in the kitchen: the pianist's wife and son; my mother and me. Both women had nervous ways: their eyes were unnaturally bright, their lips trembled a little when they spoke, their hands shook when they reached to restrain us. I knew these ways.

At the vehement height of the living-room discussion, the mothers fell silent and sipped their tea in mute prayer. The pianist's son and I, already far advanced in the art of making ourselves invisible, crouched under the table, and between the legs of the table I could see the grand piano and the piano tuner. His face was rapt as he tapped and listened, tapped and listened. Once, while the verbal wars raged, he looked up and said: "Would you two old volcanoes please shut up. Unless you don't give a damn if I can't get the pitch right."

He was calm and reasonable. Never for a second did it occur to him that all power was not his. My mouth fell open. I waited for mayhem. But my father and the concert pianist were as kittens in the piano tuner's hands. They apologized. They wandered out to the garden.

Magic, I thought. Black magic.

*   *   *

The piano tuner does not make value judgments, the dogmatics of pitch are not his concern. Wars are fomented around him, but he takes the requested frequency of the A as a given and tends to the pianos of orthodox and heretic alike. It is difficult for him to follow why the critics rage and the performers imagine a vain thing. He turns his back and cups his ear toward his tuning fork.

He does not care for the limelight, he works backstage. Composers, performers, and conductors come and go, they rant and rave, they have to stamp the world with their egos. There are far too many of them. They all entrust their lives and their reputations to the skill of the piano tuner, they are utterly dependent on him. When they cringe in pain, those high-wire walkers, when catcalls or critics inflict savage wounds, the piano tuner shrugs. They make their own fate. Those who stand in the stage lights must burn. Their curtain falls.

In the wings, life goes on much the same.

I wanted to shake Felicity. By the time I realized what was happening, I wanted to shout: Get off the stage! But it was too late. And in any case she would only have said, bewildered: It was an accident. I thought I was in the wings. I turned round and the spotlight caught me.

9

"We're safe here," Felicity said. "For the time being anyway. Until we decide what to do." She moved the kerosene lamp across the table, a soft shuss of metal over pine, and a puddle of light fell on the dish of oranges and grapes. "Have some. And more wine."

He would have preferred his Scotch, or else beer, but was for some reason hesitant to mention it. She refilled his glass and he sipped, thinking: The Scotch is in the car. I could get it.

But these shadows and loops of foggy light made him passive. Mildly uneasy. He was snagged in Therese's candlelight dinners, the strain of special occasions, the obligations. Memories of wakes pulled at him; in his mind the dear departed gathered, he saw the flower-massed niche, the tapers flickering, the sleeper gift-boxed in mahogany, present and not present.

He glanced toward the other room where the torn woman, an arc of mysteries, huddled on the bed in a dead sleep. But she lay beyond the lamp's amber bloom and the darkness surrounding her lapped out at him between washes of light.

"Why don't you have electricity?" he asked edgily.

"I prefer it this way. I come here to escape. No phone either."

"Oh shit," he said. "Therese." He drained his wine at a gulp. "Where's the nearest?" And when she raised a blank eyebrow, added irritably: "Telephone, telephone. The nearest telephone."

"You'll have to drive back into L'Ascension. About ten kilometers. We came through it, remember?"

"What the hell will I tell her?" He flinched from Therese's martyrdom, from the bruise that her mournful

54

non-reproaches would inflict. "She'll think I was . . ." He pushed back his chair—the wooden legs gave a little screech of exasperation against the wide pine boards—and paced jerkily up and down the room. "What a joke. The one time I'm innocent. She'll never believe this."

"You can't tell her," Felicity said sharply. "You can't tell anyone."

They stared at each other.

"Listen." Felicity picked up the lantern. Gus was pacing about. "Stop it," she said, and stood in front of him. "Listen to me. This is a crazy thing, what we've done. A crazy thing." They stood trapped in the cocoon of light. "It's not like sneaking some extra liquor across."

Gus sighed.

Under stress, Felicity noticed, he had an odd little gesture of running the pads of his fingers across his cheekbones, tracing the eye sockets, the length of his nose, the curve of his lips. Over and over. As though checking that everything was still in place.

"If we're caught," she said, "it won't be like not declaring a case of Chivas Regal. This is serious. A crime."

He said slowly, his fingertips sprinting around his face, "But not wrong."

"Oh please, don't get noble. You have no idea what it costs to be noble."

"But what else could we do?"

His submissiveness, the docile fatalism, produced a kind of vehemence in her. She swept around the room opening and closing things (the dresser, the casement window), the lantern swinging wildly from her left hand.

Jesus, Gus thought, as the lunatic tongues of light slurped at corners, at ceiling, at the dark doorway beyond which the unknown woman burrowed into her dangerous secrets. "I'm going to get my bottle of Scotch," he said. "It's in the car."

"Oh for heaven's sake." Felicity put the lamp back on the table with a mild thump. "Sit down." She refilled their glasses with excessive energy so that a quick tidal arc of white wine whispered across the table. In spite of herself,

55

she was arrested by the way the light caught the lip of the spill. Seymour would have done that well, she thought. In an earlier period. She drank quickly, several mouthfuls. She took a deep breath. Go easy, she warned herself. She knew she was too intolerant of slow thinkers.

"Listen," she said again, gently, offering patient rationality like Camembert with the wine. "Instinct is instinct. It's not noble, it's not right or wrong." Index finger dipped in the puddle of wine, she drew tangles. "But we're not shackled to it afterwards. There's a space. And after the space, one can reassess."

Gus's mind glazed over. He had no visa for the country of talk. In school, when a teacher had said: Look, it's simple, self-explanatory, but if anyone is unsure of exponential . . . he would slip through classroom walls to where everything waited—girls damp with willingness, cars asking to be driven, the best deals, the way to live. This woman reminded him of schoolteachers. She was a talking machine. She could be blinked away.

"It seems to me," she said, "that various humane avenues are open."

Blink, blink.

But her voice hummed on. He had a sudden craving for an uncomplicated anxiety—such as smelling of another woman's perfume. He focused on Felicity's tanned shoulders, smooth as butter, and tried to go back to that distant moment when she had been simply a blonde in a blue Datsun and he had thought of licking her neck. Had explored a fleeting fantasy of being holed up with her in the same motel during a freak blizzard. Or of being alone with her in a cabin in the woods. He remembered something he had once plucked from a fortune cookie: Be careful. Your wish may come true.

Suppose he leaned over and dipped his tongue into that dimple beside her shoulder blade?

Her dimple glared.

"These are our sensible options," she said. "I could drive into L'Ascension and get a doctor and the priest. The priest can approach the local chief of police. It'll go better for us that way."

56

Gus was aware of an inner disturbance, the Niagara of wine hitting a deep lake of Scotch.

"I don't mean we'd get off scot-free," she said. "But we'll be forgiven. Humanly speaking. And probably legally."

"The falls," Gus said, and then blinked at the words, astonished, wondering where they had come from, what they meant. He followed their trail and saw a man in a rubber dinghy bouncing around lightly as fluff at the lip of the Horseshoe Falls, all the tourists screaming, leaning out from the railings, offering helping hands and panic. A rope and a lifebelt are thrown, but the man moves sluggishly, apparently stunned, stupidly peaceful, rushing on to the fatal drop.

"That really happened," Gus said earnestly. "I saw it on TV."

Though what it had to do with now, and them, he could not say.

Television, she thought with exasperation. It figures. And irrationally: He watches every kind of junk. He has the attention span of a five-year-old. He's drunk. He's dangerous.

"We have no idea why those people were smuggling themselves over the border." She spoke slowly, with exaggerated emphasis. "Compassion, it's instinctive. We don't have to be martyrs to it. It's not a very intelligent emotion." She began pacing again. "A doctor and a priest. Beyond that, we don't have the right to take the law into our own hands." She opened the dresser doors, closed them. "We don't have the right."

And when he said nothing, she closed a door with particular sharpness. "It would be arrogant and it would be stupid," she said.

But then, Gus thought, isn't everything we do? Isn't it preordained?

Once, he remembered, as he lay between conjugal sheets, a chaste space of years of mistakes running down between the pillows, the fragrant fog of the day's indiscretion had risen like a mist and settled into the rift between Therese and himself. He could not even remember the perfume-wearer's name, though he had filled it in on a form that very day. Some youthful slip of a housewife, with a baby asleep in a corner crib. It was frightening the amount of yearning lurking behind suburban walls. So available. As easy as knocking on doors with an offer of Whole Life or Term and a set of premium tables.

He had got as far as listing assets on the factfinding sheet, and then he had said, "I need to know what coverage you already have. If you could tell me which policies—"

"I'll get them," the young housewife said. "Just a minute." And disappeared into the bedroom.

She had reappeared in panties and bra and a smog of perfume. She must have doused herself in Essence of Need, he thought, and felt awkwardly tender. She tipped her long legs all the way up and back and he could have drowned in her.

In the act of mortal sin he often asked himself: Why is this wrong?

But clearly it must have been, or she would not have lain there on the rug, when it was over, with tears streaming down her cheeks.

"Oh Jesus," he said. "I'm sorry."

"No, no." She shook her head and went on crying and made some gesture of despair that brushed his arm like an injured wing.

Reassembling himself in her bedroom, he had seen the atomizer on her dresser. *My Sin* by Lanvin. He had bought a bottle, later, to take home to Therese; he reached under his pillow to touch it. He could present it and presto, her hurt and the indictment would vanish. Maybe.

"I tried it out," he could say. "I wasn't sure if you'd like it. I wanted to keep it a surprise but I suppose you guessed when you smelled the bedroom."

He had lain there knowing he was not going to give Therese the little gift-wrapped box, wondering why. Perhaps he was simply better, more practiced, at living with guilt than with cheap salvation. He never deserved absolution.

But also, in his helpless and destructive way, he felt heavy with—well, for want of a better word, with love—for both women. For Therese and for the girl crying on her living-room carpet, a bruise on his memory. He could not, somehow, violate that fleeting encounter by denying that it had taken place. Could not commit double sacrilege by negating her smell, not even to lessen his wife's humiliation, which he must atone for some other way.

He had reached across the chasm of bedding and touched Therese's cheek. It was streaked with tears. So much sadness, he grieved, and turned to take her in his arms. Across far too many barricades. She stiffened and turned her back to him.

He wondered if remorse and compassion were tumescent for all men, or only for those trained by the Christian Brothers to keep morbid score of lusts for release in the orgasm of confession.

He had given himself up to the distress of the blood-throb that would have to wear itself out, unused. It was almost pleasurable. A tiny payment to be entered in his vast ledger of debits.

"Stupid," Felicity said again. "And perverse. A kind of moral arrogance."

"Yes," he sighed. No matter what one did.

"We'd need to be perfectly clear about one thing: it would be a lifetime decision." Like giving birth to a retarded child, she was thinking. "You can't unmake that kind of burden."

He realized: She's trying to convince herself, to extricate us. He watched her anger with idle fascination, as one watches a fly struggling in the arms of a cobweb.

"Don't you see?" she asked. I'd be painted into a corner, was what she thought. Locked inside one frame forever.

He picked up the lantern and went into the bedroom, sleepwalking, to see if spells could be broken. He stood beside the bed. Felicity, watching from the darkness, thought: Rembrandt, *The Nativity*. That match-flare of epiphany in one corner of a canvas of darkness.

Gus was bred on miracles. The ankle bone of Brébeuf, salvaged from Iroquois-flayed remains, had rescued an aunt from epilepsy. His own mother had warded off a fourth miscarriage with daily prayer and the clasping of an anointed linen handkerchief blessed at Ste. Anne de

Beaupré. Gus himself owed the recovery of a lost wallet to St. Anthony, could attest to the powers of his St. Christopher medal, and owed the non-pregnancy of a secretary to the special intervention of saints in the seventh week. He was as intimate with manifestations of the divine as he was with mortal sin.

He did not, consequently, resist the notion that the torn dress spoke to him. In times past, as he well knew, men had been commanded by wounds, by the voluble mouths of stigmata. The black rents addressed him in a whisper, clear as thought: Have mercy on us, they said. Do not abandon us.

Or perhaps he was in thrall to the woman's face.

Perhaps he sniffed the sharp, salty quim of atonement.

He felt the nether gathering of his wine-limp blood, a tidal miracle. He felt he might smash anyone who had laid a hand on her. He returned to the living room and set down the lantern.

"It's no use," he said apologetically. "If you go to the police, I'll have to take her. I'll make a run for it."

"Oh really?" The heroics of alcohol, she thought witheringly. "And where would you go?"

"Away," he said loftily. "Somewhere."

"A fugitive. For the rest of your life."

"Until she's . . . back on her feet. Until she can make her own decisions."

"Oh, I see." Felicity laughed. "Just until she's back on her feet."

There was a silence, a strange truce. Felicity filled their glasses again. Each stared into private thought. What they do, Gus told himself, is send them back where they came from. He visualized this: the face above the torn dress, pale as hard-chilled butter, in a Ziploc freezer bag, labelled, dated, returned to sender.

"Your own juices would freeze," he said.

"What?"

"Like those days that are thirty below, with a windchill factor thrown in." He was running his fingers around the map of his face again. "You know"—he gasped as though the air had turned suddenly arctic—"the way it hurts to breathe."

"What are you talking about?"

"The truck. The meat van."

"Ah."

"They must have been desperate."

"I wish you wouldn't," Felicity sighed. "You don't seem to realize we'd be criminals."

"Oh well," he said, with a weary gesture of one hand. He had always been that, a miserable worm in the sight of God. (Absolve me, Father, for I have sinned . . .) "But listen, there's no need for *you* . . ."

"Oh please. And do wipe that look of sanctity off your face. We have a duty to talk sense into each other."

"It's no use," he said politely.

"This isn't fair. It isn't fair. Why us?"

Why not us? he wondered.

"And what about your wife?" Felicity needled. "What's she going to think of this, a spare woman in the basement or wherever?"

"Oh God. Therese." The euphoria punctured.

"You see. And I'm in the middle of arrangements for the next exhibition. Ivories from Rome, paintings from northern Italy, manuscripts from Paris and Oxford, transport, insurance, you name it I haven't time for complications." This trip itself, after all, was in order to *avoid* complications. "I'm right in the middle of the end of an affair, among other things," she said dryly. "So what am I supposed to do? Kiss the manuscript collection goodbye?"

He repeated blankly, "Manuscript collection?"

"Yes. The Braques and Chagalls are going in a couple of weeks. Did you see them?"

"What?"

"My gallery in Cambridge. I managed to get two Braques and three Chagalls on loan. If you missed them, they're going to Montreal next. The Galerie St. Joseph, I think."

He stared at her. "But . . ." he said bewildered. He was not sure what he thought the people who went to museums and art galleries would look like. He did not expect them to look like Felicity. "I've never been to one of those things," he said.

61

She raised an eyebrow in surprise. "What do you do, then?"

"I sell insurance."

"Good God. You're kidding."

"Oh, scum of the earth, right?" he said bitterly. "You'd think we handed out VD instead of rent to widows."

"I'm sorry. I didn't mean . . . That was awfully rude of me. I just . . . I don't think I've ever actually met one before, I mean someone who—"

"Forget it. Goes with the job." Though whenever it happened he would think of Mrs. Fitzsimon, who had got through wake and funeral in dry-eyed shock and then broken down when he handed her the check. Oh, thank God, she sobbed. Thank God. You mean we don't have to move out of the house?

"I'll tell you something," he said somberly. "There are two ways you learn the real truth about people, and I've done them both. Waiting tables and selling insurance." He swallowed a mouthful of wine and shook his head. "You wouldn't believe. The most respectable people. Doctors, professors, newspaper editors. The way they speak when they figure you don't count, it's interesting. I can tell you, you learn a thing or two."

"I expect so," Felicity said.

They stared into their wine in silence. They sipped. They refilled their glasses more than once. They seemed to be waiting for a decision to make itself.

Gus rallied. "I have to call Therese. She worries." When she floated into vision like this, she came with that tired look that distressed him so much, that look of a woman whose husband is always on the road, whose four daughters promise endless anxiety. She came pulling fretfully at the graying curls on her forehead, brow furrowed, worn out from financial precariousness, so that he would want to scoop her up in his arms and carry her off to their bedroom and anoint her with solace and lick it off—a form of comfort useless to her, threatening only another child. Instead he would bring flowers, or buy her a whole book of lottery tickets, confident always of miracles; even lighting a candle at St. Jude's to that end, pointing out to God that it was not for himself he asked, that in fact he would not touch a cent of the winnings. In his dreams he was the Knight of Happiness, the hero who slashed through thorns, trailing jubilation. But it always turned out that he had embezzled her newspaper money; or the money set aside for the girls' confirmation dresses; or the candle money kept in a raspberry jelly jar against the saying of requiem masses for his late father-in-law. Or some other misappropriation of funds equally appalling, and wasteful, and sacrilegious.

He rested his elbows on Felicity's table and put his head in his hands. "Poor Therese," he sighed. She would be sick with anxiety at this moment, imagining car crashes, desertion, the running up of bills. "She deserved a lot better."

Of course she would never have married him if he hadn't so cunningly deflowered her. But then the baby, his one and only son, had died anyway, a judgment of God. Whenever he thought of it some rupturing took place inside him, a curse of transposed labor, and he would cringe with pain. Love was at him again. It was a sort of cancerous malady coiled inside him, gnawing away, lashing out in sudden stabbings at unwary moments. A congenital disease. Certainly it mocked him. He loved far too often, too easily, too *catholically*.

"I am a clown," he told Felicity lugubriously.

She was somewhere else. Somewhere distant. She blinked, focusing. "Pardon?"

He searched back for what he had said, caught hold of the words where they lingered, and produced them, mildly puzzled. "I said that I'm a clown."

"Aren't we all? And on strings."

"If we do this," he said, glancing at the bedroom doorway as though children who were to be fed poisoned candy lay beyond it, "I hope we'll be able to sleep again."

Felicity laughed sourly. "Oh, that's asking too much." She began walking about the room again. "Either way. No matter what we do." She sighed. "Thank God for the law. When in doubt, pass the buck and fall back on what is lawful."

63

"I wish you'd keep still," he said. "Why do you open and shut doors like that all the time?"

She was startled. "Do I?"

"You're doing it now. It's getting on my nerves."

"Let's go then," she said. "I'll take her in my car. You can stop in L'Ascension to call your wife, and then you should drive right on."

He was offended. "What sort of a rat do you think I am? We'll brand ourselves together."

"*Brand* ourselves?"

"*Band* ourselves, I said. Band ourselves together. It's as much my fault."

"I know, I know, it's not that. We can stay in touch. But it's a matter of strategy. It'll be simpler this way. No risk of contradicting each other's story under cross-examination. Besides, this is the kind of dumb thing police expect of a woman; you know, falling in love with condemned men, marrying them on Death Row, that kind of nonsense. We're subject to aberrant pity, no one is surprised. So as soon as you're safely back on the highway, I'll get hold of the priest—and he can decide which doctor."

"Priest?" He seemed to have missed something.

"The priest will take care of everything," she said. "He'll see that nothing . . . nothing unpleasant happens."

Gus thought: She has the kind of trust in priests that only Protestants have these days. Or Catholics over sixty. "But why a priest?" he asked. "You're not a Catholic, are you?"

"No. But La Magdalena is."

"Who?"

"La Mag— Oh. Silly of me. But she reminds me of a painting of Mary Magdalene."

"Oh." He digested this. "How do you know she's Catholic?"

"Everyone is, where she comes from." Impatiently.

Of course, Gus thought, flushing. I'm ignorant. Stupid. I sell insurance. But the torn dress had spoken to *him*. He picked up the lantern and walked into the bedroom again. La Magdalena. It was true that she had the face of a saint.

If we lift her, he thought, she might break. He turned to Felicity. "We can't move her again. You go for a doctor. I'll wait here."

She paced the other room. She opened and closed closet doors and windows. She came back to the bedroom.

"That won't work, to have two of us involved. They'll never believe we both acted on the same impulse. It's too improbable. Do you really want the police at your office? Immigration people? Reporters?"

"We can't move her," he said stubbornly. "We can't. She's exhausted."

"All right then." She took a deep breath. "We'll leave her here. I'll bring the priest back."

"This is wrong," he said, but without energy. He knew it was too late. It was like arm wrestling. After a certain point, there was nothing that could reverse the momentum. But he said it again, a protest cravenly registered, a bell tolling: "This is wrong."

"Whatever we do is wrong now."

"All my life," he said, "I've had this nightmare. I'm somewhere very public and the police arrive. Everyone's watching and wondering and I know damn well they've come for me, even though I don't know what it is I've done. I'm sweating like crazy and I tell them, I tell everyone, I'm shouting it: 'But why? What for? I haven't done anything.' Then as soon as I say it, I have this sick feeling in the pit of my stomach that I *did* do something. Maybe I was drunk, or maybe I did it in my sleep, it's just out of reach in my mind, but whatever it is, I'm guilty of it."

He filled his glass shakily, slopping more wine across the table.

"Crazy, eh? It'll come back tonight or tomorrow night, for sure. Used to have it all the time when I was a kid." He gulped at the wine. "Ever have a dream like that?"

Felicity drew endless circles in the spilled wine and did not answer.

"Jesus," Gus laughed self-deprecatingly. "Dumb question, eh?"

Jesus. He might as well have unbuttoned his fly, exposed himself. The sick things one told after a few drinks.

Only Catholics had dreams like that. He drank another glass of wine greedily, as though it were water. We're marked from baptism, he thought. We're trained to spend our lives in hell so we'll consider purgatory a good deal.

And perhaps the last glass of wine did it. He was pitched, phosphorescent, into the refining blaze of purgatorial fire. There was a sound of shattering—the falling away of his earthly body; or perhaps the crashing to the floor of the wineglass.

"Headlights," Felicity said. "From the crest of the drive. Don't worry about the glass, I'll clean it up. Damn. They could try low beam, they must have seen our cars by now." She had found an old rag in a corner cupboard and was mopping at the mess on the floor. "Why don't they dip their lights?" Goddam city tourists looking for a cottage they'd rented for the weekend. "Happens once in a while. Cars take the wrong turn, can't find a place to turn round."

It seemed endless, the blinding glare, the obscene invasion of privacy. A garrulous car engine, the loud conversation of tires on gravel. Then an idling, but still no dipping of the lights. This was interminable. Then voices.

"City drivers!" Felicity said irritably. "Can't even tell when they've made a mistake."

She went to the door and was bathed in the lights. "What are you looking for?" she called. But there was no answer. Felicity had to shield her eyes. "They must be able to see me," she grumbled to Gus. "What are they trying to do? Blind me?"

At last: a ritual of reversing, a swinging away of the lights, a diminuendo of sound.

Silence.

"So," Felicity said. "Let's go."

Words fell into Gus's mind like dust dislodged from the low ceiling beams. *What you have to do, do quickly.* He examined them warily, poked at them with a finger of thought, but they gave back nothing. He did not know where they had come from.

He followed Felicity into the darkness where the cars waited.

10

A jag of lightning reached down like a tuning fork.

Gus's aerial sang.

The highway waited for rain but was rough-housed by bluster, a dry, electric flirtation. Once L'Ascension was behind him, the winds swooped like birds of prey. Splat, the windshield parrying. Perhaps, before Winston, he would drive into rain. No doubt storm clouds were brewing over the Great Lakes and sending foraging parties on dry runs eastward. He tacked into them, exhilarated.

"I was so worried," Therese had said, a catch in her voice. Or perhaps it was simply storm interference on the telephone connection. "*J'étais en train d'imaginer* . . ." She always lapsed into French when upset. "I don' know what," she quavered. "Somet'ing terrible . . ."

Her consonants, as ever, seduced him. He was helpless before the segue of her syllables, the unpredictable stresses and intonations. "An accident has arrived, isn't it?" she faltered.

No, no, he assured. Safe as churches. Just a darn muddle-up at the border, a bunch of refugees, everyone gets penalized. Luck of the draw, darn it, waiting and waiting and not a chance to make a phone call. But at last, thank God . . . begun to think they'd never . . . in just three hours, if he kept to a steady ten kilometers over the limit.

Grâce à Dieu, she said. *Grâce à Dieu*.

The best-told lies, he thought, skirt closest around the truth. It is the telling detail that convinces, the gospel of trivia. The flies, he would say. And the smell—you wouldn't believe! Like a freezer on the blink, full of rolled roasts and people. Endless delays—what else would you expect?—and more questions than a driver's license test.

In all probability tomorrow's paper would give impressive confirmation. Television, even, in full living color. *Incident at the border*. Perhaps there would be a photograph of the van, the carcasses swaying on their hooks. Your father, Therese would tell the girls with awe, was there.

A sales rep for history.

Though he would have to warn them to say nothing beyond the house.

On cruise control, he set course for hearth and home. Therese would be mellow with relief. His daughters were dreaming the dreams of innocence by now, tucked in their beds, adrift in lace veils and seed pearls and their First Communion; homework done, their packed lunch boxes lined up and waiting for morning. No, tomorrow was Saturday. Well anyway, all would be well.

Also, it was bound to make a difference coming home innocent. Virtually innocent. How could it count now, that grappling in a hotel room a century earlier in the day? And in another country on the far side of the border. Another country altogether.

His aerial sang to him, humming in the wind.

Te absolvo, it chanted. The Lord be with you.

And also—he lifted up his voice in tuneless antiphonal grace—and also with you. Amen.

Blessed art thou, thrummed the aerial, among clowns and philanderers.

Amen, he sang.

He was frequently an optimistic pessimist. When the wind was right, he could soar above the evidence of his life and education. A host of guardians (the nuns and priests of his school years, keepers of the faith) hovered on his lee side, withholding judgment.

Therese, he would say. I have flowers for you (though they are still at the florist's until the shops open in the morning). And in a week, two at the most, I'll have money for the confirmation dresses, white lace on the bodice and cuffs. And by summer, a pool in the yard, you'll see.

Oh yes, oh yes, it was possible. Blueprints for the

68

good life had fluttered down on the sales conference like confetti. *Whatever the mind can conceive, the mind can achieve*: it was on the conference note pads, on every page, in gleaming embossed letters. This was the promise, an article of faith, and the convention speaker had a Cadillac to prove it. And a recipe too, a fail-safe series of steps: one day he was taping a magazine picture of that Cadillac to the cracked slum walls of his life, the next he was dangling the keys in his hands and papering his penthouse with speeding tickets. I wanted that car so bad, he told them, thumping his pulpit in the Grand Hyatt conference room, I could feel the wheel in my hands before I had two half-dollars to rub together. That wheel had a mink collar on it. I could feel the mink between my fingers, I used to fall asleep stroking it.

Fantasize, fantasize, that was the key. It isn't raining rain at all, it's raining swimming pools, sundecks, a Corvette for Therese. It's coming down silk dresses for the girls. The power of the mind, he could spin his own life out of it. Apparently. New York was swarming with people who would swear to it: I visualize, therefore it is. I believe, and it comes to pass.

And therefore the woman, La Magdalena, whose torn dress had spoken, was safe. He was not turning a deaf ear, he was not deserting. And it was not required of him to break the law—surely a sign in itself of the Good Living seal of approval. He was drafting her future.

Happiness would dominate, and material comfort—he would weave both in. The priest, smitten when Felicity's lamplight fell on that face, would have a brother in Immigration who would wave official wands. Experts would offer favorable testimony. Although unspeakable things had been done to the woman (the doctor would undoubtedly reveal this), she had been blameless throughout, virginal in spirit; she would recover. Wise men from the upper reaches of government would offer gifts that would include a work permit. Certainly she would not be deported. New language would come to her, French and English both, and at nursing school she would win gold medals. A doctor, bewitched, would worship from far and then near, showering her with many Catholic children and a gabled house with backyard barbecue and wall-to-wall plush, the deepest velvet kind, top of the line in the Sears catalogue. There would be a silk dress for every rip in her shapeless black tent. Her son would become a Supreme Court judge or possibly Prime Minister, one of her daughters would become a nun, and the rest would marry well. On the living-room mantel of her later years there would be a row of framed portraits—the granddaughters in First Communion dresses that took the breath away, so fragile with lace and purity. And when, after a full rich life, La Magdalena died, the flowers would come in truckloads, a whole city in the cortège, tributes to immigrant success in the True North strong and free, requiem masses in Latin and French and English, her grandchildren rising up to call her memory blessed.

Gus saw that the life he had given her was a good one and he was pleased with himself. He rested after his labors. It was absorbing work, though strangely tiring. A virtuous lassitude swamped him, an earned drowsiness—like the pleasure of a beer in the shade after the lawn is mowed. Or like watching the Sunday afternoon game when all the ladder work and cleaning is done, the storm windows snugly in place for the winter, his bruised fingers a badge of merit that even Therese would honor.

It was also possible that Felicity's wine had something to do with his state of ineffable peace.

And so he coasted along, grateful that La Magdalena's life had gone so well. On high beam his lights picked out the phosphorescent letters of the *Au Revoir* sign. *Vous partez* . . . it reminded him, and he flashed past it into English-speaking territory. Bye-bye, Marthe, he called over his shoulder to the sister-in-law who would speak to him in English even more rarely than he would accompany Therese and the girls on visits to the Montreal relatives. *Au revoir* to all that, the Quebec border dwindled in his rearview mirror. This was the country he loved, this was the ribbon of highway that reeled him back every time, God knew why, to Winston-on-the-lake, Winston-at-the-edge-of-the-world.

Where? fellow salesmen would ask, convention-jovial, in the lavish hotel lounges of New York. And *why?* they would demand, though not all of them plied such great cities as their teasing suggested. Some indeed came from even smaller and obscurely named townlets in remote upstate reaches, but they knew that everywhere south of the border was Significant Geography. Confident at the hub of the world, they would marvel at Canadians, affectionately incredulous, mocking: Do you insure against death by snow-job, then? How's business among the Eskimos? Heard the one about the moose who got snow-goosed? You couldn't help liking Americans, they were so guilelessly predictable.

Gus laughed into the jaws of the wind. It was screaming off the Great Lakes at such a pace that his Chevy bounced along like an early experiment of the Wright Brothers. And the granite outcrops, snouting out from their veneer of coarse soil and tormented pines, laughed with him, a long laugh that stretched all the way north through empty rockmeadows to Hudson Bay. He sang an old army song at the top of his lungs:

> Gee, mom, I want to go
> Back to Ontari-o
> Gee, mom, I want to go
> Ho-o-ome.

Mostly he did not quite believe he had not grown out of this rock. He had a secret version of his history that he always looked at after a few drinks: once a seed fell like a pine cone and lodged in a pocket of snow. And the green shoot of Augustine Kelly came forth, blossoming into a Sunday altar boy and a weekday terror at school, until it came to pass that he bumped into his fourteenth year and his teachers and spiritual mentors had had enough. To work, they said, it will straighten you out, since school is achieving nothing. He got a job washing dishes at Joe's Grill.

Currents passed through him in those years, his sap gave off blue sparks, his stamens crackled, the pistils of clover and young girls and lonely widows gave off a

71

scorching smell that singed him as he passed. His father died of whiskey, leaving nothing but debts.

At the wake his mother moved between the lilies and spoke to Father Dougherty. "Augustine's going the way of his father already," she grieved. And Father Dougherty spoke to the faithful, murmuring here and there of obligations. A conference was held and Gus rose in the world. On condition that he attend Mass every Sunday he could graduate to washing dishes, and eventually to waiting tables, in one of the grand old hotels on the lake.

Gus turned off the 401 so that he could drive in along the lakeshore. He loved this view of Winston. Now, as thirty years ago, it lay below him tricked out in night lights: the lake pinching itself into the St. Lawrence River, the causeway, the limestone domes and spires, the old fort. He crossed the causeway and coasted by the hotel where he had waited tables for so many years. He remembered the summer when the pert young French-Canadian waitress joined the staff so that she could practice her English. The walks along the lakeshore with Therese. Memories, memories.

Ah, the elegant dinners in the fine old hotels of Winston. Inhale. And they were still in the air: the emanations of damask and starch, the roast beef, the port wine, his fascination and nostalgia and alienation, the same old blend, the smell of unbreachable distances. Even now the Gus Kellys of the world only entered this section of town to scrape plates and clear tables. It was still, in its way, a fort.

Not that it mattered particularly.

Augustine Kelly had no aspirations to move in on history. A cramped place. No room for barbecues or swimming pools or stands of pine. Or even for driveways, with people owning only one side of a wall.

He drove on.

Out of the eighteenth-century enclave. Past the three-tiered nineteenth-century brick (dripping with a lace of pigeon leavings; eaves trough jostling eaves trough, wooden porches slumping softly with rot). Past the shopping center where the long strip of upper-case energy

72

began: Hamburgers to Go! Jock's for Used Cars—Will not be Undersold! Furniture City! Be Cool—Add a Pool! Beyond the flashing lights. Beyond the neat new houses with their L-shaped living rooms. Beyond roads that were curbed, to where the fences petered out. To where the edges of the town turned fuzzy on the map or ribboned out along highways. To where the properties heaved themselves nonchalantly around vague surveyors' markers, pleated themselves between one winterlock and the next thaw, and went slipping wetly away like lovers compliant under rampant pines. To where three centuries of settlers' events, brief flecks of commentary, were barely noticeable in the expansive statement of prehistory.

His lights picked out Therese's car in the drive, its rust holes cruelly visible, the bodywork a cascade of metal lace. By Christmas, or thereabouts, he would wave his wand and lo the Volkswagen, ugly duckling, would be a swan of a Corvette. *To Therese with love.* He would tie an enormous red ribbon around the entire car. And the keys? In her Christmas pudding, perhaps, the happy chink of her spoon discovering them . . .

He cut the engine so as not to wake the girls. Doused his lights. Therese would be waiting in their warm bed. In the kitchen he bumped into something and leaned on it for a while. It was very late, he was very tired, it was difficult to stay upright. There was a strange, sharply sweet smell, and vague stirrings of sound. Night creatures. For some reason he did not want to turn on the light. This innocence he was bringing Therese, this return that was free of any other woman's mist, and these new sips of power and a different future—they were delicate growths. He was reluctant to subject them to harshness. The hundred-watt bulb, in his experience, was not a great sustainer of newly germinated hope.

It was very penetrating, the smell, very puzzling.

Therese would be wearing the soft blue nightgown he had given her for her birthday. Blue for come unto me. The color of welcome, of dew, of lips moistly parted. When he took her in his arms . . . He steadied himself against the wall for a moment and concentrated. What had

73

the speaker at the conference called it? Self-scripting, that was it. He wrote the coming scene: when he took her in his arms . . .

He stepped on something soft and violent. Cat. There was the sound of a maddened bull-violin in full rut. Claws in his ankle.

He bit his lips on the cry of pain, but could feel something escaping, his euphoria hissing out through the bloodied pinpricks in his leg like air from a punctured tire. He clasped his hands together, squeezing till the knuckles glowed whitish in the dark. Trying to hold the hopefulness in.

Light assaulted him and he flung his arms up, resisting it.

"Ah, *mon Dieu*," Therese said. Quietly. Tiredly. With resignation. "You're drunk again."

Something slipped out between his fingers, brushing him, he could feel the soft tickle of it, hear the air sigh. The white dove of his innocence. Gone.

Across the floor, exposed to the light, gleaming slickly, trailed a short gray rope, a knot, pungently perfumed. A pretzel of cat vomit. Or perhaps—oh surely not?—his own.

"I've got flowers for you," he said thickly. "In the florist's."

His words swam gamely against some obstruction in his mouth. His tongue was tossed like a lost canoe paddle. Rocks loomed. He had to let her know: I'll get them first thing in the morning. As soon as the shops open.

Therese smiled her sad smile.

Spreadeagled on the bed he could see himself in her eyes: the cross that she bore.

Sleep claimed him. He paddled its dark river lazily hazily and came to a dream. A loverly cream of a dream. He recognized it. He knew a dream when he saw one. It reached out its finger of light.

After that it was easy: just a shipping of his paddle, a waiting, a momentum of the current. He was borne on a stream to the heart of the cream of a dream, where choirs sang and an altar lamp burned. And where she lay golden

74

on straw, the woman of all desire. Her face pierced him, so untouchably beautiful. His fingers wept.

"You may stroke my cheek," she said.

When his fingertips touched, blue fire leaped from his body. All his senses stood on tiptoe. The rents in her black dress sang like mouths: Come to me, come to me, come. Her skin was white as marble, violet-veined. When he spread his body over hers there was a smell of burning. A spasm shook him: desire as conflagration.

What have you done? sang the choirboys, their pure eyes wide with shock.

And from the antiphonal echoes: What have you done, have you done? It was spreading like flames, an entire congregation singing it, watching him from every niche of the cave, from the side chapels, from the far reaches of the city, the massed spectators demanding: What have you done?

His hands were black with soot, there was blood on the straw. A stain oozed from his pores, foul-smelling. He looked with horror at his cloven feet.

And then the cock crew three times, a shrill jangling.

He leaped awake, sweating whiskey.

"Hush," Therese said. "It's not six yet. Go back to sleep. I'll answer it."

11

How would it sound?

"I found a woman half frozen under a side of beef."
Felicity rehearsed variations, and then she thought that she
would have a cup of coffee in L'Ascension's one and only
café. After the coffee she would walk the two blocks to
St. Sauveur and ring the rectory doorbell. It was not so
terribly late. She supposed that priests must be used to
being summoned at all sorts of odd hours.

She had once attended Mass at St. Sauveur's. She
counted back. Fifteen years ago, her first July at the cottage. And the church visit—not a common event for
Seymour—was because of Jean-Marc, who was with them
for the summer. Jean-Marc had just arrived the evening
before, the reunion was still fresh and untarnished, and
Seymour was stirred by an image of himself as a benign
family man.

Not that the morning had gone well.

"Maman says you're Protestant," Jean-Marc announced.
He was speaking to Felicity though not looking at her.
"You shouldn't be coming."

He was ten years old, and Felicity was eighteen. She did
not blame him for hating her.

"Jean-Marc!" his father said. "That is quite enough."

It is possible that between the *Gloria* and the *Agnus Dei*,
both of which he murmured so angelically, Jean-Marc
considered various means of doing away with Felicity. It is
certainly probable that Seymour, who did not bother with
the responses at all, was taking advantage of the prayers
to study profiles. Felicity, as so often happened, was in
another time and place, with her father.

"Here is *one* view of God," he had said, as they stood
in the missionary chapel from whose pulpit he preached

76

on Sunday mornings. (This of course was before word of "irregularities" reached the Missionary Society.) It was a simple and austere building, whitewashed mud over bamboo, and bare of ornament except for the plain wooden cross on the Communion table. "One perspective. And perhaps not the best one for this part of the world." They went outside to where the light came at them like a tiger, and a vermilion gash of flowers spilled violently over a wall. "If you see what I mean," he said.

"And this is a different perspective, another glimpse," he explained in the temple, a place of tumult that was a wonder to her, a vast monument to sun and shadow. In the central sun-white courtyard a circus parade turned and turned: elephants, flower sellers, the chanters of the thousand names, the gongs, all the colors of sound. And in the surrounding caverns the long penumbral notes of space, the suggestion of a nothingness more potent than matter.

"But of course," her father had said, stroking her hair, "you can't catch God in any of these nets."

"Who liveth and reigneth," said the priest of St. Sauveur in provincial French. "World without end. Amen."

"Amen," Felicity said, and the candles quavered. She heard the sharp intake of breath, the raised eyebrows of the Boston aunts. Really, Felicity! they said. *Papists!* Another net, another glimpse, Felicity told them, and they pursed their lips. They had rescued her from her past and from her father, not that he could often be mentioned. Sometimes she heard them whispering a litany among themselves; "renegade," she heard, and "tragic waste." We do wish, they told Felicity once, that your father hadn't been so *enthusiastic*, that he'd settled down into *respectable* religion.

"Maman says you're young enough to be my *sister*," Jean-Marc muttered viciously after the Mass, while his father was talking to the priest.

"That's true," she said quietly. "Your father and my father were friends. A long time ago."

"Your father's dead. Maman said."

77

The priest came over and put his hand on Jean-Marc's head. Felicity studied the hand. It was old and weathered, a hand that had mended fences and chipped ice from outdoor pumps and chopped firewood, that had baptized and married and buried. Seymour should draw it, she thought. She waited for its blessing.

The priest murmured something in Jean-Marc's ear, his hand on the boy's shoulder. Felicity waited. The priest nodded to her, not quite meeting her eyes, and moved away.

"Goodbye, Father," carolled Jean-Marc, triumphantly possessive.

"Goodbye, Father," Felicity, wistful, echoed.

Felicity stirred her coffee. Would the same priest come to the door? Would he recognize her? She would like to please him. (I've brought you someone, Father, one of your own.) He might put his hand on her head in benediction.

But perhaps he would not trust her. She was "weekend people," flitting in and out. She was English-speaking. Perhaps she should discuss it with Jean-Marc first. She went to the phone booth and dialled his number. She counted six rings. Then a seventh, just in case. Out. Well of course, on a Friday night.

Her coffee was nearly cold now. She swallowed it quickly, grimacing. She ordered another and thought: Of course I am procrastinating. She had newspaper clippings in the file Jean-Marc considered morbid, she knew what could happen. The eyes of La Magdalena floated in her coffee like black moons. Like soft discs waiting for crows.

But a cause, Felicity pleaded with them, is like a boa constrictor. It can take in a whole life at one gulp, the way it took my father's life.

The coffee sucked itself into a well around the spoon, La Magdalena flapped her black dress like wings and flew away. I'm sorry, Felicity said; the priest is the best I can manage.

She paid for her coffee and walked out into the night. Past the bakery where tomorrow's bread was giving off

78

its warm yeasty fragrance. Past the general store. She averted her face from the butcher's shop. (There was a sharp smell of blood and fresh guts.) She walked on by several small clapboard houses with window boxes full of geraniums. She trailed her hand along the stone fence of the church of St. Sauveur. She came to the rectory, took a deep breath, and rang the bell.

12

"I was not altogether surprised," Father Bolduc told the police, "to find no one at the cottage."

The woman, he said (her name was Felicity), must have been in a state of shock, although she had been able to drive with perfect competence and had at first given every impression . . . but first impressions could be so misleading, and he could smell alcohol. And very soon, even more strongly, he could smell moral torment, which had a very distinctive odor.

He actually said that to the police. He said it again to me last week, describing that night, and said it without a trace of embarrassment or irony. Such people amaze. I remembered him; he was elderly even when I was a boy; or at least, I had thought of him as elderly back then. A well-meaning old man, but obtuse as only the pure in heart can be.

He did not remember me—fifteen years is a long time— and I saw no reason to point out my connection with the cottage. I was on the trail of Felicity's absence, checking out every nook and innuendo and cranny.

"Unmistakable," he said again. "The odor of moral torment."

He enjoyed his own homilies. He had been rolling that phrase around in his mind, he liked its bouquet, it had aged in his mouth. He shook his head lugubriously. "Moral torment," he sighed, savoring the taste.

The detection of it, he told the police, was an advanced spiritual skill. In his calling, over the years, he had become adept. He liked that phrase and repeated it. "In my calling, officer, a man sees many . . ."

"Of course, Father," the police hastily conceded. "The nature of your calling, we don't dispute it. Though not

80

something we can take down as hard evidence, you understand."

Father Bolduc understood. He was simply filling in certain gaps. He sensed, with spiritual antennae that over the years had become highly . . . he sensed that the woman had witnessed something traumatic and was unable to speak about it. This was not a question of language. Her French was quite good, though rather formal. Learned in a classroom. But she seemed deliberately vague about why they were going to the cottage. Something about a woman in need of help; he had to read between the lines. Some sort of guilt, of complicity, was very apparent, and he had recognized the struggle of someone wanting to make a difficult confession.

"Of course," he said, "if she *had* made confession, my hands would be tied."

The police had driven down from Montreal and did not have quite the same order of patience as L'Ascension's elderly constable.

"Could you get to the point, Father?" they prodded gently.

Father Bolduc said sternly that the nature of wrongdoing, and its effect on the soul, *was* the point.

"Of course, Father," the police agreed. "But we mean, from our point of view. In the way of actual occurrence."

Father Bolduc had recognized the cottage. It used to belong to that painter, the famous one, a godless man.

"Quite godless," I could not resist interjecting, delighted. "And god*awful* too."

Father Bolduc was not gratified by my agreeing with him in this particular way. "We are all the children of God," he reproved. "Even those who reject him are precious."

I said dryly: "The Old Volcano despises the precious. On esthetic grounds alone."

"I'm afraid I don't quite follow . . ."

"It's nothing," I said. "Not relevant. You were saying that his cottage . . . ?"

"No, no, it *used* to be his cottage," said the priest.

81

According to gossip, he had given it to one of his mistresses, though hardly anyone ever saw her. In fact, according to some there was no such person; and according to others, she was what you would expect of an artist's woman. He was unable to say whether the woman who had come to the rectory in the middle of the night was the mistress in question.

At the cottage he had waited on the steps while she lit a kerosene lantern—a task that seemed to take an unconscionable length of time. Her match and then the flame had gone out several times. She had talked incessantly but in a way that was difficult to follow. At times she seemed to be speaking of political matters. He remembered thinking that this was a very peculiar emergency. "I thought this woman was injured," he said to her. "I thought there was some urgency involved."

Yes, she said, flustered. There was. And then she managed to get the lamp lit, though she went on talking in a more or less incoherent rush. "I'm counting on you, Father," she said, "to ensure that she will be safe." She mentioned—he was sure that she mentioned—Mary Magdalene. In retrospect, of course, all of this made sense.

"The Magdalen, you will remember," he explained to the police, "was the harlot who came to Christ."

It was when he caught the word "rape" that he began to realize.

"You see, I've had this experience before. They always have to tell me obliquely. It's a dreadful and violent thing, of course, but the sad truth is, they know they are partly to blame."

He sighed. He regretted to report that she—the woman Felicity—had been provocatively dressed. When he saw the two wineglasses (one smashed, the picked-up pieces in a little heap on the counter) he knew it was the usual story.

"You see," he explained, "up to a certain point she had been willing."

Until they entered the cottage, he said, Felicity had given every indication of genuinely believing there was another woman inside. Indeed, she appeared absolutely stunned when she saw the bed. Until that moment she had been able to deny her own involvement. She had convinced herself that it had happened to someone else. This was a not uncommon defense mechanism. And shock—in the clinical sense—would have played its part. A kind of necessary amnesia.

Father Bolduc shook his head, pondering the complexities of intention and innocence. A theological line, precarious though it was, had to be drawn.

"I think, you know, it must have been quite violent," he said heavily.

There was not just the blood on the bed. There were spots across the floor and on the porch steps. Also the intensity of the woman's need for repression had to be considered. When he had seen from the tire marks that *two* other cars had been present, pieces of the puzzle began to fall into place. One extra glass, two extra cars. It had begun with a flirtation, one man invited in, and then the others had arrived. Another summer gang rape, not uncommon in these parts, weekend people and alcohol and isolated cottages—a devil's brew. This was why he had called the police: to avert further violence in the area.

The police appreciated his concern but there were, from a legal point of view, problems. Apart from the blood on bed and floor—which could after all have been menstrual—there was no real proof of violence. True, the smashed wineglass was suggestive, but a number of interpretations was possible. It could not be considered hard evidence.

"You must understand, Father," they said, "that unless and until the woman presses charges, no crime has taken place as far as we are concerned."

Father Bolduc did not understand. He knew what he knew. But he would content himself with prayer for Felicity who had been so strangely oblivious to him on the drive back, who had left him at the rectory and fled, who had been in such patent moral torment. The stink of it was still in his nostrils.

Felicity! I'll say when she phones from some room with a view of the Aztec ruins. You have to do something about this odor problem. And I'll tell her what the priest in L'Ascension said.

Honestly, she'll laugh. You're outdreaming me, Jean-Marc.

13

From L'Ascension Felicity drove to Montreal, her eyes on the past.

She never forgot the day she had last seen her father though she rarely spoke of it to anyone, especially not to Seymour, who plundered the memories of those close to him. He had painted her father chasing God (as he put it)—the shape of a man plunging into cobalts and hot pinks and a jungle of greens. This was recent, part of his "violent period," his experimentation with acrylics and strident colors. But she recognized her father.

"I wish you would leave him alone," she said when they met at his retrospective.

"I paint whatever I'm impelled to paint," Seymour said. "He's been floating up lately, all our old college arguments. Persistent bugger won't leave me alone. I think he still has hopes for my soul."

This was the kind of comment that gave Felicity involuntary spasms of jealousy.

She said tartly: "You know nothing about tropical colors. Pure second-hand Rousseau and Gauguin."

Seymour roared with delighted laughter. "Oh Felicity," he said. "Your father's daughter." He stroked her cheek. "Let's get the hell out of here. Let's go back to my studio."

And she did, of course, though not without a moment's compunction for the gallery's poor press secretary who actually caught hold of Seymour's coat lapels in an effort to stop him from leaving. Please, he implored, there are people who've been *promised* interviews, I've given my word. He was wringing his hands.

"If my paintings needed my small talk," Seymour told him gaily, "they wouldn't be worth a retrospective." And he waved farewell with a bottle of champagne plucked from an ice bucket in passing.

"I do hope this means you're being unfaithful to someone," he said when they reached his studio. "I love trespassing."

"You're incorrigible."

"So your father always said. About this businessman in Boston, this Aaron fellow." He poured champagne over her and began to lick it off. "I keep tabs on you, you know. Can you really have sunk to a *businessman*?"

"Tell me about the first time my father brought you home."

"Oh your aunts," Seymour laughed. "Your ferocious aunts. It was such fun to ruffle their feathers."

(A dreadful man, the aunts always said. A perfectly dreadful man. Felicity, my dear, of all the men in the world, how *could* you? We certainly never wanted to see him again.)

"Did you make passes at them?" Felicity asked.

"Well of course I did. Your Aunt Norwich had splendid breasts, though she kept them behind a deal of upholstery. She squealed in the hallway when I felt them, a pure gesture of esthetic appreciation, I might add. Of course your Aunt Ernestine was madly jealous, and your father said he was disgusted. He was hot on the track of truth and I loved to goad him."

"He never mentioned you. Never."

"God swallowed him whole. That predatory cobalt you noticed. It's not a tropical flower, you delicious shrew, it's the bite of truth." He bit the soft flesh of her inner thigh. "Why don't you move back in? I miss you."

She ignored this. Absently, she stroked his silver though still abundant hair.

"The last time I saw him," she began, but stopped.

Seymour said irritably: "He had an annoying habit of self-preoccupation. It runs in the family."

"Look who's talking."

"He elevated fervor to an art form. For his ordination portrait, I did him as St. Sebastian."

She sat bolt upright, incredulous, outraged. "Ordination portrait?!"

He laughed. "You didn't know about that, did you?"

She was speechless with accusation.

"Your aunts were incensed," he chuckled. "They bought it to silence it. My first professional income, you could say they started me on my way."

"But they've never—"

"Of course not. That was the point."

And where, her eyes asked, is it now?

"How would I know where it is? I should think, somehow, it still exists. Even your aunts, I would think, I would hope, couldn't have brought themselves to destroy it. Must be in a bank vault somewhere. I was still dabbling in realism, so it's something of an actual likeness. Then the war got him, then God. But I caught him in the first flush of that passion for selflessness, which of course is the worst kind of egotism. He must have been hopeless as a father."

"He wasn't."

"What does a child know?"

"You know nothing about our life over there. Nothing."

Seymour laughed. "You think you're free to invent him as you wish. I know more about both of you than you'd ever dream." With his tongue he stopped her from answering, and then said by way of evidence: "We were both in New Guinea when word of Hiroshima came. It did strange things to the rest of our lives." He drew fingertip swirls on her breasts, the route maps of convoluted lives. "He went lusting after God, and I went to the devil." He laughed again. "The last time I saw him, the day he sailed off to hunt down his own Holy Grail, he said he loved me because I sinned boldly."

"If somewhat repetitively," Felicity murmured through a mouthful of his flesh.

"Heartless bitch. You don't love me at all."

"Don't be silly. Of course I do."

Pensively he stroked her pubic hair. "He said I'd paint my way to salvation eventually."

"He wasn't God," Felicity said. "He could be wrong about things."

"You're an idea of mine, remember that. You should never wear clothes. Once you put on a dress, you're very ordinary. Anyway, what does a child know?"

A child, Felicity thought, knows everything; but one matures into so much uncertainty.

She had become grateful for the tactile, the visual, the quantifiable: the glissando of tires on the highway, the song of speed, the meteoric pines flitting through high beam between L'Ascension and Montreal, the pungent statements made by butchers, blood on the fingers.

What a will to live, she thought. It is something new in this part of the world. Like the discovery of electricity or the conquest of space. There will be unpredictable changes.

But where had the woman found the strength to crawl away and hide? And what of her trail of blood?

With a flamenco swirl of her torn black skirts, La Magdalena alighted in the passenger seat. I am inconvenient, she said.

Felicity, sniffing at the smear of blood on her fingers, conceded: I would much rather have imagined you.

La Magdalena rattled her castanets. I have offered you a moral reprieve, she said.

Felicity laughed: I don't believe you. I can feel your hooks in my flesh. There's a catch somewhere.

There was a rattle of drums. I am inconvenient, La Magdalena said again, but I don't coerce. You are as free as you wish.

I know your type, Felicity accused. You'll gobble me up. And I won't have it! One martyr in the family is enough.

"The trouble with integrity," her father used to say, more to himself than to her, "is that you can never be certain if you're inspired or simply misled."

Frankly, La Magdalena said, I spit on that. I couldn't care less about your integrity or lack of it. I'm bleeding out here in the woods.

"And the trouble with heroics," Felicity's father said,

"is that one always inflicts difficulties on the innocent. Anyway, your grandparents are right, Felicity. This is no way to bring up a child."

"I'm not going to go," Felicity said.

"You'll love Australia," he promised. "And your grandfather's house—the air smells of your mother's hair. And you'll love school too. I can't deny you the normal things. All this"—they were passing a gaunt cluster of men and women, skeletons wrapped in skin, sitting motionless behind their begging bowls—"will never be real to anyone over there. How can it be? I can't leave them, there aren't enough doctors. But it's not a fit life for a child."

"If you send me away," Felicity said, "I'll be so unhappy I'll just die."

"No one ever dies of unhappiness," he said. "It's too comfortable for both of us if you stay here, which is not a good sign. Always be on guard against being too comfortable. *That's* what kills."

"What bullshit," Seymour laughed when she told him. "But typical of him. That sort of nonsense should have died out with hairshirts and flagellation, when the saints went the way of the dinosaurs."

On the last day she saw her father, the long and slender snake boats were drawn up high on the sand. "What can I teach the fisher people?" he asked her. "They know more than I do. I give what I can in return: see the clouds growing over their eyes? Those are cataracts."

"I'll hide in one of the boats," she said. "I'll go out with you. I'm not going to go to Australia."

"You'll come back here for school vacations. Now run along and help Didiji pack your things."

"I won't go."

But he was already mingling with the fishermen, bundling nets, dragging the boats to the water. Seawater came gurgling up the keel tracks like an afterthought and foamed around her toes. She stood alone on the beach and watched the flotilla move out. "I'll be back by dusk," he called. She heard the beating of gigantic black wings—thump, thump, thump inside her head—and cried out to him in sudden fright. He waved. Above the slap of bamboo paddles she heard his laughter. "Don't wait!" he called.

Touching, La Magdalena said, but you survived. And frankly, I'm for survival.

Well, exactly. Felicity parried all the voices. So why should I put myself in jeopardy? I've had enough trouble, I've paid my dues. If our positions were reversed, you'd go for safety. And yet I did take an enormous risk on your behalf, I was prepared to shoulder *all* the responsibility, I released that hapless innocent you'd beguiled with your eyes.

Who asked you to? La Magdalena said.

I'm still covering for you, Felicity persisted. I've convinced the priest you don't exist. And Jean-Marc will back me up if it's necessary. My stepmother, he'll say, has an overly vivid imagination.

La Magdalena put her thumb to her nose. I can manage, she said, with or without your help. She flapped her skirts and flew out of the car window, but her shadow hovered like a vulture's and darkened the windshield.

Felicity, Jean-Marc would say, amused and mildly exasperated, have you picked up another stray?

Honestly, the aunts would say, stirring their tea and arranging the damask pillows, the things you *invent*, Felicity!

She drove into the outskirts of Montreal and called Jean-Marc from a telephone box. It was now well after midnight. He answered on the fourth ring, his voice smudged with sleep.

"Jean-Marc, I'm sorry to call so late. Did I wake you?"

"What?" She pictured him surfacing from dreams, his hair tousled. He was twenty-five now, but still a child in her eyes. "Felicity? Where are you?"

"In Montreal. Did I wake you?"

"It doesn't matter. What's happened?"

"Can I come by?"

"Naturally."

"I'll explain when I get there. See you."

She waited several minutes after ringing his doorbell

and then rang once more. "I fell asleep again," he apologized. "I wasn't sure if you'd really called or if it was part of my dream."

They hugged, and she said contritely: "I shouldn't have, at such a barbaric hour."

"Nonsense. I'm always happy to see you. Whenever." He yawned and rubbed his eyes.

(When she calls from wherever it is she's gone, it will be just the same as that night. It will be at some wretched hour and I'll be weak with relief.

"This is an all-time record of non-contact," I'll say. "I was beginning to think you'd disappeared for good."

And she'll say contritely: "I'm sorry, Jean-Marc. I got sidetracked by something a bit bizarre. I'm in a phone box a few blocks south of Mexico. Can I drop by in twenty minutes or so?")

Jean-Marc rubbed his eyes again, in case it was just a wish in full bloom. "Coffee?" he asked.

"Thanks. You look haggard."

"School-board pianos; had to work late. Gave me a lot of trouble."

"I called a couple of hours ago from L'Ascension. Thought you must have been out with a girl."

He leaned against the door to his kitchen, watching her. She was never still. She was moving along his bookshelves, absorbed by his recent acquisitions. She doesn't want to know, he thought. She refuses to know. And he himself had hopes of outgrowing his obsession.

("They all look like your stepmother," the Old Volcano laughed. "What's the matter with your imagination? Can't you stand on your own two feet?"

At least, I could have told him, I don't chew them up and spit them out. I keep to civilized rules.

Oh well, I imagine him telling all and sundry, he may be a piano tuner, but at least he's not gay.)

"Oh your books, Jean-Marc," she said. "They're taking over the house."

(It's true. A modest obsession: to recreate on a private scale the library at Alexandria. Pianos and books, what else do I have?)

Felicity's breathing began to grow more regular. She sat in his armchair and closed her eyes, inhaling deeply. "Oh I knew I'd feel better once I saw you. It's so *calm* in your house, Jean-Marc."

"So what's the trouble?" he asked. "Is it him?"

"No, no. Nothing to do with him."

"He hasn't been exposing himself in public? Or crying on your shoulder because his latest student nymph ran away with the printmaker? No vulgar volcanic eruptions?"

"Jean-Marc," she said gently. "Don't be so harsh. You keep trying to invent a monster. It's your only imperfection." She stroked his arm and for a moment he kept still and held his breath, but then turned into the kitchen and busied himself with the making of coffee.

"You've seen him then?" he asked over his shoulder.

"Not for a couple of months. I dropped in on his latest show when I was in New York, and he happened to be there."

"*Happened* to be there." Jean-Marc laughed, and the coffee mugs turned restive in his hands. A brown comment seeped into his carpet. Felicity was looking at his books again and said soothingly, "He seemed very . . . serene. He said—"

"Oh, *serene!*"

"He said he'd been hoping you'd come down for the opening, that he'd sent an invitation."

"Fliss, I know perfectly well who sent me the invitation."

"I did *not!*" She turned from his books. "He asked how you were. He said he wished—"

"Liar." But he said it fondly, handing her a mug of coffee. He remembered the day she had found him sobbing in the woods near L'Ascension. He had run away. He was never going back. And she had simply held him until he was too exhausted to pound her with his fists anymore. He was still a child then.

Felicity sighed. "Oh well." She made a resigned gesture with her hands and shrugged. "Fathers. They're bound to disappoint. I'm sure if you'd only visit—"

"I prefer to keep the border between us, as an outward

and visible sign. Anyway, enough of the Old Volcano. What *is* upsetting you?"

"Ah." She took a slow mouthful of coffee. "It's going away. Perhaps I shouldn't talk about it in case she jumps out of the words."

"Oh Fliss, not another stray. It took me months to get that so-called jazz pianist off my doorstep. He didn't want work, he was a junkie. He stole three rolls of my best piano wire."

(The truth is, from the age of eighteen, I've always felt it was me looking after Felicity. She's not anchored to everyday, she floats away. Her days are baroque, they curl into each other like acanthus leaves, she lives somewhere between now and then. She moves in and out of her life.

She picks up people—men especially—through sheer inattentiveness. I've watched it happen. There must be something magnetic about her total indifference. Strays adhere to her like lint.)

"I know, I know," she said. "You won't have to get involved this time, Jean-Marc. I tried not to get involved myself. You talk as though I go looking for complications, but I try to avoid them. I *have* avoided this one. I'm avoiding her now. Which is rotten of me."

"You're hopeless." She always made him feel light-hearted, as though she had arrived with clowns and balloons. "You can't turn anyone down. Your sympathies are totally cockeyed." From his father on down.

"No, really, Jean-Marc, anyone would have done this. It was instinctive. In fact, someone else did do it. I have his card." She began rummaging through the large, worn leather sack (a weird and exotic thing, talismanic, a relic from childhood) that served as briefcase and handbag. Only art curators, he thought, who are permitted eccentricities, could get away with such a carryall. "I know it's somewhere here," she said vaguely.

He grinned. She would forget what she was looking for before she found it. He stirred his coffee vigorously to stop himself from brushing the hair out of her eyes as she sorted through muddled and magic contents.

93

"Okay," he said. "So who's in the cottage this time?"

"Well, no one at the moment, that's the problem. There was a woman . . . at least, I think . . . Do you remember Perugino's *Magdalena*?"

She had that distant look in her eyes, the one he associated with his father's studio in New York. He had dropped in unexpectedly once. Canvases stacked all over the place, the loft like a fully rigged ship sailing into an exhibition. He went exploring through tropical islands inhabited only by her eyes. Acrylic jungles on Masonite. Passionflowers six feet across. He sailed past brilliant matted vines through which her lopsided eyes glowed like a tiger's. Post-abstractionist symbolism was what critics were calling his father's stuff then. (For sheer idiocy and irrelevance, he still found it hard to choose between art critics and music critics. He pictured them as frantic little men, ramming the gloriously nonverbal into grinders to come out as words. Mincemeat intelligence. "I like to send them scurrying for new labels," his father laughed, "and then, once they've stuck on a new one, I like to confound 'em. It's my duty. I keep them in business.") Jean-Marc sailed on between monsoons and coral reefs where her underwater eyes swam at him from seaweed taller than himself. Queensland surf licked at his ankles, he could hear the sun. Bellbirds called from Brisbane gullies. He slipped round a study of eyes and crows that was big as a mainsail—and there was Felicity sprawling naked on a sofa while his father painted her.

He had felt embarrassed, bewitched, awkward, angry (he was sixteen at the time), but neither of them seemed in the least aware of his intrusion. Felicity had a glazed look in her eyes. He remembered thinking she had gone off somewhere else and left her body behind to take care of the boring business of a sitting. He simply stood there transfixed, half hidden behind the redoubt of stacked canvases, until his father turned and saw him. Confusion. A forest fire in his cheeks. And then the Old Volcano erupting into roars of laughter at the embarrassing evidence of his son's adolescent excitement.

Whenever he saw that abstracted look—that studio

94

vacancy—in her eyes, he was swamped with a muddle of desire and of murderous rage toward his father.

She was talking in her faraway voice. Something about a refrigerated truck. He blinked and struggled to attend.

"I've been reading about this, Jean-Marc, I've got clippings in my file. Death squads, corruption, it's a nightmare. The ones who are sent back disappear or are killed, there's evidence—"

"I wish you wouldn't keep that file. It's morbid."

He felt an impulse to pound the persistence out of her, as he had done in the woods of his childhood, though it wouldn't have any effect, it wouldn't discourage her, "because when I was ten," she said then, "just like you, I stood all by myself on a beach at the edge of the world and screamed at the sea."

When he visualized this, he saw her in miniature, a child with wispy golden hair and her bizarre leather bag over her shoulder trailing in the sand. He imagined the snake boats with prows like cobras craning their scaly necks to peer at her, a child waiting forever at the crinkled edge of an empty ocean.

"It's *ironies* I keep on file," she was saying. "It's *irony* I collect. You have to be fleeing an approved dictatorship before you count as a refugee. It has to be the right kind of suffering. Jean-Marc, are you listening to me?"

He jerked himself away from the beach at the end of the world.

"Fliss, I never know when to take you . . ."

"Look, here it is. I knew I had it somewhere in here. The card of this man who sells insurance. That should convince you."

"Convince me . . .?" he echoed in bemusement. "The man who sells insurance?"

"You haven't been listening," she reproached. And she told it all again while he tried to follow. "The priest thinks I'm crazy," she said. "He thinks I invented her, but he did see the blood on the bed, so I don't know what . . ." Like a sleuth, he was listening for the subtext.

"What about Aaron?" he asked.

"What?"

"Isn't that his name? The one with the wife and two daughters, the businessman with refinement." He was not quite able to keep the razor-blade edge from his voice.

"Oh," she said. "Aaron. That's over."

"Again?"

(And naturally I deduced that was the real reason behind all this fluster. Why wouldn't I? How could I possibly have separated all the talk of La Magdalena from a dream or a typical thought on the wing? I know Felicity. You have to get under the skin of her reasons.)

She was looking at her watch and riffling through his books. She could never be calm when sitting still. "Do you think it's too early to call him?" she asked.

"Call who?"

"The insurance guy. Augustine Kelly."

"Why do you want to call him? I thought you . . ."

"Because I didn't anticipate the . . . And then there's the blood. Suppose the priest subsequently . . . ? I think it's only fair to let him know, in case there are complications."

Jean-Marc laughed. "Your mind works like a switch-back ride through a hall of mirrors. It's impossible to keep up."

"Do you think it's too early to call?"

"At three in the morning? Are you serious?"

"I suppose you're right."

She was moving along his bookcases again, taking down books as though she planned to cram for a morning exam. It surprised him that the Old Volcano had not painted her as a woman sleepwalking on water through the middle of a howling gale.

"Do you suppose," he said fondly, "that we could snatch a few hours' sleep?"

She rubbed her cheek against his hair. "You sleep. I'm too wound up. I'll read for a while."

He leaned into her embrace for a dangerous minute then pulled away. (As a patient leaves an anesthetic, tempted by the narcotic, knowing it is necessary to resist.) When he stood, he was considerably taller than she. This helped him. He breathed deeply, inhaling detachment. He was troubled by her translucent flush, by the unnatural brightness of her eyes. He asked, with an almost entirely clinical concern, as though gathering data on a piano that needed attention: "How much sleep are you getting? On the average?"

She raised her eyebrows, surprised, perplexed. "I don't really know. I don't keep track. I suppose as much as I need. It's always hectic getting ready for a new exhibition."

If he had known that was the next to last time he would see her, he would have smashed his tuning forks and burned his library rather than fall asleep. He would have woken himself up properly when he heard her—or dreamed he heard her—on the telephone at an hour when birds were barely stirring. There were fragments he thought he remembered—her hair tumbling over him, the kiss on his forehead, a bemused comment: "His wife answered, and hung up on me. At least I guess it was his wife. Now why would she do that?"

"At six on a Saturday morning," he mumbled. "Why wouldn't she?"

"Oh dear," she said. "Is it Saturday?"

In his dream she was swept away on a fishing boat that flew.

If there was any night in his life he wanted to have over, it was that one.

When he woke in the middle of the morning, she was gone.

14

A blood spot in the yolk disturbed him. Gus watched the egg as it skated about the pan, spitting butter, and felt an unpleasant heaving along certain internal muscles. Nevertheless, he would be unable to throw the egg out. He thought of it as live. Eating it would be a solemn and chastening duty, a sort of *memento mori*, like receiving the Host at Mass.

There was a note on the refrigerator door, appended to it by a butterfly with flaring black-tipped orange wings and a magnetized belly.

> Have taken Sylvie and Jeanne to their figure-skating lessons. Tina is playing in the Dicksons' basement with Peggy. Kathleen is allowed to sleep in, but don't let her sleep too long. She has to help Sister O'Sullivan with the altar flowers at 11. Vic's Hardware called, the lawn mower is fixed.

He read a multitude of reproaches in these lines. With a sigh he flipped the eggs over, swallowed back an urge to be sick as the blood spot was seared by hot butter, and went over to the kitchen window. Sunlight greeted him like a dagger between the eyes. He leaned against the window molding, eyes closed, and asked himself how it was that he never remembered about hangovers while he was drinking. He counted to ten then squinted at his lawn. Dandelions spattered its surface and slid around in the sun like egg yolks. He felt sick again and had to close his eyes. A mathematical problem absorbed him: if weeds grew twice as fast as grass, and if there were three times as many broadleafed undesirables as there were blades of good Kentucky bluegrass, and if he had mowed this lawn 1,437 times in the last decade, how many transgressions did it take . . . ? The problem was too difficult to formulate. And why was it that uncut grass did not grow at a uniform rate? Why was it so tufted with hummocks and valleys, a shaggy terrain that humped itself into the wind? Swaying. Running in wavelets toward the house. Oppressing him.

He sighed, poured coffee, and slid the fried egg greasily onto toast. Its blood spot, like a devil's eye, watched him. As he ate, he could feel his throat muscles flinch from the close observation, one by one. In the beginning of all things, he thought, is a blood clot. This was the starting point. He must have been eating the heart of a chicken-to-be. He monitored its descent down interior tunnels until it splashed into some lake behind his navel. There was actually a sound similar to small waves breaking over rocks. The coffee, he supposed; a lake that heaved uneasily, brewing inner storms. He ate some dry toast.

In a loose way, he believed in signs and portents. Blood meant that harm had been done. There was a need for expiation. For various reasons yesterday and last night did not bear close scrutiny; but reparations, he knew, were called for.

He ignored his queasiness, he turned resolutely away from a craving to crawl back into bed, he set his course bravely, tacking into the day. He washed his few dishes. The stove top was noticeably speckled with brown flecks of butter, so he rubbed it with the wet dishcloth. To his dismay, a film of dullness spread itself in the wake of the cloth like a blight. He squeezed the cloth out, held it under cold running water, and tried again. No improvement. The stove top made him think of a marsh, motionless beneath its opaque gray skin. He acknowledged defeat and went to see if Kathleen was awake yet.

As soon as he entered her room he had a sharp and profoundly disturbing sense of *déjà vu*. A dream came back to him: long hair across a pillow, a woman on a bed.

But he could pull nothing specific from the fog at the back of his mind. Or did not want to. There had been a woman in a New York hotel room. He did not want to remember that. And then another one somewhere else, he did not want to remember that either. He had won a trip to New York, there had been a successful sales conference, he had drunk the usual conference amount (far too much), he had come away with a pocketful of magic formulae, he had managed to drive home without getting himself killed. And hadn't there been some muddle-up or other at the border? He was hung over, he had slept in, his wife was upset or angry or both, and no doubt for good reason.

Full of untarnished possibilities, his eldest daughter (his second-born) drew her sweet sleeping breaths. A slow and untroubled sighing. Yet the sweetness was not after all absolute; a slightly sour morning smell reached his nostrils and he felt saddened—as when a hearse passes on a fine summer's day. An intimation of mortality. He thought of his first-born asleep beneath the stone marker, and crossed himself. A comforting gesture. He did it again, to exorcize the dreams, and felt better.

Kathleen, her long hair drifting across cotton percale forget-me-nots, was watched over by a jostling crowd of young men in various poster poses: shirts open, silver medals nestling in chest hairs, jeans tight in an apparent advertisement for gender. Keep smiling, the young men had scrawled across their thighs. Some had written: To all my fans, with love. And one, larger than life, his protuberances chiselled into high-relief denim, had actually written: To Kathleen, with all my love, Johnny. This intimate greeting had cost Kathleen—or, in point of fact, her father—fifteen dollars and a large self-addressed stamped envelope; for which Johnny and his manly attachments (though scored with a gridwork of fold lines) looked soulfully grateful.

Kathleen stirred and turned over and the gallery of young men, rank upon rank of guardian angels, fluttered and stirred with her. Gus tolerated them, skewered as they were to the wall by their upper corners, decently restrained, and certainly preferable to the ones who left bicycles lying in his driveway. When he leaned on his car horn, the latter stared at him with faint insolence as they shifted their bikes. They moved with a slow, casual

arrogance, and he considered the cut of their jeans porno-
graphic. It was intolerable to think of those acne-faced
boys, with their unwholesome hands, touching Kathleen.
He certainly hoped that Therese had explained what was
what to the girls, though when he thought back to the
awful innocence of Therese at eighteen, he felt extremely
uneasy. On the other hand, she knew only too well the
penalties for naiveté.

How fearful and astonishing to have arrived at this
place: to have a daughter who was sixteen and beautiful,
an arranger of altar flowers, a collector of glossy pinup
sex and innocuous sleaze. Like all philanderers, he wanted
to shield his daughters from men. The fragility of their
innocence caused him anguish. Sometimes when he was
watching the Sunday afternoon game, Kathleen would
bring him a beer and would rumple his hair and give him a
quick, furtive kiss on the back of his neck. At such times
he would have to read the *TV Guide* with great concentration, holding it close to his face because of the small print.

Very quietly he tiptoed from her room. He could not
bring himself to propel her, just yet, into the day's quota
of imperfections. Let her sleep and dream on.

There was the lawn mower to be picked up, and then
he would stop by the florist's for the peace offering.
Carnations for Therese, pink and white. These were her
colors, the soft pastels, pale as the faces of martyrs. Insipid,
perhaps. But he brushed this thought aside quickly and
guiltily because—like a small dark spider—it had fallen
into his mind from out of nowhere.

At Vic's Hardware he saw a man whose uninsured
condition was a source of concern even on a Saturday
morning.

"Hal!" he said. "How're things?"

"Fine, just fine! Good to see you, Gus."

"How's Sally?"

"Great, just great. And Therese?"

"Couldn't be better. And your little one?"

"Peggy. Just as cute as a button," said Hal, beaming.
"Apple of my eye."

"Sure makes me lose sleep when I think how you haven't,

you know, *provided* . . ."—Gus hesitated tactfully—"if anything should happen."

Hal laughed. "Now don't start that again, Gus. I plan to dance on my hundredth birthday. Got no plans to leave them in the lurch."

Gus, truly unable to comprehend a lack of anxiety about one's family, shook his head lugubriously. "Not the sort of gamble I'd take for *my* wife and kids. But it takes all kinds, I guess."

Hal, counting out lengths of copper piping, missed a beat. He ran his hands along the slender cylinders, seemed to be pondering the idiosyncrasies of his bathroom, and then said: "Okay, you win. Figure out something that won't cost me more than ten or fifteen a month, and drop over next week."

This was the method that had won Gus the trip to New York. He was something of a phenomenon in his company. He had the peculiar distinction of bringing in the largest number of sales, yet one of the smallest incomes, of any agent in the province. The finer points of fiscal analysis and persuasion eluded him, but he was a *believer*. Protecting the family: it was quite simply one of those things—like standing for the national anthem or helping old ladies across the street—that any decent man did. When his branch manager was being kind about the low dollar volume of Gus's business, he called Gus "our knight in shining armor" or "our guardian of the *little* people, who need it most, heaven knows!" At other times, he said, "For God's sake, Gus, think *bigger*. Think rich."

What Gus needed, his manager believed, was some old-time-revival sales pep; to brush pinstripes with Million Dollar Round Table types. He hoped a razzle-dazzle convention would do the trick. Think success, he told Gus when he handed him the hotel reservation for New York.

Gus was thinking success at the florist's, visualizing good outcomes, waiting confidently for the magic. The florist's was one of his favorite places. It reminded him of a travel agent's poster of Tahiti. Begonias mobbed him, African violets lifted up their purple skirts, gardenias lay

102

fragrantly at his feet. Therese came toward him, languid between the potted chrysanthemums and the Boston ferns, her hair streaming over her bare shoulders and breasts. She was wearing nothing but a flower behind one ear.

Beside a lagoon, in soft sea grasses, she lay down and he covered her with the carnations, one by one. I don't know why the other women have happened, he told her. They just crop up from time to time like dandelions. I never give them carnations.

It doesn't matter, she said. I know they mean nothing. They have nothing to do with us.

Pink and white convolutions of petals, a voluptuous blanket, almost hid her. Only the tips of her nipples were showing. He kissed each one and murmured fondly: It's so long since I've seen them. You never take your nightgown off in bed.

Oh, murmured Therese, moving liquidly to accommodate him. The carnations! And it's so warm here, so warm.

He began to peel off his clothing.

"Can I help you?" The voice came sighing between the grasses. "It *is* warm, but we have to keep hothouse conditions."

Gus peered through *ficus benjaminas*, a humid forest of them, to where a maiden tossed her long brown hair and smiled. Her eyes were full of leaf shadows.

"Can I help you?" she asked again. Her lips were very close to him and smelled like petals. "We have roses on special. And also the potted mums."

"Carnations," he said bemused. "I had carnations in mind. They're more—"

"Oh yes. I quite agree." He could smell her gardenia skin. "This way, sir."

He followed, bewitched, through forest paths. She scattered blessings as she went, pausing to encourage the crotons, to cull an imperfect leaf or two from geraniums and Swedish ivies. *Dracaena marginata* waylaid her, she dallied over the gloxinias, the movement of her hips was miraculous. Gus gave thanks for the natural world.

103

She was wearing a clinging white knitted shift embroidered in royal blue across her breasts. *Jill's Flowers*. The letters moved like a field of bluebells as she breathed. Philodendrons, gawking from their overhead baskets, brushed her thighs with their trailing and variegated tendrils. Gus also was tempted to touch.

"Help yourself," the wood nymph offered. She indicated plastic tubs of carnations, an extravaganza of fluted petals. She bent over them and her buttocks moved inside her shift as silkily as tulip bulbs through spring soil. He bent over beside her, his cheek almost touching hers.

"Are you Jill?" he asked.

"Not *the* Jill. She's my aunt." She was selecting blooms, red and pink and white, their long stalks glistening wetly as she lifted them out of their buckets. "But my name's Jillian too." She proffered her samples. "Do you like the red ones? They're my favorites."

He was mesmerized by the pulse in the hollow of her neck. Fragility always overwhelmed him.

She seemed slightly and charmingly nervous. "Don't you want to help pick them out yourself? Men usually do."

He took the red carnation from her hand and touched its flower to the dimple in her neck. As though dubbing her a Lady of the Realm or conferring magic. Her dimple throbbed delicately. "The red's for you," he said. "Since it's your favorite." He tucked it behind her ear.

She blushed furiously, and he wanted to drag her behind the begonias, down to the Tahitian lagoon. As she turned her head away, bending over the carnation tubs for safety, the long stalk of her ear ornament bounced across her shoulder blades like a kite tail and she took refuge in laughter, becoming arch and flirtatious.

"You'll get me in trouble," she said, looking through her lashes. "Your wife will be in here returning the flowers."

"How did you know they were for my wife?"

"I can always tell. We're experts on men as well as flowers."

"Ah." He was disconcerted. Perhaps they assigned

grades, depending on the kind of flowers ordered. He wondered how he measured up.

She said teasingly: "It's carnation-picking time."

He turned to the business of choosing whites and pinks with her help. Sometimes their arms brushed, a delectable accident. Fumbling for stems, his hand skirmished with hers underwater. Once he dropped a flower and as he stooped to pick it up, the back of his forearm came into fleeting contact with her thigh.

She said: "You'll want greenery with these. It's out back in the storage room, if you'd like to help choose . . ."

He kissed her, out back, by the glass-doored refrigerators in which chilly roses bloomed by the bucketful. In the presence of orchids, they touched various parts of each other. These things happen under hothouse conditions. Someone, a shrill and impatient customer, rang the counter bell in the front of the shop. Such is life.

"Perhaps," Gus said, flustered, "we could meet for a drink some time. Later today, maybe? Or next week?"

"Wait here. I'll be back."

He was left with the bridal arrangements and corsages-to-go. Wreaths of lilies tied with black ribbons were reproachful. Therese's face appeared inside a circle of sad laurel. Therese! he said. Wait! I can explain. I'm bringing flowers. But it was not Therese. It was a woman in a torn black dress. He was startled. She seemed to belong in a dream. She seemed to be someone he once knew but could not quite place. She moved behind a wedding bouquet. Jillians come and Jillians go, she sang in her black bride's voice, but who can keep count of your betrayals?

Who can keep count? sang Therese of the wreaths.

Bunches of baby's breath joined in choral accusation, there was a swelling chorus of asparagus fern, judgmental.

I am a clown, Gus confessed. And a lecher.

He gathered up his sad carnations, left the requisite money, and fled through the tradesmen's entrance into the back parking lot.

Therese accepted the flowers graciously, as clear evidence of guilt. Resignation suited her. She wore it well, like a dress that has become threadbare but is still comfortable and attractive. She had the air of someone who carries on by instinct in the face of exhaustion and predictable humiliations.

"Thank you for mowing the lawn," she said quietly. And then: "Sister O'Sullivan called to see if Kathleen was sick." Though Therese had never mastered the pronunciation of the English *th*, her absent *h*'s were expressive. *T'ank you. Kat'leen.* It was unbearably plaintive.

"I'm sorry," Gus sighed. "I couldn't bear to disturb her. I thought she'd wake in time."

"That's okay, daddy," Kathleen said brightly. "I hate doing the flowers with Sister O'Sullivan. She asks a million nosy questions. She thinks all of us girls are sex maniacs."

"Kat'leen!" Therese's voice was shocked but weary. She knew the worst would always happen. "Please to tidy your room."

When the children had left the lunch table, she said neutrally: "Your phone call early this morning. It was the woman." (*T'is morning. T'woman.*)

Gus, innocent, raised a puzzled eyebrow. "What woman?"

You know, her turned back said.

He was frowning, summoning up business contacts. "What did she want?"

Therese made furrows in the sugar bowl. "She would not say."

Gus felt a momentary panic but could think of no sins likely to announce themselves in this way. "Must be one of the secretaries. Something must have come up with a client while I was away. Or else they wanted to check that I was back."

"It was not a secretary. The woman has said she is calling from Montreal."

"Montreal?"

After seconds of total blankness, Gus remembered the dream in full clarity. And then that it had not been a dream. He remembered the woman who had something to do with art galleries, the delays at the border, the torn black dress. The crime.

106

"My God," he said. "What did she say?"

"She has not left any message." Having stated her case, Therese would press charges no further. She knew how to suffer.

"Oh for God's sake, Therese," he said. "It's not what you think." A rare innocence made him angry. "It's not in the least what you think." He was on a crescendo now, energized by the absence of guilt and by anxiety. "I need to know every detail. Could it possibly have been the police?"

Therese blanched. "The police?"

"What did she sound like? Did she have a Boston accent?"

"I . . . I don't know." Therese was shaken.

"What number did she leave?"

"No . . . no number. She . . . hung up the phone."

"*She* hung up?"

Therese was not a good liar. A rash of guilt spotted her cheeks. Gus decided on a strategy of wounded silence, but there was something acrid in his mouth, the taste of fear. There must have been trouble with the police. Fountains welled from his underarms; his shirt drooped against him like a wet sail. Felicity—that was the woman's name. He had her card somewhere. Therese watched in alarm as he rummaged through his suit pockets, turned his briefcase inside out.

He found Felicity's business card.

There was a Boston address and a Boston number, but pencilled on the back were some digits with a Montreal area code. He dialled from the hallway phone, the Montreal number. He let it ring twenty times. He could not believe she would not answer. Immediately, he dialled again. No answer.

Therese, alert to new disasters, watched him wild-eyed. "*Qu'est-ce qui arrive?*" she faltered.

If he had not been so worried, he might have enjoyed being the wronged one. He understood, suddenly, why it was addictive; why withholding forgiveness was irresistible. He said tersely, turning the knife: "If there's a call, I'll be in the driveway. Working on the rust holes in your car."

107

As he assembled the sanding blocks, the acrylic filler, and the primer, his motions were heavy with virtue. For months he had been promising to do this, putting it off. He had thought of it as a tedious job, but now he wondered why. There was something restful, sensuous even, about stroking the metal with the sanding block, banishing ugliness. Scrape, scrape, scrape. He blew ferrous particles from the block and watched them float away between the pines in dark, rosy puffs. He tested the sanded edges of a hole. They were freshly silver, the color of a soul after penance.

Stroke and lift. He fell into a comfortable rhythm. A film of brownish red, luminous in the sunlight, dusted his arms. He might have been a tarnished priest bending to obscure rites of purification. He blew himself clean.

After all, he thought, as hole after hole was scrubbed immaculate, I did nothing wrong. If the police come, I will tell them the truth. The woman looked pitiful, not quite human. Anyone would have helped her. I did it without thinking. If I stood on a dock and saw a child fall in, I wouldn't stop to remember that I can't swim, I would just dive in. And then afterwards, Your Honor, when we realized we had broken the law, we turned her in. We did the right thing.

The right thing. This thought assaulted him in a sudden cloudy funnel of rufous filings. He was almost choked. *Have mercy upon us*, sang every laceration in the metal. *Do not abandon us.* The torn black dress flapped like a mad thing in the summer wind. It wrapped itself around his face, it shrieked in his ears. His nerves were in a panic.

Something has happened to her, he knew. To La Magdalena.

I betrayed her.

They are sending her back to . . . to whatever it was she was fleeing from.

He knew only this: it was apparently worse than slow death by refrigeration.

He had difficulty breathing. A coughing fit took possession of him. Metal filings were clogging up his lungs. He felt that if Felicity did not answer his next call, it would become completely impossible to breathe. But he could not call her. He was afraid to find out what had happened.

With renewed frenzy, he plunged at the rust. He was the man that ate the corruption that ate the car that Therese drove. The savage scouring calmed him, his breath cleared a passage through the dust.

"Daddy?" Kathleen said. "Can I help?"

From the convulsive way he turned, she might have been a policeman or an immigration officer. He stared at her with a blank dread. It was impossible, impossible, to untangle right and wrong. Existence was rust-riddled beyond repair, a pockwork of errors. He moved, he did harm: that was an axiom.

"I'm sorry, daddy. I didn't mean to startle you."

"No, no," he said distractedly.

"Can I start on the other side?"

In tandem, they scraped at the metal. It was some solace for Gus to think of the car as his life. He furrowed his own back, concentrating on the pockets of rottenness. The clamor of his muscles filled up the space of his mind, there was no room for thought. The pain began to be seductive, a comfortable self-flagellation.

"Daddy," Kathleen said, "can I ask you something?"

Her voice came in rhythmic fragments, punctuated by dust. Gus went on scouring the right foreleg of the car, biting deep into the flesh.

"Will you promise me not to get angry?" Kathleen asked.

One, two, three, and return to the start of the stroke. He had given himself over to the beat of it now, a mindless pleasure.

"Daddy, I'm not asking this just to be . . . I mean, it's not because I believe it. When Jonathan Springer told me—he said it in front of a whole group of my friends—I was so angry I ripped up his math homework. I said he was a filthy liar. But then . . . but then, some of the kids looked away as though . . ."

Dust covered them. They moved like two figures in an inferno.

"Jonathan Springer said that he saw you in your car in

the lane behind the school stadium . . . he said there was some woman . . . that he often . . .''

Gus had moved on to the flank now. He ignored the wincing of the car, he was merciless.

"And another time, he said he saw you in Sandy's Bar with . . . with Miss Matthews, our gym teacher. I told him she was a client. I told them that's the way insurance agents do business, over coffee and all that."

His sanding block made long, sweeping gouges across the flank, toward the rear thigh. He was heading for the car's privates, he had a sharp instrument.

"Anyway, everyone knows Jonathan Springer is a liar. He's such a pain. Like, he wants to prove that everyone's parents are like his. I feel sorry for him, really. You can't believe anything he says. It's just that . . . well, it was when the other kids looked away. It won't make any difference, daddy. Well, it will, I guess . . . but I mean, I'll still love you just as much. I just don't want to be the only kid who doesn't know, daddy, that's all. I would just like to *know*."

He was raking at the inner flesh between the rear wheels now, his hands bloodied with rust.

"Daddy, why is mummy crying in the bathroom?"

Over the trunk of the car, he stared at his daughter in despair. The dirge of his abused muscles ascended. He was clothed in red powder, the sun set him on fire, he writhed in flames. Only the sheltered areas beneath his eyebrows and nose were free of dust, and to Kathleen he looked weirdly owlish. His ghostly eyeholes frightened her. She thought with alarm: My father is even unhappier than my mother.

The world seemed suddenly fragile as tissue to her, full of gaping holes through which she might fall and fall forever.

"Daddy," she said urgently, beginning to giggle with a panicky hilarity. "Oh daddy, you should see yourself. You look like a clown."

15

On Beacon Hill the aunts waited with Sunday tea. They lived on Chestnut Street in a house dating from 1820 (at *least* that early, they always said, with a knowing and mysterious smile), where nothing untoward or unpleasant would ever be so rash as to intrude.

"I had horrible dreams last night," Felicity told them. "It's because I drove straight back to Boston. I didn't come by way of L'Ascension, I didn't even try to look for her. I convinced myself she'd rather not attract extra attention."

"Listen!" Aunt Ernestine raised an index finger, her expression ravished. She leaned into the slow movement of a Beethoven sonata. "Lovely," she whispered. "Lovely."

"Telefunken," Aunt Norwich told Felicity.

The Misses Sayer, as they were called on Beacon Hill, restricted themselves to the better recording labels.

"Suppose she dies out there in the woods?" Felicity asked. "Suppose it's true, those reports about the death squads, suppose she's deported?"

"Felicity, my *dear*." Aunt Norwich poured more tea. "Such a *melodramatic* imagination." And in such poor taste, she implied. And all for the want of another cup of Earl Grey, which had calming properties. There were very few problems that could not be cured by Earl Grey provided it was properly steeped and made from loose leaves. Aunt Norwich murmured incantations over the teacups as she filled them. They were Royal Albert's Springtime Bouquet, her favorite pattern.

"Do you remember," Aunt Ernestine smiled in fond reminiscence, "the time Felicity heard starving children calling to her?"

111

"Hordes of them," Aunt Norwich said. "We told her she'd heard squirrels in the attic."

They beamed at each other, delighted. They were connoisseurs of eccentricity. Only Beethoven pleased them more than the finer family oddities.

And it turned out to be bats, they chuckled.

"We always knew you'd do something artistic, dear. Actually we rather thought you'd become a writer, making up stories the way you do—"

"Though goodness knows, Norwich, with the kind of novels being published—"

"Oh indeed, we much prefer. . . . How are the arrangements for the Florence thing coming along? Weren't you having trouble getting one of the paintings, my dear? The one you particularly wanted?"

"Wasn't it a Perugino?" Aunt Ernestine asked.

"What? Oh. Yes. Still negotiating." Felicity was stalled eye to eye with La Magdalena, she could not get around her. "Perhaps this is what happened to daddy," she said. "Perhaps he ran into Circe. A nightmare looks you in the eye and it won't let you go—"

"Felicity, my dear, do sit down."

"—even though you know it might be pointless," Felicity went on, "you have no way of knowing the rights or wrongs of the situation—"

"Felicity, all this motion is very bad for the African violets. It distresses them. They are very sensitive to their environment. You really must be more considerate."

"—you even wonder if you're quite rational, if you really saw . . . But it won't let you go. It won't budge. It marks you out. You don't want to get involved, but you find you can't *not*."

The aunts let Beethoven have his say, and when he paused Aunt Norwich offered an opinion: "I don't think these pastries are quite as good as last week's, do you, Ernestine? A shade too much butter perhaps. I must speak to Mrs. Goodman about it."

"It could be the butter." Aunt Ernestine pondered possibilities. "Or maybe the cream in the creamcakes is too rich."

"Or you might have brewed the tea too long. It can go to the head if it's too strong. I hope she won't do anything rash."

"Of course she won't, will you, Felicity? That would be history repeating itself. Very tiresome."

"Your father was a terrible disappointment to us."

"Such a promising young doctor," Aunt Norwich sighed. "Dreadful waste."

"Of course the war . . ."

"Yes, yes, it didn't help. But the tendencies were already there, you must admit. He didn't *have* to go to the front. It could easily have been arranged . . ."

"And after the war he just couldn't seem to . . ."

"Do you remember, Ernestine, that dance not long after the Japanese surrender? The Marblehead Ball? It was just before he went off to India—"

"And the Westbury girl came."

"We had high hopes that night. They danced until dawn, remember?"

"She would have made all the difference."

"We didn't know that the Australian girl was already . . ."

"And they could hardly have known each other. Ten days in Brisbane on leave, and then back to New Guinea. I blame the Japanese—"

"Though we would never dream, Felicity, of holding you responsible for the circumstances of your conception."

"If he'd been free when he danced with the Westbury girl . . ."

"Wasn't Seymour at that party?" Felicity asked. "I'm sure he's mentioned it."

Some tea leaped from Aunt Ernestine's cup and she mopped at it with a linen serviette.

"From what Seymour has said," Felicity went on, "it wouldn't have made any difference. Not my mother, or the Westbury girl, or anything you could have done. Seymour says that God swallowed him whole."

"Oh really!" The crocheted tips of Aunt Ernestine's collars quivered. "It is quite unnecessary, really it is quite lacking in a sense of what is proper, to bring God into the conversation."

113

"I blame that dreadful man, that . . . that *painter*." Aunt Norwich was so agitated that a Royal Albert cup was almost chipped. "You *know* Springtime Bouquet has been discontinued," she said reproachfully. "If anything untoward happens, it will take months to track down a replacement."

"Norwich is absolutely right. He must shoulder a good part of the blame. There was something vulgar about him . . . a quality of . . . of unwholesome *enthusiasm*. It was like a disease."

"Nothing was done with moderation."

"A whole generation was infected. Everything to extremes."

"And to think, Felicity, of all the men in the world—"

"You almost broke our hearts all over again."

"We were glad when all that . . . when your incomprehensible fascination was over."

"Seymour says"—Felicity felt her way carefully—"that he did an ordination portrait just before they went off to the war. He says that you have it. My father as St. Sebastian."

She observed them closely. She knew the secret codes of agitation, the scent of lavender and attar of roses shaken loose from silk underthings set a-tremble. But how magnificently they stood guard against the unacceptable. What a flawless duet they played. She would never know who were the better liars, the grander mythmakers: her aunts or Seymour.

"She's in fine form today," Norwich smiled.

"Her imagination has always been extraordinary, though a trifle melodramatic." Ernestine might have been speaking of one of her prize-winning African violets. "She has a fine sense of the symbolic."

"That's what makes her such an excellent curator. Wouldn't you say this is what distinguishes her exhibitions? A mythic dimension?"

"And a startling originality, of course."

They smiled secret smiles and sipped their tea.

Certain things were simply not permitted. No guest under their roof could sustain a belief in anything they

114

disapproved of. You would think, Felicity told them dryly, that Beacon Hill was the gateway to heaven. The aunts did not perceive this as irony. Well, they said modestly, we have found that all things, when looked at from the right angle, lead to contentment.

Nevertheless, nevertheless, Felicity worried. "Whether you look at them the right way or not, there are certain things, certain intractable things . . . If you'd *seen* La Magdalena's face—"

"Ah! Didn't I tell you, Norwich? As soon as we knew she'd watched that documentary, I said this would happen. I said there'd be dreams."

"She takes history so personally."

"She keeps that dreadful file."

"And the Perugino. It's her taste for myth again."

"You *must* see, Felicity, that it's a projection."

On account of your deplorable childhood, their litany went. You were conceived in a pagan country, born into riots. And then your mother (of whom we know nothing, who was not even an American) abandoned you from Day One. Then your father went chasing obsessions while you grew into ruin. Who could say what the years in India had wrought? And then Australia. Now how could any place so remote not do harm? You acquired a very unreliable view of the peripheral in those countries, they said. You give it undue importance. All this before we managed to bring you home, and not without legal complications. You were thirteen already. It's been uphill work.

"These occasional signs of a relapse," Aunt Ernestine said gently, "are therefore not surprising. But naturally they concern us."

"We've taken care of everything," Aunt Norwich assured her. "You are not to worry. You mustn't think we're indifferent to matters like this. We make the appropriate donations, we take our own kind of action. In all things, the proper channels should be followed."

"But sometimes," Felicity protested, "the proper channels seem to be on the wrong side. Or else dreadfully, if not wilfully, misinformed."

115

"It is not nice, Felicity, to impute anything but the purest of intentions to the people in charge of the proper channels. It is not our place to question. It is simply not done. It is impolite."

They offered more Earl Grey and applied a poultice of Mozart. The Sinfonia Concertante for Violin and Viola, K. 364, Isaac Stern and Pinchas Zuckerman performing with the New York Philharmonic, Zubin Mehta conducting. With the latest in digital technology. And also, they said, we have a little gift. The *Très Riches Heures* of the Duc de Berry in a new facsimile edition. Do you see how the ducal arms appear on the walls of heaven? One feels such affection for the artist.

Of course this was the country Felicity preferred to have come from, the world of gold leaf and lapis. This was where she wanted to belong. Behind a parapet of art and history. Within the aunts' walled garden where all was well, where all manner of things would always be well. Certainly the elements are improbable, she conceded to herself; a fifteenth-century face in a side of beef. She would have *liked* to believe that this was an arrangement of her scheming imagination.

She smiled at the aunts, those purveyors of soothing magic.

"The first time I saw you," she began to remember fondly.

Oh, they laughed, it begins much earlier than that. When we were children ourselves, we knew you were coming. It goes back to before we were born, it goes back to our youth, it goes back at least as far as the Marblehead Ball.

But this was a ritual, and was always performed to the making of apple wine. Even as Norwich fetched the aprons and paring knives, and as Ernestine brought the barrel of apples up from the cellar, the telling began. Whatever the variants—and they looped and embroidered them differently each time, according to the age of the apples and the weather and their whim—it was all the same story.

As the spirals of peel went slinking into bowls that

116

might have held half the world, so the stories uncoiled themselves, and curled up again into new shapes, and twisted and laced their way into past and future and each other. Sometimes the aunts had been mere children, peeping from the stairway at the Marblehead Ball. Often and again they had watched, blood warm, from the womb of their dancing mother, your grandmother, my dear, they said. Though since you are not twins . . . Felicity demurred. You see, they would reply sadly, shaking their heads, you are thinking from the wrong set of rules. And in any case, we were seventeen and eighteen respectively, shy debutantes, stepping out at our first formal occasion.

They had been in fact of marriageable age and alarmingly beautiful—this was beyond dispute—dispensing rejections with a grace that left young men tongue-tied and drove them to ordination or poetry. For the aunts had hundreds of suitors who came pining from near and far. The aunts were legends in those days. Men murmured talismans as they passed, men staggered from the sudden weight of their own genitals, men consulted witches to find charms that would win the lovely Ernestine, that would soften the ravishingly remote Norwich. But the aunts knew all there was to know about happily ever after, and they laughed (in ever such a ladylike and mysterious way) in the faces of their suitors, and they spurned them every one.

But on other occasions the aunts had been old and wise, past the time of their hundredth birthdays, on the night of the Marblehead Ball. They had looked back on the meaning of their youth and danced only with an old man in black.

The paring knives flashed and the bowls (they had always been in the family, they had come over on the *Mayflower*, they had carried the porridge of Columbus) were brimming either with the sliced flesh of the apples or with rind. You must not think that the aunts discarded the rind. A certain amount (kept secret) gave the wine a baroque bouquet, for apple peel is baroque by nature and the aunts approved of the eighteenth century. An infusion of apple peel in Earl Grey will do wonderful things. When

117

the rind was a dappled mix of red and green, it took curlicues to excess, it looped itself around Ernestine Sayer and Norwich Sayer, soothsayers at the Marblehead Ball. Depending on the mood and the temperature of the apples and the state of the lilacs, it allowed for a guest with a tarot pack at the epochal ball; though sometimes he had a slide rule that told fortunes with mathematical exactitude.

There was also, on occasion, a hornèd artist—a dreadful man—who made unpredictable and showy appearances and insisted on unveiling the future in oils and acrylics. Though none of the guests ever liked him. (On this point the aunts did not vary.) They would turn their backs and get on with the next dance, and *pouff*, he would disappear.

But whatever the means of foretelling, the future was always felicitous. For once they knew about the lost child, the aunts went out into the highways and byways of time and found her and brought her home. In their walled garden, where the lilacs bloom right through the winter, she was safe from all harm and she flourished.

A speckled snake of apple peel slid around Felicity's wrist.

"This reminds me of my *ayah*," she said. "We used to make the curry paste together." She could feel the stone slab and the roller, smell the bruising of coriander, see the cumin seeds bleeding into the coconut, and the purple-skinned *brinjal* waiting to be cut into cubes. "My *ayah* used to sing me stories while she worked. When daddy was away—he was nearly always away—she used to sing the legend of—"

"Oh dear," Aunt Norwich said. "I've cut my hand."

There were bright beads of blood on her palm and a single drop lay like a scarab on the apple pulp.

"We shall have to concentrate," Aunt Ernestine said. "Though your blood will add a certain piquancy to the wine, Norwich."

"I believe we have reached the last apple," Aunt Norwich said.

When the right proportions of rind had been stirred into the pulp, and the secret ingredients added and the blessings murmured, then the mix was left to ferment through whatever variations it thought proper.

Aunt Ernestine put away the aprons and paring knives, Aunt Norwich took down a corked stone bottle and three glasses, Felicity gathered up the Sunday supplements of the *Boston Globe* and the *New York Times*. In the cobbled garden, under a flowering dogwood and the lilacs that always bloomed, they sipped apple wine. Wisteria kept watch over the gate in the high brick wall and a little stone boy in a shell held out his hand, while Felicity read about the world. From the stone hand of the little boy, a fountain curled around the shell and over it and through the ground cover of myrtle and ivy and violets.

"She was such a little hoyden when she came to us," Aunt Ernestine said fondly, studying Felicity's profile. Felicity did not look up from the *New York Times*.

"A scarecrow," Aunt Norwich confirmed.

With an imagination, they reminded each other, as fertile as the mulch they put on their lilacs.

"You must remember, Felicity," Aunt Ernestine cautioned, "that you cannot believe the half of what you read in the papers."

"I do hope, Felicity," Aunt Norwich sighed, "that you are not going to clip out any more of those dreadful stories. Such things are always with us, there is no point in getting morbid. It is better to use the proper channels."

Felicity lifted up her eyes from the ephemeral and un-reliable newspapers to contemplate the garden that had always been there. And the aunts, white witches, who were now perhaps seventy, or perhaps a hundred, or perhaps more, smiled back from their youthful untroubled eyes. All is well, they promised. And all manner of thing shall be well.

Felicity, I'll say, when she calls in from wherever she is. You'll love what I've done with the aunts.

Though maybe she won't.

Maybe she'll say: Jean-Marc, you've never even *met* my aunts. I won't have you making fun of them.

But it's her own fault. She's told me a thousand and one

tales about them. Felicity weaves her past as she goes, she spins out memories, the facts of her life are as clear as riddles.

On the subject of your aunts, I'll tell her, I've been restrained compared to some of *your* versions. When I think of certain anecdotes, when I think of your flippant tone—

That's different, she'll say. I love them.

Tra la, tra la. Kathleen is the same. She alone is permitted to criticize her father. I am expected to agree at appropriate moments (when her mood requires it); I am rebuked for concurring. You don't know him, she says. He wasn't like that at all.

A full and frank confession: I do not understand women. Or anyone else I've ever known, for that matter; which is why I appreciate the reliable mathematics of pianos.

Still, Felicity is Felicity. You can't sail round her. And I know her aunts and her *ayah* and her grandparents (none of whom I ever met) better than I know anyone except Felicity herself, with the possible exception of Kathleen— but that's something recent. Whereas Felicity and I go back forever, we go back to before she left the Old Volcano, we go back to that day I was running away in the woods near L'Ascension. At *least* that far. We may even go back as far as the Marblehead Ball.

Jean-Marc, she'll dream, you're impossible. I hope you're not upset, I did mean to call earlier. There's a frightful racket—can you hear me?—because of these two old volcanoes arguing. I'm hiding under the grand piano. Maman says hello.

Really, Jean-Marc! the aunts will say. This is quite improper. You're beginning to laugh her laughter.

16

In the middle of the regular Monday morning staff meeting at the Winston branch office of the Greater Life Insurance Company, Gus heard a stifled scream. It was a long, thin, eerie sound, like the distress of a bird whose nest has been violated. Or like the kind of high-pitched throat noise made by a mute person who is in pain. He knew it was the voice of La Magdalena.

Everyone else heard it too.

There was a sense of disturbance.

Bob Wilberforce, the branch manager, pressed the pause button on the video machine. "You okay, Gus?" he asked.

"It wasn't *me*," Gus said.

They were all looking at him strangely. "Sorry," he said, embarrassed. "Yeah, sure. I'm fine."

Mr. Wilberforce released the pause button and Reggie Jackson flickered back into motion. His face was in close-up. "It's all in the head," he said. "Whatever's goin' on inside your head, that's what's gonna happen when you come up to bat. First you gotta be winning inside your head."

Reggie's face began to float backwards from the camera, his Yankees shirt came into view, his whole body was suddenly rocketing in reverse, getting smaller and smaller, until he was just a tiny white figure at home plate as seen from the eye of a cruising blimp. First the baseball diamond filled the screen, then the whole green field, and then the funnel of the packed stands. There was a pause in the blur of distancing. The ball park hung there, motionless, waiting, like a bauble at the stretched limit of an elastic string. Music indicated that something of great significance was about to occur. The room was hushed with expectant tension. Gus wondered how it felt to be

Reggie Jackson, exposed there so tiny and alone, at the vortex of the watching world.

Then slowly, slowly, as though he was moving in a dream, Gus seemed to be on a languid slide toward the pitcher's mound. Or else the pitcher, along with Reggie, was beginning the leisurely elastic return to a distant hand holding a stick.

The upper stands disappeared. The benches and bleachers slipped off the sides of the screen. The outfield went.

And there was the pitcher rubbing his hand on a piece of rosin. The bases were loaded, the crowd was going wild. The pitcher maneuvered a wad of something around in his mouth and spat toward first base. Reggie's disembodied voice floated over the trajectory of spittle. "You can't afford to listen to anything but the words inside your own head." Now the pitcher's face in close-up, readjusting the wad in his cheek. And Reggie's voice: "There was a stretch early in the season I struck out several times in a row. The crowd took to booing from the moment I stepped out of the dugout. Didn't make any difference. You can't let it get to you. I never quit believing in myself. I went right on—"

Click.

Mr. Wilberforce, finger on the pause button, looked out over his lectern at the sales force. "I want that to sink in," he said devoutly. He leaned on his pulpit and his eyes rested on the members of his congregation one by one. "The essence of higher sales is right there. I want everyone just to concentrate on those words while I rerun Reggie for a bit."

With bowed heads and reverent demeanor the sales force reflected on the week's First Lesson.

There was a blur of images rushing to return to their starting positions, the spittle flew back into the pitcher's mouth, Reggie's voice clambered out of a moment's squealing static and continued: ". . . the words inside your own head." Two beats, the mole on the pitcher's nose, the deformity of the wad inside his cheek. "There was a stretch early in the season I struck out several times in a row. The crowd took to booing from the moment I stepped out of the dugout. Didn't make any difference. You can't let it get to you. I never quit believing in myself. I went right on listening to the words inside my head."

Now the video screen was arranging itself as a frame around the ball, which moved forever in a slow and beautiful arc toward the batter, trailing streamers of voice-over. "And that voice said: You can do it, Reggie. You're the greatest! Just listen to the winning."

"And I just kept listening to the sound of that thwack." Reggie's voice was still unfurling, looping itself like ribbons around the trajectory of the ball. "I listened to the sound of a ball being hit out of the park. I listened to the sound of winning."

Now the languid ball was falling, floating, falling towards Reggie's bat, and Reggie's body was turning to meet it in a slow-motion ballet that was exquisite to behold. Ball and bat touched. They kissed. The kiss was voluptuous, a soulful smack, and now everyone knew that this was the sound of a ball being hit out of the park, the sound of winning, the sound of that crucial home run against the Red Sox in the Eastern Division play-offs for the 1978 World Series.

Bob Wilberforce blinked his eyes rapidly. More than one member of his sales force surreptitiously fumbled for a tissue. Grown men wrestled with bronchial disturbances.

Just as the ball was winging its dreaming way out of the park, just as Yankee stadium was teetering on the brink of delirium, Gus heard La Magdalena scream again. He was caught off guard and lurched convulsively in the manner of one waking from a fall in a dream. No one noticed or heard. Everyone else was jogging around the bases with Reggie, preoccupied. No one heard Gus's gasp of pain. This time she was digging her fingernails into the soft flesh of his forearm.

A national executive of Greater Life stepped out onto home plate and surveyed the suddenly deserted baseball diamond, the empty stands. Reggie's voice spoke to him from the clouds. A light shone on his face. He repeated

123

Reggie's words, he read his text, he began a short sermon. He had a voice like Aunt Jemima's buttered syrup.

Do not abandon me, La Magdalena whispered.

Gus glanced nervously around. He massaged his bruised forearm.

The Aunt Jemima voice was oozing its sticky way around the room, lapping at the sales force. It flowed through home runs and hard work and never giving up just because you might strike out a few times. It covered all bases, it bathed all agents. It stressed the importance of listening to the inner voice.

Do not abandon me, La Magdalena whispered.

Since it was difficult to know where the sound was coming from, or how to help, Gus closed his eyes and tried to visualize the cottage outside L'Ascension. But all he could see was the pond of lamplight and the dark shore of the room beyond it where the face of La Magdalena hung like an icon, pale and luminous, and streaked with tears.

What does it mean? Gus wondered. And what had Saturday's phone call meant? And what had it meant that no one answered at the number he had been given? He felt ill with the same sort of apprehension he felt in a dentist's waiting room.

On a flip chart Bob Wilberforce was drawing forceful lines with a black felt marker. The lines gathered themselves up like twigs and began to whirl in front of Gus's face, faster, faster, their black skirts rising over long white legs soaked in blood. He could not contain his sense of dread, he needed air, he rose to his feet, his chair made an unseemly comment to the vinyl floor. Bob Wilberforce stopped in mid-exhortation. From the way a chasm formed to let him through, from all the startled upturned faces, Gus knew that he must have looked dreadful.

He *felt* dreadful. He felt as though he had received word of a death.

He felt conspicuous and embarrassed.

At the door he paused and rallied himself, holding on to his dignity and a chair back. He was aware of the clammy tide of sweat in his palms. "Sorry," he said. "Must be something I ate."

He waved a secretary off—"Just need to put my head down on my desk for a few minutes"—and swayed down the center hallway to his own office. He felt as though he were walking along the deck of a rolling ship. He shut his office door and sat down. He was shivering a little. His hands were shaking. There was a sour tincture of panic on his tongue. He felt horribly queasy.

He knew what he needed.

He took Felicity's business card from his pocket and dialled the Montreal number. This time he was answered on the first ring.

"Hello," a male voice said. "This is Jean-Marc Seymour. Because of heavy bookings there will be a wait of at least three weeks before your piano can be tuned. At the tone, please indicate the make and approximate age of your piano, and also your name and phone number. Your call will be returned as soon as possible."

Gus hung up. His head was throbbing now, his lips numb from being bitten. He turned Felicity's card over and dialled her Boston number. Someone answered on the second ring. "Hello?"

He recognized her voice. "Felicity?"

"Yes. Speaking."

"Thank God. This is Gus." He swallowed. He had to know what had happened, he was afraid of finding out. He made a false start, coughed, cleared his throat, plunged in. "My wife said you called on Saturday morning. What happened?"

"Pardon?"

"What happened?"

"Who is this?"

"Gus. Gus Kelly. Don't you remember? We—er—you know . . . the border."

"Oh!"

"You remember me?" he asked.

The silence seemed interminable. "Hello?" he said. "Hello? Are you still there?"

"Yes," she said, so softly he had to strain to hear.

125

"You don't remember me?"

"Yes. Yes, I do." It was clearly an admission she would rather not have made.

"In L'Ascension," he began, "after I left—"

"She's gone."

"What?" He felt the lurch of dread again (as when the dental assistant beckoned him into the chamber of horrors). He said faintly: "Already? They've sent her back? But I thought—"

"No, no. She's *gone*. Vanished. When I went back with the priest, she wasn't there."

He asked nervously, cupping his hand around the receiver and dropping his voice: "Why are you whispering?"

"I—I don't know." It was increasingly difficult to hear her.

"Where . . . do you think she is?" he whispered.

There was another long silence, though he could hear her breathing.

"To tell you the truth," she said slowly, her voice thinner than air, "she disappeared totally. Right out of my mind. I was hoping she never existed."

"But she did," he said. "She does."

"Yes," Felicity sighed.

"So then where . . . ?"

Felicity did not answer. The woods? they both wondered. Montreal by now?

Aggrieved, as though she had criminally mislaid something priceless, he accused: "She was *injured*, she had no money, she—"

"Don't!" Felicity sighed. "Please."

"We should never have left her alone, I knew we shouldn't, I *said* we shouldn't . . ." His outrage flagged and dwindled. Another long silence as each began to realize: the albatross has gone.

Then Felicity offered: "Perhaps she had people waiting for her. You know, friends. Or relatives. I believe there are church groups in Montreal, something like the old Underground Railroad for runaway slaves."

"Remember that car? The other car?" Gus asked suddenly. "They turned their lights on the cottage?"

126

"My God, yes." Her voice was warm. "It was deliberate. I'm sure you're right."

"It's out of our hands then," he said.

"Yes."

They were both relieved. But then Gus remembered
something else. "And the priest? What happened? Didn't
you report—?"

"He just thought I was a bit crazy. Neurotic or something. A woman afraid of being alone."

"Well then." Gus inhaled deeply. (No fillings necessary,
the dentist might have said.) "Nice meeting you. Good
luck with that show."

"Show? Oh, you mean my exhibition. Thank you. And
for you too, all the best with . . ."—she was obviously
uncertain about the aspirations of insurance agents—"all
the very best."

Gus hung up. He felt expansive. Benign. With an air of
modest accomplishment he tipped back his chair, put his
feet on the desk, and touched his fingertips together in
an Eiffel effect, an elegant gesture—the kind one saw in
advertisements for expensive watches on successful wrists.
He was savoring the pleasure of arrangements that had
gone well. It seemed to prove something, this happy ending. He had been mapping it out even as the woman had
had the presence of mind to get away from the cottage. It
was just as promised. And who, after all, could begin to
doubt speakers paid such fabulous fees (so he'd heard) to
address an audience of fifteen hundred people in a New
York hotel where even the bellhops wore black suits and
bow ties?

It was a little tip I picked up from my friend Reggie, he
said to an imaginary interviewer. Think it, see it, make it
happen. It works. You should try it.

He leaned back in his chair—at an executive angle, as he
could see from his reflection in the window—and realized
he was a man who, from his own desk phone, made calls
to Montreal and Boston; a man who made such calls as
nonchalantly as if he were telling his wife to bring the kids
down to Lino's for a pizza. He was a man who made, on a
regular Monday morning, *international* phone calls.

More than that, he was someone who chatted to people involved with Culture. Capital C Culture. Oil paintings. The kind of stuff you had to go to auctions at the Holiday Inn to buy. A contact of mine in the art business, he might say casually over a beer to Bob Wilberforce one day, is putting together a little show. Some Oxford and Florence stuff. She's given me some good leads. Perhaps I should, you know, expand my horizons, travel a bit more.

Debonairly, in what an observer would have had to acknowledge was an unpremeditated and exceedingly graceful movement, he swung his feet down from his desk. He brushed lint from polyestered thighs and heard his pocket handkerchief prophesy of lightweight woven wool. *Pure* wool. His suit buttons spoke of new spheres of influence. His star was rising.

He reached for his fourteen-karat Bic pen and made a few notations on a scratch pad for Headquarters. Mission accomplished, he wrote. Miss Moneypenny gave her special 007 rap on his door and stuck her head around it.

"Gus? Mr. Wilberforce wants to know if you're okay?"

"Uh—" he said, hastily covering up classified information. He wished she would not open the door without waiting for his answer. How many times had he . . . ?

"Should I call your wife?" She sounded concerned. "Perhaps she should come and get you?"

"No, no." He rested his head in his hands. "It's nothing. Some sort of dizzy spell. Seems to be gone now. Just give me a few minutes."

He waited for a while after she had closed his door in case there were to be any further oracular hints or warnings or instructions. But his inner voice was silent. After all, La Magdalena was safe now.

With a small shock of recognition, he thought: Of course we did it on purpose. We left her there alone. We wanted this to happen.

Probably, he thought, it would have been simpler if that first time we'd stopped, when Felicity's car ran off the road, before we even got to L'Ascension, closer to the main highway . . . Nevertheless, it had all worked out for the best. For good measure he pictured the underground

128

church network in Montreal as a hearth by which La Magdalena could warm herself.

And he saw Therese too, putting new patches on Tina's jeans, smiling over her needle and thread. The carnations were nodding at her elbow. All was well.

He squared his shoulders and walked resolutely back into the hard, real world where Bob Wilberforce was laying out game plans. Gus, he said, glad to have you back in the dugout. It's a hitter's game. Now we can all see that since New York you've got the ball and you're running with it. You've got momentum. You've got the largest client pool in the agency. Your bases are loaded, man. This is your chance to move up to the majors.

Waves of energy passed through Gus like pleasurable electric shocks.

It was expected that they would all gain yardage. It was expected that each and every one of them would hit a few out of the ball park. It was expected that collectively they would meet the new company objectives, set a new branch record, and win Bob Wilberforce a week in Barbados.

The ball was in their court.

They were asked to bow their heads for a moment's silent contemplation of that fact; they meditated on the great scoreboard in Head Office; they pledged themselves to regard each precious minute as being in the bottom of the ninth.

And then it was time to hustle. They dispersed into the infields and outfields of the city.

Gus touched all his old bases. At Mister Donut he lined up three client interviews in the space of ten minutes, two with customers, one with the girl behind the counter; all certain sales, each of which would add at least five dollars a month in commissions to his income. He was off and running.

It was a good place to do business. He chatted with police constables as they came in on their breaks. (Now there, if ever, was a group who needed insurance!) Factory workers ending shifts contemplated their possible demise over coffee and a custard-filled. High-school students—the clients of tomorrow—stopped to shoot the breeze with

Gus while skipping classes. There was a stream of store clerks from up and down the street. Supermarket checkout girls. Bank tellers. And from the fashion boutiques, the slinkily clad and high-heeled attendants whose legs went all the way up to their thighs.

Jillian from *Jill's Flowers* came sashaying in.

And La Magdalena chose that very moment to manifest herself in a glazed double-chocolate doughnut. How *could* you? she asked. And so soon after leaving me? I meant *nothing* to you.

Gus was so agitated that he knocked his cup of coffee off the counter, scalding his arms and legs. Flustered, he mopped at the mess with paper napkins, keeping his burning face low, crouching and running along beneath the counter's overhang to the door. He escaped to his car before Jillian realized he was there.

He did not know until well after he had turned into the on-ramp for the 401 that he was heading east for Montreal and L'Ascension. And then he realized he had been planning to ever since he woke on Saturday morning.

17

Felicity replaced the receiver. She looked at the business
card of Augustine (Gus) Kelly, For all your insurance
needs, then ripped it neatly into four pieces and dropped
them into her wastepaper basket. End of episode. Canada
vanished and the weekend never was.

She knew better than most people how simple it was
to rearrange the past, that yesterday was an hypothesis
existing purely by the grace of today. Every week she
snipped crowded centuries into manageable clusters of
years, she billeted them in suites of rooms, she labelled
them in catalogues. Florence and Umbria: the battle for
supremacy. This was now an event. It had all the attributes
of an event. It had a chronology, a geography, leading
figures, an accompanying text. It was discussed in the *New
York Times*, that arch-arbiter in ontological matters.

Felicity—and any number of journalists and art
critics—could also toss the present into yesteryear with a
mere flick of the phrase. Neo-Renaissance. Twentieth-
century Florentine. Umbrian revivalist tendencies in post-
abstractionist painting. The dark could be made light, and
the fashionable passé. No style of painting was so lost in
disrepute that it could not be "reassessed," no reputation
so assured that it could not wane. Some painters vanished
overnight, others mushroomed into vogue.

(For the past, as Felicity knows and I know, is a capricious and discontinuous narrative, and the present an
infinite number of fictions. The braiding of the two is the
very stuff of a curator's bag of magic. A historian's too,
for that matter, and history is what I'm writing.)

Felicity was busy conjuring up the Florentine-Umbrian
saga in her Cambridge, Massachusetts, office when two
gentlemen materialized at her door. They looked out of

131

place, overly solid for the gallery's arrangement of empty spaces. They sensed this and rubbed their ankles together awkwardly. A damp cloak of unease hampered them. Almost furtively, they examined their boots, suspecting that they should have removed them and left them at the street entrance.

"Name's Trog, ma'am," said one, flashing an ID card. He cleared his throat apologetically. "FBI. Like to have a few words with you."

They came into her office and shut the door behind them. "This is Mr. Hunter." Mr. Trog jerked his thumb at his colleague. They pulled up chairs and sat facing Felicity across her desk. "We'd just like to chat a bit," Mr. Trog said. "But then I'm afraid we have to take you in for questioning as a possible witness in a murder case."

Felicity was never surprised by the extraordinary, which was altogether too commonplace in her experience, but it did have a way of pitching her into temporary disorientation. A wheel would spin in her head. Which year? which country? which language? she would think in a daze, waiting for the wheel to stop at the right answer.

The wheel stops, she is on a beach, the shadow of palm branches falls across the sand, the fishing boat and her father are getting smaller and smaller, the waves bigger. Nothing can be done about it. The palm trees are thrashing at the sky, her *ayah* is calling for her.

But why? she asks her *ayah*. Now they are at the Trivandrum airport. Why isn't he here to say goodbye?

Because the tide hasn't turned yet, her *ayah* says.

But the wheel is spinning and she is somewhere else again. In her grandparents' garden in Brisbane, there is a gardenia tree six feet tall. A passionfruit vine climbs around her window. She is happy, though fishing boats often arrive in dreams. There is a knock at the door but she will not go with those who have come for her. She does not want to see the box containing her grandmother. She climbs out her window, she runs away, she hides in the gully behind the house. Bellbirds call her and she follows the sweet haunting sound. The bush is full of solace.

But there is a knock at the door. Whatever uniforms

they wear, whatever accents they speak in, the messengers look the same. There is bad news, there is no one to explain in Malayalam, the wheel is spinning, she has arrived in Boston, there are two policemen in her office. She recognizes them, they have come so often, their news is old. She knows where she is now.

"*Entukontu?*" she asks.

But as soon as she sees the word curling toward the two men like a thin twist of smoke, she sees that it is in Malayalam, her *ayah*'s tongue, and is embarrassed. An improper alignment. Swift adjustments are made.

"Why?" she repeated. "I don't understand."

(She did not say: "There must have been some mistake" —because there are always mistakes and it is pointless to be amazed.)

Mr. Trog produced a photograph. "Have you ever seen this woman?"

The photograph was a large black and white, rather grainy. There was a face distorted beyond anyone's recognition by bruises and knife slashes. All that could be told with certainty was that this was the face of a woman with long dark hair. The hair was matted with what appeared to be blood.

Felicity said faintly, "I can't tell."

"How about this?" Mr. Trog produced a second photograph.

When the wheel is not spinning, when Felicity knows which year of her life she is in, a different thing happens in moments of distress. Her body becomes a cage full of small white birds in a panic. The cage is overcrowded, teeming, a myriad tiny wings are beating frantically. Felicity has to empty her mind of everything else, she has to concentrate on calming the birds, she focuses on the leaping pulse behind each fragile white breast until it is still. The wings flutter to rest. Then she can speak.

She looked at the second photograph. When she spoke her voice was almost entirely steady. "I think I recognize that face from a painting."

"What?" Mr. Trog drummed his fingers on the desk. They were thick fingers with knuckles like small tumors,

133

behind one of which was a signet ring that would never come off again without being cut. "We're not talking about paintings," he said irritably, looking about him for somewhere to leave his air of uneasy deference. His finger-drumming had a military sound to it. "We're talking about murder. Have you or have you not ever seen this woman?"

"I'll show you." Felicity's voice was calm as a dreamer's. She took a catalogue from the shelves behind her: *Treasures of the Pitti Palace*. She flipped through the colored plates to the ever-faster accompaniment of Trog's drumming fingers until she found the Perugino. "You see?" she said.

But Trog brushed the book testily aside. "The woman was known professionally as La Salvadora," he said. "Her real name was Dolores Marquez and she was under government protection, she worked for us. Her body was found up in Quebec, Canada, where you went on the weekend. Dumped in the forest. Forty-six stab wounds, some apparently done as ritual marks. She was found not far from a cottage owned by you. Canadian police have run a very thorough check and we're cooperating. At this point, you are a possible witness but not a suspect."

"I see," Felicity whispered.

"You are allowed to make one phone call, and then, I'm afraid, you must come with us."

Aaron, she thought. He knows all the best lawyers. But his secretary would not put her through. I'll give him your message, the secretary said. Tides turn, Felicity thought.

"I can't get through," she told Trog, "but it doesn't matter."

Mr. Trog did not care for irregularities. Cases could be thrown out of court over just such details. Investigators could be demoted.

"You have to reach someone," he said. "Call someone else."

So she dialled Seymour's number in New York. But either he was not in his studio or had disconnected his phone.

"There's no answer," she said.

Trog's fingers were galloping, a rat-a-tat-tat of impatience.

She dialled Jean-Marc's number and spoke briefly to his tape.

"There's no one else I could call," she told Trog.

Trog shook his head to indicate that he had never expected an interrogation in an art gallery to go well. He led the way to a black cruiser and they drove her to an unmarked office building in the heart of Boston.

This was what the interrogators knew: that the body of a Hispanic woman had been found near Felicity's cottage; that the murder had been an act of great brutality and ferocity and appeared, from the number and direction of the stab wounds, to have been committed by more than one person, probably by three; that death had occurred some time on Friday night; that Felicity had spoken to a local priest and had mentioned a woman; that she had been drinking and appeared to be in a state of considerable emotional distress; that there was blood on the bedding and floor of her cottage.

Further, and perhaps related to the above facts: that a truckload of illegal aliens had attempted to cross the border on said Friday afternoon; that a print-out of border computer data indicated that Felicity's car had been following said truck; that the truck had driven from Boston that day, as had Felicity.

This was what the police hypothesized: Given that the number of illegal aliens from Central America had now reached epidemic proportions in New York and Boston and Montreal, that this number was increasing almost daily, and that the level of associated violence was also sharply increasing, a careful compilation of data showed that extremist groups of both the left and the right were active in all said cities. Ritual political murders were becoming common. Wealthy businessmen and their families, who were legal immigrants or residents, were being kidnapped and/or killed by the leftists. Subversives, flowing across the borders in illegal droves, were being eliminated by right-wing vigilante groups monitoring the external fomenting of disruption within Central America.

The Quebec atrocity had all the marks of either a left-wing or a right-wing murder, and (because of the woman's work) either side could think it had cause.

It would appear that various people knew when the truck was to arrive at the border.

It would appear that a contact and a meeting place had been set up.

Would Felicity kindly outline her ties with extremist groups?

I am having another nightmare, Felicity told herself.

"I have no such ties," she said.

Then why had she followed a truckload of illegal aliens from Boston to the Canadian border?

She had never seen the truck until a few miles before the border, she said.

"And what exactly happened at the border?"

"There was total confusion," Felicity said. "It was difficult to know what was happening."

Nevertheless, what was her version of what happened?

Felicity gave a brief account, omitting only to mention the scarcely believable appearance of a fifteenth-century artist's model in a frozen carcass of beef.

This report from Father Bolduc, the police wanted to know; this talk about a woman at her cottage?

"Father Bolduc misunderstood me," Felicity said. "He's told you, no doubt, there was no one at the cottage. I . . . I became afraid, that's all. Afraid of being alone. Because of the other car."

Aha! Trog pricked up his ears. What was this about a car?

There had been an unknown car, she said. But she knew nothing. She had simply been afraid of summer hooligans. No, because of the dark, she could not describe the car.

Would she please comment again on the woman in the photograph? Had she or had she not ever seen the woman?

It is impossible to tell, Felicity said. When I look at the photograph, I think of a painting.

Trog was becoming increasingly impatient. Smoke-screens, he muttered. Whenever detainees threw up

136

smokescreens, he knew they had something to hide. What political organizations did she belong to?

I am not a member of any political organization, Felicity said. I am not political.

And yet, Trog prodded dryly, your family has made donations—substantial donations—to numerous political groups. Your aunts are very wealthy women with financial and political clout.

My aunts, Felicity replied, are even less interested in politics than I am.

How then did she account for their donations to a number of Central American social agencies and church groups, many of which were known to be fronts for political groups?

Their reasons, Felicity said, are purely humanitarian and charitable, not political.

With reference to Central America, Trog said, there is no such thing as nonpolitical.

My aunts and I are nonpolitical, Felicity insisted. They knew more about the fifteenth century, she explained, than they did about the next election.

"Is that so?" Trog leaned close with the air of one who knows that his victim, given enough rope, will hang herself. His eyes were glittering with triumph. "Your apartment was searched this morning," he said. "We found a very interesting collection of newspaper clippings in a file. Very interesting indeed."

He beckoned to Mr. Hunter who hovered like a presiding spirit, possibly benign. This is always rough, his eyes said to Felicity. It has to be done this way, part of the job. Don't be too angry with us. His eyes never left her face as he handed over a folder. She felt his gaze and glanced at him and sensed he was aware of the tornado of panic inside her, that he sympathized.

Trog took a clipping from the folder and handed it to Felicity. She read the byline: Texas (The Associated Press):

A freight train plowed through a group of illegal aliens walking across a railway trestle in the dark, forcing some to jump into a creek 30 feet below and killing four

137

of them. At least seven were injured. As many as 50 aliens may have been on the bridge when the train approached late Saturday night at about 40 mph, said the county sheriff's dispatcher. Authorities arrested 14 aliens who escaped injury, and searched yesterday for more victims in the creek and for other aliens who may have sought cover in the mesquite that dots the rugged coastal plains south of Corpus Christi.

"We've been searching all night," said the agent in charge of the Border Patrol office here.

He said the aliens were walking north across the trestle when they were surprised about 10:10 PM by the Missouri Pacific freight train traveling south. As the train approached, some of the aliens jumped from the bridge, some tried to outrun the train and some tried to avoid the locomotive by standing at the edge of the trestle. "I'm sure it was mass confusion out there," he said. He said that the uninjured aliens who were arrested immediately after the accident were taken to the sheriff's office to be processed and sent to a detention center. He said authorities think most of the aliens were from El Salvador.

"Well?" Trog demanded. "If you're not political, why did you clip this?"

"It's part of a collection," Felicity said. "It belongs with Magritte and Escher and some stories by Borges."

"What are you talking about?" Trog was drumming his fingers again, a peremptory sound like a firing squad.

Felicity sighed. "The absurd has an awful fascination for me." She spoke wearily, not expecting to be understood. "I collect items. I find it . . . I suppose I do it because . . ." Her hands moved, speaking of the inadequacies of language. "It's my immunization program. I mean, the desire to understand is itself absurd, isn't it?"

"Is it now?" Trog's voice was heavy with sarcasm. "And I suppose it's absurd—just a coincidence about which, of course, you know nothing—that some of those people on the bridge in Texas wound up in a truck at the Canadian border."

138

Even her febrile nerves were perfectly still with astonishment. She stared at Trog with awe, with reverence almost: How could he carry on in his line of work? How did he resist being crushed under the weight of the world's irony? She searched his eyes intently. Mr. Hunter watched Felicity as though he could only breathe when she did.

Trog appeared to be bearing up very well in the teeth of staggering assaults on the hegemony of reason. "And this one?" he asked, pulling another clipping from the folder. "What about this one?"

There was a medium-size headline: *In chaos, businessman finds stability.* The byline was San Salvador.

Despite the troubles, this is as good a time as any to make money in El Salvador, businessman Eduardo Esfinge says.

It isn't always easy, however. Four years ago, Esfinge was sitting in his office in a large Salvadoran bank when government troops stormed in, bearing rifles and the curt message that the bank now belonged to the state. His stock holdings in the bank would be converted to government bonds, he was told, like it or not.

Two years later, Esfinge received another rude visit at the showroom of Secretosaal, a retail sewing-machine business that he had started after his banking career was so unceremoniously ended. A troop of young toughs, saying they were Marxist rebels, invaded the store, held a gun at his head and, after examining his account books, requested a "donation" of 20,000 colones—about $5000 at today's rate of exchange.

But Esfinge sees profit where others see bullets and danger. Other sewing-machine sales companies have abandoned their markets in areas of the country where the guerrillas and the Salvadoran army are in daily fights for territorial advantage.

Secretosaal, which Esfinge started in 1979, leaped into the breach. "We know when we load up a truck with sewing machines, we could have problems. The guerrillas could burn it, the army could requisition it, anything could happen, and we'd lose our butts," he said.

139

But Esfinge, who holds a business degree from the University of California at Los Angeles, does not let this worry him too much. Scattered through El Salvador, he says, are a lot of tiny tailor shops, clothesmakers, shoemakers and repair people who need sewing machines, war or not.

"I went out east into the troubled areas and people said, 'From day to day we don't know who'll be in charge—the guerrillas or the army—but we still have to make a living. Life goes on.' "

Last week Esfinge's sales manager ran into one of the hazards of traveling El Salvador's roads. He was stopped by a band of armed rebels who demanded money for their cause. "There was no problem," Esfinge said. "You pay the 10 colones and go on your way. We do the same when the army stops us."

Esfinge's biggest problem is employee absenteeism. People are always getting killed or "disappeared." "Every week, someone joins *los desaparecidos* (the disappeared ones)," he says. "It's a constant problem."

Is it the army or the guerrillas who "disappear" his workers?

"I do not ask," he says.

Though a nuisance, the problem is not insurmountable. There are always people waiting for jobs.

Last week he opened a second distributorship in the beleaguered provincial capital of San Miguel—which was without electricity most of last year. His company slogan, "One stitch at a time," is painted across the bullet-pocked front of his warehouse, a building he was able to buy cheaply after it was abandoned by its previous tenants, who lost it in a shootout that left eight dead. The tenants were apparently Marxist rebels using the building as a hideout; although some neighbors claim that the building was a private arsenal of several army officers and that guerrilla cadres carried out a successful raid on it.

"Either way, it doesn't matter to me," Mr. Esfinge says cheerfully. "The sewing-machine business is booming. Both sides have to wear clothes," he points out, "and I am very optimistic about the future."

140

"So," Trog said. "You're not political."

"Did *you* read this?" Felicity asked him.

"Naturally I read it. And with very great interest in your motives for clipping it."

"But surely you can see? For the same reasons. Language itself has become absurd."

"Oh it has, has it?" Trog pushed his tongue into his cheek in a parody of patience. "And of course you are completely ignorant of the fact that this man's son lives in Boston? That we know perfectly well he smuggles in cheap labor for his parts factory in Medford?"

Felicity leaned toward Trog and asked with an intense curiosity: "Does any of this seem real to you?"

Trog floundered momentarily in her eyes. For the space of several seconds he was taken aback. Sounds full of bronchial irritation quarrelled in his throat. He blew his nose.

"A few years in this business," he said harshly, "and you've seen and heard everything. Nothing surprises me. *Nothing*. I don't even think about what seems real and what doesn't. I've seen a slip of a girl, butter wouldn't melt in her mouth, and she hacked up her boyfriend into little pieces." He was moving toward the door, his body providing a curious subtext of angry twitches and comments. "You think it would surprise me that someone in Highbrow Art is into political murder? That someone who looks like . . . looks like . . ."—but here words failed him. "No, ma'am. *Nothing* surprises me." He seemed to blame her for this—either for being capable of butchery, or for being incapable of surprising him. He glared. A vibration passed through him like ripples surrounding some core of disturbance. At the door he paused: "You're under surveillance, but you can go now. Your car is impounded for forensic testing. You can't leave town without my permission."

Taxi drivers, who must themselves be subject to a thousand natural daily shocks, can rarely be counted on to treat us with great sensitivity in times of stress. At a red light, in heavy traffic, Felicity's driver swivelled and bellowed into the back of his cab: "If you don't tell me where the hell you want to go, you can get out right now. *Right now*, lady!"

Apparently he had already asked her several times for a destination. Apparently she had not answered.

She watched his face with interest as it mutated through a spectrum of reds. A fleck of spittle hung in his mustache like a Christmas decoration and the hairs of his eyebrows were so long and wiry that they climbed toward his hairline in winged and matted ladders. She thought: Seymour would love that face.

"Out!" screamed the taxi driver. "Out!"

She obeyed him meekly, picking her way through traffic like a child of the May through daffodils. Car horns flocked around her like geese rising. But when she paused to look uncertainly through the windshield at a driver, he let his engine stall and got out of his car and offered his arm with a charmingly archaic flourish. She smiled at him and he sucked in his stomach and led her to the curb. When he asked if he could take her somewhere for coffee, however, she looked sadly into his eyes and sighed and regretted that she had an appointment.

Not that she could remember what it was.

But she was disconcerted by the frequency with which these invitations to intimacy mushroomed around her. The earlier she politely extricated herself, the better; complications set in so quickly.

She moved along with the hubbub of pedestrians, noticing every few minutes people she thought she knew. She had constantly to try to match up the two columns in her mind, to find out if she was in the right country, the right segment of her life, for that person. Mostly she would have to conclude: No, no, it couldn't be; that was someone I met in Italy when I was working on the Tintoretto exhibition; or else: that was someone I knew as a child, someone in Australia.

Her feet began to ache. Luckily, a restaurant detached itself from the city backdrop and waited conveniently in front of her. She thought, though she was not certain, that she had seen the restaurant before. Perhaps she had even eaten there on one or more occasions. Obediently, she followed a waitress who was weaving between tables of worn golden oak. The place was full of potted azaleas and weeping figs and the smell of dark roast coffee. She found peaceful harbor in a corner screened by greenery and ordered espresso.

Perhaps she was still on her first cup of coffee, perhaps her second, when someone parted the curtain of benjaminas and asked if he could join her.

"Uh, well," she said, dismayed. "Actually, I'd rather . . ."

But he had already sat down opposite her. This time she was sure it was someone she knew, though a name and context would not reveal themselves. But yes, definitely. From the recent past, she was sure. In a minute she would place him.

"I hope you'll forgive me," he said. "Of course, I was following you. But not for the reasons you think."

She smiled non-committally, waiting for further clues, but he seemed tongue-tied and nervous. He ordered coffee. He adjusted the position of his chair several times. He stacked the table's supply of sugar packets into an unsteady tower. When the tower collapsed, he began again. It was as though he would not be able to speak until his tower reached a certain height—if indeed he had anything to say.

"What fascinates me," he blurted suddenly, "is the different ways people behave under interrogation."

Click. Three things fell into place simultaneously: he was Hunter; she should have been back at the gallery; La Magdalena had been murdered. It was as though a big cat had pounced. She could feel the renewed frenzy of the trapped birds, a wild pulse against the membrane of her body. Within minutes the cage would break open from the pressure. Bruises would flower darkly on her face and arms.

"I don't think we've ever had anyone quite like you," he said. "Such extraordinary *calm*. It makes you seem almost . . . not quite human."

Felicity stared at him in amazement. So he knew nothing about the panic, was deaf to the trapped birds. Realizing this, she found it easier to will them to stillness.

"Of course the whole thing is a ghastly mistake," he said. "A nightmare coincidence. We realize that, or you couldn't stay so unperturbed. Just the same, most people would go to pieces. There's something about you . . . Unless, of course, you *are* guilty. One of those psychotics, no conscience at all. But I don't think so, no, I think probably . . ." and his voice trailed on and on, curling like cigarette smoke around her ears. ". . . what you *really* know about Dolores Marquez. You needn't be afraid, you'll find me very understanding. Whenever you're ready, there's no hurry, except that it is crucial we know exactly where . . ."

Her eyes were stinging. Coffee scalded her throat. She almost gagged. What she was trying to swallow was a bitter indigestible fact: the murder of La Magdalena (La Salvadora. Dolores Marquez). She saw again the stricken eyes, the torn dress: black ciphers. She considered the meaning of randomness: If she had not felt a compulsion to run from Aaron that very weekend? If she had crossed the border half an hour earlier or half an hour later? If she had stopped to think soberly before rash action? If she had taken stock when her car ran off the road? If they had bundled the woman—exhaustion, injury, and all—into the car and taken her to L'Ascension? If she had peered beyond impulse and seen murder, where would she have acted differently?

The fog of talk that rose from Mr. Hunter drifted around her, muddled with caffeine, opaque. Here and there, single beads of words were becoming visible in the mist: "tranquillity", "irresistible", "erotic". Now, accidentally making contact, he was tracing something on her wrist with one finger. These were hieroglyphs she knew. Comfort and protection in many forms were being suggested. She watched his eyes for a specific translation.

"Seizing the moment," he said, "especially two people whose inner vibrations," etcetera, "and so deeply attracted . . ."

Felicity winced. An ongoing puzzle: why men always assumed that attraction was reciprocal. And why so many, on no discernible evidence, convinced themselves that she

144

had mysteriously summoned them, felt themselves impelled to present what she thought of as the Galahad face: devout, confessional, confident of intense consummation, embarrassing.

And yet, at this moment, she was tempted. Partly because once a certain point was reached, it was simpler to get away afterwards than to extricate oneself before.

(In heat, so Felicity tells me, men are afflicted with a loss of decent embarrassment, with intemperance, and with tenacity; they cling closer than limpets. Afterwards, like fat cats, they roll over into temporary oblivion.

Thanks for telling me, I said.

Oh Jean-Marc, she said, I don't mean men like you.

Thanks a lot, I said, not pursuing it.)

So Felicity thought it would be simpler, but there were other temptations as well: the promise of a respite from thought; the possibility of swamping all questions, however fleetingly, in physical sensation. And then there was his size and strength and the potent identification tag in his coat pocket. When he turned to get the attention of the waitress, she saw beneath his jacket the gun in its holster, tumescent against his thigh, a seductive organ. She felt aroused yet drugged, as though she had readily consented to hypnotism. She was surprised by primitive instincts.

I am capable of the commonest kind of lust, she thought with interest. The sordid garden-variety kind. And the realization was obscurely comforting, an indicator of coarse-grained solidity and ordinariness, the mark of someone to whom phantasmagoric things did not happen, of someone not responsible for a murder.

Mr. Hunter believed that something had been decided. Perhaps he had believed this from the moment he sat down at her table. Or from even earlier: when he produced the folder of newspaper clippings and she had looked at him; or perhaps from when he had first walked into her office at the gallery, thousands of hours ago. And perhaps something had indeed been set in motion far back. Certainly their fingers were already intimate. His hand had trailed declarations of passion back and forth, back and forth; and her forearm—its soft blue-veined inner skin—had not resisted. Leaning toward each other to speak—as they now seemed to be doing—they tasted each other in the air between.

"Let's go then," he said.

She breathed in his words, peremptory as the gun against his thigh, and submitted with a sort of drunken willingness. Swagger bored her. But anything that might have interfered—a satiric instinct, a ripple of mockery—was rammed into a back corner of consciousness. For the moment, she wanted to settle for what he was offering: a jigger of physical comfort, a quick draft of mindlessness, cheap protection from one of the dungeon masters who just might have a key to the way out of the morning's labyrinth.

In his car, an unmarked one, she let his thigh press against hers and felt something warm and spicy—like an inflamed syrup of cloves—leak from between her legs. *De profundis*, she thought, *et in extremis*. She had to put a hand over her mouth to hide the smirk. One has to be grateful, she told herself, for the involuntary appetites.

But then, as an alarm clock rips through the tissue of a dream, she took stock of where she was. He had stopped outside her own apartment, and if Felicity had any cardinal rules, this was the first of them: she never slept with a man in her own apartment. Never. How could she be certain he would leave?

"Not here," she said urgently. "We have to go somewhere else."

He was breathing into her ear, an act, she had concluded, that must have been widely advocated in high-school locker rooms as erotic. The hot buzz of his words set her follicles on edge.

"I'm afraid there's a wife and kids at my place," he murmured to her earlobe.

"Somewhere else, then." She tried to explain that his desirability was fast ebbing away, that unless they moved to neutral ground . . . But he believed he knew this script.

"Oh baby," he moaned. "Why do you all have to go

146

through this routine at the last minute? It wastes so much time. Especially when I knew from the moment I saw you that I could make you happy."

Felicity could have laughed. He might as well have thrown a bucket of iced water over her. Did men have any idea how often they used that line? But now the whole tiresome ritual of extrication had to be gone through; and she would have to acknowledge, from sheer habit and some strange inability to do otherwise, every one of the old taboos: no damaging of his esteem; no hint of sexual rejection.

"I'm sorry," she said gently. "We can't go to my apartment for the same reason we can't go to yours. My boyfriend—"

Hunter laughed. "You forget, baby, that I've already been in your apartment today. With a search warrant. Not the slightest evidence of a male about the place. That's why you're so hungry for it. Mmm."

He was breathing fumes on her ears and neck. He was expecting spontaneous combustion. She could smell stale cigarette smoke, cheap machine coffee, and slightly rancid breakfast bacon. Easing herself away, she said, "He's married, so he's careful not to leave evidence."

Hunter laughed again. "Who are you trying to fool, sweetheart?" He pushed his hand between her legs, ripped violently at her pantyhose and panties, jabbed at her, his thumb swimming through syrup, diving like a porpoise, tunnelling, cavorting. "Why is it that the more desperately a woman wants it, the more she pretends she doesn't?" She wrenched away from him, reaching for the door handle. This excited him. He clamped her hands together and held them against his crotch. "Oh, I could tell it when I emptied your bedroom drawers," he said. "I know everything there is to know. I sniffed all the lacy little pretties, especially the ones in the laundry basket, and they all smelled very, very hungry to me."

Felicity felt a chill of revulsion and of real fear.

In spite of long odds, intelligence will often outmaneuver brute force. She lunged for the car horn, watched the impact of one blaring discordant note on passing drivers, and in the few seconds of his disorientation, swung herself out of the car and melted into the general bewilderment. She hailed a cab.

This time she remembered she was going to the gallery.

When she stepped into the sanctuary of its hollowness, she understood why even Trog and Hunter had felt constrained by deference. The world was muffled here, held at arm's length. Such noise as there was came filtered; there was an antique, old-gold quality to it, a patina of hush. Even the footsteps of browsers were muted, more an image, a representation, of sound. Other centuries prevailed, and other modes of seeing; Chagall, for example, insisting that people floated. (Trog, at the end of a kite string, could twist in upper air currents.) In the central courtyard the tranquil faces of icons promised: time and individual disaster are nothing; from our vantage point it is difficult to tell the difference between joy and suffering. This was true. Felicity looked at the faces of saints in ecstasy and martyrs in agony. Yes, it was true, once the distance was great enough.

She was grateful for the earlier centuries. Grateful that the present so quickly became the past and that the past was so pliable to the touch. The Ponte Vecchio, circa 1490, for example. She wandered across it, marvelled that the hawkers of cheese and olives already knew nothing of Dante, dead a mere two hundred years. Never 'eard of 'im, they said. 'Ave some olives, luv. Goldsmiths beckoned her, dangling bracelets like bait. Students in wine-splattered gowns ogled her and joked. Dante? they said. Well of course, but he's so passé. A little embarrassing. Not to be considered typical of Florence. Somewhat blind (they winked knowingly at each other) to the sensual realities of the flesh. All this Beatrice stuff; everyone knows nothing ever happened between them. Perugino, now, and that wench he keeps in his studio, that's a different story.

She meandered through Medici gossip, she listened for Savonarola in every piazza, the bright details of history buffeted her. She tripped on a basket of fish. The Arno stank. She was searching the crowds for Perugino, who had smuggled an Umbrian girl into Florence. The girl had been murdered by the Medicis. She watched for a man obsessed with a woman in black, haunted by the memory of her eyes.

Felicity sat at her desk and phoned Rome and Florence. She talked with others who sailed in the Renaissance, who were anchored safely outside the here and now. They discussed ongoing restoration, government permission and aid and interference, travel arrangements for the largest of paintings, insurance, the political and nationalist connotations of certain canvases. They gave every indication of expert awareness of today. This was their finest act of camouflage.

Somewhere toward the twilight of the Umbrian and Florentine schools, a secretary came slipping down between the tall colonnades that flanked the Uffizi, leaning into the fog of the desk lamp.

Was there some sort of problem? she seemed to be asking.

The Italian government, Felicity said, still has reservations about some of the requests.

No, no, the secretary said. Problems, she meant, with the two gentlemen who came in the morning, who were, according to Old Joe at the front desk, though this was surely ridiculous, from the FBI. Staff members were wondering if something was missing from the permanent collection?

Ah, Felicity said. That. No, no one should worry in the least. There was nothing the matter.

Would Felicity object, in that case, if her secretary left now, since it was well past five?

Felicity smiled ruefully. Of course not. You should know, she remonstrated gently, not to set your clock by me. Leave early tomorrow to compensate.

Felicity stretched luxuriously into the emptiness. She preferred to be alone with her own people, the crowd of framed witnesses. Possibly, some day, the gallery would acquire one of Seymour's portraits. She liked the thought of her lopsided eyes continuing to look down on the flagstoned courtyard after she had gone. She wandered over to the windows of her loggia. Dogwoods flirted with their shadows, students leaned on their bicycles and unwound long, languid arguments as though summer would go on forever. And over there, blurry in the golden haze . . .

Giddiness seized her, she hit an air pocket of the present. He was there, leaning against his car, the gun blatant on his hip, confident, menacing, waiting. Hunter.

What now?

She paced the room, agitated, assessing. She paced the hallways where her people watched, sympathetic, no doubt, but impassive. A Titian head averted its eyes. In some situations, Gauguin admitted, the simple intensities of color may not suffice. Braque offered only a rhomboid solution, impenetrable.

The telephone rang.

She jumped, returned, breathless, to her room, and answered it.

"I just want to reassure you that you're under my personal surveillance at all times." Hunter, like hot treacle, flowed into her ear. "No one else can touch you, you're in my keeping."

Felicity hung up. Her hand was shaking. She dialled her aunts' number. No answer. Their tea-and-symphony night.

She tried Seymour again. No answer.

Aaron. She could not resist the temptation. He always worked late. But his secretary was still there too and said coolly, "I'm afraid he's not available. I gave him your message." (And how could Felicity blame him?)

Stay calm, she told herself. At the very worst, from the law's point of view, I did something impulsive and misguided. (In the corners of her mind, there were whisperings that the nature of her transgression was not catalogued in the broad tables of the law.) Below her window, Hunter waited.

She would feel, not safer perhaps, simply less *exposed*, if someone knew. It would be so soothing to hear Aunt Norwich say: Really, Felicity, such a melodramatic . . . It would be even better to turn to someone who acknowledged the seriousness . . .

Augustine Kelly! She rummaged in her wastepaper basket until she found the four pieces of his business card. She taped them together.

It was now after six—too late to phone his office. She summoned Winston, Ontario, from the electronic ether and his wife answered.

"Could I speak with Mr. Augustine Kelly, please?" she asked, crisply professional. "This is a long-distance call, and it's urgent."

In the three seconds' silence, and then the click, she read the solitude of several people.

She put her head in her hands and closed her eyes and watched until she could no longer tell whether the tossing black dot was a fishing boat or a fluorescent lightfleck on her retina.

Alone.

Of course, after the initial panic, one finds one can always go on. One turns and settles for the *ayah*'s hand, the next step. I'll go on working, she thought, until the aunts get home from the concert. I'll spend the night with them.

Telephone. As though an electric shock had been administered. Wary, she watched its shrill seizure. She raised the receiver an inch, cut off the call with her finger, and dialled Montreal.

"Oh Jean-Marc," she said to the tape. "I'm so frightened."

18

Felicity knows about fear. There are two kinds, she said when I was ten years old. I was bawling my eyes out in the woods. I was running away for good. I had pummelled her till I had no energy left.

"It's all right, Jean-Marc," she kept saying. "It'll be all right."

Maybe a certain kind of devotion sprouts out of desolation, I don't know. They say that baby monkeys, taken away from their mothers and wrapped in terry cloth, fall in love with the piece of cloth. At ten, I suppose, one is desperate to find someone perfect, and it couldn't be my own mother, who was just beginning to move away down the long corridor of new possibilities with a widowed carpenter. Her bitterness toward the Old Volcano slopped over on to me. (Really, how could I blame her? After each visit, my clothes stank of him. Literally. An odor of oils and paint thinner and self-indulgence.)

"There's the fear," Felicity said, "that you're all alone in the world." She was stroking my hair and I let myself grow still and settled my head against her shoulder. Her skin was creamy and smelled of gardenias. Even her hair was fragrant. It made me think of ferns and darkly brilliant flowers. (She has always smelled of the tropics. She still does.) And her voice went murmuring on: "That particular fear's easy to handle. You just say to yourself, 'I *am* all alone and I don't mind. I like it that way.' You see, Jean-Marc, the truth is that *everyone* is alone, and all the people who matter to you are going to leave you sooner or later. You expect it, so it doesn't bother you."

"My father leaves all his girlfriends," I said. Pure reflex. The habit of turning any knife that lay to hand.

"Yes," she sighed. "Of course he does."

I thought about how I was going to stab him one day with the pointed handles of his paintbrushes. His blood would come squirting out like color from a new tube of paint and I would dip a brush in it and make great smears of red across his paintings. I also thought about the time I was going to find him bleeding on his studio floor because someone else had stabbed him first (some enraged and abandoned woman), and how grateful he was going to be that I had arrived in the nick of time, and how sorry that he had never realized, and so on.

"The other kind of fear," Felicity said, "is much worse, and I never quite learned what to do about it, though Hester said there was a trick."

"Why?" I asked. "What is it? Who's Hester?" I forgot I hated her. I forgot I was never going to speak to her. "Tell me about the other kind."

"I don't like to remember it," she said. "Anyway, I don't think you'll ever have to worry about it."

Tell me, tell me, I begged.

And so she did.

Once upon a time, she said, there was a Moreton Bay fig tree so big that if you sat under it, with your back against the trunk, you couldn't see the sky at all. It grew in one corner of a schoolyard in Brisbane, Australia, and the teachers said it was at least two hundred years old. No doubt it's still there, but I've never been back to see.

The tree spread itself like a great umbrella whose points almost touched the ground. Under this canopy the light was murky and green, no grass could grow, and roots lay in waiting in the dirt: long, bony fingers that might reach out and grab a passing child. Perhaps for this reason children avoided the cave beneath the branches. But also, and mainly, on account of the trenches.

There are ghosts in the trenches, a boy told Felicity. (She was ten years old, and new to the school, and many things seemed strange to her.) The boy pulled his mouth into a skeleton's slit with his index fingers, made his eyes go big and whitely blind, and let a long, ghastly, ululating cry slide out of his throat. That's the sound they make, he said. When it rains, you can hear them.

The trenches began in the corner of the schoolyard and ran along inside the fences like two arms of a compass set at ninety degrees. Each arm was about fifty feet long. Beyond the damp and shadowy circle of the tree, these old indentations were choked with soft grasses and wild flowers. They looked harmless and inviting: places to roll in, to hide in, to jump across.

But under the tree, where nothing grew, there was something frightening about the two scarred and naked wings of the ditch. They made one think of open graves. Or of the empty eye sockets of the giant creature whose root-fingers scrabbled at the ground. In the rainy season a porridge of red clay leaked into the eye sockets and made horrible sucking sounds.

At home, Felicity asked her grandparents: "What are the trenches for?"

"Good heavens!" said her grandfather. "Haven't they filled those in yet?" He shook his head mournfully. "There'll be an accident some day. A broken leg, or worse. What are they waiting for? The next war?"

"What are they for?" Felicity persisted.

"For in the war," her grandmother said. "When the air-raid bell rang."

"You see, we thought we might be bombed," her grandfather said. "After the Japanese bombed Darwin, all the schools in Queensland had to dig trenches for air-raid shelters. There used to be sandbags along both sides. Your mother was teaching at your school then. Look, I'll show you."

There was a drawer in an old dresser that was crammed with photographs. When anyone opened it, the pictures would spill onto the floor like fish out of a burst aquarium. A waterfall of the past. All the pictures were a sort of creamy brown color, not even proper black and white. It took her grandfather a long time to find the one he wanted.

"There!" he said at last.

154

Felicity saw the Moreton Bay fig and long lines of children wearing old-fashioned clothes and a young woman with cropped curly hair. The woman's back was to the camera and her soft, lacy dress was caught in below the waist and fell to halfway down her calves. She was holding the hand of a child and pointing to the line of sandbags.

"That's your mother," Felicity's grandfather said. "During an air-raid drill. The school bell used to ring and everyone had to stop whatever they were doing and go immediately to the trenches."

Felicity looked intently at the back of the mother whom she had never met. But the people in the photograph seemed to be on the other side of a thin white cloud, as though sunlight had been spilled on the picture and had stained it with too much brightness. The harder Felicity looked, the hazier her mother became. If only she could make her turn around.

"Are there ghosts in the trenches?" she asked.

"Of course not," her grandmother said.

But a teacher said yes, there was a ghost. One air-raid drill had lasted for hours. It was during the rainy season and the children and teachers had huddled together, cramped and wet and shivering, listening for Japanese planes. When the bell sounded the all clear and the roll was called, a Grade Two boy was missing. They found him in the corner of the trench, under the tree, hunched up into a little bundle, his arms locked around his knees. He must have fallen asleep and slumped, face down, into the red mud. The coroner said death by drowning.

"When it rains, you can hear him crying," the teacher said. "So stay away from the trenches under the tree. They're dangerous."

An unnecessary caution. The circle of shadow around the Moreton Bay fig was taboo. Except for Felicity. And except for Hester. But then, they hardly counted. They were both peculiar. Like the boy who had drowned in the mud, they would pass into folklore.

Felicity was peculiar because she was wild. She could catch cricket balls like a boy, without flinching, and could climb the straight columns of the palm trees. Monkey girl, monkey girl, the children chanted, and threw pebbles at her. She would find her desk and her pencil case filled with nuts and leaves. Strangest of all, if you got her really mad, she would burst into some other language that no one knew. Jabbering. Just like a monkey. Every week she tore a dress. The teachers shook their heads, but were never angry. She's Evelyn's child, they would whisper. Poor little Evelyn who fell in love with a Yankee soldier. Poor little Evelyn who died in India.

No question, Felicity was the teachers' pet because of poor Evelyn. And because of the way she could read. In the fifth grade she could read better than most Grade Eights. The headmaster, Mr. Barlow, used to send for her and make her stand in front of the Grade Eight class. Grade Eighters were giants whose limbs hung over shrunken desks. Their arms were like vines run amok. They were a jungle crop of glowering eyes.

Mr. Barlow would take the Grade Eight Reader and open it just anywhere and hand it to Felicity. She would be expected to sight-read aloud. She hated doing this. Each time she prayed for a page that would be too difficult, but Mr. Barlow never found one. He would beam and pat her on the head and send her back to her own classroom. There, Miss Richards would smile and tweak her curls, oblivious to the fog of scowls rising from arithmetic books. Oh, Felicity was certainly peculiar.

Hester was also peculiar, but for quite different reasons. She was older, maybe as old as thirteen, but had been "kept back" in the fifth grade. She was slow. Her left leg was one of the seven wonders of the school, being only about one-quarter of the thickness of her right leg. The skin on it seemed to be stretched tight, and was very shiny, as though Hester worked on it with wax and a polishing mitt. She walked as a person walks who has one foot on a low fence and the other on the ground. On her left foot she wore a boot instead of a shoe, and the boot had a stirrup attached, from which iron rods ascended and disappeared up under her dress. It was rumored that she wore an iron cage under her panties. It was also rumored that she wore the cage *over* her panties, and that each night her mother had to unlock it and drain off the day's pee and shit.

Felicity knew this was not true because of what had happened in the girls' lavs. (Though one had to say, "Please may I go to the lavatory?" to teachers, among themselves the children always spoke of "the lavs.") The doors in the lavs could not be fastened. They swung to and fro with a metal shriek. If you were sitting on the toilet, you had to hold one leg straight out in front of you so that no one could push the door open and stare. Though of course this happened all the time. Everyone did it. You pretended you didn't know there was someone already inside, and then you sang:

> Higgledy-piggledy rub-a-dub dum,
> I can see your big fat bum!

The best thing, when you had to go, was to take a friend who stood guard at the door while you went; then you stood guard while your friend went. But Felicity, being new and strange, had no friend to guard the door. And neither did Hester.

At first, on the day Felicity learned that Hester did not have to pee into an iron cage, she thought there must have been a terrible accident in the lavs. So much commotion! But then she heard someone say: It's only Hester Ironpants. And indeed, several girls were helping Hester to show off the full length of her metal underwear. Her arms and legs were being held as though she were a letter X, and the skirt of her dress was pulled up over her head like a bag. She did not look human at all.

Felicity watched with the same awful fascination as everyone else. Just above where the leg cage passed through a metal garter, the left hip and buttock were unnaturally shrunken. Felicity thought of a balloon that has gone down, even though its neck is still tied—how it becomes a spongy wrinkled smallness. Disgusting, somehow. And contemptible. Around this shrivelled-up bum there was a system of metal bars and leather straps tying the whole contraption to the waist, and the skin

157

that showed between was horribly pallid—the way skin goes under a Band-Aid that has been worn for several days.

Everyone felt slightly sick, and then, for some reason, angry. Perhaps that was why someone began kicking. The X, with its bagged head, did not seem to notice. It did not flinch. It did not struggle.

"People who've had polio," one girl observed sagely, "can't feel *anything*. My dad told me."

Now there was real curiosity. And further experimentation. Thud, thud, thud. A redness, and then a spreading bluish darkness, became visible on the matchstick leg. It was hard to reach it between the iron bars. The girls had to aim carefully. They became more and more accurate, but there was never a reaction. No cry. It was true, then. The X couldn't feel a thing!

Time to try something new.

Between the inverted V of leather straps that framed the crotch, hairs grew. A wispy tuft, bedraggled, but the real focus of fascination for many of the girls whose hair "down there" had not yet started. Someone produced a stick. At first, to universal gasps and giggles, the hairs were "combed." Then the skin behind them was softly poked. Then, in a bold hand, the stick made a swooping dive and rose into the crack between the legs. And now at last the X reacted with a violent spasm and a muffled cry from inside the skirt that covered its face.

A spell was broken.

Some children ran away, others cheered. Flushed triumph for the stick-wielder, who jabbed again and again.

But Felicity went berserk.

Monkey girl! they shrieked as she lashed out with her fists. Wildcat! Reffo! Nevertheless, they fled from her as she jabbered in her monkey talk; and when they had all gone, Felicity led Hester to the one place where they would be left alone—to the circle of shadows and ghosts beneath the kind branches of the Moreton Bay fig. They sat in the dirt with their backs against the trunk. Felicity sat with her legs crossed, and so did Hester, after a fashion, except that the leg in the cage stuck awkwardly out in front of her.

"Can't you feel *anything* on your leg?" Felicity asked with awe. "You really can't?"

Hester's face had a blank look. She might have been asleep with her eyes open. Her breath came noisily and quickly in and out, in and out, with the sound of a man sawing wood. But apart from this she seemed very calm, as though nothing had happened.

"It used to hurt," she said at last. "But I learned a trick."

"What trick?"

"As soon as they start, I pretend my leg is made of wood."

"But . . ." Felicity paused delicately. "You felt the stick part?"

Hester didn't answer. She reached in under her skirt and touched herself. When she pulled out her hand, there was blood on it. They both stared at it with a thrill of horror. A fearful and magic sign.

"I'm going to tell," Felicity said. "I know who did that, with the stick. I'm telling."

"No!" Hester grabbed her arm and dug her fingernails in. "Promise me you won't tell. They just do it worse the next time if you tell."

"If anyone does it again . . ." Felicity vowed, her fists doubled up.

"I just have to practice, that's all," Hester said. "I have to practice pretending that part is made of wood too."

Weeks passed.

Felicity and Hester always went to the lavs together. Felicity stood at the swing door with her fists in full view. No one bothered them. They spent their lunch hours under the Moreton Bay fig. They made up stories about the trenches. They talked to the boy who had drowned in the mud. Sometimes he brought the woman in the lacy, old-fashioned dress. She would be holding his hand but she would never turn round. Please, they would beg. But she never would.

Sometime in November, when the jacarandas were in bloom and the grass was turning brown from the heat and

159

the days were drowsy with the sweet smell of frangipani, an inspector from the Department of Education came to the school, and Miss Richards received a message to send Felicity to the Grade Eight classroom again.

"You can give her anything at all," Mr. Barlow told the inspector. "Anything at all."

The inspector picked up a Reader from one of the front desks and flipped through it. He made a decision and ran the pad of his thumb down the center crease. Those two pages, Felicity could see, would not dare move again until he gave permission.

"So you're Evelyn's child," he said. "Do you remember your mother?"

"No, sir."

"Well, young lady, let's see if you can hold a candle to her. Let's see what you make of the chariot race."

It was about a man called Ben Hur, and his lifelong enemy Messala. Just as she was getting to the thrilling part, just as she was dying to find out who would win the race, the inspector said, "Stop!"

Like a Roman consul, he took the Reader from her and put it back on the desk it had come from.

"All right, Johnson," he said. "Carry on from there, will you?"

Johnson was much too big for his desk. He was nearly sixteen, another "slow" student who had been "kept back," and his voice, when it came out, seemed much too big for its body. Perhaps on that account it had trouble finding its way. It stumbled. It doubled back on itself. It got lost between lines.

"Enough!" groaned the inspector. He covered his ears with his hands. The class giggled nervously.

"Next boy!" he said. "Continue!"

But this was not much better. The whole front row, all boys who had been "kept back," one after another, tripped and fumbled through the next few paragraphs at a snail's pace. As each boy was released from his forced labor, he glared at Felicity over the edge of his book.

I don't want to do this, her eyes pleaded back. Mr. Barlow makes me. She did not in the least blame them for

160

hating her. Her hands were coiled into fists at her side and her fingernails cut into her own palms. She wondered what would happen if she were suddenly to hammer the inspector.

"Stop!" he cried for the sixth time.

He handed the Reader back to Felicity.

"Now, young lady. Show these gentlemen how it should be done."

"Please, sir," she said. "I don't want to."

The inspector raised an eyebrow in astonishment. "Well," he said dryly. "I'm afraid that's beside the point. Little girls have to do as they are told. You can start at the top of the page."

Felicity stood there trembling. She was afraid not to begin, but she could not, simply could not, read on.

Mr. Barlow, the headmaster, stepped in. (Everyone knew Felicity was Mr. Barlow's pet.)

"You see what you've done?" he accused the front row. "There, there," he said to Felicity. He put his hand on her shoulder. "Run along back to your room now."

Felicity's feet felt heavier than a box full of Grade Eight Readers. The floor might have been covered with red clay mud, it was so difficult to lift one foot after the other.

"I'm going to build a boat," she told Hester that afternoon. They always stayed late after school, peaceful beneath their tree. It was not really safe for Hester to walk home until most of the children had gone. "I'm going to sail back to India. My *ayah* misses me. And when I tell my father what they do at this school, he won't make me leave again."

"But your father's dead," Hester objected.

"No, he's not. Not really. That's just what everyone thinks. But he stays out in the boats with the fisher people. Anyway, my *ayah* is there. And you can come with me if you like."

They drew boat-building plans in the dirt with a stick. There were problems to be worked out: how to make the boat watertight, where to store enough food. Perhaps they stayed later than usual. It was so quiet; quiet in the heavy, still way that promises an evening thunderstorm.

161

But it was not a downpour that trapped them.

Hester saw the boys first, and Felicity saw Hester's eyes go blank and her body stiffen like wood. She turned. The whole front row from Grade Eight was there, standing at the edge of the shadow like black crows watching for the soft parts. She could have run, of course, or climbed the tree. She was as fast as any of them. But she couldn't leave Hester.

It was like a dream, everything in slow motion. But when Johnson clamped a hand over her mouth, she woke up and kicked and struggled and fought. This delighted the boys. There were four of them holding her, laughing. One of them pulled off her underwear, but then they held her like a trussed chicken.

"First," Johnson told her, "you gotta watch what we do to Little Miss Ironpants. Just so you know what's coming."

" 'Cause you gonna get something even bigger and better, Little Miss Smartypants," someone else promised.

If they had not clamped a hand over her mouth, Felicity would have been much too proud to scream. Now it was a challenge. Not for a minute did she stop kicking and biting—until someone twisted her arms up behind her back. It did not seem wise to provoke further pain at this point, and she pretended to give up.

Hester lay very still. She did not make a sound. In fact, once they had ripped off her panties and pulled up her dress, they didn't even need to hold her. Then Johnson took off his pants and Felicity saw with shocked fascination that his thing was about six times as big as it should have been. All the boys, except the two now holding Felicity, took off their pants. They all had things as big as five-shilling firecrackers, sticking straight up and out like skyrockets waiting to be lit. She couldn't understand it. She had seen boys peeing behind bushes with their little pink dicks. Nothing like this. Perhaps it came from being kept back.

She bit the hand clamped over her mouth and kicked again like a mad thing. This brought a stunning blow to her head, and then, after she had fallen, a fist like a

162

sledgehammer punched her in the soft place between her legs. She could feel the pain everywhere, even in the tips of her fingers and at the ends of her hair. She began to be afraid, and the fear gobbled up her anger and her energy and something else she couldn't define. She wanted to die very quickly.

"Make her watch!" Johnson yelled. "Barlow's bloody little pet. Make her watch!"

One of her captors sat on her legs, and the other, who had his hand over her mouth, forced her head sideways to make her see. But she defied them, she closed her eyes, she couldn't watch.

The boys were breathing hard, like race horses, and making snorting and whinnying sounds. Then there was a cheer. "Attaboy, Johnson! Kaboom." Laughter. More scuffling. Grunts.

I am made of wood, Felicity said to herself. (She could hear her own voice like a scream inside her head.) I am made of wood, I am made of wood. But it didn't work. Nothing dimmed the siren of pain that jangled on and on and on: the weight on her legs, the hand on her mouth, the throbbing bruise at her head and groin. But all this was nothing compared to the fear. The fear was like a great shark-toothed mouth that was chewing her up, mincing her, turning her into liquid.

"Oh Christ!" yelped the boy who sat on her legs. "What the hell . . . ? You filthy little slut!"

For a moment her mouth was free, and she screamed full force.

"Christ!" someone said. Something soft—her own underwear—was rammed between her teeth. She gagged and vomited and swallowed her vomit and gagged again. General disturbance. "Christ," she heard Johnson say. "You dumb bugger, Adams, you've made Ironpants bloody as hell."

"Push them into the trenches," someone said. "It'll look like they fell, and they'll get hell for being there."

She remembered the fall and the impact of Hester's body against hers. Then nothing.

When she opened her eyes and sat up, bells banged in

163

her ears. There was a frightful smell. She became aware of several things at once: that Hester was staring at her with blank eyes, that they were in the bottom of the trench, that her own legs were wet and sticky, and then—with a sharp spasm of disgust—that she was streaked with her own shit.

Hester reached over and took her hand. She was smiling. "It worked!" she said. "I can make that part wooden too. I didn't feel a thing."

Felicity opened her mouth to say, "I'll kill them," but sobbing sounds came out instead. She couldn't stop them. They went on and on.

"You just have to practice," Hester comforted. "Soon you'll be as good as me. I didn't feel anything. Truly."

A tiger had Felicity in its paws and wouldn't let her go. It shook her and rattled her as though she were nothing but a handful of birdbones. It made her dribble a vile-tasting greenish fluid. "The teachers," she blubbered. "The teachers . . ."

But Hester said: "You must never tell anyone. Never. If you tell, they just do it worse the next time."

On the day Felicity found me in the woods, the day I was running away for good, I wanted to know if they ever told.

"No." she said. "We never did. You're the first person to know about it, Jean-Marc."

Fifteen years later, on the day Felicity called from Boston and told my answering machine that a man named Hunter was trailing her, I thought of Hester, and so—I am sure—did she. I play that tape over and over, listening to the break in her voice. *Oh Jean-Marc, I'm so frightened.* I rewind, I replay, I strain to catch the message beneath the words.

I make discoveries as I write; I wonder why I did not think of this when I began: that meeting (or vision or misapprehension or whatever it was) at the border, that moment when Felicity first saw La Magdalena, she must have thought of Hester. She was defending Hester again. When her car ran off the road, it wasn't the cow and the crows she was thinking of, it was Hester.

164

Though how do I know what she thought?

Her stories bombard me, they seem to have become my own memories, they writhe and change and regroup in the way true memories do. They are like the photographs in her grandfather's dresser, a deluge of the ever-present past.

About one thing, though, she was wrong.

The fear of physical harm is not worse than the fear of being alone. I cannot believe it is. I cannot believe anything is worse than this. At four o'clock, when Kathleen had not arrived, I called her aunt's place.

"I'm not allowed to visit you today," Kathleen said. "I'm sorry, Jean-Marc."

So I stayed home alone and played some Chopin. Felicity used to sit in the room and read while I practiced Chopin. I was playing a mazurka to cheer myself up but all of a sudden—I don't know what it was—the notes made a gap in the air. A void. And a thought jumped out at me: What if I never see her again?

Vertigo.

But of course she always breezes back.

When she calls from a kink in the equator or wherever, I'll be very nonchalant. I've had the weirdest dream about you, I'll say.

Oh dreams! she'll laugh.

And I'll laugh too, and this attack of angst will vanish. I know what brought it on. It's playing that tape, the break in her voice, the catch of panic, it's putting it down on paper. But probably, when I think about it soberly, Hester couldn't have been further from her thoughts. For all I know, Hester was a story she made up to distract me when I was ten years old. Perhaps I should delete it. After all, this whole enterprise is for Felicity's entertainment when she reappears.

And also for Kathleen.

I'm really doing this for Kathleen, who needs to believe that her father will show up. And perhaps he will, who knows? I've been running along in a black mood, but it's impossible to be morbid about Gus, whom I've left heading east on the 401.

19

From the turnoff outside Montreal, the road dropped
gradually toward L'Ascension. Gus was surprised. He did
not remember so many twists and turns. At times he
seemed to be driving in large, looping circles. Had he not
passed that same farmhouse five miles ago? But of course
they all looked much the same.

When he got to L'Ascension, he would have to call
Therese. Obviously he could not get back to Winston
by nightfall. But what would he say? I realized, once I
had crossed the Quebec border, what I was doing but by
then . . . I don't know what got into me, I found myself
outside Montreal so I thought I might as well . . .

He could hardly say: This is a matter of life and death;
and yet he believed it might be.

What exactly did he think he *was* doing? How could he
make sense of it, even to himself? Either La Magdalena
would have been absorbed by some refugee network in
Montreal, or she would still be in hiding near the cottage.
If she were still in hiding—exhausted and desperate—was
it likely that she would reveal herself to a man who had
consented to turning her in?

All he knew was that he was under some sort of compulsion. That he could not do otherwise. That he felt summoned.

He found that when he tried to picture La Magdalena,
he could not evoke her face with any clarity of detail. He
could see a luminous circle (like the haloed face of an icon)
and the brilliant black eyes. A moon with craters. The
more he tried to focus on the pale glow, the less clear the
outlines became. Everything was swallowed up in a kind
of aura, as though he had looked into the sun.

What am I doing? he asked himself in a sudden panic.
Where am I going?

166

He seemed to be in the middle of a dark wood. He must have strayed from the highway onto a side road that was becoming narrower by the minute, a country lane. Pines swarmed on either side, their branches almost touching overhead in a dark ceiling. When had the pavement ended? He was aware of deep, bone-jolting ruts and of occasional welts of granite outcrop that strafed the underside of the Chevy. Sometimes a not-quite-levelled tree stump jabbed ominously at the muffler.

Had he somehow got on to a hiking trail? He wondered how far back he had taken a wrong turn, and where he would find enough space to turn around. The track dwindled into nothing, snaking away under a quilt of pine needles. Gus reversed, watching for a gap between trees. In the leeside of a massive white pine, he thought, there might just be room to maneuver if he pulled sharply left . . . And then the back wheels locked themselves into a ditch.

He felt curiously resigned about this. More than resigned. He had a strong sense that the impasse was entirely fitting, that what he really wanted to do was walk into that trackless twilight under the pines. He did not bother to lock the car or even to wind up the windows.

Under the trees the light was thin and aqueous. He could smell decay—a fragrant, resiny sharpness, a sweet rottenness. Addictive, perhaps. All his senses seemed to stretch themselves out. He walked on into shadow.

If the sun had been visible through the green above him, he would have been less surprised by the heat. Perhaps the pine needles—so seductively yielding to the feet—trapped the warmth and held it, a natural hothouse for seedlings. He removed his coat, hesitated a moment, then folded it loosely and left it at the foot of a tree. A little further on, he discarded his tie. He unbuttoned his shirt and rolled up the sleeves.

Now there was nothing to distract him from his voices. He heard Kathleen's: *Why is mummy crying?* And Therese's: *A woman called long distance.* And La Magdalena's. Hers, dinning inside his skull, was without sound, infinitely sad. A siren's call. A wounded siren's call. But all of his voices, all of his women, were wounded.

167

He walked faster and faster. Always the deeper shadow lured him on, a camouflage for shame. If he could enter the heart of the darkness, where he belonged, he might be able to stand the sight of himself. Perhaps he could discard his life like a stale skin or an extra layer of clothing. Begin again.

But how? When his flesh leaned willy-nilly toward comfort even while he despised himself? When he had a mortgage to pay and First Communion dresses to buy and every time he turned around, so many pairs of sad eyes watching him. When in fact very soon he would have to button his shirt, pick up his tie and coat, reassemble himself, walk back along the track to a road, hitch a ride, find a gas station, rent a tow truck, etcetera, etcetera, etcetera.

And to pay for the gas for this unbudgeted joy ride, to pay for the tow truck, he would have to sell another quick handful of Mister-Donut-sized insurance policies. And if he could just want the Corvette for Therese a little more urgently, he could graduate to a bigger and more elegant treadmill.

So palpable was the sense of pointlessness that it took on form before his eyes: it had the body of a toad and the face of a ghoul. In a kind of horror, he clasped a tree and beat his forehead rhythmically against the trunk. Anything to expunge the view of himself as loathsome and of his life as a bad joke. He wished that a merciful bolt of lightning would strike him. Then at least Therese would collect the insurance, then at least the family would be decently provided for.

Tapping his head did nothing to ease the torment. He had to run from it. He began to jog. His shirt billowed out behind him. He tacked into his despair. The pine woods were endless and there was very little light to give direction. Probably he ran in circles. He ran and ran, hoping for something definitive like a heart attack.

When at last he had to stop because the pain in his lungs was intolerable, he threw himself on the ground and closed his eyes and waited till the dizzying light show inside his head subsided. Perhaps he actually slept for a few minutes, or else simply passed through a brief hiatus in consciousness because of a shortage of oxygen.

168

At any rate, when he looked around him he was surprised to see that the edge of the pine forest was at least two hundred yards away and that he was halfway up a hillside. Below him and to the east lay a village, and he recognized the church spire. L'Ascension. He had not after all gone so far astray. He concluded that he must be only a couple of miles from Felicity's cottage and that he might as well walk there before seeing about a tow truck. Probably he would be able to see the cottage from the top of the hill.

Afternoon sun was beating down on his back, fiery. He was ascending through a wall of heat, shading his eyes, trying to see the house and barn and sloping fences that seemed to sit like an elaborate finial on the top of the slope. Shapes danced like phantoms in the blinding light. Nothing was clear.

And then suddenly it was.

Just under the brow of the hill a clump of trees gave him respite from the glare and he could see the barn and a small apple orchard and a large iron-wheeled farm wagon under the trees. Someone was standing in the wagon picking apples. A woman in black.

He began to run again, but as soon as he moved beyond the trees the sun hit him like a blow and the woman was swallowed up in a dazzle of light. When he reached the orchard, the wagon was empty.

But it was La Magdalena, he was sure of it.

He followed the track that led from the apple trees toward the farmhouse. No signs of life. The house was shuttered and still, but certainly not deserted. There were well-tended flower beds, a stack of chopped firewood ready for the winter, a cat on the porch. He peered through the front windows but could see nothing beyond his own reflection. He shaded his eyes and looked down the hill toward the southeast. He thought he could see Felicity's cottage.

That's where La Magdalena went, he decided.

He had to take the track back through the orchard. Under foot, fallen apples were turning soft and brown and the air was sharp with their sweet fermentation. It was like walking through a cider press. He became aware

169

that he was very thirsty. Perhaps he should veer toward L'Ascension first, buy a drink, make some phone calls, hire a tow truck.

Then he saw her again and stopped dead, afraid the image would disappear.

She was standing under a tree, transfigured by light, her head tilted back, watching the sky through the leaves. She had her back to him, though he could tell that she held her black skirt gathered up into a pannier in front of her. He imagined it to be full of apples.

He did not move.

There was a ring of light around her head. While he watched, she moved a little and apples fell from her skirt and rolled into the grass. She stretched her arms up into the patch of sun that fell between the leaves and began to stroke herself with her hands, as though she were bathing in the light.

Gus was trembling. He clutched his heart because it was booming like breakers on a reef. Equipped with no tools for articulating to himself a sense of the ineffable, he was simply obscurely aware that nothing would ever be quite the same again.

A squirrel moved.

The woman started and turned, but the light falling on her through the leaves was so strong that his eyes began to water and he could not see her. Nevertheless, he knew that she was looking at him, and that her look was dense with meanings that could not be read in such a glare.

He took a step toward her and stretched out his arms—perhaps in reassurance, perhaps in desire—but he might as well have fired a gun. She was off and running downhill through the trees, her hair streaming like a black pennant.

He knew it was pointless to follow.

He went and stood in her patch of sun and picked up one of the apples that had fallen from her skirt. When he bit into it, he felt as though he had partaken of grace. Exhilarated, he hiked down the hill into L'Ascension and arranged for the tow truck.

170

20

Do you think I'm not aware of what is happening?

Do you think I don't know I'm really writing about Felicity at ten years of age, lost in the dark world, trying to make the woman in the photograph turn round?

Do you think I don't know I'm also writing about myself? That I'm not aware that the woman under the apple tree is really Felicity?

Of course I know.

This is a very common phenomenon. Give a medical article about a new disease to any ten people and they'll all become alarmed. They'll all recognize symptoms and warning signs in themselves.

We impose our own lives on the world: the self as template.

I recognize, therefore I grant meaning.

But I am also writing about Gus, who panicked (along with the rest of us) that his life made no sense, that it lacked a core. He was after the burning bush, the sublimely beautiful, the all-compassionate, unconditional lover. (You think I don't know that my Felicity, my version of her, is suspect? That her photograph is blurred with light? That she has, as it were, her back to you? Look to the beam in your own eye! I read Dante, you read Dante, we're all of us looking for Beatrice, all in the dark wood together.)

And remember: I know Gus. I listened to him for long, drunken, maudlin confessional hours. (I'm getting to the part where we met.)

I know what Gus dreamed of.

I know what he saw, or thought he saw, in the orchard.

171

And I know that other side, the one he was scarcely aware of, the net of illusions that he himself cast. Remember: I am intimate (*emotionally*, let me stress) with his teenage daughter. And she sees him ringed with light.

21

"Really, Felicity," Aunt Norwich said. "A man from the FBI? Honestly, my dear. In *our* street?"

Aunt Ernestine smiled indulgently as she poured the coffee. "Another peach, Felicity?"

A languid and graceful ritual, breakfast with the aunts: omelettes and toast, fine china, fresh fruit. And how could Felicity speak of murder in front of this perfect peach, so demure on its fluted Royal Albert plate? How could she discuss surveillance while slicing it with a pearl-handled fruit knife and fork, the finest of old sterling? She speared a slice and held it in front of her. She rubbed the rose-gold pelt against her lips. She licked at the juice with the tip of her tongue, dreaming of mangoes and of Brisbane and of how the sun used to touch her skin when she fished for tadpoles while her grandparents dozed on deck chairs under the flame trees.

Aunt Ernestine made a small clicking noise of disapproval. Felicity closed her lips around the tines of the fork and savored the flesh of the peach in private.

She rehearsed telling them again: "That woman I told you about, the one at the border. She's been murdered." Perhaps reiteration would convince both her aunts and herself.

The telephone rang, and Felicity had such a visceral vision of murdered and pulpy flesh that she had to dispose of the chewed peach slice into a linen napkin. The aunts stared at the telephone as at an unmannerly intruder. They did not accept callers until after lunch. They waited for its tantrum to finish.

With each shrill syllable, Felicity's nerves became more jangled. The ringing went on and on. The aunts sipped their coffee with peaceful indifference. Peaches fell into

173

perfect segments at the touch of their pearl-handled knives. Felicity twisted her linen napkin into knots. The ringing went on. It was unendurable.

Felicity pushed back her chair and fled to the hallway.

"Really, Felicity," Aunt Norwich said in mild surprise. "It only encourages people. If they don't know any better than to . . ." But Felicity was out of hearing.

"Yes?" she said, breathless but curt, expecting the worst.

"You are the art curator who drives the blue Datsun." It was not a question.

"Yes."

"You do not know me." The voice, a female one, enunciated English carefully, as a second language. "I speak on behalf of a group. We wish to thank you."

"Thank me?"

"For the rescue."

"For the . . . ? Do you mean . . . ?"

"Yes. La Desconocida."

"La Des . . . ?"

"The unknown one. It is better not to mention her name. But we have received word and we thank you. It was bravely done."

"But hasn't she been . . . ? I was shown a picture . . . she's been murdered."

There was a pause, and then a regretful: "Already the nets are out."

"Pardon?"

"They want other information from you," the voice replied. "It was someone else who was killed, not she. We have spoken with her this morning."

"This morning!" It was like waking from a nightmare. "Oh thank God!" Felicity said. "Is she still in my cottage?"

"She is with friends."

"Ah," Felicity said. "I knew it. The other car."

"The other car?"

"It doesn't matter." For Felicity there were more pressing riddles. "So it's true she's under protection? She's a government agent?"

174

There was a short laugh. "Is that what they told you?"
Felicity was nervous. "She works for . . . someone
else?"

Another laugh. Or it could have been a kind of sob of
exasperation, bleakly amused. "For whom, for God's
sake? For the hopeless?"

"Who *are* you?" Felicity demanded, desperate for a
sticking-point in the quicksand. "And how did you know
where I—"

"Everything is dangerous," the woman said. "Especially
talk. We want to know: Will you help?"

The nightmare settled around Felicity again, like a bird-
catcher's net. "I don't know," she faltered.

"We understand. But if you want to know more," the
voice said quietly, "come to Central Square. You know
it?"

"Of course," Felicity said. "Who *are* you?"

"Come to El Centro Salvadore, 136 Massachusetts
Avenue."

"But . . ." A nervous tic in Felicity's lip made it difficult
to speak. "The FBI . . . I'm being watched."

"Naturally you are being watched. If only it were by the
FBI. If you want to do nothing more, we understand. In
any case, we thank you. La Desconocida herself thanks
you. Goodbye."

"Wait! If I come to Central Square, whom shall I ask
for?"

"Just come to El Centro Salvadore, 136 Mass Ave."

There was a click.

Felicity stared into the receiver. A miraculous mani-
festation issuing from it would not have surprised her.
Agitated, she flipped through the telephone book to the
federal government listings. She called the FBI. Could she
please speak to Mr. Trog? There was, she was informed
after a pause and the sound of riffled pages, no such person
at the Boston office. Could she, then, speak to Mr. Hunter
or leave a message for him? The Boston office had no
knowledge of a Mr. Hunter.

Felicity returned to the breakfast room, trembling a little,
and drank her coffee. She needed it. Twittering about her

175

like cooing doves, the aunts spoke of this and that, but
Felicity was not listening. Alive, she was thinking.
Dolores Marquez-Magdalena-Salvadora-La Desconocida
is alive. And in spite of everything her spirits lifted. But
then . . . if the murder was false, how authentic was the
deliverance? If someone who distrusted Trog and Hunter
knew so much, knew how to reach her, just how many
people were watching her and what were their intentions?

She looked at the aunts moving between the silver
coffeepot and the old lace curtains, and they seemed to her
as distant as a fishing boat in the Indian Ocean. I will
always be alone, she thought. I will never be safe. I am
one of those people marked at birth, like my father. The
people who need dangerous work done smell us out, the
way horses and dogs smell fear on human beings.

She drifted upstairs to the bedroom that had been
hers since she was thirteen years old, and looked down
into the street. He was still there. Hunter. He was sitting
in his car, his thick forearm resting on the window. Even
the way his hair fell in oily clumps over his forehead
seemed sinister to her now, and she was alarmed that she
had ever thought of him as gentle and sympathetic. It
revealed some fatal incapacity on her part to assess people
correctly.

What could she say to her aunts?

You were right. It appears that the woman I met at the
border has not been murdered; and the man in the street is
not from the FBI. Nevertheless a man, some man, is out
there watching the house and I am afraid of him and I have
to get to Central Square without being seen.

Really, Felicity, they would say. You've let your coffee
get cold.

Hear no evil, see no evil, speak no evil, Felicity thought,
and you can protect yourself from a great deal of distress.
If only she could acquire the knack.

The gardens on Beacon Hill are beautiful but secret—
perfectly scaled triumphs of azaleas and dogwoods in col-
loquia, of shy statuary and of gluttonous ivy in elegant
containment behind high brick walls. Many of the gardens

176

are interconnected, part of a grander scheme of aristocratic cooperation, or cosmic harmony in little. Though the aunts' garden is not part of this continuous landscaping, a wicket gate behind the lilacs permits access to it. One can pass unseen for the length of the street, there are hidden doors to laneways and side streets, there is private access to the Common.

Felicity made brief and vague explanations to the aunts, who assumed she was leaving for her gallery. But where is your car? Aunt Norwich asked. Ah well, Felicity said, it was impounded by that man from the FBI. Really, Felicity, they chuckled, as she faded from their morning.

Once she reached the Common she felt safer, though a thought, like a burr, snagged in her mind: Just how many watchers *were* there? Why was that gardener staring? Why did that child point at her? She rubbed her eyes. She was running full tilt at paranoia.

But really, there were too many people about and the watchers would lose track. The world was in motley. Punk rockers with dangerous hair. Children on roller skates. Dreadlocked black teenagers with ghetto blasters in full voice. Girls blooming with suntans and hope. Everyone was young, except for the gentlemen on benches who turned in their sleep and pulled sheets of newspaper up to their chins for comfort.

At the entrance to the Park Street subway station, she had to pass through a crowd gathered around a sword-swallower. The man was on his knees, his head tilted back so far it was at right angles to his shoulder blades. His Adam's apple moved convincingly and the sword blade slowly disappeared, inch by inch, down his gullet. Mildly curious, Felicity watched as she fished in her purse for a token. Was the feat anatomically possible? And if not, how was the illusion managed? She found her token. As the sword hilt clicked against the man's teeth, she moved away and descended to the gritty bowels of the Park Street stop. Miasma. She loved the subway, as steamy and murky and full of the unexpected as a tropical rain forest. Everyone in transit. An underground world of equals,

177

every face pale and phantasmal as the nimbus of a wandering soul. Felicity felt at home in such places.

The Red Line train came snorting into the station, rattling its scales and plates, spewing out hundreds of people, sucking in hundreds more. It snarled and screeched and rushed on into darkness, earthworming below Boston, surfacing to slink across the Charles River, plunging back into the city's intestine. Past Kendall, where no one ever seemed to get on or off, to Central Square, where the phantoms rose into sunlight like bits of discolored froth and were blown in a myriad directions.

(I was there just weeks ago, sniffing into every cranny of the disappearance. I feel an urge to interject with fresh-picked facts. Hear now the voice of the piano tuner turned interpolator, tourist guide, and stage manager.

Oh Jean-Marc, Felicity will laugh, you're having another didactic attack.)

Nevertheless . . .

Though Central Square is only a mile or so from Harvard Square, it is not part of the same world. The latter is bohemian, intellectual, and affluent. Its students may dress shabbily, but their style is expensively shabby. Rumpled chic. Harvard Square may be dirty, but the dirt has panache.

And Central Square? Neighbor and poor relation, it is nothing but asphalt, tawdriness, and poverty. It is crowded with the unemployed and the unemployable. Grittiness is pervasive. There is nothing picturesque about the dirt in Central Square; it is simply filth. And yet it is more cosmopolitan than its neighbor; of the faces in the street, white ones would barely make a majority. For the rest, human confetti: black, Hispanic, Vietnamese, Chinese, and the unidentifiable.

Because of her gallery, Felicity knew Harvard Square like the back of her hand. But it was years since she had had any reason to go one subway stop east, years since she had been at such close quarters to squalor. Woolworth's is Woolworth's anywhere, she thought, except in such places as Central Square, where it is more so. A stink of oil eddied rancidly from a grubby-looking popcorn machine.

178

Everywhere the din of traffic and transistor radios. Cheap sneakers hung like bunches of vinyl-scented bananas in dime-store lobbies. Clutter was aspired to: as though consolation could be found in the sheer *quantity* of shoddy goods. On the leeward sides of telegraph poles, torn fragments of inflammatory pamphlets whispered among themselves, little covens of conspirators.

Felicity had thought that a cotton skirt and blouse would be sufficiently unremarkable—an assumption worthy of the aunts in its benign ignorance. Now she saw that she was marked. Conspicuously alien. This was far more than a matter of her clothing, though her clothing was noticeable enough. It had also to do with the condition of her hair, her teeth, her skin. On all sides she saw evidence that dental care is by no means universal in America. Every step advertised her foreignness. A woman on welfare walks differently from a woman with an earned income.

(End of *mise-en-scène*.

Jean-Marc effaces himself.)

A cat among birds, conspicuous, her footsteps delicate, Felicity tried to slink along Massachusetts Avenue looking for Number 136. Numbers were not easy to find. Storekeepers worked on the principle that the mailman and anyone who needed to know already knew where they were. She found 132 and she found 140. Between the two was a sliver of building occupied, at the street level, by a record store whose entryway made up the entire frontage. It was one of those places that is locked up by means of a folding steel curtain. She could not see a number. Only a sign hand-painted in lurid pink letters: *Scoop's Poopdeck*.

The store, about the width of a wide hallway, was a two-aisled supermarket of sound with a horse trough of rock records down the middle and a welter of every kind of disc stacked like tattered wallpaper on either side. There were two turnstiles, one in, one out. Having been catapulted in, Felicity had to follow the first half of the alphabet of rock down a long, tubal passage to the K's

179

at the U-turn, and then back through L to Z toward the cash register by the exit. Every few feet she had to suck herself in to get by a gyrating automaton wearing headphones plugged into the wall. Wired for sound, these robots snapped their fingers, moved their hips, sometimes sang along much too loudly with the private pipeline of music.

"Hey!" called one black teenager, removing his headphones. "Hey Leon! Look at this!"

Leon pushed his headset back like a visor and flicked his dreadlocks off his shoulders. Both young men watched Felicity's progress around the tubal U with gleeful curiosity. She might have been Mother Goose in a crinoline. Certainly, as she smiled with shy politeness, she felt encumbered by something not unlike miles of petticoat. The two young men shook with laughter. They made deep sardonic bows.

Felicity blushed and hurried on past W, X, Y, and Z to the cage-enclosed cash register. Cigarette smoke hung in clouds. Two men, one black, one white, were dimly visible through the fog. Felicity wondered how they could see. Her own eyes were stinging and watering.

"Hey, Scoop!" yelled Leon, from reggae section D-E-F. "You're keeping the Duchess waiting."

Scoop, the white keeper of the till, leaned forward in his cage and breathed fetid air over Felicity. Discreetly, she leaned away. Not wise. Scoop's face, a violent relief map of acne, twisted with hostility. A slow lava of blood and mucus seeped from the scratched peaks of his malady into craters on his cheeks.

"Yes, your ladyship?" he asked, picking a scab on his chin with leering pleasure. "What can I do you for?"

"I'm looking for Number 136 Mass Ave," Felicity said. "I was wondering if you could—"

"Well you ain't found it," Scoop said. "So why don't you bugger off?"

"What number *are* you? I couldn't see any—"

"Why?"

"Pardon?"

"Why d'ya wanna know our number?"

"Well, because it would help me find 136 if I . . ."

Scoop's black partner, who must have played basketball on many a back-street lot, leaned out over the top of the cage and said thickly: "Lissen, candy-cunt, bugger off before we do a little number on you ourselves."

This remark was a huge success. Way to go, Big Ben! several customers called. Laughter scudded towards the turnstiles like gases escaping from something noxious trapped in the elbow joint at K. Felicity was only too eager to bugger off, but Scoop and his gargantuan sidekick instituted a game. A switch had been tripped, the exit turnstile locked.

For several seconds, mortified by her own ineptness, Felicity pushed at the bars which refused to turn, the back of her head pelted with catcalls and mock encouragement. She could feel color spreading out from her neck like a rash. Quite suddenly, Scoop flicked the switch again and she hurtled into the street. Laughter splattered on the pavement around her like broken glass.

Head high, cheeks flaming, she walked away. Anywhere, any direction. And quickly. In a sheltered doorway, she stopped for breath.

Perhaps I have muddled up the digits, she thought. Perhaps it is 316 or 163 that I should be looking for. But neither number helped: 316 was a crack between Papa's Pizza and a used book store; 163 was part of a gas station labelled over its office door—black decals on the glass fanlight—as 161–169.

Perhaps there are several sequences of numbers, she thought. Perhaps I am in the wrong part of Central Square. She walked east along Mass Ave almost as far as MIT, but no new sequence of numbering began. She walked west toward Harvard Square. Nothing.

Then it must be next to the record place, she decided. I must have missed a doorway.

As frustrated and determined as she was nervous, she went back to Number 132, a Vietnamese restaurant. She walked slowly past its doorway, monitoring every inch of frontage. Its east wall was flat up against the K to Z of rock and reggae. Eyes down, heart pounding, she crossed this danger zone quickly. And now she was in front of Number 140, an unbelievably dingy cubbyhole with "Central Square Watch Clinic" painted across its grubby plate-glass window.

Felicity went inside. Watches, hundreds of them, from fobs on chains to Timex specials, hung in bunches from hooks. Every inch of the walls was covered. She thought of satellite moons, so many tiny white faces. They seemed to multiply before her eyes like pale mushrooms under ferns. Perhaps this explained the dank vegetable smell. Tufts of Timex sprouted from the counter, copulating perhaps in the gloom.

"Can I help you?"

Felicity squeezed her eyes tightly shut in an attempt to adjust them for twilight. When she looked again, he was perfectly visible: a gnome-like man on a stool behind the counter. A jeweller's monocle was growing from one of his eyes.

Oh, she thought, with involuntary fascination. This I have to describe for Seymour. The man wore a circlet of silvery hair. A tonsure. His skin was as pale as the dials of his myriad watches, but seemed faintly luminous, as though it had been long deprived of sun and had evolved a capacity to provide its own light. Entranced, Felicity quite forgot why she was there.

"Of course," the little man said (it was either his voice, dry and faint, or the ticking of a thousand wrist watches), "I have all the time in Central Square, if not in the world. But the question is, do you?"

He laughed at his own joke and she saw the flash of gold in his teeth. On the counter a gold watch lay in sections, its wheels kicking feebly. She thought irrationally: Perhaps he runs a gold scrap service for a dentist.

"Take your time, take your time," the man chuckled. "Or take some of mine, as you prefer; it's a wide selection. There's a time to pick and a time to choose."

Felicity remembered why she had come in. "Actually, I just wanted to ask directions. I'm looking for Number 136 Mass Ave, but it doesn't seem to exist."

"Ahh," he said. And the search took on metaphysical weight merely from the inflection of his voice. "All

182

conceptions exist. Perhaps you want Mass Ave in Harvard Square."

"No. Central Square. Definitely. That's what I was told."

"Then perhaps it would be better if you told me who or what you are looking for."

"Yes, of course. Silly of me. It's a place called El Centro Salvadore."

"Ah," said the man, squinting through his monocle. He poked at the insect insides of a watch. It lay on its back, helpless, its cogs flinching from his metal probe as he pushed into cavities here and there. Perhaps he runs a dental practise himself, on the side, Felicity thought. He seemed to have forgotten her, and she, watching him, forgot she was waiting for an answer. There was something mesmeric about the delicate way he nudged at the fly wheels, touching nerves, setting off spasms of movement, putting a gentle stop to flickering activity. She leaned closer and into the pale emanation that seemed to come from his face, and then she saw the numbers tattooed on his forearm: 000136.

Without lifting his head, the watch repairer raised his unmonocled eye and they stared at each other from almost point-blank range.

"Which side are you on?" he asked quietly.

"Side?" she faltered.

"Why did you help her?"

Riveted to his one eye, Felicity felt the throb of strain on the nerves of her own eye sockets. She was aware of a tic that was beginning to swallow up one side of her face. He could be mad, she thought. Or he could—impossible though it seems—be talking about Dolores Marquez. Or he could be responding out of another language, another story altogether, and it happens that our syntax and chapters coincide.

"I don't know why," she said. "It was instinctive. Anyone would have done it."

The answer seemed to please him. He smiled and nodded over his work, but said, "Not everyone. Strange, isn't it?"

He had taken up the most delicate of tapered, silken-haired brushes, and was removing dust from a watch, dust that could not be seen by the unaided eye.

"There is a barber shop," he said without looking up, "on Milk Street."

His silence, and his attention to the watch, went on for so long that at last Felicity prompted, "A barber shop?"

He blew gently on the watch and picked up another tool. "Do you know Mr. Scoop?" he asked.

"Pardon?"

"He's watching us."

Startled, she turned and saw Scoop's grotesquely pustuled face pressed against the grimy window.

"Who is he?" she asked nervously.

"My neighbor."

"Yes, but I mean . . ."

"All finished," he said. "Just needed cleaning." He lifted the instrument from its vice, clicked on its case, attached a blue ribbon band, and placed it in her palm. "As promised," he said. "To be delivered to the barber shop today." He nodded in dismissal. When she reached the sidewalk, Scoop was already back inside his teller's cage in the record shop.

Felicity walked east and asked the first policeman she saw where Milk Street was. Not far, he told her. Turn left into Compson, then left again, then right. It's just a lane, really.

She found it without difficulty—an area of unmitigated asphalt where the summer heat crouched like a lion, snarling, waiting. Walls rotted, paint peeled, buildings bulged with tenants, dandelions—the only green and living things—flourished in sidewalk cracks, while sad parodies of gardens rampaged in a brown and weedy neglect. Noise triumphed. An eerie and invisible noise: for though practically every sound of urban living could be made out in the cacophony, the street and its parking lots were weirdly vacant. She had the sense of being in a rowdy ghost town. Each house was a pressure cooker, seething and shaking and boiling and threatening to blow its lid off.

184

There were babies crying, mothers yelling, ghetto blasters blasting, children and teenagers shrieking, playing, fighting. And from a barber shop, the most astonishing barber shop Felicity had ever seen, came a babel of high-decibel Spanish folk music that threw everything else into background sound. A concerto for barber shop, with orchestral slum.

The shop itself was bright orange except for a pulsing neon barber pole. Over its door (closed, but bidding *bienvenido* on a cardboard sign) a mounted speaker hurled music out to the city.

Impervious to this tumult, plaster saints—decidedly tropical in hue, large as life—crowded into a narrow display box behind the plate-glass window. Jesus, fuchsia-robed, bared his Sacred Heart; a sticker beside the wound on his delicate left hand said $25. As Infant of Prague he cost a little more, but came in gold-sprayed and glitter-dusted tulle and satin brocade. For $18.95 St. Francis would preach a technicolor sermon to pets in any apartment. Come unto me, said Our Lady of Guadaloupe—patron saint of primary color, $32.50—all ye who pine for bougainvillea and the bright song of sunwashed adobe, and I will give you a warm memory of your mothers and grandmothers, vividly swathed.

Felicity pressed her nose to the window, overcome with a sharp longing for the loud, gaudy courtyards of temples, for the extravagant fragrance and color of Brisbane gardens, for her *ayah*, for her father, for her grandparents, for Hester, for the sun at its arrogant and undiluted nearest. Who knows how long she stood there with her nose pressed against the past? When the barber shop window swam back into focus, she noted its *pièce de résistance*, a thing of wonder.

For sheerly exuberant tastelessness and tropical excess, she could think of nothing to rival it: a hand with a thirty-inch span, in the palest of rosebud flesh tones, dripping red paint from the wound in its palm. This was not all. From each fingertip and from the pad of the thumb sprouted a saint as long as a finger joint and flashier than papal finery. Saints Peter and Paul in lapis and indigo; our

185

multicolored Lady on the middle finger; St. Anne bluely indexed; and on the thumb, like a triumphantly juicy cherry, the Sacred Heart itself. An expensive hand, this. A tag dangling from the knuckle of the pinky demanded $49.95 of the devoutly undiscriminating.

Felicity pushed open the door and went in, blinking against the dark, conscious of the abrupt cessation of talk and laughter. Her eyes adjusted. She saw the barber chair and its occupant, the barber, and four other men, presumably waiting their turn. All were staring at her as if she had horns.

She said nervously, "I'm looking for El Centro Salvadore."

There was a stirring of feet, but otherwise no response.

She produced the watch. "I was asked to deliver this."

"Ah," the barber said, and pocketed it. "*Gracias.*"

The men continued to stare at her, uneasy, perhaps hostile. The barber had a comb in one hand and a pair of scissors in the other and his fingers worked the scissors open and shut, open and shut, as though his hand were slowly digesting the inexplicable fact of her presence.

"I was told you might be able to help," Felicity persisted.

"No speak English," the barber said decisively. It worked as a cue. He turned back to the business of the haircut and the men who were waiting their turn picked up torn and much-thumbed Spanish magazines and read them studiously. Felicity felt ridiculous, standing there; but she also felt irrationally afraid of walking out of the shop and making her way back down Milk Street. She knew she would feel the men's scrutiny, perhaps their catcalls, falling on her back like long shadows.

Stubbornly she said: "Does El Centro Salvadore exist? I was told 136 Massachusetts Avenue and the watch repairman sent me here."

"Ah," the barber said, cautiously courteous. "Mass Ave, *sí, sí.* Pedro will show."

Rapid Spanish on the wing. A man, presumably Pedro, was given instructions. He motioned to Felicity to follow: back down the raucously vacant dandelion trail of Milk Street, back along the side streets to the corner of

Massachusetts Avenue. Then he pointed in the direction of the now familiar cluster of shops. "Mass Ave," he said, nodding somberly and repeatedly.

"But I've *been* there," Felicity complained, "and I was sent to you."

"*Sí, sí,*" he said. "You go." And he turned on his heel.

She felt giddy with frustration. The barber shop is El Centro Salvadore, she decided, but something has gone wrong. Or else I'm being very rigorously screened. Or perhaps someone is playing an elaborate and horrible game with me. Or then again, the entire thing could be meaningless coincidence. Deduction roulette. Pick an interpretation and impose.

The acquisition of knowledge, she thought, is like water over sand. She knew—or thought she knew—that she had lifted a woman from a carcass of beef; that the woman's blood had stained a bed in her cottage; that a man calling himself Hunter had followed her; that he knew about the woman at the border, La Desconocida, the unknown one, whose name may or may not have been Dolores Marquez, who may or may not have been murdered. She knew that an unknown woman had telephoned her, had spoken of La Desconocida, had known about Trog and Hunter, had sent her into a hall of mirrors.

I will back up a few days, Felicity thought. I will stay with Aaron.

She wanted to change her mind about last weekend's trip to the cottage, to find a way out of the maze, to return to sanity.

She was passing Scoop's Poopdeck again, walking quickly, anxious now to take the subway on to Harvard Square, to reach the haven of her gallery. But Leon of reggae persuasion and dreadlock hairstyle was leaning against one of the turnstiles: Cerberus of the sidewalk.

"Hey!" he called. "Her ladyship is back!" He turned and winked at his delighted audience in the store. "I think maybe she's got the hots for me."

Peripherally Felicity saw him swagger after her. She felt the grit of public laughter. Scoop's catcalls, pus-like, dripped through the air.

187

Nothing can happen, she told herself firmly. Her heart was hammering; it might have been auditioning for one of Scoop's rock bands. Nothing could happen on a crowded street in broad daylight—though perhaps it would be better not to descend into the subway, perhaps better to walk all the way to Harvard Square. In the jostle of people waiting for the light to change near Cambridge City Hall, mocking Leon rubbed himself against her from behind.

She could have sworn she heard his urgent whisper: "Listen, I'm more scared of you than you are of me. There's a pub just past the Post Office. The Plough and Stars. Wait for me."

The light changed and the crowd bore her across the street. At the far side she turned, but Leon was impossibly distant, mimicking some woman's walk (her own!) for the benefit of a small audience of vastly amused cronies.

She crossed to the Post Office and walked on. I have more than paid my dues, she told herself. I have no obligations. I do not want to be involved any further. I am going straight back to my gallery, she decided, even as she turned into The Plough and Stars.

22

I began as a simple filer of facts. I was recording the truth, the gospel according to Jean-Marc. I told myself that the truth must be tempered because mere accuracy was false. And this is not a fabrication. I was scrupulous, I was after something three-dimensional, I was on the trail of a metaphysical balloon.

I began by guarding not only against error, but against the spirit of error. I know the temper of the times, when politicians never lie but merely "mis-speak" themselves, when heads of state smile winningly through demonstrable contradictions. I have tuned a piano while children watched news clips of the historic D-Day invasion.

"An uncle of mine was killed there," I told them.

"It's not as good as *Indiana Jones and the Temple of Doom*," the children said. "Or *Star Wars*. We like that even better. We've got it on video now."

I know truth is an old-fashioned plant, like sage or thyme. I know the difficulties, but I am steering for the essential rather than the merely literal.

I temper, I stretch, I embroider.

And then self-hypnotism sets in. (Form, after all, is important. One is concerned with the shape of the whole.) One begins to flex new muscles, to sense power, to acquire a taste for it. This is the Pygmalion factor: one falls in love with one's own creation, one rather enjoys playing God.

(A confession: The piano tuner is getting a yen for the stage.)

Perhaps, when Felicity finally calls, she will disappoint. Perhaps I am better at her lines than she is.

I have begun to dream her dreams.

A beach with rocks. Every few seconds I am drenched:

the waves seethe into crevices, froth upwards in fireworks of foam, retreat, hiss, whisper, gather themselves up for another siege.

Felicity! I call. Take care!

Because this is what I see on the rocks: the Old Volcano with his easel, impervious, is painting on through cataclysms of spray. Felicity's boat is coming closer and closer to the rocks, he has arranged it, he plans compositions of disaster.

Felicity! I call, but a sea fern is growing out of my mouth.

"You bastard!" I scream at the Old Volcano. He thinks he can make the whole world after his own image. He paints, and therefore things are. "You bastard!" I scream. But he does what he wants. He always has.

Felicity's boat is held in a fist of spray, it is poised in air, in an instant it will be smashed on the rocks. "Oh Jean-Marc," she says mournfully as she passes over me, like a stricken bird, "why are you making him do this?" And then impact. Fragments.

When Felicity calls in from wherever, she'll enjoy that dream.

Oh Jean-Marc, she'll laugh, dream me another. You're always imagining I'll come to harm.

That was last night's dream.

When I told Kathleen, she said: "But my father isn't cruel at all. He wasn't like that at all. You are always making him out to be stupid. You are always saying he hurt us because he never knew what he was doing. It isn't true. He did love my mother."

Kathleen follows her own trails these days. It's natural. They've been missing for months.

"If you want to stay here for the night," I tell her, "you can sleep on the sofa. The pianos will keep you company."

"My mother wouldn't let me," she says. "She doesn't trust you. And nor does Aunt Marthe."

She only loves me because I knew her father.

But the day Felicity called from a tavern in Central Square, I had still not even met Augustine Kelly, and Kathleen was hidden behind the future. When Felicity

190

called, she said: "Jean-Marc, this is either an absurd game or a deadly one or both. If no one shows up in the next ten minutes, I'm leaving."

"Never mind that," I said. "What about Hunter?"

Because I hadn't had a chance to speak to her since I'd played back her tape. I hadn't been able to free myself from the break in her voice when she'd called and said, "I'm frightened."

"Fliss," I said gently, "the whole world is out of tune. That's the way it is." She was right to call me. I've never had any illusions. I'm not afflicted with a sense of responsibility the way she is. There's the difference. One note at a time, that's my motto.

"The world is full of jerks like Hunter," I told her. "Don't let him get to you like that." She's not aware of how she encourages men, she has no idea what she does.

"And as for Dolores or whatever her name is," I said. "You can't take the whole world on your shoulders It's a disease, this belief that you're responsible. I agree, I agree, it's all a nightmare, it's horrific, it's absurd. But it's not our concern. It's against all common sense for a woman to hang around taverns alone."

"And the main thing," I told her, "is that you need more sleep. You need someone to look after you—but not someone who will merely *use* you."

She let that pass.

She will never hear a word against the Old Volcano.

"Why don't you come up here for a while?" I asked. "And rest."

But she didn't.

She kept right on course for the rocks as though there were nothing she could do about it.

All right, Mr. Piano Tuner, you say. Enough of red herrings. Enough of disarming admissions about dreaming Felicity's dreams and remembering her memories, about putting on the masks of Gus, of Dante, of all the flounderers in dark woods.

We will not be so easily fobbed off, we will not be

deceived. Do you think we cannot see through that chapter of conceits in Central Square, the games, the false trails, the elaborate smokescreens, the entire futile hunt to find out what happened to Dolores (Hester, Felicity)? Confess now. The whole truth. Let us hear you say it: *Felicity herself, c'est moi.*

Touché! I hear you crowing.

Oh come now.

Do you really think you have made an original discovery? The androgyny of Jean-Marc? His own quest for a father? His own meditations on individual accountability? His own hunt through a maze of riddles for a woman who has been missing for a year?

Come now, this trick is at least as old as Shakespeare. "These are all lies," said Rosalind from behind her Ganymede mask: and we know she was a boy actor playing a girl disguised as a boy who was pretending to be a girl to snare Orlando in the Forest of Arden.

Seriously, is any of us not aware that Dante is Beatrice? That he took on her plumage and presumed, from behind her mask, to discourse on the Empyrean, to bind and loose, to hurl his critics into the Inferno, to pose certain questions, in effect, to God himself?

And is it possible there exists anyone who has not detected Shakespeare's voice in Rosalind's, pining in code for the dark lover of enigmatic gender? *O coz, coz, coz, my pretty little coz, that thou didst know how many fathom deep I am in love!*

(There is, after all, a report that he wrote the part for himself. That cocky young actor, as a rival playwright, Greene with envy, muttered over his beer in a Tudor pub. That upstart crow, that *Johannes fac totum*, that Shake-ass, that fag, that Rosalind!)

In any case, all this conjuring is both true and not true. There *was* a Rosalind, there *was* a Beatrice, there *is* a Felicity. How many changes can be rung on the human condition? Is it surprising that I feel at home in Felicity's skin? That sometimes she slides into mine? The truth is, I seem to know more about Felicity's life than about my own. I understand hers better. I've given it more thought.

192

This seems also to be true with Gus and with all of the characters I record. I seem to *recognize* them, I remember the view from their eyes, as though I were a salamander that slips into the envelopes of other people's lives.

Don't obfuscate, you say. And you produce your little list of indictments. Specifically, you want to know:

1) Why does Jean-Marc pretend he took Felicity seriously when she called from her gallery and from The Plough and Stars?

Why does he pretend he made suggestions that might have dissuaded her from the journey toward her disappearance?

Why is he tormented with guilt?

Why, depending on the light, does Dolores resemble Hester resemble Felicity?

2) Why does Felicity's father, receding into the Indian Ocean in his fishing boat, have a cargo of paintbrushes?

Why does he have bushy eyebrows like the Old Volcano?

And why, when Jean-Marc remembers that phone call from Central Square, does he feel ill all over again with panic?

Why does his mind veer off toward Gus, who was rushing only slightly more slowly toward disaster?

23

Vaguely troubled that Therese was still not answering the phone after his car had been towed from the ditch, Gus headed west. Driving always soothed him. After ten miles he decided: She has taken the girls to the new shopping center, a very sensible thing to do, since his daughters enjoyed it so much. She was a good adapter, Therese. He could not complain. And he would make it up to her. Perhaps he would take them all out for dinner tomorrow night.

He wound down the window and crept another five miles above the speed limit for the sheer pleasure of the bluster of headwind. He inhaled optimism. Perhaps it was the rush of oxygen, or the strange exhilaration aroused by his vision of La Magdalena. He decided he would contact Felicity in the morning as a courtesy gesture. Just to let her know they had been wrong about Montreal (the church basements, the underground railroad), but that all was well.

The other car, he would say. Probably just weekend people after all. My guess is she sleeps at your cottage. She lives on apples and rainwater.

"Did you check the cottage?" he imagined Felicity asking.

Well, no.

"Why not? When you drove all that way?"

Because, because . . .

(Because, Gus, one doesn't tamper with visions of transcendence. Because, like all of us, you want to add a dimension of the ineffable to your unbearably mundane life. But even I, who am busy creating you from bits and pieces of information, and from that long, drunken conversation at which we have almost arrived, cannot put

194

these thoughts into your mind. There are rules. Limitations. Even a master piano tuner cannot make a LeSage sound like a Steinway.)

Gus himself could find no answer to the question he made Felicity ask. Because, he said. Because. He was preoccupied with the memory of a woman washing herself in light. And then the look she had given him when she turned, the look he had been unable to see for the glare. He felt as though he might spend the rest of his life deciphering that look. He felt he would never exhaust the meaning of apples falling from her skirt and of her hair streaming in the dappled shadows beneath the leaves. His skin tingled and was tender, almost bruised, to the touch, as though from sunburn. Or as though it were the kind of new, delicate tissue that grows over a wound. Certainly he felt that he had stepped out of an old scuffed layer of himself and left it somewhere between the pine woods and the orchard.

You've got to know what you want, said Reggie, a constant companion, before you can go for it.

And now I do, Gus said.

Go for it, Reggie urged.

But the gas gauge showed almost empty and Gus had to pull into a service station first.

"Super or regular?" asked the attendant at the pumps. She was as young and flawless as the summer evening, dressed in baggy blue denim coveralls and a pale pink T-shirt. When she leaned under the hood to check his oil, her ash-brown mane fell forward over her face and her breasts in petal-pink interlock spilled sideways out of the coverall bib.

"You shouldn't," Gus offered, solicitous. "You'll get oil on your . . . on here." He was about to stroke the soft shirt through which an animated nipple was budding. But something restrained him.

"Lucky for you, mister," she said calmly. "I get mauled by more travelling men than there are hairs around your balls. And that's exactly where I'll kick you if I have to."

He was astonished, but not by her sassy mouth. He was astonished because he had not touched her. It was a miracle. La Magdalena, framed in light, smiled on him from between the windshield wipers.

He said absently, "She has a strange effect on me."

He saw himself standing beside Therese in church, his thigh brushing hers but his thoughts pure, their daughters in white veils and circlets of orange blossom with their first pale Communion wafers on their tongues. La Magdalena watched from the choir stalls. She was wearing a diaphanous gown and he could see her breasts, though the meaning was as far removed from the carnal as are the breasts of the nursing Madonna in a painting. I will nourish you, La Magdalena promised. Her eyes were lowered in prayer.

"Who has?" asked the girl in coveralls.

"What?"

"Who has a strange effect on you?"

But Gus was elsewhere and did not answer.

"You need oil," the girl said, holding the dipstick up to the light. She took a canister from a display rack beside the pumps, snapped off its plastic cap, and poured through a funnel. The *glug glug* reached Gus's ears between dreams of apples and breasts and daughters, and he turned to watch the girl again. Her movements were quick and deft. She was obviously at home with cars. The gentle rocking of her unsupported bosom filled him with tranquil pleasure.

"You're very beautiful," he said.

"Is that the beginning of another pass?"

"No." And it wasn't. The miracle held. "I was admiring the way you do your work."

"I love cars. My mum and I run this place between us since my dad buggered off. You want to come in for a drink before you drive on?"

"Is that a pass?"

She laughed. "First we lure them in, and then we rape them."

"Our problem, Mr. Kelly," said her mother over tea with a dash of gin added, "is that we are quite partial to male company, but as soon as it sets up camp, so to speak, we realize we're better off without. On the whole, we find we prefer cars. Better rhythm and spunk. They're

196

capable of nonstop performance, and they don't cheat on you."

Gus liked the mother. She chain-smoked and her voice filtered its way out through gravel. Streaked with axle grease to the elbows, she kept pushing a wayward coverall strap back on her shoulders and a lock of hair out of her eyes. Hair? Thatch. Probably once ash-brown like her daughter's, it had aged into mousiness and wiry rebellion. Various combs, plunged into the growth like surveyors' markers, tried to keep it in check.

"Lynn here is more sanguine about men than I am," she said. "As long as they don't paw her in the first half hour, she thinks the age of chivalry has not passed. Me, I don't waste energy on romantic illusions."

"This one's okay, mum," Lynn said, as though discussing grades of gasoline. "A bit dreamy. The gentle kind, that you can have a proper conversation with." And to Gus, by way of extenuation: "My dad lit out without leaving us a cent, so we've had to be tough. We're kinda proud of ourselves."

"So what do you sell, Mr. Kelly?" The mother blew a smoke ring around his head.

"How do you know I sell anything, Mrs.—"

"Em. Just call me Em. Short for Emmelina, would you believe?" She laughed and it was like a chorus of uninhibited bullfrogs. He loved the sound.

"Gus," he said, reciprocal. He could feel the tea and gin purring in sundry odd places: behind his fingernails, in the pulse behind his knees. "So what makes you think I sell anything, Em?"

"Oh, you have all the marks of a man who spends his life away from home in order to keep his marriage intact."

Gus spluttered into his tea and gin and both women laughed, though Lynn, quickly contrite, said, "That was mean, mum."

"I'm going to change," Gus told them solemnly.

"Aren't we all?" Em was full of good cheer, dispensing insouciance with smoke rings.

"I mean," Gus amended, "I *am* changed."

"That happens," Em said absently. She seemed to know

197

exactly what he was talking about. "The kind of moment when you *know* . . . For me, it was in a grotty public washroom in Toronto, filthy limericks on the walls, mirrors busted. And I saw my face with a crack running right through the middle of it . . ." She trailed off, reading earlier pages of her life.

Lynn leaned forward and took from her mother's forgetful fingers the last burning rind of a cigarette. She stubbed it out, lit another, and transferred it from her own lips to her mother's. Em accepted it with an abstracted smile and patted her daughter's wrist. So much brightness, Gus marvelled, blinking rapidly. There is scarcely room in the world for darkness. His eyes were watering. (It must have been the cigarette smoke.) He had to turn away.

Em stirred, returning to them, and poured more tea and gin all around. "So," she said, as though summing up a long peroration. "The sun just keeps on rising and setting."

"Are you always so contented?" Gus asked, mesmerized.

Em raised an eyebrow. "Contented?" She pondered the word, turned it around in her mind. "I guess so," she said. "But then, I'm lucky. I've got Lynn here. Terrific kid. And I've got me a good franchise, I'm hooked on cars, and I rather like working my butt off."

"I guess I'm lucky too," Gus said. He pulled out the pictures of his wife and children and displayed them. "I guess the problem is I haven't been doing the right things to make *them* happy."

"The little ones are real cute," Lynn said. "And who's this one?"

"That's Kathleen. She's sixteen now."

"Same as me."

Gus was shocked. He had not thought of Kathleen as someone old enough to roam unleashed in the wide adult world, old enough to chat with sleazy men who would look at her body, who might not be as self-disciplined as he himself . . . as self-disciplined as one could wish.

"Well," he said, suddenly anxious. "I really should be moving on. I'm heading for Winston."

"Already?" Em's voice was full of regret. "The decent ones always leave soonest. And I made a whole pot of tea."

"Just one more cup?" Lynn suggested.

"Well . . ." It was not every day that he met someone with whom he could discuss the turning points of the soul. This was not something a man should toss lightly over his shoulder. Another cup, a few more minutes, how could it hurt? A simple matter of courtesy. A statement of thanks. Perhaps he had more than one cup. Perhaps Em was not overly precise about the quantity of gin added. When Lynn suggested a round of three-handed bridge, he thought it would be a good way of sobering up before he drove on.

Over bridge, further chapters of past history were exchanged. Confessions and aspirations were aired. I suppose, Em mused at one point, that I should ensure things are taken care of for Lynn, if anything happens.

Heck yes, Gus said. I get nervous with anyone who hasn't. It's like driving with brakes that don't work.

And so, between the second and third rounds of bridge, an application for $25,000 Whole Life was filled out and signed. They played a fourth round to celebrate and drank more tea and gin. They became more intimate.

"I never wanted to cheat on Therese," Gus said. "But somehow, I don't know, it was always happening before I realized it."

"Past tense, I notice," Em said. "Men always believe they've reformed."

"As a matter of fact," he said, "something happened today."

"Don't tell me," she laughed. "A miracle."

"Maybe."

"And maybe not," she said. "But you shouldn't be too harsh on yourself. No one has brains in the glands. Universal problem. Me, I'm just beginning to learn. Getting hooked on do-it-yourself sex. So much less trouble, especially once you've got the hang of building up a good library of fantasies. You may notice, Gus, that I've been casting my bloodshot eye over your body. Memorizing. I'll try you out tonight."

199

Gus spluttered with nervous laughter, not sure whether to take her seriously. Her sardonic eye held him, unwavering. Blushing, he said, "Can't think of a nicer person to be a fantasy for. Hope I work out."

"Don't you just love him?" Em asked Lynn. "I mean, I can almost bring myself to want him around over breakfast. Always a danger sign with me."

With dry gallantry, Gus reached for her hand and kissed it.

"Hey," Lynn said. "I found him."

Gus kissed Lynn's hand too. "Do you know, I'm still a virgin?" she sighed.

"Enough of that," Em said. "My two of hearts trumps your king, Gus."

"Congratulations," he said. "You win me."

"Lucky me. Must be time for coffee, before we all yield to temptation. And we don't want the RCMP pulling Gus over for a breathalyzer test."

"Oh God," he said, looking at his watch. "I think I'd better call Therese. Tell her I'll be a little late."

But he did have a signed application in his briefcase. He was on legitimate business. He could explain—though perhaps he would skim the main points, edit a little. He dialled his home number and let the phone ring twelve times before he gave up. It was very late now, all the shopping centers closed. Perhaps they had gone to a friend's house. Anxiety set in. He saw ambulances, bottles of clear fluid suspended high over hospital beds, plastic tubing. He drank his coffee black, embraced Lynn and Em chastely, took off like a drag racer.

He kept to a steady speed, his anxiety sobering him. I am changed, he kept telling himself. Everything will be different now. He had a deep conviction, not susceptible to proof, that he would never forget this day.

And he was right.

The house was in darkness. There were two sealed envelopes on the kitchen table, both bearing his name, one in Therese's handwriting, the other in Kathleen's.

He opened Therese's letter first.

There was no salutation.

200

I am sorry, I cannot take it any longer. I never know where you are, I never know if there'll be enough money. I've always lived with that and I could go on living with it. But I will not live with your women phoning here in my own house. Don't try to find me. The children and I will manage.

Therese.

Then he opened Kathleen's letter.

Dear daddy,
Please don't let this happen.
I'm not supposed to write to you but I'm going to run back in the house and leave this at the last minute. We are going to Tante Marthe's in St. Hyacinthe. I'm not supposed to tell you that. I love you. Kathleen.

He called Therese's sister immediately and asked for Therese.

"She won't speak to you," Marthe said.

"Let me speak to Kathleen then."

"No one will speak to you," Marthe said, and hung up.

Gus dialled her again. "Tell them I'm leaving immediately," he said, before Marthe could cut him off. "Tell Therese I'm coming to see her. Tell her I love her, tell Kathleen I love her . . . tell Sylvie . . ." He went on intoning his litany of loves even after the line went dead.

He was completely sober now. He was back in his car and driving east again. Of course I deserved it, he admitted to himself. But she does not know about the change. He would explain. He would iron things out. He would perform, and willingly, any penance she required.

He had no map of Montreal and when he reached it, in the wee hours of the morning, he could not remember exactly how to find St. Hyacinthe. How many years—eight?—since he had gone with them on a visit to Marthe? He spent a frustrating hour getting lost in the center of the city before he found an all-night gas station and obtained a map. He got lost again in St. Hyacinthe. When he finally found Marthe's house, it was four in the morning. He rang the doorbell, at first gently, and then when no one answered, loudly and repeatedly.

Marthe's head appeared at an upstairs window.

"Go away," she said, "or I'll call the police."

"Are you going to make me sleep in the car for the rest of the night?" he demanded.

"Yes," she said.

Miserably he tried to make himself comfortable in the back seat. He dozed and had a horrible dream of a slaughterhouse where bloody carcasses passed by on a conveyor belt. Inside each one, like a pea in a pod, was someone he knew. His wife, his daughters, La Magdalena. A man in a black welder's mask was pushing a button and a mechanical cleaver was slicing the carcasses one by one. Gus lunged for the man who was pushing the button. The man turned—it was himself. He could not switch off the slicing machine. He woke in a sweat.

It was 5 A.M.

He began to drive aimlessly around the streets but he had to stop. Too many visitations. Instead he walked, arguing with his accusers. You can't let it get you down, Reggie said. And Therese: It's no use, it will never be any different. La Magdalena appeared. You really should let Felicity know, she said, that I'm grateful for the use of her cottage.

At a phone booth he stopped and dialled the answering machine at the Montreal number she had given him. Just to have something to talk to. But this time the tape did not speak. Instead, Jean-Marc, jolted from a nightmare, invited him to come around for coffee.

24

The question, possibly of interest to you, and certainly to me, is why did I do it?

Kathleen says I did it because I thought it was the Old Volcano come round at last.

"And from where," I laugh, "do you get that fantastic idea?"

"From your dream," she says. "The dream he woke you out of. The one you told me about."

"Oh Kathleen, Kathleen." I shake my head fondly. Show Kathleen an inkblot and she sees the return of a prodigal father.

"The mountain that shakes," she persists. "The Old Volcano."

An ingenious interpretation. At times Kathleen astonishes me. Oh dreams, Felicity will laugh. What cannot be construed?

In fact, it was one of those chaotic and senseless dreams that pick up the day's trivia and thoughts and memories the way blue serge picks up lint.

In the dream I am tuning a grand piano with a recalcitrant high C. Nothing works. After each adjustment of the pin, I play the scale. Once: good. Twice: off pitch already. As though truth may only be attained for seconds at a time.

Exasperated, I climb onto the sounding board itself, nesting down into the ribcage of strings, the better to get at the faulty pin. With the speed and illogic of dreams, the piano is a raft crossing a choppy sea, there is a fellow passenger, and both of us, when the boat beaches abruptly, are thrown onto the sand.

Climbing. That is the next fragment I recall. Round and round and up, a corkscrew mountain, both of us looking for something but we don't seem to know what.

Sometimes I am leading, sometimes he. In the apple orchard at the top, three women stand in a cart. One is Felicity, and one is Hester. I do not recognize the third. This is Dolores, Felicity says. She reaches out her hand to be helped from the cart. Our fingers are touching, I am reaching up to her, she is floating down toward me like a cascade of apple blossom, she rains perfume, I seem to be drenched. And then an earthquake speaks inside the mountain and we are all of us hurled into space.

Free falling. We flail about in a dark trench waiting for the all-clear bell, but when it rings a voice moans: Lost; it's hopeless. Over here, I call. The all-clear bell rings again. This way, I say into the receiver, and give directions.

"That's not the way he was at all," Kathleen says. "He never felt lost, he was an eternal optimist. You always try to make him out as a helpless bumbler."

"When I dreamed the dream," I laugh, "I hadn't even met your father. You think he's in the air, you think everyone breathes him in."

"And he certainly wasn't involved with that woman, that Dolores Marquez, the way you think," she pouts. "I know that for a fact. Aunt Marthe's right, Jean-Marc, you have a dirty mind."

"What?" I laugh, dumbfounded.

"Don't worry," she says. "Felicity wasn't his type at all. Not at all!"

"Kathleen!" I am not shocked, not really. "Have I ever laid a finger—?"

"Oh, not on *me!*" she screams. "Not on *me!*" She slams down the lid of the piano I am working on, narrowly missing my hands, and runs from the house. It's natural. The strain of the disappearances is telling on us.

It would be so easy for me to take advantage of her. Like father, like son, the Old Volcano would guffaw. A hundred years or so ago, he dressed up in Felicity's memories and seduced her. Oh Seymour, she cried, what a great big history you have! All the better to impale you, my dear, said he, as he wolfed her down.

But I am not the Old Volcano.

I am a chronicler of clues and memory.

25

"People see smoke," said Leon, "they assume fire. They see dreadlocks, they assume black, not Latin. Good camouflage."

Felicity raised an eyebrow. "You're telling me you're *not* black?"

"You see? It works." In the tavern darkness, the whites of his eyes shone like milk glass. "My real name is Angelo," he said, "and I'm here without papers. But I'm lucky."

"Why are you lucky?" Felicity asked.

"I was once here legally. Went to high school in Connecticut, so I don't sound foreign. Most of us have to pretend to be Puerto Rican to get the sweatshop jobs."

"Most of us?"

"Yes."

"I meant: Who is *us*?"

Leon looked uneasily about him and rolled a cigarette. "I'm talking too much," he said. "Like a starving man in front of food. Can't handle temptation." He lit his cigarette and inhaled. "You're dangerous. I can taste my need to trust you. Deadly."

Felicity drank her beer. "Nothing has been logical since I woke this morning," she sighed. "Not one single thing."

"Oh logic." Leon—or Angelo—shrugged. "I'll give you a course in Advanced Logic. Lesson One: He who trusts least, lives longest. Lesson Two: A day without a deportation or a death is a good day."

Felicity doodled in spilled beer with one finger. She drew a thin line between herself and Angelo. She drew barricades. Fortifications raised themselves around her, gray columns: shafts of stale cigarette smoke lifted themselves up, were sucked into the cheap glass lampshades. Currents eddied in many directions. She could feel an undertow.

205

She hooked her feet around the chair legs, bracing and battening down, anticipating headwinds, funnel effects, freak tides.

"Who telephoned me this morning?" she asked.

They stared into each other's eyes, neither blinking. An era passed. "What the hell," Angelo said at last. "What you did for Dolores—you must be all right. And I hear you've had a taste of the opposition. So here goes." But he finished his cigarette and lit another from it and finished that, like a horse balking at an impossibly high jump.

"The phone call?" she prompted. "Who was it?"

"Sister Gabriel. She's legal, an American citizen, which makes her omnipotent. Under divine protection, you might say." Now that he had begun, he talked at a breakneck pace as though there might not be time to say everything. "She used to teach school and deliver babies and such stuff in the Guazapa region, but got kicked out."

"And what . . . ?" Felicity paused. She felt queasy, stirred by a compulsion to ask as well as an enormous reluctance to do so. "What does she . . . what do you . . . want of me?"

"For now, a tiny thing—though who knows what is tiny? It could always end up costing your life. A mysterious accident, they happen all the time. Or they could disappear you." He watched the effect of his words. Her eyes did not waver from his, but they gave away nothing. "Or possibly I won't ask anything of you," he said. "Depends on my courage too, whether I can take the risk. We're afraid of everyone, including you."

"Afraid of *me*?"

"How do I know you're not with *la migra*?"

"*La migra?*"

"The immigration people. Always decent. Infallibly polite and sincere when they ship us back to our deaths. One stray comment, one moment of misplaced trust, and I'm done for. If I'm sent back . . ." He drew his finger across his throat and she saw the slash, smelled something foul, like shit. She wrinkled up her nose in shock.

"That's the smell of fear," he said.

"How do you know this would happen?"

"It's already happened to my father and younger brother. My younger brother was a mistake, they meant to get me." He sucked in smoke, made a decision, recited a biography as though rattling off something distasteful, rote homework. He was the son of a reasonably prosperous businessman in Morazin province. His father had dreams for his sons: an American education, business or law school, entrepreneurial energy, the vanguard of benign reform. And then last summer . . . "Nothing daunted my father," he said, "but it wasn't easy times for a business. He wanted my help for a year before I came back here for college. So I went back home, I made the deliveries for him . . . had to drive to the craziest places . . . a sewing-machine business—"

"My God," Felicity said. "There was an article last year . . . I clipped it, I have it in my—"

"Quite possible, he loved to—"

"But they said that you . . . Trog said you smuggle cheap labor across the border for your own factory—"

He laughed sourly. "Is that what they said?"

"A parts factory in Medford."

Angelo looked alarmed. "I did work there," he said. "Two jobs back. They're unpleasantly close on my tail."

"And last summer?" she prompted. "When you went home?"

"Home from green, green Connecticut," he said bitterly. "I can't believe how green I was. Spouting American high-school idealism, liberty and justice for all, the whole fantasy. Incredibly stupid of me. You go away a few years, you forget."

The usual story, Angelo said. The knock at the door in the middle of the night, the disappearances, the bodies found in a ravine the next day. Except that Angelo was out on a village delivery run.

"Why do you think it was you they wanted?"

"Because I was the one with the big mouth."

"Who did this?" she asked.

"Who knows? Could have been the guerrillas because

207

we were pro-America. Could have been the army because we talked reform. They didn't say, we didn't ask."

"You can apply for refugee status," Felicity said. "It's a clear-cut—"

"Did apply. Didn't get it. No hard evidence of risk, they said. That's when I went black instead of trying for Canada. I take one day at a time. Sometimes I take calculated risks, like talking to you."

"I can give you my word—"

"You're a calculated risk," he said. "But we scavenge for ports in a storm."

Felicity felt weighted with lead. She had a sensation of burning faggots being piled high around her chair. Whatever he's going to ask, she thought, I won't be able to say no, and I'll be afraid to say yes. She said morosely, "I wish I hadn't crossed the border when I did."

"Oh *borders*," he said savagely. And then: "Look, I'm not going to twist your arm. I don't think I'm going to ask anything at all. You've already saved a life. Well, prolonged it anyway. Everything's temporary."

"I was going to notify the authorities," Felicity faltered. "I do believe they would have been humane. But I'm relieved she's safe."

"No one's safe. ORDEN is active and so are extremists on the left. Everywhere."

"Orden?"

"Paramilitary. Ultra right-wing. They have ties with a number of U.S. groups. They stalk us here, and send death threats to the remnants of our families back home. So does the left."

"It's difficult to believe," Felicity said.

"I expect so," he said coldly.

"I'm frightened," she said, "because you knew how to contact me. I'm frightened of Hunter."

"We shouldn't have contacted you. We only do it because we're desperate. I won't ask anything. You've done enough."

"Who is Hunter?"

"We're not sure," he said. "Possibly CIA. Possibly ORDEN—one of their local links, the vigilante type, the

208

kind of right-wing zealot who . . . And then again, possibly he's a thug for the left, they have their own kind of fanatic." He drained his beer mug as though imbibing recklessness. "I've been trying to decide whether it's crueller to tell you or not to tell you . . ."

A whirlpool sucked at Felicity. She felt dizzy, and drank quickly to steady herself. Against her will, she pressed: "To tell me or not to tell me what?"

"The extent," he sighed, and trailed off. He rolled another cigarette and signalled for a jug of beer. She waited, afraid he would finish his sentence, afraid he would not. When the jug came, he filled their glasses, raised his in a sardonic toast. "You won the lottery," he said. "You're a VIP. From your point of view, you saved the wrong person. Everyone's after Dolores Marquez."

Felicity closed her eyes and saw the flame trees, the twitching cow, the crow flying off with its eyes. I was marked from birth, she thought helplessly. But the crow-demon has choked, said her *ayah*, and has fallen to earth like a stone. You turned away too soon.

You are a teller of tales, Felicity accused. And a dreamer of dreams. And my father was a madman to leave me alone in the world.

You are possibly right, he called from his fishing boat. I accuse myself of madness and arrogance. And yet I don't know how I could have done differently.

You've tainted me, she wept. I'm marked.

Angelo waited. Felicity felt infinitely weary. She seemed to be reading lines for a part she had been trying to refuse all her life. "Why is everyone after Dolores Marquez?" she asked.

"Her husband joined the guerrillas. But the guerrillas believed he was a government spy and shot him. Both sides seem to think she knows too much. Some say she's a guerrilla commando in her own right, others say she's an army informer."

"And is she?"

Angelo shrugged. "I won't swear to anything. I've been told she sends back reports to the army on all of us. I've been told she'll betray me to the left. Who knows?

209

Somebody sent my mother a death threat, somebody sent *la migra* to my door. It could have been anyone." He raised his beer again, in a mock salute. To insanity, perhaps. "The thing is, I met Dolores on the back roads, we hid in ditches together from army bombings, we bribed border guards together, she fucked them to get us both through. Doesn't necessarily prove anything. Probably she doesn't trust me either. But I'm a gambler, why not? My bet is she has only two allegiances: to her children and to survival."

Her children.

Oh unfair, Felicity thought. Below the belt. I don't want to know about her children. Felicity knew what she wanted to do. She wanted to wake up into last week. Before Friday, before the border. All this, she wanted to convince herself, is about a painting. About a dream about a painting. About Perugino's way with expressive eyes. She looked around her: an ordinary smoky tavern halfway between Harvard Square and Central Square. Student couples discussing love and summer school. Obviously nothing irregular could happen, nothing fantastic. She had stumbled into someone else's nightmare, that was all.

Angelo's face was green and bearded with smoke. His dreadlocks twitched about his shoulders like snakes. He was talking, talking, words dribbled from his mouth like bile, he had no right. He took out black pictures as though the dark made them safe. Flash cards, all dirty, flouting the obscenity laws. They're all done in invisible ink, he said; they disappear in the clean, clean light of America.

You have no right, Felicity said. I don't want to hear. But his voice and his visions surged on in antiphonal chant, piling up bodies in ditches and garbage dumps, telling of mutilations.

Really, Felicity, a chorus of voices reminded. *Really*, what *will* . . . ?

These things are excessive and hallucinatory, she said. They cannot be real. They are in such bad taste.

Oh definitely, agreed Angelo. In very bad taste. There's a cauldron in my mind full of toads. Once in a while, he said, I lift the lid and let a memory or two escape. Because they vanish in American air. They're invisible here.

210

Felicity watched one of his memories spill out and disperse itself.

A raggle-taggle group is walking along an unpaved road. When the A-37s fly over, swooping low and dropping bombs, the people dive into ditches and under bushes for cover. When the planes fly on, they straggle back along the road. There are a lot of children, little ones, who are hungry and tired, but no one can stop. They have to reach Tenango by nightfall. An A-37 flies over. In the ditch there is a woman on top of Angelo and she is moaning in labor. The plane moves on, Angelo helps the woman back onto the road. She gives a cry and leans against him, he is supporting her by the armpits, she is squatting, moaning. She gives birth, he severs the cord with a sharp stone, she picks up the baby, they move on. Angelo asks her name and she says Dolores Marquez.

"I can't listen to this," Felicity said. "Stop it."

Angelo did not hear or could not stop. "The baby was dead before the next morning," he said. "We didn't have time to bury it. We left it under a tree and covered it with some branches but I looked back and saw the vultures and crows before we'd gone a hundred feet."

"Stop it," Felicity begged, protecting her eyes with her hands.

"But she has two other children," Angelo said. "They're with her mother in a village near Copapayo. At least . . . we hope so."

Felicity was rocking her head in her hands, exorcizing visions. Really, Felicity, whispered the aunts.

"It isn't possible," she said. "It isn't possible to give birth like that."

"None of it's possible," said Angelo. "None of it's real. But it happens."

He was moving his beer mug in circles, creating a whirlpool, and she saw that it was full of blood. He drank it calmly. I'm going to wake up now, she said. I'm going to leave. I'm going to get out of bed and make coffee. These are sticky nightmares, Angelo warned. It's harder than you think to escape. But no one would blame you. Go quickly, while there's time.

"Damn you," she said. "Damn you." She could not move.

Angelo's hand reached out of the dream with a memento from the other side. A photograph.

"These are her children," he said. "And her mother. This was her talisman. We all need a piece of magic to keep going.

"The thing is," he said, "there's no telling what bitterness will require. We become the puppets of our personal wounds. Maybe her bitterness will require her to turn me in: to *la migra*, to the army, to the left. Maybe for her I have the face of Judas, maybe I smell of the man who shot her husband, who knows?" He shrugged. "If she has to, she has to. But I'll take my chances."

"It was the birth," he said. "Being there. I feel responsible for a life. I'll never live long enough to have a child of my own, so I . . ." He forgot to keep talking. He was looking at a tree under the sign of the vulture. "We all have to have an unrealistic obsession," he said. "Something stronger than fear, something to keep us going. For her, it's those children. For me, it's her." He picked up the photograph of her children and stared at it. "That's why I paid her fare on the meat truck. One thousand dollars, and cheap at the price, since the driver got caught, poor fool." He shrugged. "I get four dollars an hour washing dishes, all cash, no taxes. What else am I going to spend it on?"

"Trog said . . . About the murder . . . You're sure it's not . . . that she's not . . . ?"

"If she'd been killed, they wouldn't be trailing you. It's *her* they're still after."

He sipped from his tankard of blood. "What I'm asking," he said, "the little thing I'm asking, is that you get the photograph back to her. She needs it more than food. There was a last-minute panic with the meat truck here, someone tipped off *la migra*, but the truck got away (or so we thought). I found the photograph after the dust had settled."

Felicity picked up the photograph, and once she had touched it, thought: I am branded now.

"I have this impossible dream," he said, "of keeping her

212

alive until it's safe to go back. This crazy beautiful dream."
He laughed. "A serviceable obsession. I've pencilled the
Montreal contact address on the back of the photograph.
Ask for Casa del Diablo, it's a restaurant."

"Oh no," Felicity groaned. "What do you mean, *ask for*?
Do you mean I have to go through another circus like
today's? Trying to find a number that doesn't exist.
Making a fool of myself, wandering from a watch clinic to
a barber shop—"

"Barber shop!"

"The barber shop with the tacky religious statues in the
window."

He was startled. "You went *there*?"

"Wasn't it part of the cloak-and-dagger scheme?"

"What scheme? What are you talking about? Why did
you go there?"

Felicity began to feel that inner sensation of frenzied
wings again. "The watch repairman sent me. Who is he?"

Angelo had the look of a man who is cornered but is
planning to make a run for it, to fight to the end. "He's
our watcher, that's all. Sympathetic. He gave Dolores a
cash job, no questions asked. You should have told me he
sent you there. Tell me, the statue of the hand—"

"What a dreadful piece of kitsch! Quite extraordinarily
tasteless."

He leaned across the table and grabbed her wrist.
"Listen," he said urgently. "Can you remember the
arrangement of the signs on the fingertips?"

"The signs? You mean the saints?" Felicity closed her eyes,
summoning up the image. "I remember that the Sacred
Heart was on the thumb. And Our Lady of Guadaloupe
was on the middle finger, I think . . ."

"That's that, then," Angelo said and began to laugh. He
laughed till beer dribbled from his mouth and tears rolled
down his cheeks, and the laughter bounced back at Felicity
from every surface like ping-pong balls, like tiny skulls,
like the ricocheting heads of gargoyles. Angelo rose into
its deafening fog and lurched drunkenly out.

She was alone in a dingy pub with a creased Kodak
snapshot of two children and an old peasant woman.

213

26

Euclid might be adduced: the lifelines of Felicity and Gus, having intersected once, were destined never to meet again. Does this help? Geometry as salve?

Or I could posit a sarcastic Prime Mover.

All in all, however, it might be simpler to resort to the exotic. In India, I understand, human history is seen as the *lila* or sport of the gods. This makes good sense. Perhaps it was this that seduced Felicity's father: a release from the Western compulsion to find *meaning*. If nothing is meant to make sense, if it's all a cosmic farce, then everything is so much more tolerable. Or at least less intolerable. So Felicity says.

In South India, she tells me, there is an inside-out version of the Sisyphus myth. Perhaps the monsoon, so essential and capricious, is conducive to stories of this kind. A man pushes the familiar rock up the same steep hill, but his purpose is not to get to the top and the story is not about futility and despair. After each hard-won morsel of climb, the rock plunges back to the bottom and the man dances and laughs and claps his hands. He puts his shoulder to the rock again, he sweats, he grunts, he gains fifty feet—for the sheer pleasure of watching that boulder get nowhere.

I like that story.

What I am groping for is something to lessen my sense of guilt—although any sane person would surely agree that it is quite irrational to feel guilt. (Would *you* have taken her seriously if she had called you from The Plough and Stars with such an improbable tale?) But the fact remains that if I had not been so bemused by the garbled story of a birth, if I had not on that account tuned out a thousand and one extraordinary details, if I had not

214

interrupted, if I had given her a chance to tell me that Dolores Marquez had not after all been murdered, if I had just *listened* . . . this story might have been different. I would not feel I had aided and abetted two obsessions.

At the time, it seemed like a fantastic game. Felicity being Felicity. And Gus? Well. A philanderer's remorse. A Catholic with guilt and visions. These can be taken seriously?

And yet, if Gus had not just left when Felicity called back again from her office; or if I had not told him that his Magdalena had been murdered; or if I had not assured Felicity that Dolores was still at her cottage . . . If Felicity had called me earlier than she did, if she had filed more progress reports . . .

"I've met him," I told her. "Your insurance salesman."

"What?" She was back in her office but still seeing the tree that grew under the sign of the vulture.

"Augustine Kelly. Likable, but a hopeless innocent."

"You've met him?" Nothing makes sense, her inflection said.

"I know." (I can answer her thoughts, we have always been this way.) "It's a long story. But he's been here and we've talked for hours."

"I don't want him to know," she said urgently. "He's too trusting, too dangerous, he'll talk. It's all so much worse than we could have guessed. And now the photograph. And I'll have to get it to her."

"Get it to who?" It's not easy to follow her threads.

"To Dolores Marquez."

"Wait a minute," I said. "On my tape, if I recollect rightly, she'd been murdered, you'd seen a photograph of the body, you were frightened, you were being watched—"

"I still am," she said. "He's out there now. I can see him from my office window. But he's not from the FBI, and my car hasn't been impounded, it's in the lot, but it won't start, it's been tampered with. And she hasn't been murdered, I already *told* you that."

"No you didn't."

"I did. When I called from The Plough—"

215

"Well," I said. "How relieved she must be. So when Gus keeps insisting he saw her—"

"He *saw* her!" There was a leap in her voice. "Is he with you now?"

"Just left, and in appalling distress, poor fellow." (You have to cajole Felicity out of her black moods, you have to listen to the lower currents of her words.) "The murder was the last straw, and of course I wasn't aware it had un-happened. In his cups he has a tendency to confuse his wife and your mystery woman. Obsessed with both of them, anyway. I pointed out that he couldn't have seen her because—"

"But he could have! Tell me, was it in a restaurant off rue Maisonneuve?"

"No, no, not in Montreal, Fliss. You fail to appreciate the symbolic scope of his vision. He saw her near the cottage. Remember that old farm on the hill?"

"When was this?" she demanded.

"Yesterday afternoon."

"That's strange," she said. "Angelo gave me a Montreal—"

"The murder certainly threw him into a frenzy. He thinks he had a warning. Mind you, he'd been drunk and maudlin for hours, confessing all over my carpet. I think your Magdalena is a necessary distraction for him, an obsession to hang on to for the time being. Until his wife—"

"Near the cottage," Felicity said again. She sighed. "Another wild-goose chase, I knew it. I have this awful premonition . . ." She was not entirely coherent. She spoke of Trog and Hunter and Central Square and Angelo. She spoke of her father. "That's how it happened," she said. "Suddenly it makes sense. He never meant to leave me like that, he got caught in a riptide, there was nothing he could do."

"Fliss, what on earth are you talking about?"

"I think I'm caught in one," she said.

I waited for a translation, but she had gone off into one of her brown studies. She's given to long-distance thinking. "Fliss," I said dryly, "this is an expensive way to say nothing."

But all I achieved was an absently murmured, "I'll have to get hold of Angelo again, but how . . . ?" and then another long pause.

"Don't you think this calls for a touch of irony?" I asked.

"Some things don't, Jean-Marc."

"Aha. Success. At least you're listening to me."

But the volley petered out. Silence at $1.25 a minute.

"Fliss?"

She said something softly, but I didn't catch it. "I didn't hear . . ."

"I don't believe it." It was clear this time, though she seemed to be saying it to herself, or to the air. I will admit to a second of fear, to a garish scene played out in a split second in my mind: Hunter (I see him as one of those men grown into his function, a gorilla of a man whose fingers are gun muzzles, a billy club protruding between his legs), Hunter coming at her like a riptide.

"What?" I asked, a shade frantically. "For God's sake, Fliss, what—?"

"It's Seymour," she said wonderingly, and there was a break in her voice. "Oh it's Seymour."

"Well, hosannah, hosannah," I said. "The Old Volcano still active."

But it was wasted. She didn't so much hang up as forget she was holding the receiver. I could tell from the sounds of grope and clatter.

27

Felicity did not analyze why she moved between the phone and Seymour. By stealth, behind her back, the receiver found its way to its cradle, as though she were hiding a furtive conversation.

Not that this helped.

"Must be the piano tuner," Seymour laughed. "You get that maternal translucence. Very fetching." He moved about her office, picking up things and examining them in his usual proprietary way. "Still calling in, is he? Still running under your wings for protection?"

"I called *him*," she said.

That startled him. He could never imagine himself as anything but the center of everyone's circle. He raised an eyebrow. "Why?"

Could she even begin to sift all the reasons why she turned instinctively to Jean-Marc? She said only: "You don't even know him."

No.

It's not going to work.

Wishful thinking.

I know perfectly well they are more likely to discuss the properties of tuning forks than me. I might as well not exist once she sees him again. It defies explanation. It's an obsession. Like her idealization of her father, an irresponsible innocent (a Protestant Gus with a medical degree), tediously fixated on Doing Good. Two of a kind, he and the Old Volcano. Two forms of exhibitionism. Watch me, watch me, and to hell with everyone else.

No doubt the Old Volcano has planned a similarly flamboyant exit. Apotheosis in oils. Stop press: LAST

218

CANVAS! ARTIST PAINTS HIMSELF INTO A CORNER.

Hah.

So His Omnipotence has arrived, and Hunter disappears in a puff of smoke. Angelo and La Magdalena are so much dew in the rising sun. And what shall we do with the Rising Son? Put him in the long boat until the riptide takes him. Sometimes, Felicity, the limits of our extraordinary relationship are strained.

Enough.

This is not helping the enterprise. There is a riddle still to be solved and I have to make a more serious effort to discover what it felt like to *her*, because the key to the mystery could be right there: Felicity and the Old Volcano.

But I'll have to do it later. I'll have to come back to this. After I've tuned a piano or two, taken some stridency out of the air, tempered things. Note by note, that's how it has to be done. And then there are other, easier pieces of the puzzle that can be attended to first. Gus, for instance. Nine hours of drunken monologue, an encyclopedia of information.

Poor Gus. There is nothing original about a man who has just been abandoned. A comic stereotype. He rages, he drinks, he wallows in self-pity, he burdens with lamentations anyone who will listen, he panics, he lusts every which way, he is impotent. He feels himself to be going under, he clutches for an icon above the flux line, he invents a love (or recalls one) that soars like a helium balloon above his carnal ineptitudes. His suffering is appalling. It is unique and also banal. Embarrassing. Transforming. The stuff of kitsch and great art and religion.

When Beatrice snickered at Dante and turned away her face, he had his revenge, he swallowed her whole, he fashioned her after his own liking—immaculate and divine, untouchable by Dante or anyone else, forever and ever, amen. When Felicity left the Old Volcano, he raged and mourned in oils through a thousand and one paintings that made him famous. Everywhere he or anyone else looked, her lopsided eyes followed. As now, from over my desk. (I own only one of his paintings, because she gave it to me.) He was cunning, the Old Volcano: he reduced her to the rules of his own imagination, confined her within his own borders, a painter's perfect revenge.

And Gus? He added two saints to the St. Christopher medal dangling from his dashboard. He took them everywhere with him, divine protectors: St. Therese and Our Lady of Sorrows.

28

There was scarcely room for Gus in his own Chevy, surrounded as he was by so great a crowd of witnesses, all the saints and holy martyrs and the women he had wronged. His wife, his four daughters, Jillian of the flower shop (still waiting for him, perhaps, by the bridal bouquets), the young mother whose name he could not even remember scattering insurance policies and perfume as she came, the girl in the hotel room in New York, all the girls in all the hotel and motel rooms and back car seats of his life. They wore long white robes and sang the *Kyrie Eleison*, dropping it note by note into his ears, a soprano ointment. They waved their palm branches before his eyes. They made it difficult to drive.

Down the corridors of their singing, dimly, he could see the veil that hid La Magdalena from his eyes. Now she had a name: Dolores Marquez. He said it several times, the way he had said the rosary as a boy, experimentally, cautiously, half afraid of its potency. Dolores. She was brighter than the sun. Even through the veil she blinded him. The blood of her martyrdom flowed like a river, it lapped at the banks of his General Motors upholstery (torn in several places), it welled out of the ashtrays, it fed a tributary system in his eyes.

Murder!

The word bubbled up out of his mind like a toad. Horrible. If it was true, the whole world was a swamp. He might as well go under, he could taste the mud. He felt queasy and not entirely sober. It was over thirty hours since he had slept. Perhaps he had leaned unduly on Jean-Marc's whiskey. His bloodshot eyes flickered some blurry warning and a hundred car horns suddenly trumpeted the imminence of the Day of Judgment. Shaking,

221

he pulled into a gas station and drank three cups of black coffee. Blinked. The world came into slightly better focus.

He tried Marthe's house one more time. He made a fool of himself hammering at her locked front door. Already, but to no avail, he had made more phone calls than there were years in his marriage. Marthe's fault. She must have taken her phone off the hook, she was poisoning Therese's mind, she had never approved of Gus.

Anglais, she sniffed at the wedding. (In Montreal, this means simply: Not French.) Show me *un Anglais* you can trust, and I'll show you a man who's taken French leave of his own history.

Where was she keeping Kathleen? And the little ones? He sobbed at the thought of his unfathered children.

Therese's face appeared at an upstairs window, as cold and remote as the moon.

"*Trop tard*," she said. Too late for tears. "If you don't go away, I will call the police."

How was it possible? For better or for worse, she had sworn. Till death us do part. "You're not giving me a chance," he pleaded. He wanted to speak of his transformation, of new beginnings, though his tongue was not entirely cooperative.

"Look at you," she said. "You should be ashamed to let the children see you in such a state. Listen to you."

"But you don't understand . . ."

"Nor do you," she said. She was not vindictive, only impossibly weary of it all. "I'm all used up," she told him. "I've been chewed and spat out. There's nothing left. You'll have to feed off someone else."

"But something has happened . . ." How could he speak of a miracle, of rebirth in an apple orchard, when he was shouting up from the street?

"Please go away," she said tiredly. "You only make it harder for the children when you go on like this." She closed the casement.

Gus sat on the curbstone, seasick. He had to wait for the sidewalk to grow calm. His life was threatened by high waves. Reggie! he cried from the depths. I'm going under.

222

And Reggie called over the storm: You gotta find something to hang on to. You gotta *believe*.

Then he saw La Magdalena's sad and beautiful face in the heart of a peony, right there in his sister-in-law's front garden. Unsteadily he rose to his feet. She was beckoning him. Come, she said. Her body was embroidered with wounds. To L'Ascension, she said. The scene of my transfiguration. And he followed without question.

His car battled high seas. He had to make temporary harbor for gas and more black coffee. There was a television set on the snack counter in the gas station and he saw three murders between one cup of coffee and the next. Dread seized him. It was not a safe century to live in. On the road again he drove in a state approximating prayer, vowing restitution and making deals: if these horrors could be reversed, he would do such and so with the rest of his life. All of it was noble.

There seemed to be a pain about the size of a football lodged in his chest cavity, slightly to the left of center. If he had not needed both hands on the wheel, he could have reached in and got it. He knew what it would look like: a bloodied wad of threads—his writhing muscles—knotted around Therese's tears and La Magdalena's wounds. He was beginning to have difficulty with his breathing. He knew it was essential to avoid even a stray thought about the details of the murder, he could not afford to glimpse even one of the forty-six stab wounds. He was so sober now that he could feel the sharp edges of seen objects against his eyeballs, and the signpost to L'Ascension came at him like a guided bowie knife, a gouger, blinding white. He managed the turn, then had to pull off the shoulder of the back road and close his bloodshot eyes till the throbbing subsided a little. Its message was clear: he had left her alone at the cottage; she had been murdered; therefore he was guilty. Fresh paroxysms of pain jolted him. There was a thrumming axis from his eyes to his chest.

He went back to dickering with God and scaled down his side of the deal: if he could just find some clue as to why, to all the whys, then he would devote his whole future, etcetera. He started the car, his crowd of passengers lurched about his ears with the unexpected momentum, they burst into startled song. L'Ascension flew by his window, the dove of a departing spirit. He was dropping through loops of dirt road toward the cottage.

Visions scudded towards him: gargoyles, apple orchards in flames, griffons on bat wings, bloodied sides of beef. He prepared to swerve for the Other Car, a hearse, its headlights always blazing. One scorching nick of those lights and a driver was dead. There was a web of tire marks around the cottage, a geometry of malediction. The Other Car circled and reversed, circled and reversed, driving Gus closer to the eye of the web. He rubbed his fly legs together and prayed.

He turned a last loop in the road and saw the cottage.

There *was* a car.

Two men on the cottage steps, beer, cigarette smoke. Evidently he had made a mistake. The cottage looked like Felicity's, but then all cottages looked much the same in this part of the world. It was odd the way those men drank their beer, unsmiling, with excessive concentration, as though they had been waiting for an interruption. As they came towards him, there was a suggestion of swagger, almost; of defiance.

"Sorry," Gus said. "Looking for a friend's cottage and got mixed up. I'll just back out of your driveway."

"Who were you looking for?" one of the men asked. He looked strangely familiar and there was something about him that made Gus nervous. Better not to answer, he decided. He started his engine and called over it, "Sorry to bother you." He was trying to remember where he had seen the man before.

"I believe you have a flat tire," the man called back.

It was true. Gus could feel the crippled lurch of his car. Must have been something sharp on the driveway.

"We'll help you fix it," the man offered. Gus could not quite remember him. "You might as well have a drink with us first."

Gus was wary of people who did not smile, though the man seemed convivial enough in a restrained way. Perhaps they were simply the kind who did not know how to let themselves go, who fished and hunted from obsession or social obligation rather than for pleasure. They opened a new case of beer. The talk was of local lakes and of the trials of cottage owners: vandals, transients, squatters, border smugglers, summer violence, unsuitable people buying up the surrounding land or renting it for the season or just appearing, like gypsies. Something that was said almost tripped a switch in Gus's mind, but he lost the clue again.

"Haven't we met somewhere before?" he asked.

"Possibly," the man said. "We're hunters. We get around."

"I'm Gus Kelly."

"Pleased to meet you, Gus. Have another drink."

Such attentive hosts, they were, and such good listeners. They kept Gus plied with drinks and questions, they commiserated about Therese. When he spoke of strange events, they did not sneer but took an interest. Encouraged, he poured out his heart. He talked himself into an ever greater thirst.

There's more beer in the cottage, he heard one of them say, so he went after another bottle. Inside it was exactly the same as Felicity's cottage. Same casement windows through which the Other Car had flashed its lights, same large wooden closet she had kept opening and closing, same table they had sat at, same kerosene lamp, same bedroom off to one side. Perhaps cottages were made on assembly lines.

Dolores Marquez appeared and stood there in her torn black dress, her face pale. He reached out to touch her but his hand moved through space. I have had too much to drink, he confessed. She smiled sadly and vanished. He had to go into the bedroom, he had to touch the bed, just to touch it. Even the arrangement of bedroom furniture was the same as in Felicity's cottage. Same kind of quilt on the bed. He bent to touch it and saw the dried bloodstain and then he saw the shoes: an old, worn black leather pair, misshapen, cracked, alive with fungus. Peasant shoes.

The pain was back in his chest and eyes. There were lights popping in his head, his breath staggered in the

225

effort to reach his lungs. The walls were closing in on him. Through the window the Other Car dipped its headlights and leered.

It happened here, he thought, and felt violently ill. Dizzy, he went back to the porch. He passed between the two men unharmed and lurched down the steps. "Left something in my car," he mumbled. They fell silent and looked at him strangely. They circled him. Now he could see their horns and cloven feet. He leaped into his car and started it. Your tire, your tire, they called. But he was not fooled. He reversed, but the car skewed itself sideways, he had to do a three-point turn. Their eyes were red in the early evening sun. Their thirst for blood was up. He could taste his own terror rancid on his tongue. He accelerated and was free. He flew. He ignored the car's wild limp, he drove flat tire and all, cavorting and swerving like a damned soul in a lake of hot pitch. He did not stop in L'Ascension.

On the highway he pulled into a service station and vomited copiously behind the trucking area while his tire was changed. I abandoned her, he thought. (He meant Dolores Marquez and Therese.) I am damned forever.

Where could he go? Where could he hide from his own crimes? He found himself back in Montreal, the oldest part—narrow streets, narrow houses, dilapidation. He found a boarding house as derelict as his life and paid for a room. It did not surprise him that the place smelled of rotten meat and vomit. He followed the wide road of stink along a corridor to a numbered room. He turned the key.

In his room there were further signs: the mirror over the dresser was cracked; and a fur of mold, which had been gathering quietly on the walls all summer, was running amok. Moss everywhere. Hummocks of it on the ceiling, the windows bleary with slime-green growth, the floor busy with slugs and earthworms.

A fitting place.

He knew he was living in hell.

Really, Jean-Marc, Felicity will say, how terribly gothic. How *Catholic* of you.

But Kathleen likes it. It could have been . . . she admits.
(She has his letters from that time.) Poor daddy, she sighs.
(His letters appear to have been written on crumpled toilet
paper from an infernal outhouse.) It was mummy and
Aunt Marthe's fault, Kathleen says. They lied to me, they
never let me know he called and tried to see us.

Poor daddy, she sighs again.

29

There is an old Baldwin piano in Outremont that survived a bomb blast. This was back at the time of the Québecois turmoils. Some of the pins and strings melted, keys were scattered like loose teeth. A predecessor of mine had restrung it, but new strings take time to settle down, sometimes years, a lifetime even. When the instrument's history was given me over the phone, I was not hopeful. Don't expect miracles, I warned. But the Baldwin surprised me. Damage, like violence, ebbs and flows, I suppose. I worked for an afternoon, and the new owner was delighted—not that he's any judge of tone—but the thing is, even I was delighted.

"I'm surprised," I said. "I thought the mutilation would be permanent."

"Oh that." He brushed away old history with a wave of his hand. He is working-class French, a policeman, frugal and aspiring. Politics embarrasses him. He picked up the Baldwin for a song in a Westmount garage sale because he knows a good deal when he sees one, and because he wants the best for his children who take music lessons from *un Anglais*. "That's a long time ago, all that," he said.

"Not so long," I told him. "I can still remember."

"Ah," he smiled indulgently. "You're young. The young think disasters are unique."

When I came home, Felicity was in my living room. That's her style. She's always had a key, and still does. Now do you understand why I can't get too upset about the disappearance? It's true a year has gone by, a long time, longer than ever before, but just the same, I'll come home one day and she'll be there, chatting with Kathleen. I got sidetracked, she'll say. I was climbing some Aztec ruins and I didn't notice the time. When I looked at my watch and saw a year had gone by, I was truly . . .

I've heard so much about you, Kathleen will say. And my father . . . you knew him, Jean-Marc says . . .

Heavens! Felicity will laugh. I almost forgot. He's on his way.

"Jean-Marc!" Felicity cried, jumping up when I came in fresh from the Outremont Baldwin. I am never prepared for her bear hugs. She smelled of something exotic and musky, like forbidden flowers in a rain forest. "I hope you don't mind?"

"Why would I mind?" She always makes me laugh, she always makes me feel as though the circus has arrived. I had to go into the kitchen. I hadn't slept for a week, wondering where she was spending her nights. I hadn't slept since the phone call that was interrupted by the Old Volcano.

"You were wrong about the cottage," she said. "I went there first. There've been vagrants, squatters, frightful mess. Dishes left dirty, a pair of men's shoes in the bedroom. Everyone says it's getting worse, some people are selling, they've had enough." She was picking up things from my kitchen counter, putting them down again. "Anyway, no sign of Dolores Marquez. He couldn't have seen her. He must have been mistaken."

"So," I said. My voice sounded casual. Unwavering. "Why has he turned up in Boston again?"

She wandered back into the living room, she couldn't keep still, she examined the books on the coffee table, took others down from the shelves, put them back again. "Your library is taking over the house," she said. "You've put up more shelves, I see. Soon you'll have to move out. I see you're into Dante again." She flipped through the *Inferno*, put it down again. "My God, you should just see that mess in the cottage. Must have been teenage boys." She stopped suddenly in the middle of the room, colliding with a thought.

"So," I said pointedly, because he's always there between us, the Old Volcano, and Felicity is such an old pro at changing the subject. "Where is he now?"

229

She blinked at me, wide-eyed. It took her several seconds to disengage from her thought. "Oh," she said. "That. I was hoping you'd know. Is he *sure* he saw her in the orchard?"

"What?"

"You said he saw her. Or thought he saw her."

"Saw who?"

"Dolores Marquez." She's impatient if you can't read her mind. "That's what you told me."

I couldn't help smiling. I never know if it's one-track tenacity or brilliant subterfuge. She always makes life seem deliciously absurd.

"Oh Fliss," I laughed. "Honestly."

"Do you know where he is?" she persisted.

"Gus Kelly? Haven't a clue. Haven't seen him since his visit a week ago, poor drunken bugger. Wish I'd had a chance to tell him the murder was cancelled."

"That's not very funny, Jean-Marc." She took a deep breath. It seemed to be a sigh of relief. "Well then," she said. "I don't see that there's anything more I can do." She opened a window and leaned out to watch the street. I joined her. Our forearms touched on the sill.

"Where'd you leave your car?" I asked.

"There." She pointed to a maroon Ford.

"Good grief," I laughed. "How dull. What happened to the wild blue chariot?"

"Don't laugh, Jean-Marc. Its brakes had been tampered with, among other things. I'm scared to drive it. I'm scared to drive any one car for too long now. I rented three different ones along the way."

"Are you serious?"

She ran her fingers through her long hair and her hands were shaking.

"Fliss," I said carefully. "Are you running away from him?"

"It's all so crazy," she said. "There *was* a Casa del Diablo at the address, but it was a blind alley. A complete dead end."

"Fliss."

"What?"

"Don't evade," I said. I was seeing the two of them,

Felicity and the Old Volcano, standing there with the receiver forgotten between them. "What happened?"

"I had to be careful. I told the waiter Angelo sent me and I had a message for Dolores. There was no reaction, so then I said Dolores Marquez. Nothing. I tried her other names, La Salvadora, La Desconocida. Nothing. I didn't think I should show the photograph . . ."

"Dammit!" I shouted. "Stop treating me like a child!" I admit I lost all self-possession. I admit, in retrospect, this was stupid. I know perfectly well Felicity can worry at a single thought for hours. I went storming around the room at full throttle while she followed, chirping and skipping, a distressed mother dove in the wake of a fledgling. She followed me into the kitchen.

"Jean-Marc," she said. "Is this about Seymour?"

I had to laugh.

"He asks about you," she sighed. "I wish you could forgive. I wish you'd visit us."

She never quits trying, Felicity. On the subject of fathers, she's a hopeless romantic. I stared at her. I do wonder (still) if the extent of her blindness is possible. And also the extent of her obsession. It is really beyond understanding, what she sees in him. "Visit us?" I said. "Are you telling me, are you actually telling me . . . ?" But words failed me.

She turned away. I'd never seen her blush before, not that I can recall. Actually blush. "I couldn't go back to my own apartment," she said. "It's been ransacked."

"Oh well, naturally," I said. "Reason enough."

"One of the reasons."

"So what are you doing here?" I asked. "Been abandoned already?" I was clutching at straws, I admit it.

I know she showed me the photograph. I remember a grainy surface, an old woman, two children. A part of me must even have listened, heard, absorbed, because afterwards I pulled details back from somewhere. But I know I didn't consciously take in much at the time. I know I was aware of my anger as of a time bomb, ticking, ticking. I know I wanted to protect myself from twin possibilities: from grovelling, and from committing mayhem.

231

Mr. Piano Tuner to the fore. El Magico, the mathematician, transformer of discord into smooth tones. "I think you'd better leave," I said coolly. "You know how he hates to be kept waiting. When he snaps his fingers, I'm sure you'll want to be there." I can be, when occasion calls, a master of arch savagery. I can dart in with the quip modest, the reply churlish, the reproof valiant.

But I went too far. I have never seen her since. If only . . .

Ah, your "if" is the only peacemaker.

When she calls at last from wherever she is, I'll say simply: "I'm sorry, Fliss. On whatever terms you want, you're welcome."

30

Felicity woke in the middle of the night and stepped ashore into Seymour's Boston studio. Beneath her feet the floorboards were cool as wet sand. She could hear gulls calling from a dream: this way, this way. Behind her, Seymour rocked gently on waves of sleep, the dark lapping at the edges of his sixty-third year, the white sails furled around him, the rigging slack.

In the act of leaving, she turned back to look at him again. He was dreaming energy, even in sleep he never stopped wrestling with age. All his hair was gray now, and soft as down. His body was covered in tightly wound coils of it, a skinsuit of chain mail with only his vulnerable parts exposed. She was tempted back. He was as familiar and as natural and as dear to her as the country of memory. He could not be lost. She laid her cheek against his thigh and breathed in his yeasty smell and nuzzled his prick. It stirred in sleep, and half in sleep he pulled her onto himself. She rode him gently, not wanting to disturb him, but he woke and laughed throatily to find himself moored to her. He slid to the edge of the bed and stood and walked with her growing like a passionflower from his root, her legs locked behind him. He was always defying his age. He paraded her around his studio, showing her off to the canvases old and new.

(Braggart! his son might have said, if he'd been there. Old goat on its hind legs!

Jean-Marc! Felicity might say. This is quite indecent. I had no idea you were such a voyeur.

You should have thought of that, I'll say, all those nights when I was a boy in the next room.)

"I had to come back," Seymour said. "I have a whole series in mind and you're the only possible model. I needed

233

you." (There were a number of questions his son might have asked. Has your latest nymphet run off with the paintbrush supplier? for example. But his son was not there.) "Not that I ever stopped painting you. You've always been there in my blues."

She rested her head on his shoulder and nibbled at the hollow of his neck.

·"It's time for us both to settle down," he said, as they rolled on the bed again. "I'll move all my work back into this studio, and we'll stay here from now on. What do you say?"

She stroked his hair and smiled and said nothing. She had never really thought of him as absent. She had her own ways of staving off loss and change.

"This Aaron," he said. "Are you still seeing him?"

"Does it matter?"

"What a question." He bit her nipples lightly, playfully, warningly. An imprint of possession. "A *businessman*! And I thought I had taught you discriminating taste. You'd rather be with him than me?"

"Don't be silly." She found it hard to understand his jealousy. He must have known why she had left him. (There's no point in trying to hang on to anyone, Jean-Marc, she once said. The more you try, the worse your chances.) She did not try to articulate this for Seymour. She talked with her hands. Her tongue explained to his flesh.

"Listen," he growled. He wanted to eat her. "Don't go whoring after abstractions like your father did. Don't talk to me about essence and mutability and renunciation. I want to touch and taste and smell. Don't tell *me* it's all the same whether or not you have this. And this. And this."

"Well?" he demanded, minutes or perhaps hours later, "is anything else like that?"

She smiled. "Nothing else," she admitted.

"This businessman, this Aaron. You used to spend the whole night with him?"

"No. Never."

"With anyone else? Ever?"

"Never with anyone else. Only with you."

234

"But then you left me," he said. "It was a cruel thing to do."

"That was a long time ago. I couldn't afford to be left."

"I would never have left you," he protested.

"Of course you would have. You keep coming back because you never had the chance to leave first."

"It's a rotten lie, but maybe it's true. Anyway, all these years, and I still can't sleep without wondering where you are. It's time we both settled down."

But she knew it was too late. She knew the riptide had her. "It's the photograph," she said. "It has a lien on me, it obligates me."

"It does nothing of the kind!" Seymour fumed. "It's just your wretched father's approval you're chasing. I want you to cease and desist."

"Do you remember Perugino's *Magdalena*?" she asked.

"Perugino," he sniffed. "The Mantuans bought his soul. He turned decorative after 1500. Dreadful stuff."

"But the *Magdalena* was earlier. Do you remember it?"

"Of course I do. Exquisite face."

"Dolores Marquez is her double," Felicity said. "Don't you think you can see the likeness in the little girl?"

He studied the photograph. "You have to stretch your imagination," he said dryly.

"Is it just me?" she sighed. "Everything's fantastic, everything's unreal." But then, she thought, so are so many things the Associated Press swears are happening. "The aunts think I dreamed the whole thing."

"Oh your aunts. They are very reliable weathervanes. They know which taboos must not be broken." He wadded the bedsheet into a microphone and mimicked some recent interviewer: "Could you tell us, Mr. Seymour, why your recent canvases appear to be a descent into a gratuitously violent form of post-modern narrative expressionism?"

"I would rather have dreamed it," Felicity said.

"I don't think you dreamed it," he said. "But I do think you're playing with explosives. These are violent times. I forbid you to have anything more to do with it."

235

31

The days clustered like crows and flew away. Seymour, at Felicity's request, went back to her apartment to get her clothes—the bare necessities. "It's unbelievable," he said. "You'd think a herd of elephants had been through it. I insist you come with me so you'll know the kind of mentality you're up against."

"I already know," she said. Each morning she found a reason for not going back there to look.

"But we have to go back for the paintings," Seymour said.

"We can do that later. Some other time."

"And we have to notify the police."

"But then I'd have to tell them about the border."

"Whatever side of the fence it's on," Seymour said, "it's a rank weed, violence. You can't be silent about it."

"I don't know," she said. She was thinking of Hester (*If you tell, they only hurt you worse . . .*) and of Dolores Marquez. "I'll think about it," she promised.

But the days went by and she saw no more sign of Hunter. She began to wonder if he had crawled out of some dark hole in her imagination. She disconnected the studio phone. (They both hated interruptions.) She went to her office each day, a safe world. She took refuge in history and efficiency, the next exhibition took shape, all its details budded and blossomed according to plan, except that the Perugino stayed in the Pitti Palace in Florence. She still kept up a newspaper file. These recent events in your life, the file told her, are no stranger than the daily electronic chatter of a thousand wire services.

Sometimes she called Jean-Marc, but the conversations were a little strained. There were so many topics to be avoided. Her car, she acknowledged, had been fixed and

Seymour had driven it to the studio. It shimmered outside in the street, an impossibly blue reproach. She did not drive anymore.

"And Hunter?" Jean-Marc would ask.

"Oh Hunter." She would laugh a little, embarrassed, self-deprecating.

Each day she took the subway to Harvard Square and walked to her gallery. She kept her eyes and her thoughts firmly on the Renaissance, a time of astonishing beauty in art and considerable brutality in politics. And civilization had survived it, an encouraging thought.

She flew to New York, she flew to Rome and Florence. She even stopped for a meal in Perugia. It had not changed much, she suspected, since the painter had left for Mantua, lured by rich patrons. Now there was a restaurant or two, a gas station. Otherwise, probably, it was much the same as in 1500. She described Perugia to Jean-Marc, but spoke mainly of paintings: those staying in Italy and those on their way to Boston. It was sad about the late Perugino canvases, she said. But after Mantua, he was fearful of offending—always the kiss of death for an artist.

Every Sunday Felicity took tea with the aunts and discussed the health of their wisteria and other such topics of interest. (Jean-Marc declined to sigh with her over this; he considered the festooning of a garden wall with wisteria, like the tuning of a piano, to be an accomplishment of no small significance.) Seymour was not invited to Beacon Hill. Felicity is going through a phase again, the aunts told each other over scones with jam and Devonshire cream.

At night, Felicity sat hunched in an armchair in the studio while Seymour painted. He worked as though time and paint were running out. He was febrile with energy, he could not sleep for excitement.

Felicity could not sleep for fear of her dreams.

Instead, with eyes open and glazed, she would drift back into the tropics. She staved off visions with details of bougainvillea and frangipani, she summoned up petals and stamens and leaves, the memory of primary colors comforted her. She braided lifelines of jasmine and scarlet flowers. It's time I went back, she thought.

To Seymour she said: I think I might organize a Gauguin exhibition next. She began to daydream the taste of mangoes. I would need to visit Tahiti, she said, for the catalogue notes.

She's imagining things again, the aunts said. She has dark circles under her eyes. She's not sleeping well. They clicked their tongues. It's that dreadful man, they said.

"If not Gauguin and Tahiti," she said to Seymour, "perhaps Mexico, or somewhere further south. When you think of it, Central and South America have always exerted a pull—El Dorado and so on. Perhaps: 'The Latin-American influence on the European Imagination.' What do you think?"

"I think it's a congenital disease," he said. "Your father's damned hankering after martyrdom. You can't leave well enough alone."

"I've been hearing bellbirds again lately," she said. "I used to hear them in the gully behind my grandparents' house. I expect there are bellbirds south of Mexico. When you think about it, it's ridiculous that I haven't been back to the tropics in all these years."

32

Gus had to move into the adjoining room in the boarding house. Too much moss. It bred in the fur lining of his mouth and escaped when he breathed, propagating itself like an obsession. It grew out of the moldings and the corners, it trailed pale green tendrils from the window frames. Over the bed a canopy moved like seaweed, the floor was soft as peat moss, the air sharp with rot.

The next room was worse.

He cleared a space in a third and camped there. He was always soaking wet. At night he sweated booze, it rose in a mist to the ceiling growth above him and fell again as gentle rain. His morning dew stank of Johnny Walker.

There was purpose and ritual to every morning. First he would state a proposition. If Therese would simply talk to him on the phone, or if Kathleen or any of his children would talk, then he would stop drinking, he would go to them immediately, he would etcetera etcetera to the greater glory of God and the happiness of his family. He would then dial Marthe's number; she would hang up rather vehemently; he would drink a little whiskey neat, for comfort and consolation.

Once Marthe paused long enough, before she hung up, to tell him, "Your voice sounds like a dog barking."

He was not surprised. He knew he was an animal. He looked at himself in the cracked bedroom mirror and saw the hairy face of a gorilla with a thatch of slime green on top, moss hanging from his ears like seaweed. He roamed the streets and got himself a dishwashing job. (From the kitchen he came, to the slop bucket it was fitting he return; dishes to dishes and dust to dust.) Sometimes he thought he saw the men who had been at Felicity's cottage. Sometimes they seemed to be following him. He was afraid his mind was going. It just shows that we never know, he said to fellow customers in the Mister Donut near his boarding house. There's horror around every corner. His air of conviction sent shivers along the spine. He acquired a small following. He could have written a lot of business.

On a number of occasions, Dolores Marquez appeared to him. She was brutally murdered, he told his audience in Mister Donut. Forty-six stab wounds because I abandoned her. And now she haunts me. He would drop whatever he was doing and follow her. He dropped a column of dinner plates and lost his job. He followed her through a labyrinth of sleazy streets to a Spanish restaurant in Old Montreal, and they gave him a dishwashing job. Through steam and soapsuds he would recite the catalogue of his life's errors; his need to achieve expiation was overwhelming. He would call and confess to Jean-Marc's tape.

Sometimes Jean-Marc himself would answer. "Where are you, Gus?" he would ask.

"In hell," Gus would say. "I'm a destroyer and a killer."

"Listen," Jean-Marc would tell him. "It's all a mistake. She hasn't been murdered at all. I gave you wrong information."

But Jean-Marc didn't understand. He couldn't see the true horror of things. "Are you back in Winston?" he would ask. "No," Gus would say. "I'm in hell. Will you call Therese and Kathleen for me? Marthe knows my voice, she hangs up."

"But I don't even know them," Jean-Marc would demur. "Look, why don't you come on over for a drink?"

"I can't," Gus would say. "I'm in hell."

He said the same in daily letters to Therese and Kathleen. He used whatever paper came to hand in the boarding house—pages and pages of promises and confessions. The postmark was Montreal, but he gave no return address.

One day, as he was scraping the remains of tacos and enchiladas from a stack of plates, Dolores Marquez appeared in the kitchen, and he brushed her arm. Flesh! An electrifying sensation. She was wearing an apron. She set a load of dishes in the sink.

240

"Are you really real?" he asked. "Are you really Dolores Marquez?"

She put her hand over her mouth in sudden fright. Her eyes darted about like black moths in front of a lamp. She never spoke. He had never heard her speak. He brushed the damp hair from her eyes, he touched her cheek.

"Do you remember me?" he asked.

She smiled her sad smile.

"I've found Dolores Marquez," he told Jean-Marc's tape. "You were right, she hasn't been murdered. I'm looking after her. She can't speak English, but she doesn't speak Spanish either. Pedro—he's the owner, and legal—says it happens to some of them. Too much shock."

Gus wrote a letter to Kathleen:

> I am making things right. You told me that day we were sanding the car that you just wanted to know. So I'm telling you the God's truth before you hear it from anyone else: Dolores Marquez sleeps in my room, but it's not what anyone thinks. I will swear on the Bible. I'm *responsible* for her, that's what it's about. You're my favorite, Kathleen, even though that's a sin. I wish you would talk to me. I wish you would visit. You can leave any messages with Jean-Marc Seymour, he's a friend, I'm enclosing his phone number and address.

Jean-Marc answered his doorbell, and a teenage fury pounded his chest with her fists. But she stopped in mid-assault, bewildered.

"I thought you were a woman," she said. "Isn't this where my father . . . ?" Jean-Marc was briefly astounded. It seemed the ghost of Felicity past. But then, of course, it was obvious. "You must be Kathleen Kelly," he said. He found her belligerence charming.

"You know about me?"

"I know your father."

"Are you one of my uncles?" she sniffed.

"I beg your pardon?"

"You look a bit like my father," she said. "I have all kinds of relatives we haven't seen for years. I thought maybe you were related."

"No, no. Just a friend." He was mesmerized. She had Felicity's hair and eyes, the same nervous gestures.

"Where's my father?" she demanded.

"I'm afraid I don't know, though he calls quite often. Somewhere in Montreal, I think."

"He's run off with another woman." She tossed her long hair. She ran a hand along one of his bookshelves. "He's abandoned my mother. He doesn't care about us in the least."

"That's not true," Jean-Marc said. "Your father's gone chasing his own salvation. He thinks about you all the time."

"Oh!" she said. She threw her arms around him and sobbed on his shoulder.

Jean-Marc felt a mantle alight on his shoulders. Old shackles fell from him, new powers were granted. He understood how gratitude and adoration could be addictive. It's as simple as this, he thought, as he stroked her hair. He saw an endless mirrored corridor of clowns. He heard the Old Volcano laughing. The glands are banal, he thought, and without subtlety. And life is such a stale joke—it's all managed with circles and mirrors, it's all been done before.

Abruptly she pulled away and picked up her mitts and scarf from the chair where she had tossed them. It was September, and the summer warmth had gone.

"Mummy will be waiting," she said. "And Aunt Marthe!"—she wrinkled up her nose—"You'd think she was running an army!"

"Please don't leave," Jean-Marc said.

She raised an eyebrow in surprise.

"If you stay long enough," he cajoled, "your father will call and you can talk to him."

She pulled off her mitts again. She pressed his hand to her cheek with gratitude and he thought: After all, we are far closer in age than the Old Volcano and Felicity. And Felicity was only eighteen when . . .

"How old are you, Kathleen?"

"Sixteen," she said.

33

On a strap-hanging morning on the subway, between one armpit and another, Felicity saw Hunter. He was watching her as a small boy watches an insect. The boy removes one wing, he pinches off a leg, he crushes the lower abdomen: merely to see what will happen.

Felicity's fear was so sharp and sudden that she lost bodily control. Humiliation. She could feel the warm trickle of her own water on her legs. When the train stopped at Harvard Square, she could scarcely breathe. She stayed close to the surging heart of the crowd that rose up to daylight, she flowed across the street in its shelter. When the tangle unravelled into side streets, she shivered from exposure. She was afraid to look behind her. She hailed a cab and got off at her gallery door.

At her desk, she rested her head in her hands. She could do nothing about the agitation of her muscles. The eyes of Dolores Marquez burned in the twilight of the gallery: This is the way it is, she said. A daily diet. You get used to it.

Felicity looked at the photograph in her wallet. The two little girls and the old woman stared impassively back. They told her nothing. She looked at her other photographs: her father was mending nets, preoccupied; her mother would not turn around. No messages there either. Nothing. She could not call the studio, since she herself had disconnected the phone; and when Seymour was working, he had nothing to say.

"And there is nothing you can do," Jean-Marc told her over the phone. "Except take care never to be alone. You didn't ask to have that photograph."

(Naturally I wasn't going to tell her that Gus, in full raving flight, thought he had found the woman. No point in stoking one obsession with another.)

243

"You didn't ask to have the photograph," I repeated.

"No," she sighed. "And yet I have it."

Perhaps that was when I began to feel truly alarmed. I can read her tones of voice, I'm an expert on Felicity's silences.

"Fliss," I cajoled. "You're not going to do anything rash and pointless, are you?"

"Rash." She weighed the word, turning it over. "Pointless," she said, prodding it. As though it might reveal something of the mystery of compulsion. I knew it was only a matter of time before she threw herself into the current of some action. Some futile gesture of expiation. Fear of Hunter and the disapproval of her own fear would drive her to it.

"I have too much, Jean-Marc," she sighed.

All the fifteenth century at her beck and call, she meant. And her own niche in art history; and the aunts and the Old Volcano and me. I can read her sighs. She had never gone hungry, she meant. She had never offered a dead child up to the crows. She had never had to flee for her life in a refrigerated meat truck. She was born in a goddamned hairshirt. She had her father's God-hungry blood in her veins.

"I know what you're doing, Felicity." I was working up a rage of anxiety. "It's arrogant of you, it's sick. You're chasing a myth. It's blasphemy, what you're doing. You think you've been singled out, you think there's some special plan, you think you've been chosen. Hah. You think God or anyone else gives a shit what car you're behind at a border? You have a very perverse understanding of the random, that's your problem. You're thirty-three years old, for God's sake, it's high time you—"

"Jean-Marc," she said, "you're shouting."

"Listen to me, Felicity, just listen. One art historian, one gallery curator, can save a painter or two from oblivion. One well-tuned piano is worth a roomful of concert performers. They're pricks, those soloists, every last one of them, and totally dependent on us. We're *sane*, you and me, we don't *want* center stage, so don't you dare do a prima donna exit . . ."

244

"Oh Jean-Marc, don't you see?" She was laughing. "We're all chasing the same thing, don't you see? It's stupid, I agree, but we're doomed to it. The piano tuner as God, I never thought I'd hear you admit—"

I slammed the receiver down.

"Shit!" I told Kathleen. "It's the Old Volcano all over again. An infectious disease."

I could still hear Felicity's laughter. A weird sound. Not mocking, not cruel. It made me think of the man who watches the boulder crashing down a hill in South India.

34

"You're not eating," Seymour said. "I don't trust so much translucence. It reminds me of your father."

Felicity turned from the window. "I saw Hunter today. I'm frightened."

"Your eyes," Seymour said. "It's the eyes."

Perhaps their fevers were contagious.

"There," he said. "In the window seat, stay there. With the light behind you." He bit the top off a paint tube, he squeezed paint directly onto his brush, he did the window upright and the sash, a stark cross rising from her shoulders like a falcon.

"You're not listening to me," she said. "You've been working as though you're possessed. And another thing: you're not eating properly. I'm worried."

"Take your shirt off. And don't interrupt. There isn't time."

He worked.

She went roaming in her own preoccupations.

At dawn he said, "I haven't got it yet, but I will." He massaged his hands. "Are you tired?"

"I don't know," she said, surprised, stirring in the thicket of a memory. She watched him, concerned, as he rubbed his stiff hands. There were age spots and knotted veins. "You're working too hard," she said.

"Jesus," he murmured, stroking her hair. "You're not sleeping or eating properly. You're so gaunt, so luminous, I can't tell which I want to do more, paint you or fuck you or eat you. They all feel the same to me these days."

"You shouldn't worry like this," she said. "You'll live to a hundred and three."

*　　*　　*

Felicity stopped at the newspaper kiosk by the subway entrance in Harvard Square. Instinct. The pressure of a stare on the curve of her neck. She scanned the magazine rack. *New Yorker, Atlantic, Esquire,* all those sedate fictions. Not there. Something coarser and grainier. She could smell the musk of violence. Of something unfashionable and not at all in good taste. Her eyes roved across *Le Monde, Die Welt, The Times.* Beyond sports, beyond the soft, sanctioned pornography, beyond even the news magazines and tabloids.

Over a plain black cover she met his eyes.

He was leaning against the Ticketron window, flipping pages, the magazine held high to shield his face. Hunter. She felt again the despicable craven lurch of several bodily functions. She wanted to demand: Who are you? but only a wisp of fear passed through her lips. She could not move.

"Did you want that?" a clerk asked Hunter.

"Just looking," he said.

He placed the magazine, open, behind the slats of the rack near Felicity and walked away. Felicity stared at his message: a naked woman spreadeagled over the front of an army truck, her ankles lashed to the bumper, her wrists bound to a rope running over the hood. A jackbooted soldier was sticking the muzzle of his submachine gun up her vagina.

Felicity had to lean on the magazine stand because of her dizziness. She clasped and unclasped her hands. She looked into the passing crowds but could not see Hunter. She paid for a newspaper so that she could keep leaning on the stand for support. The newspaper was smeared with blood. She saw that she had punctured her hands with her own fingernails.

The riptide, she thought. There's no escaping it now.

She went down the subway steps—she had to hold on to the rail—and took the train to Central Square.

Our Lady of Sorrows rises massively above the flotsam of the square. Out of place, Felicity thought, and out of time. She knelt in the great Gothic cave and peered into the

247

shadows beyond the banks of votive candles. It was amazing: another border crossed. The sun, the hubbub of Central Square, the very look of the twentieth century, all extinguished by the heavy west doors. She was awed by a tradition that could sustain, at the very core of urban dissonance and flux, such a sanctuary to the inner life. The heartbeat of the silence thudded softly in her ears. What could Hunter do in the face of such weighty hush? She would anchor herself to the calm. A phrase came to her: Rock of Ages.

Just one perspective, her father said. One glimpse. You can't catch God in any of these nets.

Only the red lamp above the altar, an unblinking eye, watched. The place was impassive. Baptisms, marriages, deaths, it had absorbed them all. A man stepped out of the eye of God. So it seemed. He was gliding up the aisle, his face was round and pale as a Communion wafer. She could hear the whisper of his black gown against the floor. He turned into the confessional alcove.

Felicity waited.

Her eyes were growing accustomed, the twilight was settling into shapes. There were perhaps five or six other people, devout elderly women, here and there among the pews. One of the women made her way slowly and painfully toward the confessional. Two canes, tap-tapping down the nave, supported her. The echoes answered: tap, tap. As she passed Felicity, the candlelight fell on her gnarled hands, the veins showing like purple knots, the fingers shockingly twisted by arthritis. A sadness pierced Felicity. So many frailties, she thought. How does anyone manage?

She waited. She read the booklet containing the Mass for the previous Sunday. She murmured the responses, they ran on such ancient grooves of entreaty. She studied the parish bulletin: its cover sketch of Our Lady of Sorrows, its phone numbers, its list of Masses: daily at 7 A.M.; Sundays at 7 A.M. and 11 A.M., Spanish Mass in between at 9. She scanned the list of staff: Rev. Dennis O'Dowd at the top; and lower down, one of six parish assistants, Sister Gabriel Vergara.

Felicity realized she had expected nuns to be hovering in the nave like ministering doves. She realized she had been listening for the silken rustle of black and white habits. She had thought Sister Gabriel, miraculously recognizing her, would quietly kneel at her side. They would exchange news.

I found Casa del Diablo, Felicity would say, but Dolores Marquez wasn't there. I don't know how to find Angelo without wandering around Central Square and asking for Leon, and so endangering him. And now Hunter is following me again. What does it mean, and what do you want me to do?

The silent nave gave back no answers. Sister Gabriel did not appear.

What possible sins could be occupying the woman with twisted hands? How could they take so long in the telling? The silence thudded, the beats were like a doomsday clock. When the canes came tapping their way out toward the square, Felicity gathered up her own shortcomings and all her questions and moved toward confession.

"Father," she said to the grille. "I am looking for Sister Gabriel."

"My child!" There was a startled edge to his voice. "Have you forgotten the act of contrition? You must begin: *Bless me, Father, for I have sinned.*"

"I am not a Catholic, Father. I need to see Sister Gabriel."

Silence. The silence bloomed and grew, it was palpable. Perhaps he had left and had gone padding back down the nave, soft as a cat. "Father?"

"Sister Gabriel is not available," said the voice behind the grille. "Perhaps I can help you?"

The dark in the box was seductive. Velvet. There was a faint fragrance of candle wax. Against such a backdrop Felicity watched her own thoughts take on form. They danced in front of her voice. They eddied across the partition. And the voice beyond the grille: mellow, caressing, inspiring trust. A watcher of the visible thoughts. Protestant thoughts. The thoughts of a *lapsed* Protestant. Felicity understood the craving to confess, the temptation

249

to shed the past like an old skin, to step out again newly minted.

She began to speak. All the fragments of memory and fear, event, threat, hallucination, gathered themselves up into a flood and poured through the little sluice gate beyond which the priest waited. She told him everything. She spoke of the border, of Dolores Marquez and Hunter and Angelo and Sister Gabriel, of the photograph and the Montreal address that had yielded up no meaning. She spoke of the dead weight of a responsibility that she did not want. She could feel the photograph like a lodestone in her wallet.

"It's like a steel trap, Father. It has me by the ankle and by the throat. The faces of her children are more real to me than my father and mother."

When Father O'Dowd spoke, she thought of shepherds murmuring to their sheep. She thought of her *ayah* and her grandparents and her aunts. She thought of a falconer, gentle but stern, calling the way home.

"There are borderline cases," he told her. His voice was full of solace. "Where is the photograph?" he asked. It did not occur to her not to give it to him. "You have done all that could be asked of you," he said. "Everything will be taken care of."

Of course, he pointed out, the Church would have to weigh every aspect, and would proceed with extraordinary caution. Misguided compassion, he said solemnly, could be a form of heresy.

"Heresy?"

"You were wise to turn the matter over to me," he said. "Go in peace, my child. Everything will be taken care of."

She was free and shriven.

She could hardly believe the relief.

She walked out through the great west doors and was surprised she did not waft upwards from the steps like a helium balloon.

Central Square greeted her like a slap in the face. Two children fought over food scraps in a garbage can, shouting in Spanish. Dogs lifted their legs against fences. The sun shone as it had to. The asphalt glared back at the sun.

*   *   *

250

That night she dreamed Seymour was painting her black. Her body itself was the canvas, she could feel each brushstroke like a scourge, her skin choking and unable to breathe beneath the caked layers of pigment. Seymour daubed her navel with red. The altar lamp, he said. Father O'Dowd, like a wisp of genie, came smoking out of the red eye. He sheared off her breasts with pruning clippers. Beware of heresy, he said.

Felicity woke with a cry.

"Don't go," Seymour murmured in his sleep. "Don't leave."

She was grateful for his arms, though she knew they would not hold.

When she woke again, he was already at work, the easel beside the bed, paint tubes scattered on quilt and floor. He worked, lately, as though time was running out. He's sixty-four, she remembered.

"All these years," he said, "and I still haven't got you properly. I want to *fix* you here before you slip away. You're going to leave me again, I know. You're not eating. I wish you'd eat."

Felicity's desk was covered with catalogues and 35-mm transparencies. Gauguin was passing through her fingers, but also Rufino Tamayo—Tahiti and Mexico, the colors, the smells—when Sister Gabriel called.

"You were looking for me?" Sister Gabriel asked. "Word reached me."

No salutation. No identification. It was like a voice from the black region of dreams, but Felicity recognized it immediately.

"Yes," she said weakly. But I've finished with this, she wanted to say. I've been absolved. I've discharged my duty. She waited for her heartbeat to stop thundering in her own ears. Don't ask anything more of me, she begged silently. "Father O'Dowd told you?"

"No," Sister Gabriel said. "You were seen going into the church. You're very conspicuous. You don't look like a member of Our Lady of Sorrows' parish."

"I was trying to reach you," Felicity said. "Or Angelo.

251

One or other of you. I tried to deliver the photograph, but she didn't seem to be there."

Silence.

"I can't help feeling . . ." Felicity stumbled on. "Has something more . . . ? Why is Hunter following me again?"

Silence. For so long that Felicity thought the line had gone dead.

"Sister Gabriel?"

"Please. No names."

"I need someone to tell me what's happening," Felicity pleaded. "Should I go back to the record shop? Should I meet with Angelo again?"

"Please." There was a sigh. "It wasn't you, then?"

"What wasn't me?" Felicity asked.

"Who turned him in to Immigration?"

Felicity felt something like a feverish chill beginning at her fingertips and spreading. "Turned Angelo in?" she whispered.

"He was deported. Dead now, of course." Sister Gabriel's voice was expressionless. She might have been a recording. "Twenty-three machine-gun holes in his body."

"I don't believe you."

"Arrested the day after he met you, and flown back. Never reached home from the airport. We thought it must have been you."

Felicity leaned against her desk, all her body fluids seasick. The tavern laughter of Angelo was deafening. Echoes, echoes, echoes. "No," she said. "I swear to you. What possible reason would I have? As it is, I have nightmares, I can't drive my car, I can't eat. The photograph was burning a hole in my wallet. But Father O'Dowd said that everything—"

"Father O'Dowd?" Sister Gabriel's voice was very faint. She sounded impossibly weary. "How much did you tell him?"

"Well I . . . everything, I guess. I gave him the photograph."

"But no addresses, I hope."

252

Felicity swallowed. "There was one on the back of the photograph. The Montreal restaurant, though she wasn't—"

"It's all over, then," Sister Gabriel sighed. "His duty to report, he believes. He hasn't lived there, you see, so it's all black and white."

Felicity said weakly: "But surely he wouldn't . . . ?"

"Yes, he would. He has. For him, they're all tainted with the wrong ideology, they're all part of an Absolute Evil. What else can he do?" Felicity pictured the voice as a rubber band gone slack, stretched beyond its limits. "I hardly think she'll mind," the voice went on, "she's so tired. We're all so tired, we've all lost hope."

Felicity was appalled. "I always thought the confessional—"

"Oh, in *confession*! You didn't say! Thank God. He's bound then."

"Well, more or less in confession. I'm not a Catholic."

"Oh. Who knows then? I'll try to get word to her, but all our links are smashed. Anyway, there isn't anywhere left to hide except maybe New York. Not a big enough legal Spanish community in Montreal."

"Is it possible that she . . ." Felicity faltered. "I mean, all the rumors . . . You don't think *she* might have been the one who . . . regarding Angelo, I mean?"

"One never knows anything for certain," Sister Gabriel said. "I go by intuition. The people I work with . . . survival's their only ideology, their only possible one." She laughed suddenly, a harsh, macabre sound. "A misguided perspective, of course, as the bishop has told me. Though not quite heretical, he says."

"I'm afraid of Hunter," Felicity said. "Why does he keep following me?"

"It's proof they haven't found her yet."

"But does he think I'm in touch with her? Does he think I know something?"

"Do you?"

Felicity felt a skid of fear. "Even you don't trust me? But I tried to deliver the photograph. Isn't there anything—"

"Yes, there always is," Sister Gabriel said. "There are the children, there are thousands of homeless and hungry children. I want a lay worker to go back, but it's so difficult since the murder of the nuns to find—"

In a panic, Felicity hung up.

35

His canvas was very large; sometimes he stood on a chair, sometimes on a stepladder. He argued with it, cajoled it, made love to it. He often talked to himself. He was painting a radiance: it filled the room with a smoky phosphorescent gold. It throbbed. It swallowed him up. Somewhere behind this glow, like a shadow or the nub of the numen itself, were two eyes, one slightly higher than the other.

"If you'd seen her," Felicity said, "you'd know what I mean." Her mind, like fire on an oil slick, went licking along a new idea. "Suppose I could find her? Suppose I could get her to New York? You could paint her, you could do a Magdalen."

Seymour paused. It was as though the inner golden vision of light, whose spokesman he was, had passed into the gray of an eclipse. He got down off the chair and came over to the window seat where she was sitting. "Why are you doing this to me?"

"Doing what?"

(And how would the Old Volcano know how to explain what he meant? He spoke in colors and textures, not words. He meant: You are easing out again, I can sense it. He meant: I am used to tears and suicide threats and abject devotion; they are a bore, but I consider them my due. When you get that look in your eyes, when you forget I'm here, you drive me to a frenzy of possessive desire. You make me determined to have you, to pin you down. But it's like trying to catch light in a net.

No one knows Felicity and the Old Volcano the way I do. No one has seen them from such close range. And this is the secret of Felicity's hold on him: that she doesn't want to be held. She has always been addicted to

255

loneliness, which is freedom; and to freedom, which is loneliness.

(And there is also this: anyone who looks at Felicity for long thinks "otherness", or "untouched", or "essence"— depending on verbal and metaphysical capability. Hunter thinks it. The Old Volcano thinks it. I think it. Men want to put their mark on her. For Hunter and his ilk, simple violation is enough, the cruder the better—like breaking a wild horse. But the Old Volcano is hungry for salvation, all of life is bread and wine to him, sacred; he wants to devour us all. Especially, and religiously, he wants to devour Felicity.

And I? Oh yes, even I have an interest. I want to save her from the Old Volcano's misappropriation. I want to be the official biographer, the final authority. I am recording and preserving as faithfully as bias and loss and grief and capricious memory will allow.

Of course, the Old Volcano could articulate none of this. He could not even formulate what he was feeling. It takes a truly blind man to be a great painter.)

So he merely asked fretfully, "Why are you doing this to me?"

"Doing what?"

"You're so like your father," he said. Accusing them both, vaguely, of not revolving around him. Or perhaps it was the way the light fell on her. A physical resemblance. An old memory.

Felicity puckered her eyebrows, reading his face, trying to locate the reason for his distress. "Is it because you don't think she has a chance? Or because it would be illegal and dangerous? Are you afraid this'll interfere with your work?"

"What? Who?" He had been thinking in colors. He had forgotten what lay behind the sense that she was moving away from him. He was thinking of fragments of asteroid that slip beyond the sun's reach, the light dying, leaking away into the void like water into sand. Distressed, he grumbled, "Why do you want to go away?"

"I don't," she said passionately. "I don't." She trailed off into thought. Then she said, "Perhaps it's true what you're always saying in interviews. That I'm a figment of your imagination. You've dictated the way I *see* things. Everything comes filtered through you. At the border that day, I thought first of Perugino, and second, of how you'd paint her. And now the only way I can visualize her is as one of your paintings taking on life. It's weird. You've stolen my eyes."

"Hah!" He was back on his chair, in vehement confrontation with his canvas. "It's the other way round. You and your damn father, you won't leave me alone. You're hounding me, both of you. You're after my soul."

"My father and you," she said, "in the war. You hardly ever speak of it."

"There's quite enough darkness ahead of me. I don't reach back for more. I'm for the light these days."

"Were you ever afraid? In the war, I mean?"

"Hah. I was *always* afraid."

"And my father?"

"A maniac of a medic!" Seymour fumed. "He never seemed to be afraid of anything, the bastard. Always out there bringing back bodies, giving death the finger. I don't know. Maybe he was scared too. I was certainly scared shitless, helping him."

"Oh Seymour, you were really afraid." She slid off the window seat and coiled herself around him. An aphrodisiac, his fear. Or his admission of it. But she had an urgent question, her arms were around his neck, her eyes close to his. "How do you make yourself do something you're terrified of doing?" she asked.

He was transfixed by the closeness of her eyes. "Damn you," he murmured. "His eyes too, damn it." He reached for her hands and undid the noose around his neck. He picked her up. He carried her to their bed. "I won't answer," he shouted, as they wrestled in a desperate love. "Felicity," he whispered in her ear. "Whatever it is, you don't have to do it. *I* should be enough for you to work on, a full-blooded and foul-mouthed heathen. Don't go. Don't leave me. I'm too old and I'm afraid of the dark."

She kissed him. She kissed his lips. She kissed him all the way down his body to his crotch, she took his prick in

257

her mouth; she lavished on him her lips and her tongue and her love. She kissed him all the way back up to his lips again, and as she lay over him, riding him, she whispered, "But of course the reason I love you, and the reason you loved my father, was because you did things you were terrified of doing."

His prick suddenly wilted inside her. He held her tightly. "Heroics," he said, "are a miscalculation of youth, grossly overrated. Think of your father, think of the waste." And when she said nothing: "Felicity, please don't leave. I'm too old. I'll confess it: I'm afraid of dying alone. And besides," he whispered, "listen. Before it's too late, we could have a child. Why not? It's time we settled down."

Felicity leaned on the sill of her office window. A child, she thought, our own child. She felt like singing. Children drifted from the sky like music: their flawless faces, their curls, their laughter. Two of them had an old woman in tow and their dark hair brushed Felicity in passing.

She looked down at the sidewalk where people were waiting for buses. In the doorway of the bus shelter a man, shapeless in his light September coat, was whittling at something with a knife. A piece of wood? No. Something soft. A nectarine perhaps. Strange, this bird's-eye view. The man had a bald spot in the middle of his head. He was cutting the nectarine into sections, which he swallowed whole, one by one. When he got down to the pit, he drop-kicked it into the gutter. He looked up at her window and saw her watching him. He saluted with the knife.

She was no longer sure if it was Trog or Hunter.

The chair was not high enough. Seymour was on a step-ladder now. The canvas seemed to be growing skywards and he was ascending above a middle region of cloud, cirrus puffs only, a last barrier. He was working on an expanse of pure light in the mind of the sun. He was using acrylics: white, ocher, more white, a blended dove gray, clear yellow, white.

He did not notice when Felicity left.

She paused by her car in the street. Her crazy lapis lazuli

258

car. Weird blue, Gus had said an eternity ago at the border. She sat behind the wheel and the memory of Trog and Hunter arriving in her office came back. They were palpable presences. Her hands were shaking on the wheel, she had to lick sweat from over her upper lip. An impounded car. A tampered-with car, the brakelines cut. Heroics, Seymour said, are a disastrous miscalculation.

She waited for the trembling to pass. She started the car. She tested the brakes. She drove to Central Square, parked, and went walking. The Watch Clinic was shut up, a sign hung over its doorknob: *Closed. Liquidation Sale.* She pressed her face against the grimy glass and peered in. It was like looking into an aquarium tank that has never been cleaned: an aqueous light, the watches breeding like pearlescent fish.

At Scoop's record shop there was no one she recognized. A girl with iridescent purple fingernail polish was in the cashier's cage. She stared at Felicity with patent boredom.

Felicity walked to The Plough and Stars, and beyond it. And then back again. She put her hand on the doorknob. She could not go in. I am collecting ghosts, she thought. My head is crammed with the absent, an attic of memories, I know more dead people than living ones.

She walked as far as the Post Office, and then turned again. Back and forth, back and forth. On one turn, she stopped at the Post Office and called her aunts.

"Felicity," Aunt Norwich said. "In the middle of the week! Is something wrong?"

"Yes," Felicity said. "But I don't know how to . . ."

"If it's that dreadful man, my dear, you know we both think you'd be much better off—"

"No, it's not that. You remember I told you about the woman at the border, the refugee truck?"

"Now, Felicity, you mustn't start brooding about that sort of thing again. Why don't you come over and have tea with us? We do miss you, dear, though I'm afraid I must ask you to come alone. We can't quite . . . he's such an *awful* man . . . but we would love to see you."

"Yes, perhaps I will later, Aunt Norwich. Bye."

259

She walked back to The Plough and Stars. This time, she told herself, I will go in. The ghost of Angelo was waiting at the same table, like Banquo at the feast. She ordered a beer. Angelo's face was white, dead white. His eye sockets trickled blood. Twenty-three holes, he said, pointing them out. All the machine-gun holes laughed like twenty-three mouths, and the laughter hemmed her in. She drank her beer. The photograph, he said sadly. She needed it more than food. We all need an obsession to keep us going, and for her it's the children. The children, the children, the echoes sang. She felt queasy from the smoke and the beer. As she left she could hear him behind her, setting the fake Tiffany lamps chiming like cheap bells: the children, children, children.

We could have a child, Seymour said.

And Sister Gabriel: there are always the children, the thousands of homeless children.

She was passing a school playground and stopped to watch: steel grids on the windows, the walls daubed with graffiti, garbage rampant on a field of black asphalt—a tideline of candy wrappers, popsicle sticks, McDonald's cardboard cups, beer cans. But flowering in all directions, irrepressible, the children.

A young mother, with coffee skin and a dandelion behind one ear, stood beside Felicity at the fence and called, "Anita! Anita!" She had a baby on her left hip, and on her head, balanced there like an extraordinary crown, a supermarket bag full of groceries. It might have been the most natural act in the world. Amidst the din and litter, in her cheap cotton shift and thin coat, she stood there like a frail and exotic orchid—something that blooms once every five years, say, in the unruly heart of a jungle. Felicity heard bellbirds, and the soft sibilant lift and dip of bamboo paddles. "Anita!" the woman called again, and a child ran to her. The incongruous burden on the woman's head never trembled as she turned, a child at each side, and left the playground. Her back was straight as a young coconut palm. Her hips swayed. Felicity followed. She was chasing echoes. And Massachusetts Avenue, the filthy and wounded main artery of Central Square, budded greenly as a rain forest.

You win, Sister Gabriel, she murmured. You win.

She did not doubt that Sister Gabriel would receive the message.

There were preparations to be made, and certain things to be collected. She drove back to her old apartment.

36

An absence, whether from death or some other more final loss, calls forth compensatory action, we all know this. When the loss is not our own, we may raise an arch eyebrow. We may wink and murmur to one another of "overreaction" or "denial" or "sublimation". Such words froth at the top of the mind, empty judgments. And with love it is the same: each case both unique and predictably banal, depending on the point of view.

For this reason I prefer not to discuss my feelings about Felicity, nor about Kathleen, up to, and following, the time of the police reports. This is not a diary. It is true that I have become personal here and there, that the report has strayed from the purely investigative and objective—I freely admit it—but for esthetic reasons. For reasons of *form*.

Yes, the piano tuner has been seduced. He has the baton in his hand, the stage lights are on him, he refuses to scuttle into the wings. But he is also aware of the attendant responsibilities, the need for artistic rigor and direction.

And I realize it would not do to bore you with my nightly dreams of Felicity, nor with details of January's falling in love with May. You believe you know all there is to know about such things, you have read it a thousand times, from Chaucer on, and who am I to improve on Chaucer? Your lip curls. Ho hum. They are always the same, these affairs. Consequently I gloss over a number of weeks: the books Kathleen read in order to discuss them with me; the concerts I took her to; the way she sat in empty rooms and listened while I tuned pianos; the way we talked so avidly about Felicity and Kathleen's father. You remind me of him, she'd say. But I digress.

What is significant about those weeks is simply this: though we spoke of the absent ones constantly, we were in fact very much preoccupied with each other. During the crucial days we were oblivious; though once the police arrived, of course, retrospective remorse set in. And recrimination.

"If you'd told him I wanted to speak to him," Kathleen says. "If you'd made him say where he was . . ."

But how could I have known, how could I possibly have been expected to know, which phone call would be the last?

"If you hadn't told him what Felicity said," she mourns. "If you hadn't mentioned New York."

Oh I quite acknowledge that my haziness about the timing and content of the last few phone calls is suspicious. Transparent, if you like. (We all know what amnesia is for.)

"They were both getting paranoid," I said. "They both saw people waiting for them in every shadow."

"Paranoid," Kathleen sniffs. "I suppose their disappearance is an illusion? If you see a knife coming at you through the air, is it paranoid to duck?" But mostly she represses these dark misgivings. "He's always been like this," she laughs. "Mummy has always had irrefutable evidence of disasters, and he always turns up—slightly drunk but none the worse for wear."

I hope there will not be any glib snickering about Kathleen's way of protecting herself. I would like to point out that frequently, in the social history of mankind, compensatory action has not only taken on original and sometimes brilliant forms, but has been—in and of itself—beneficial to society.

Consider the piano in an abandoned summer palace of the Maharajah of Travancore. Felicity remembers it. Out of tune, of course. Even as a child with an untrained ear, she knew it. Monkeys chattering on the sounding board, rats gnawing away at the felt hammers, strings corroded, the whole instrument an arabesque of damp heaves. Over half the notes were silent. When she pressed them with a finger they said: *och, och.* Her ear became attuned: there were nuances in the ways the different mute keys said nothing. She was an inventive child, Felicity. It was the only piano available. She composed tunes that incorporated the silent notes, a sonata of glottal stops. All art, as Freud said, is compensation.

Or consider the *castrati* of the sixteenth and seventeenth centuries and even later. A cutting blow, you might think. Did they wither away because of their loss? On the contrary. Cropped but not crestfallen was their motto; the thorax is mightier than the sword. They bestrode the courts of Europe like giants, they towered over bass-voiced courtiers. Never forget that at the coronation of Napoleon in 1804, the voices of three hundred French choral singers and the strummings of eighty harpists were swamped, at the moment of the crowning, by the Pope's thirty Sistine Chapel *castrati*. *Tu es Petrus*, sang those male sopranos, a mighty chorus.

"Now that," Napoleon murmured to Josephine, "is a choir with balls!"

You see what can be done with loss?

The police do not understand this.

Evasion, they say. Prevarication. You are not telling us all that you know.

The police jingle facts like a handful of coins in a leather purse. Slow-thinking literalists, they tip the facts out on the table in front of you. "Look," they say, picking one up. They hold it up to the light, they turn it around, they push it in front of your eyes. *Fact*, they say. As though it had magic properties. As though they have you squirming on a hook. Now how do you explain? they demand.

The truth is, I simply cannot remember the exact sequence, or the dates, or the content of the final phone calls. (I was preoccupied with Kathleen at the time.) I remember fragments, I remember images.

When I summon Felicity back from that time, I see a shadow tied to her heels. The shadow holds the shadow of a knife. Nothing is distinct. There is a vibrato of fear in her voice. (I think of Hester.) Also a dreaming quality. She was leaning back into the sun, there are flowers in her hair. Bellbirds called her. She spoke of villages, I'm sure she spoke of villages, and of children, thousands of children. Also of the children of Dolores Marquez. Yes, because I said, "You're obsessed with that woman. And now

Kathleen's father believes he's found her, for heaven's sake."

"Kathleen's father?"

"Fliss, you never listen to me. Your border friend, Augustine Kelly, he has a daughter. Kathleen and I . . ."

"He's *found* her?" There was a fevered edge to her voice. "Why didn't you *tell* me? You said you didn't have a clue where he was."

"I did? Well that's right, I don't. He'll never say. But every so often he calls in—"

"But he's found her, that's all that matters. Oh thank God!" She was very intense. I think she was in a pay phone in Harvard Square. I think she told me that. "You have to get a message to him," she said. "You have to tell him New York, it's the only hope. And it's very urgent. They *know*, you see, they have the address, it's only a matter of time."

"Look," I said. "I have no idea when he'll call. Besides, he's mostly drunk and raving, so as far as your phantom refugee goes, I wouldn't exactly—"

"You *have* to warn them," she said. "You *have* to. It's my fault, Jean-Marc. I gave away the photograph, I *told*, and I don't want her deportation on my conscience. After Angelo, there's no use pretending—"

"Fliss, you're a bundle of nerves. Come up here for a visit. I'd like you to meet Kathleen. I want to know what you think."

"It's like a relay," she said. "And Angelo has passed his obsession on to me."

"Where *are* you?" I asked.

"In a pay phone in Harvard Square. I'm being followed."

"You need to be looked after. If you left now, you could be up here in time for dinner."

"I have to go home," she said. "Seymour's working too hard. I'm worried about him."

"Don't give him my love," I snapped.

"Oh Jean-Marc," she reproached. "I'll talk to you later."

But she never did.

I think I remember this exchange, but of course it could

be retrospective invention. A logic imposed. One thing: it must have come before Gus's call, or I wouldn't have mentioned New York to him.

"Felicity?" Gus was clearly bewildered. Weeks of dereliction and booze had passed between his last thought of her and the present. "Oh, *Felicity*! No, why?" He sounded alarmed. "Look, I'm in a rush . . . I sent Kathleen a letter. I don't suppose—"

"Yes, as a matter of fact. She paid a visit. She was looking for you. I must say, she's—"

"Thank God. Will you give her a message? Tell her everything will be fine." Listen, he said. He had to go into hiding, Dolores and he. But Kathleen was not to worry. He was being followed, he said, by some men he had seen before. There was no time to explain.

"About Dolores," I said. "Felicity thinks Immigration knows—"

"Them and everyone else."

"She says, if you could, New York is the only hope."

"New York!" he laughed. "Christ, why New York? Why not the South Pole?"

About that line, I can be definite. A joker, Gus.

Of course I have gone over my memory like an archaeologist, I have dredged up phrases and pauses, I have wracked my brain for innuendos I might have missed. I chip away at amnesia. I go over my reconstruction with a magnifying glass. In the night I listen for commas and glottal stops. I explore the subtext, I am an expert on the buried layers of the sentence.

But as Felicity's *ayah* used to say: Ivory will not grow in the rice paddy no matter how carefully you tend it.

Fact: the police say. They turn it in front of my face, they let it catch the light. It is one they have shown to Therese and Kathleen and Bob Wilberforce, to every fellow insurance agent in Winston, to a passel of clients, to the proprietor of Mister Donut. They take notes. They are gathering interpretations.

Fact: that a Chevrolet registered to Augustine Kelly crossed the border at the checkpoint nearest Winston,

Ontario, heading south, at such and such an hour on such and such a night. Only one occupant, the driver.

Fact: a gas station attendant in Carthage, N.Y., remembers the Chevrolet and the driver. Also a female passenger.

Fact: that said Chevrolet was found irreparably smashed and charred in a roadside culvert between the towns of Carthage and Utica in upstate New York. (Here the police show photographs, they spell out: high speed, sharp turn, no sign of collision or foul play, gasoline inferno from impact.) Two bodies, unidentifiable.

I push the facts back across the table. Opaque, I say. They yield nothing to me. The police pocket them again. They take out their other purse, the one labelled Felicity. Their facts come spilling out.

"Your father says you were involved," they tell me. "He hopes you may know more than he does."

"Your father's grief-stricken," they add.

One of them is a policewoman, a blonde with killer lips. I look her straight in the eye. "Oh I bet he is," I say. "Prostrate with sorrow, I should think." She blushes and lowers her eyes.

They show their photographs of Felicity's apartment building, the black remnants, the gaping holes. Arson, they say, *fact.* Impossible to identify the several victims, though some effort was made, dental records, that sort of thing, with whatever could be found in the rubble.

"Your father doesn't believe she was in the fire," they say. "He says she hadn't been near her apartment for weeks. But her blue Datsun was parked outside it, and one of the survivors remembers seeing her entering the building. Can you tell us her whereabouts on the day of the fire?"

No, I can't, I tell them. But my father's right. She wasn't driving her Datsun anymore, and she hasn't been back to that apartment since the middle of the summer.

"But she was seen," they insist.

The survivor must have been mistaken, I point out. Someone else must have driven her car, it had been tampered with by persons unknown before this. Besides, doesn't it strike you as odd, these separate fires? All this destruction of evidence? Isn't there something *contrived* . . . ?

267

"We note that it strikes you as significant," they counter. They are plodding literalists. "We note that you see a link. How often did the deceased meet in your house?"

The police have read too many spy thrillers, they live on a junk diet of television violence.

"We are keeping your answering machine," they tell me, "as possible evidence. The tapes are highly suggestive."

I don't know of what, I tell them. Political discussions, they say. That makes me laugh. How do you explain the use of code names? they ask. I look at them blankly. Hunter, they explain. And La Magdalena. Tell us about the politics of your former stepmother and of Augustine Kelly, they say. (They have one-track minds, the police.) I am brief but polite: They had none.

"Then how do you explain the newspaper file?" they demand.

Now isn't that curious? I thought Trog and Hunter had taken that file. I told them: She was a connoisseur of the absurd. She kept the file for philosophical and esthetic reasons. But you can't explain something like that to people like the police. There's no point.

If I close my eyes I see Felicity moving among hot and dusty villages. She is wearing white. A large, floppy hat, with scarlet bougainvillea ribbons, is on her head. The ribbons are tangled in her long hair, which lifts and drifts in the breeze. She carries baskets of mangoes on her arms. Pied piper, the villagers call her. Children follow like flocks of doves, they clutch at her hands and skirt. She is walking away from me, she will not turn round.

Oh Jean-Marc, she'll say when she calls. I meant to get in touch with you earlier. I'm sorry. I got involved.

I see no reason to tell any of this to the police, who, at long last, are leaving us more or less alone. All of their leads have gone nowhere.

They know no more than we do.

37

Sometimes on insomniac nights I move the police facts around like counters. I build bridges and theories. It's like playing with a kaleidoscope: a set number of givens, a flick of the wrist or the mind, an infinite number of possible configurations.

Gus, for instance.

His eyes flicked constantly to the rearview mirror. He was watching for the Other Car, for the two men he had seen at Felicity's cottage. He knew he did not dare to cross the border near Montreal (too closely watched for illegal aliens; his car known, perhaps, and associated with the meat truck from his last crossing); he would try at the checkpoint near Winston.

Don't be silly, Kathleen says. Daddy would never think of complications like that.

True. So they must have tried to hide in the empty house at Winston, and then realized it was not safe. He decided to make for New York, an innocuous border crossing on a business trip. He took precautions, he wore his one and only pin-striped suit.

"At the customs checkpoint," he explained to Dolores Marquez, "you'll have to hide on the floor in the back again. Under a sleeping bag. Same trick as last time. You remember?"

He knew she didn't understand a word, but he had to talk out of nervousness. She stared at him wanly, her huge eyes trusting, uncomprehending.

"We're in the same boat," he told her. "My life is a shambles too. Though in my case, it's my own fault." Every set of headlights worried him, he drove as though he was trying to elude the air. "To tell you the truth," he said, "my life has never been quite the same since I met you. The time I saw you . . . at least, I think I saw you, in the orchard . . ." He babbled on and on in English. His eyes lit up the road ahead. An invisible fire burned around him. He felt its heat. He glowed.

And at some point along the highway she began to talk. At first he thought he was imagining it. No one at Casa del Diablo had ever heard her say a word. She spoke, he supposed, in Spanish, a low monologue, exotic, like the sound of an Andean flute. He saw red dust and volcanoes, village churches, candles, an icon, an old woman's face, young children. He saw village squares and adobe huts and soldiers. She knew he could not understand a word. It seemed to unlock something inside her. Her talk became wilder. Sometimes she sobbed as she talked. Once she screamed.

They sped steadily onwards. Every time headlights ruptured the dark highway, he expected the Other Car. Three times he thought it drew alongside, but nothing happened. He must have been mistaken. Near the border he stopped and Dolores Marquez climbed into the back and he covered her with a sleeping bag. They crossed without incident. Gus showed his driver's license, spoke of business in New York. The official never even glanced in the back. Gus rested an arm on his window, chatted, told a joke before driving on. They flew through upstate New York, they were taking back roads, a short cut, they would connect with the Thruway at Utica. By Carthage, they needed gas and food.

Carthage, N.Y. A small town dreaming only of the ordinary. White clapboard, shutters, neat lawns, rhododendrons, September chrysanthemums in dappled bloom. The dark visions that issued from the memory of Dolores Marquez would wither in its crisp and decent air. Nothing unpleasant could happen there. There were golden eagles over the doors, flags on front lawns. A tranquil place.

Dolores, fearful, would not accompany Gus into the restaurant beside the gas station.

"You have to eat more," he told her. "I can almost see through you. I'll bring you something."

Her eyes, in their bruised gray caves, watched him soberly.

He thought, as so often, of the first name he had known her by: La Magdalena.

And though a trio of mini-skirted waitresses in the restaurant sang all about his ears, though their long hair swung over their shoulders, though they wore fetching little vests laced tightly below the bust, Gus barely even noticed.

The waitresses, who considered flirtation an obligation of the male customer, clustered helpfully around him at the counter. The least a traveller could do, free as he was to flit in and out of the small, humdrum circle of their lives, was offer dreams. One of the waitresses, with wheat-blonde hair and large, mobile, slickered lips and very long lashes, adjusted Gus's tie. He felt a tiny tremor of temptation, but immediately repudiated it.

"Yes?" she breathed, leaning so close he could smell her peppermint breath.

Gus coughed and cleared his throat. "Two hamburgers and french fries to go," he said with a certain asperity.

"My pleasure." Her voice was husky. He thought of cabarets and satin sheets. "Anything to drink?" she asked, and leaned even closer towards him. There was a tiny gold cross between her breasts. He breathed in perfume—something heavy, Eastern, narcotic. She rested her fingers lightly on his wrist. The nails were like pink, fluted shells. The nails of Dolores Marquez, he had noticed as they fed dishes to steam dragons, were raggedly chipped and her hands were red from kitchen water.

"Two coffees," he said. "To go."

And when he crossed the parking lot again with his cardboard tray and Styrofoam cups, his body tingled with exhaustion. Virtuous exhaustion. The kind an Olympic runner feels after breasting the tape, or a dieter after turning down chocolate cake. He had a vision of new snow, whiter than white, falling from the warm night. Everything shimmered. Haloes, milky gold, were looped around the neon parking-lot lights. The eyes of his Chevy burned like sanctuary lamps. Oh shit, he thought. He had forgotten to switch off his lights. Stay calm, he told himself, placing his cardboard tray on the hood. He tried the engine. A hiccup, then power, thank God—though in any case he seemed to have eluded all followers. He switched off again and handed Dolores Marquez her Styrofoam cup as though it were a chalice. She seemed uncertain what to do with it, so he himself wrestled with its plastic snap-on lid. The lid resisted. He applied pressure, too much apparently, since victory was abrupt.

They both gasped as the scalding liquid splashed them. Oh shit, he said; and then, embarrassed: Excuse me. A little flustered, he reached for the glove compartment, but the Kleenex box was empty. He did, however, have a slightly grubby handkerchief in his coat pocket and, oblivious to his own wounds, he daubed at hers. "Oh Jesus," he mumbled, "I'm sorry."

He became aware of the ghost of a smile on her lips. He was overwhelmed. Transfixed. He knocked over the rest of his coffee. Always there were fresh trials and tribulations.

He remembered, as he mopped at his soaked pants, that they were in flight; that at any moment, the Other Car, fearful nemesis, might appear. How unaware, how blithely indifferent, was the man at the gas pumps to these dimensions, to the complexities, to the *stature* of his customer.

"Sorry," the man said. "Can't take funny money. Got a Texaco card or a Visa?"

Gus folded away his Canadian bills with dignity. His look implied reproach. This between nations of goodwill? Between neighbors? He took time with his wallet in order to cover his panic. To have to leave his own trail of clues, sign his own name, trip some computer switch. Augustine Kelly, Ontario license number such and so, passed here. But he had no choice.

"Augustine!" laughed the gas attendant as he pushed the machine lever over Gus's Texaco card. "Jesus. Don't often come across a name like that. Not here in Carthage anyways. Bet no one forgets it."

Gus's fevered imagination watched the electronic passage of his name, saw it blipping its way to the heart

272

of some intelligence-eating monster whose tentacles were everywhere. It would only be a matter of time, he was sure, before some sort of worldwide All Points Bulletin went out: from the police, from border officials, from his shadowy pursuers. He had always known he would be caught and punished for something. Sooner or later.

Through the darkened back roads of upstate New York, past barns and silos and fields nearing harvest, they drove (it seemed to him) on mercy and borrowed time. Dolores Marquez slid sideways into sleep. She had almost disappeared. A shadow of a woman, thin as tissue. It seemed to him suddenly that nothing would ever save either of them—though surely grace was attached to the effort. He fixed his memory on that fleeting and shimmering moment in the parking lot, when she had almost smiled. If he could freeze time right there. If there were only a way you could stay inside such moments. If you could die five minutes after confession and Communion, unsullied as morning. Or if they could ride the night forever, in a private glowing bubble (a warm Chevy that flew out of time) so that daylight, failure, disaster, collapsed good intentions—all the harsh hunters—might never catch them.

They were nearing Utica, almost back on the New York State Thruway, and he began to believe they might make it, a smooth straight ribbon of road into anonymity. He drove faster. When he became aware of the headlights stalking him from behind, an even distance, speeding up when he did, slowing down at the same time, his fear touched the Chevy and it responded like a living thing. Its flanks trembled, it surged into a grace of speed. Surely nothing could catch him. The car behind was like a shadow tied to his wings. Faster, faster. Until, over the culvert, they made a leap of faith, a perfect parabola.

This is one of the versions I tell myself. It is not the one I tell Kathleen, who is only a child and needs to believe.

Augustine in Carthage, you say. Oh really! But how could I resist? Blame the police report. Blame the early settlers, the civic founders, the namers of upstate New

York. (Were they classicists sent down from Oxford? Packed off to the colonies? There's a Troy and a Syracuse too.) Blame Gus's mother, blame his christening. Blame the nature of things. There are only so many stories to go round.

And Dolores Marquez?

Sometimes I ponder this problem: if there were really people who wanted her so badly, she must have been dangerous, mustn't she? Otherwise who would go to such trouble? So, in spite of the fact that Gus and Felicity thought of her as mute and injured and helpless, she must have been a violent criminal, that's clear, of either the right or the left. One or the other.

It follows that I must have got her character (or the shadow of it) completely wrong. I am, after all, only a piano tuner, and I never met Dolores Marquez. Some things are beyond me, I admit it.

And Felicity?

For once I'm in agreement with the Old Volcano. She wasn't there. That is not the way she would go. Don't think I'm not tempted to describe the fire, the way it might have licked her with its hot desiring tongue, its orange lust. Don't imagine I never have bad dreams. I have, in fact, looked at the worst possibilities, looked them squarely in the eye, and survived.

I often stayed in her Boston apartment, the one where no lover ever slept, for which even the Old Volcano had no key. Feel free, Jean-Marc, she used to say to me. Any time. You're welcome. (Just the same as she is here.) I could paint that apartment from memory, I could reconstruct it: beautiful, but stark; she traveled light. And besides, she said, old buildings are their own decoration. Wood floors, white walls, fine old ceiling moldings, her paintings (a handful by young but promising artists; two by the Old Volcano), Bokhara rugs, a small jungle of plants. (She kept the tropics at her bedside. When she woke she could reach out and touch the passionfruit vine.) There were pillows on which brilliant hummingbirds flew, on which impossible flowers bloomed, vibrant things, handmade from cloths dyed in village wells. There was

274

nothing that could not be moved in two trips of a borrowed van. Almost nothing that could not be abandoned.

Once upon a time I had offered to build in bookshelves, but she had declined.

"It's only temporary," she had said.

"Until what?"

"Until I move on."

It's true, if she were planning a major move, she would have gone back for the paintings. (They were destroyed in the fire.) But why didn't you send the Old Volcano? I'll ask.

Because, she'll say, I can manage perfectly well on my own, thank you. I always have.

But you knew there was a risk, I'll say. You knew the place had been ransacked, you were being followed, your own instinct was to stay away.

I'm ashamed of my fears, she'll say. There comes a time when you have to break the taboos.

So she must have turned her key in the lock.

She must have grimaced a little because of the stale air—the dank smell. But she expected that. She expected disarray. She knew what search warrants could achieve; she could imagine the end result of an illegal search. For that very reason she had stayed away, not wanting to know what casual malevolence could do. And she'd had Seymour's appalled description; to some extent she was prepared.

Just the same, she was not braced for the extent of the mayhem: the hallway a rubble of uprooted plants and earth and broken pots. Grieving, she picked her way through the carnage. In the living room the furniture was slashed, every pillow slit and spilling its shredded foam guts, obscene drawings on her snow-white walls. She stood there stupefied. It simply did not make sense.

Her eyes clouded. Objects came sliding through vision like ships through a fog. Her heart was thumping like a piston. She hardened herself to absorb what added shock her bedroom-study would offer. She knew that that room, with her desk and her files and her bed, would have been the wreckers' crowning achievement. She had no illusions.

As she stumbled down the apartment hallway, she had a sense of having to push her way through a loathsome and dusty brocade of cobwebs. The trailing strands fingered her, disgustingly intimate. She bit her lips to stop herself from screaming. She reached her bedroom door—and then heard the footstep behind her, and turned to see the spider himself, the hunter.

"I've been following you," he says. "It's time to talk."

Felicity licks her dry lips. "But I don't know anything," she says. "I have nothing to say."

"That's why you went back to Central Square, no doubt. To leave nothing in the way of a message." He smiles his spider smile and she feels the sticky inexorable web. "There's no point in holding out," he says. "It's all over. We've got her, and her knight in shining armor. All we need now is what she told you, and we'll just stay here together, you and me, until you decide to talk."

Perhaps he went further than he meant to. Perhaps he left ghoulish evidence that needed a cover of fire.

Or perhaps she got away.

38

Kathleen and I tell each other stories. We rummage in the attics of our memories, we shake loose old sepia scenes.

Look, she says. The time daddy won St. Michael and All Angels bingo. Fifty dollars, but you would have thought a million, the way he went on. He had to buy something for all of us. Sylvie and Jeannie wanted skates, and Tina wanted a white rabbit, a stuffed one. I wanted a record, but he bought me a whole book of lottery tickets instead. Because if we win, he said, we can buy the entire recording company. Only we didn't win anything. She pauses, remembering. Giggles. "He bought mummy flowers and a black lace nightie." She sighs. "Of course, everything came to more than fifty dollars. He never kept track. And mummy was so mad, she took the nightie back." She sighs again. "He never bothered about anything for himself."

It is true, I think. And also, she wants a saint. She needs to believe. She is still a child.

"When he comes back," I say, "he'll probably buy you the earth. He's probably off in the wide world getting rich."

(And in fact, in fact, an extremely large financial settlement has been made. Bob Wilberforce, manager of the Winston branch of Greater Life, has sent Therese the check. A great Canadian, he said of Gus in his letter. Fondly remembered by us all. A knight in shining armor, a champion of the *little* people, who need protection most, God knows.

Was this lightly done by a good insurance man? I think not. People die of their own intense wishes. Gus's last great bingo game, the dream come true, the family provided for.)

277

Kathleen will hear none of this, of course. She sets great store on the fact that the bodies could not be identified.

"If anything had happened to him, I'd *know*," she says. "I know I'd know. Besides, his money plans never worked out. *Never*. It wouldn't be like him at all." She is proud of his financial disasters. She needs to believe.

But sometimes she has darker days. Sometimes the weight of circumstantial evidence stuns her. "He ran off with another woman," she says in a rage. "With a girl not much older than me! That's why mummy left him. She knew what was going on." She batters me with her fists. "And he doesn't give a damn about any of us. He doesn't even remember us." She pulls away and stares at me with glittering eyes. I am part of that tribe. "I hate men," she says. "I will never get married."

I let her sit beside me while I tune pianos. I show her how to tighten the pins, how to strike the tuning fork, how to listen. It is the minute adjustments that count. I work with what I have, I untangle the out-of-tune world. Note by note. It's something.

"He talked about you constantly," I tell her. "He never thought about anything else. Whatever he's doing, you can be sure he's thinking of you."

"He abandoned us," she weeps. "He never even writes."

"Oh well," I shrug. "Fathers. What do you expect?"

"Mine isn't like yours," she'll say quickly. Defensively. "Mine isn't like yours at all."

Ah well.

There aren't many like the Old Volcano.

I remember that night he went tomcatting. The first night I *realized* it, that is. That night at the cottage, way back, when I still hated Felicity. I was ten years old. It was before I ran away, before she found me in the woods. I hated her.

A summer night. The cottage smelled of citronella candles and my own boredom and anger. He had gone out, off, he hadn't bothered to say where. He was always thunderous away from his studio. Impossible. And my arrival didn't help. He never knew how to relax.

Eruptions every half hour. There are only two things he has ever known how to do—paint and fuck. If he's not doing one, he has to be doing the other. I used to lie on my bed at night (the one Dolores Marquez left her blood on) and listen to them in the other room. I used to string the sounds together in my mind, I used to see them moving up and down a keyboard: the base thumps, the quick trills of the sofa-bed springs, grunts that ran into chords, and then those long flights of arpeggios running up and up and up the piano to the final high C of her cry.

I hated them.

At the time, back in Montreal, I was learning to play the piano on an old upright that would never stay in tune. Each time I came home from my lesson, fresh from the teacher's Steinway, the sound of it would set my teeth on edge. That's how it was, that same feeling, when I listened to Felicity and the Old Volcano busily forgetting my existence on the other side of a wall.

I had a favorite fantasy. I would lock them both up in a room full of appallingly out-of-tune player pianos that never stopped. The tempo would get faster and faster, the discord shriller and more unbearable, it would drive them crazy, but they wouldn't be able to stop, they would have to play each other's body to a tuneless death.

The night he went tomcatting, she was reading a book on the porch. Above her head, swaying a little on its hook, was a kerosene lamp, and it threw weird moving shadows across her face. I watched from the steps. What I noticed was the way she read. Absorbed. I could tell from her face what was happening in the book. I could tell when something was witty or surprising or sad. She was inside that book. She was living in the country of its pages.

(She has always been like that.

When she calls, I'll say: Fliss, I knew you'd remember sooner or later. I wasn't worried. When you've got a certain notion in your head, you always did lose track of everything else.)

But back at the cottage, I asked, "Where's my father gone?" Just to interrupt her, really.

She didn't hear. She didn't even glance up. I tossed a

pebble at her and that worked. She was startled. Puzzled. She had forgotten I was there.

"I said: Where's my father?"

"I don't know, Jean-Marc. I guess in L'Ascension. Or maybe Montreal."

She went back to her book. I stared at her wide-eyed. I couldn't believe it. Her calm, I mean. Maman had always been frantic when she didn't know where he was. (Now that Maman has remarried and has four children in her new family, she is not like this at all. She is fat and contented and so calm that even the displeasure of the Church can't touch her. Except when I appear for a visit. I stay away out of kindness; I remind her of such a bad time. I quite understand. And besides, Felicity is my real family.)

But I still hated Felicity that night.

"Sometimes," I said, "he stays away all night."

The malevolent brilliance of a ten-year-old is something to be wondered at. I saw a cloud, or perhaps just the shadow of a cloud, pass across her eyes. She said nothing. I pressed my advantage. "Maybe he won't come home tonight."

"Perhaps he won't," she said. But I had made her look up from her book, and she never went back to it. She stared out beyond the saucer of light into the pines. It was totally dark, pitch dark, the way only a forest can get dark. But she seemed to be seeing something out there, remembering something. She forgot my existence again.

I watched her, fascinated. I was also savoring my power. I can hurt her, I thought. I can make her stop reading her book. I can show her she doesn't know my father at all.

Hours must have passed. I must have fallen asleep right there, sitting hunched on the steps, my head against the railing. What woke me was the sound of his car, driven, naturally, as though he were in an emergency or a Grand Prix race. The braking—an exhibition in itself. And when he got out of the car, I could smell it. At ten I must have had only the dimmest notion of what he'd been about, but that's what I thought of: the stink of a tomcat. I remember it vividly. I remember that the mangy striped tom who prowled the fire escape outside our Montreal apartment went stalking through my thoughts. So that when the Old Volcano opened his mouth I expected a caterwaul to come out.

In a manner of speaking, it did. Though it was one of the Big Cats who snarled inside him.

"What the hell are you doing still up?" he roared at me.

I quaked. I hardly knew him, and at ten I still wanted so desperately to please him. (This was before I discovered the far greater rewards of *dis*pleasing him.) I tried to say something, but not a sound would come out. He stood towering over me (with, as I realize now, that particular ferocity of a man who knows he is in the wrong) and bellowed, "Answer me, dammit. Answer me!" My mouth seemed to be wired shut, and I was shivering with fear.

"I asked him to stay up," Felicity said. She was totally calm. "I wanted his company. Come along, Jean-Marc." And she took my hand. As soon as we were through the door, and out of his sight, I wrenched it free. I couldn't be bought so easily. But just the same, I was amazed. I had only ever seen one other person who was not afraid of my father when he lost his temper, and that was the piano tuner. I think from that moment, I began to stop hating Felicity.

I lay in the dark (on the bed Dolores Marquez would lie on fifteen years later) and listened. I heard him pace. The cottage seemed crowded with tomcats: the way they prowl afterwards, the way they want the whole cat world to see.

"Don't you want to know where I've been?" he asked. (Spit, spit. Hiss.)

Oh, she was magnificent. A Siamese cat. That blue-eyed innocence, deliciously indifferent. They don't give a damn. They lick their paws, they smile their little secret smiles, they stretch their sleek bodies in front of the fire while alley cats watch green-eyed from fire escapes. They are languorous, erotic, exotic, aristocratic. They don't give a damn. They drive those tomcats wild.

"Does it matter?" Felicity asked.

Lying there in the dark, I could picture the casual lift of her eyebrows. I could see that look, that startled, mildly puzzled, wide-eyed Siamese stare, the way she had looked when I hit her with the pebble. And I could hear him breathing fire, hear smoke coming out of his ears. I had to bury my face in the pillow to stifle my laughter. Oh I knew right then, at ten years of age, that he'd met his match. I knew whom I wanted to study.

When she calls, I will scarcely be ruffled. Fliss, I'll say, have you been gone long? I've been working on a piano and I lost track of the time.

Because it's perfectly typical of her.

In the middle of some drowsy children-noisy morning, in a village on the leeside of the Guazapa volcano in the province of Nowhere, she will look up suddenly and think: Oh my God, I promised Jean-Marc I'd call back.

Jean-Marc, she'll say. It completely slipped my mind.

Forget it, I'll say. It's nothing. But I have a confession to make. I had this dream, this incredibly convoluted dream.

Oh a dream, she'll laugh. Write it down.

I did, I'll say. That's not the confession, don't butt in. The joke is this: I've been bitten, I've had a taste of the stage, I got carried away by the performance. The piano tuner wants to conduct. It's the *shape* of the thing, and the power, and a sense of what the audience wants or thinks it wants. I brought you to an untimely end.

I'm sure I deserved it, she'll laugh.

Kathleen and I tell each other stories.

The disappeared ones, we call them. *Los desaparecidos*. We have taken up Felicity's hobby, we watch the news, we keep clippings. See, we tell each other, there are other stories stranger than ours, verified by the press each day. A.P., Reuters, the *New York Times*, it must be true, surreal though it seems: that for no more reason than a whiff of an echo of association at two removes with a person considered to be suspicious, people can disappear. Disappear without a trace.

282

Still, Kathleen says doubtfully. This isn't Latin America. Things happen in Latin America that couldn't happen anywhere else.

That's true, I acknowledge. People are different down there. Our case is undeniably different. Any day now we'll get a phone call.

"Our car was obviously stolen," she says. "He never drove like that. It was somebody else inside." Kathleen is a child, not quite eighteen, and needs a hope to hang on to.

"You're right," I tell her. "He's still running errands of mercy, Robin Hood in a Chevy, a borderline saint."

These are not lies I'm telling her.

There's a fine distinction between what cannot be proved or disproved and what is essentially true.

Felicity's case is different again.

I know Felicity.

I know the way things slip her mind.

Any day now she'll call.

39

I knew I was right. It's happened. A sign.

Invitation to an Exhibition: the latest work. And at her own gallery, no less! Gold print, an embossed border, rough-torn parchment edges, very tastefully done. Of course she sent it. Who else has ever sent me an invitation to his openings?

Well, Fliss, I'll say, you've won. You've finally got me to come to one of them. But don't expect me to drink champagne with him—unless he makes a peace offering first.

It would be cruel to mention this to Kathleen. There is nothing, I'm afraid, to suggest that her father might come back to us, and she can be a little funny about Felicity. She gets peevish, she thinks I talk about Felicity too much. Kathleen's eighteen now—almost old enough to face reality—and she recently moved in with me. Just a business trip, I've told her. New tuning equipment that's not available up here. She gets a distant look in her eyes. Sometimes, when she walks across a room, I think of a Siamese cat.

Felicity's gallery is full of reporters and photographers and champagne buckets. Long dresses, black ties and tails, bits of chatter splattering themselves around like paint on a studio floor. Utterly unexpected . . . Post-modernist, certainly, but also, wouldn't you say . . . ? Life in the old man yet, a completely new . . . A kind of symbolist . . . Numinous, I think is the word.

All the usual brittle inanities.

A waiter passes with a tray and I take a glass of champagne. Even on tiptoe, and craning in every direction, I can't see either of them, so I join the lemmings who are making the grand tour of his latest eruptions. I can see that he is still playing with acrylics, going for vibrant violence, though there's something new too, an interest in radiance, in brilliant diffused light. It's as though J. M. W. Turner and Rousseau and a clutch of aggressive symbolists, all drunk at the same party, had worked on a canvas together,

The first one is pure sensationalism. Gratuitous, the critics will say. And the Old Volcano, pretentiously cavalier, will toss back: These are violent times. I can hear him now. Watch me, watch me. Hot lava from on high.

The first one: a crimson and beige composition around a black slash, and at one end of the black slash—like a beacon against the dark—is a halo of light. The crimson? Applied completely without restraint. It's a bloody painting. Nothing clear, of course; nothing simplistically pictorial; but I know how to read his codes. He is raiding our lives as usual, making capital out of her dreams. I know what the blood-streaked flesh tones speak of, the layered slaughterings like so much stacked meat. I recognize the black dress.

In the next one, two forms, shadowy, bend toward each other over something luminous. A lantern perhaps. A discovery. It is not clear that the forms are human, though the one on the right is like a net of floating discs. They could be atoms, they could be eyes. They float in pairs, and one of each pair is slightly higher than the other.

The next one startles me. It's a parody, I hear people saying, an artist's joke. A tribute, someone else suggests, or a backward glance. A reinterpretation of Van Gogh's bedroom. But I recognize my bed at the cottage. There is a radiance around the headboard, a smear of blood on the quilt.

Predictably, the next is a Magdalen, starkly black, an abstract rendering, but recognizable just the same. The eyes (Felicity's eyes) float loose in a bubble of light. *Homage to Perugino*, the painting is called.

And then this: a figure clothed in white samite with a gaunt cadaverous face (I think of Rouault, of all those tragic clowns) surrounded by a gaudy skirl of color: temptation perhaps; dancing girls; the worldly vanities. I close one eye and focus on the face, which has been done with a deliberate and heavy crudity of line. I recognize the eyes,

285

I recognize the hunger, the bright vacant gaze of the dreamer. It is Augustine Kelly. Unmistakable. Whom he never even met. I look at my catalogue and see that the painting is called: *To Carthage then I came.*

A stunned moment. And then I am trembling with rage. Because that was *my* idea, my creation, my performance. He is sucking me dry again. I know what you're up to, old man, I fume. The catalogue tells me that *The Piano Tuner's Dream* is next, but I have seen enough. He thinks he is pulling all the strings, he thinks the whole world is his canvas, he thinks we're all part of his game.

I'm shoving my way through the crowds now, bumping into people, knocking over glasses, slopping champagne over silk skirts, standing on people's toes. I'm looking for Felicity.

Fliss, I'll say. You got me here. But his arrogance is more than I can take. I have to leave before I kill him. I'll see you later.

There's a story the Old Volcano should read, a story by Borges. It's in my library, I think I'll send him a copy. Read this, old man, I'll say. Put this on your palette and paint it:

A man in a ruined world dreams. Night after night, he spins out dreams, he dreams a peopled world, he fills canvases with populations of phantoms, he paints them in the gallery of his sleep. He dreams words into their mouths, he dreams their dreams, he dreams their lives. They twist and turn on their phantom strings. He dreams he's the puppeteer.

His phantom cosmos is not enough, he is drunk with a larger dream: the demiurge. (We might call him the Old Volcano.) This is his obsession: to push a phantom beyond the confines of his sleep, to dream an entire man into being. He dreams with a violent singleness of purpose. He has the God-itch. He dreams his dream-being organ by organ and hair by hair. He calls him son.

He dares not cease from his dreaming, for if he does, his son will not exist. So he believes. It is—if I may comment on Borges—the usual arrogance of the artist that is depicted here. It is typical, for example, of the Old Volcano, who thinks that his paintings are the borders of reality. He paints Felicity, he paints me; the paintings are more real to him than the sitters. We cease to exist in his mind; we become mere shadows of his paintings.

But the last laugh is on the Old Volcano.

In Borges' story, the ancient gods of the circular ruins tap the dreamer on the shoulder. Sorry, old chap, they say in effect. But someone else is dreaming you.

Oh the last laugh is definitely on the Old Volcano. And the very last word is with me.

Someone else is dreaming you, old man, I'll say. I've caught the virus, your very own disease. I've got you down on paper. You're just a shadow of my words, your paintings only live in my chapters, you cease to exist once my reader puts you on a shelf, you have to reach past me to touch the world. The piano tuner has got hold of the baton.

I've pushed through to the front of the crowd now. There's a space, an emptiness, which has been cordoned off in front of his major piece. It's a huge canvas, it takes most of one wall of the final room of the exhibition.

Even I am impressed. Dazzled. (I am not ungenerous. I have a certain critical integrity.) It's as though he has painted the mind of the sun, the concept of light, the idea of God. Such is the radiance, the effulgence of the canvas, that my eyes water and I have to close them. And when I close them, dark flecks like sunspots dance inside my eyelids. They are in the shape of Felicity's eyes, they dance in lopsided pairs.

Oh, I acknowledge grudgingly. Brilliant!

When I look again, shading my eyes, I realize that the entire gallery is in fact lit by the glow from the canvas. No other lighting is necessary.

"Mr. Seymour," I hear a reporter say. "Could you comment on this extraordinary new . . . this almost mystical . . . one might say transcendently luminous . . . I find myself at a loss for words. Could you comment on the shadow of the woman behind the light? Could you tell us who sat for the painting?"

The Old Volcano's voice sounds like the creaking of a very old house. "It is the shadow of a woman who left me," he says. "The idea of a woman I lost."

And then I see him.

A shock.

It's been a number of years, and I am not prepared for how old, how frail . . . Not that this excuses him for anything.

His eyes are watering from the brightness of his own painting. His arms are dangling at his sides like broken awnings. He doesn't know what to do with them. He half lifts one towards me and lets it fall.

"Jean-Marc," he says, and his voice breaks. "You came. You finally came."

"Because I thought . . ." And I'm back in a childhood accent, I'm reduced to begging, I'm pleading with him: "Where is she?"

He stares at me.

"I was hoping you'd know," he says. "I was hoping she'd called you. She always worried more about you, I was sure she'd have . . ." His hand is groping towards me again like a blind thing, it casts about in distress.

She probably couldn't get through, I try to say. She's probably somewhere remote. (I can see her now, wearing sunlight, in a village on the far side of the Guazapa volcano. The light falls like wings on her shoulders. And there are streamers, she is trailing streamers of children.)

"The fire . . ." he falters, interrupting.

"Oh, for God's sake, she wasn't there!" (I shouldn't be shouting—though it's a strain being patient with him.) "She wasn't there," I say more gently, recovering. "That's not the way she'd . . . You know how she loses track. How she just takes off."

"Yes," he says, relieved, and his drunken persistent hands lurch toward me again. "Any day now, I expect . . ."

And she *will* call, of course, though when she drops in from wherever she is, she'll be amazed to see us standing here holding each other like this.

Oh Jean-Marc, she'll laugh, and we'll catch fire from the sound of her voice.